I0823556

A MATTER OF MURDER

A LIZZIE & DARCY MYSTERY

BOOKS BY TIRZAH PRICE

The Jane Austen Murder Mysteries

Pride and Premeditation

Sense and Second-Degree Murder

Manslaughter Park

The Lizzie & Darcy Mysteries

In Want of a Suspect

A Matter of Murder

A MATTER OF MURDER

A LIZZIE & DARCY MYSTERY

TIRZAH PRICE

STORYTIDE
An Imprint of HarperCollinsPublishers

HarperCollins Children's Books, a division of HarperCollins Publishers,
195 Broadway, New York, NY 10007

HarperCollins Publishers, Macken House, 39/40 Mayor Street Upper, Dublin 1,
D01 C9W8, Ireland

Storytide is an imprint of HarperCollins Publishers.

A Matter of Murder

harpercollins.com

Library of Congress Control Number: 2025935155
ISBN 978-0-06-327807-3

Typography by Corina Lupp

25 26 27 28 29 LBC 5 4 3 2 1

First Edition

To Tab,
my partner in crime

"It is very often nothing but our own vanity that deceives us."
—*Pride and Prejudice* by Jane Austen

"In everyone there arises from time to time the wish to kill . . ."
—*Curtain* by Agatha Christie

ONE

In Which Lizzie and Darcy Arrive at Netherfield Park at Last

"OH, NETHERFIELD PARK AT LAST!" Mrs. Bennet cried as she stepped out of the carriage that had come to a stop in front of the elegant manor house. She clasped her hands beneath her chin as she took in the sight. "I never thought I'd see the day!"

Miss Elizabeth Bennet stumbled out of the carriage after her mother, tripping over her small dog, Guy, as he made his own hasty escape. Mr. Darcy's strong hand was there in an instant, steadying her as she regained her bearings after six hours of travel. Six *interminable* hours, during which her mother had barely stopped talking long enough to take a breath. Darcy squeezed her hand gently and gave her a subtle wink, as if he knew that she had been contemplating throwing herself out of the moving carriage just before Netherfield Park came in sight.

She rolled her eyes slightly, then turned to her mother and whispered, "Mama, please!"

But Mrs. Bennet was unperturbed. "Three stories, Lizzie!

Have you ever seen such a large and distinguished estate? And to think, my Jane is the mistress of it all!"

Lizzie stepped forward so that Darcy could offer a hand to her best friend, Miss Charlotte Lucas, who alighted from the carriage far more gracefully than Lizzie had. Charlotte came to stand by Lizzie and murmured, "Well, it *is* impressive, you have to admit."

Netherfield Park announced itself with towering ionic columns, and the entrance was large enough to drive a phaeton through. It was palatial compared to the town house on Gracechurch Street that the seven Bennets—and Guy—shared. Well, six Bennets now that Jane had married Mr. Bingley and left the family home for good.

"It's very large," Lizzie conceded. She wasn't one to be carried away by extravagance, but she was finding it hard to be impervious to the grandeur of the estate when it belonged to *Jane*, her sister who had, up until very recently, shared a bedchamber with her.

Darcy, however, did not seem fazed in the least. "It's very well appointed."

"Well appointed?" Lizzie repeated incredulously, but she didn't get a chance to say more, for the front door was thrown open and there was Jane herself, coming to greet them with Bingley by her side.

"Mrs. Bingley!" Mrs. Bennet shouted, and fell upon her daughter, kissing and hugging her as though it had been years and not six weeks since Jane's wedding.

For this display of emotion, Lizzie couldn't exactly fault her mother—she had missed her older sister more than she had thought possible. She was thrilled for Jane, and a bit in awe of the wealth she now possessed. It couldn't have happened to a more deserving person. However, not a week after her nuptials, she and Bingley had departed from London, creating a distinct, Jane-shaped hole in Lizzie's everyday life.

Mrs. Bennet finally released Jane and moved on to Bingley, and it was Lizzie's turn to fling herself at her sister, no more gracefully than her mother had. Jane was radiant—she wore a new dress of cream lawn, and her cheeks were pink, and her curls appeared extra bouncy. Lizzie was achy, sweaty, and dusty after such a long day, but Jane embraced her just as fiercely. Her sister smelled familiar—violet water and fresh linen, but now there was another crisp scent under that familiarity, something that smelled refined and expensive.

"I've missed you," Jane whispered in her ear.

"And I you," Lizzie said. "Come back to London."

Jane just laughed as she released her. "I think you're going to love it here, Lizzie. This old house is full of so many rooms, you couldn't even begin to imagine."

Bingley also turned to Lizzie and greeted her with an enthusiastic grin. "Jane said that prying you and your father away from your work would be quite a Herculean task, so don't think we don't appreciate your sacrifice."

"I would do anything for Jane," Lizzie told him, "even spend a summer in the countryside."

Her bright smile couldn't quite hide her sarcasm, however. While it was true that she had missed her sister, and she would most certainly have dropped everything if Jane had called, this summer sojourn had not been her idea—she'd been strong-armed into it, and the chief perpetrator of such strong-arming had been none other than Darcy himself.

Darcy, for his part, looked utterly oblivious to her frustration. When she glanced over her shoulder, he was greeting Jane with the utmost civility. Anyone else might have thought he looked a bit on the dour side, but that was just his permanent expression these days.

The last time Lizzie remembered seeing him truly smile was after solving the case of the Mullins Brothers' storehouse fire three months earlier. Not only had they discovered the true reason for the fire, but they'd unspooled a smuggling ring, stopped an innocent young lady from marrying a true villain, and uncovered a Crown secret. To be sure, it had been a *minor* secret, and the Crown's emissary had made certain that they wouldn't be able to brag about solving the case, but it had still been a success.

The only dark spot, of course, had been Lady Catherine de Bourgh.

It still gave Lizzie chills to think that the woman was at large, and responsible for yet another murderous plot. Even more so when she thought about how that plot had included her own kidnapping. But Lizzie had been able to push aside her fears and lingering questions and bask in the satisfaction of another case closed, with Darcy by her side.

Until the first letter had come.

It had been delivered to Longbourn & Sons a week after the conclusion of the case. It arrived on a creamy expanse of parchment, lavish in its wastefulness considering the brief message it contained:

You're clever, but not as clever as I.

She'd known who it was from, even without a signature, and she'd shown it to Darcy, naturally. And her father. And Charlotte. And, well . . . everyone, really. She wouldn't admit it now, but receiving a letter from the woman herself had sent a thrill up her spine not unlike the one she'd felt when she'd first heard the news that Charles Bingley had been hauled off to Newgate for murder. Or when Jack Mullins had grasped her hand and had told her his storehouse fire was arson.

"She's taunting you," Darcy had said.

"Baiting," Mr. Bennet corrected as he studied the missive. "She wants to see how you'll react. You mustn't give her the satisfaction."

"What am I supposed to do, sit on my hands?" Lizzie was thrumming with nervous energy. It wasn't often that she faced an opponent who even recognized her as an opponent, let alone a moderately clever one.

"Do nothing," Mr. Bennet told her firmly. He refused to hand the letter back, too. "And let's hope she grows tired of this charade and moves on."

But she hadn't. Several days later, another letter arrived, this one only slightly longer.

My dear Miss Bennet, do you not think that your talents are wasted at such a firm as Longbourn & Sons? After all you've accomplished, why do you shackle yourself to men who would have you spending your time on contracts when you could be doing so much <u>*more*</u>*?*

And there it was again, that thrill of excitement . . . but there was a pinprick of worry there, too. How had Lady Catherine known that her father had her drafting and reviewing contracts? She had looked down at her desk, busy with tidy stacks of contracts and correspondence. Had Mr. Tomlinson told Lady Catherine about Lizzie's workload before his arrest? But how would he have known?

Or had Lady Catherine found herself another spy?

Her father and Darcy were made even more uneasy by this note, but they said little. Lizzie was in favor of going to the Dashwoods to see if they could track the letter's origin, but Mr. Bennet had not wanted to involve them, preferring to write to Mr. Graves, the aforementioned emissary of the Crown, for answers. Mr. Graves had written back a curt *Do nothing*, and that had been that until Lizzie had come home from a fitting at the modiste—Mr. Bingley had proposed to Jane by this point, and the Bennet sisters were all to have new dresses—to find a letter in the front hall, addressed to Lizzie.

Remember, Miss Bennet, that women always have more choices than they think they do. You can either spend your days toiling for men who don't appreciate your talents, or you can do something that will leave a far more lasting impact. Intrigued? Meet me behind St. Clements three days hence, midday. Come alone.

Lizzie's heartbeat had thrummed in her ears when she'd read the words, and she'd wasted no time in summoning Darcy and her father to Gracechurch Street to show them the message. "This is it," she'd told them. "Our chance to finally catch her."

But neither Darcy nor her father had been convinced. "It's a trap," Darcy said, real fear in his eyes as he skimmed the note. "After all she's done, she'll hardly just meet you in broad daylight!"

"I concur," her father said, rubbing the bridge of his nose. He looked more tired these days, and Lizzie wasn't certain whether it was because of the threat of Lady Catherine or Mrs. Bingley's constant chatter about Jane's upcoming nuptials. Perhaps both. "That woman has tried to kidnap you not once but twice."

Logically, Lizzie knew they were right to be worried—and Lady Catherine's multiple kidnapping attempts notwithstanding, she knew it wasn't the best idea to simply comply with a summons from a stranger, even if they had been properly introduced. But Lady Catherine had evaded her twice now, and Lizzie didn't want to give her a third opportunity.

"Graves has been tearing London apart for weeks with no luck," Lizzie argued. "Agreeing to a meeting may be our best chance at apprehending her."

"Perhaps if we all went along and hung back—" Darcy began to say.

"You mean to use my daughter as bait?" her father demanded, and Darcy shook his head.

"No—"

"Yes," Lizzie said. "Use me as bait."

"Absolutely not! I forbid it!"

Mr. Bennet didn't often go to the trouble of forbidding things, so Lizzie was genuinely shocked when he showed no sign of relenting. He did write to Graves, of course, and the shadowy man came to Gracechurch Street and left with Lady Catherine's note and a promise that he himself would stand in the church all afternoon if he had to. But Lizzie knew it wouldn't work.

And she'd had the bitter satisfaction of being proven right days later when Graves returned to tell them he'd waited six hours, but she'd never shown. After that, Lady Catherine had gone strangely silent. Mr. Bennet had been satisfied that they'd finished with the whole dreadful business, and Darcy had been somewhat sheepishly relieved . . . but Lizzie had only grown more and more frustrated.

None of them imagined what would come in the next letter.

And that was why Lizzie, her mother, Charlotte, and Darcy now stood before Netherfield Park, a carriage with Mr. Bennet and the rest of her sisters not far behind.

"Don't be fooled," Darcy said now in response to Bingley's remark about Lizzie's unwillingness to leave London. "We practically had to force her into the carriage."

Lizzie shot him a sour look. "You're one to talk about forcing me into the carriage."

She pretended not to notice her sister or Charlotte wincing at her tone.

Mrs. Bennet was, as usual, oblivious to the mood. "Oh

Lizzie, don't be cross with Mr. Darcy for insisting that we all get out of London! I've been trying to convince Mr. Bennet that we ought to take this trip weeks sooner."

"Be happy you had what little honeymoon you got," Lizzie said in an undertone to Jane.

Jane looked desperate for a change of subject. "Speaking of Papa, where is the other carriage?"

"Oh, they weren't a quarter mile behind us last time we stopped," Mrs. Bennet said. "Mr. Darcy's horses are far superior to those that Mr. Bennet rented for the journey."

Lizzie scowled at her mother's indelicate praise. Ever since Jane's engagement had been announced, her mother had not been subtle about her compliments to Darcy, and at least half the comments touched upon his wealth, as if insinuating to Lizzie that she must not let such a suitor slip from her grasp. It was a wonder Mrs. Bennet hadn't proposed marriage to him herself.

"Come, we'll call for tea so that it's ready by the time they catch up," Jane said, gesturing toward the entrance to the house.

It was about then that Lizzie remembered she'd dropped Guy's leash upon arrival, and now she turned about, looking for the dog. "Guy!" she called. "Guy, here!" Not five minutes at Netherfield, and she'd lost him already!

Darcy nudged her arm. "He's not gone far, see?" He pointed to the pristine lawn beyond the drive. The small dog was lounging on his back in the grass, tongue lolling. The sight brought a smile to Lizzie's face. Aside from a few public parks, there wasn't much grass in Cheapside—that is, not any that Lizzie would want him rolling in—and the Bennets didn't have a large garden back home. The little dog rolled back onto his belly as Lizzie continued to call his name, and then reluctantly got to his feet and trotted over to Lizzie. "Good boy," Lizzie told him, then added more quietly, "Now don't go running off. We might not ever find you again in this large a park."

Lizzie and Guy trailed after Charlotte and Darcy toward the entrance of the house, but not before passing by the line of servants standing off to the side. In all her excitement to finally be free of the carriage and hug her sister once more, she hadn't paid much mind to the receiving line. They hadn't moved from their severe formation, except for the footmen who were now scurrying to the luggage with a sharp nod from the butler. Lizzie tried not to look shocked at the sheer number of them—more than twenty people, all for this old house and their small house party! Lizzie smiled, trying to catch anyone's eye, but everyone from the lowliest of maids to the housekeeper kept their eyes downcast. Lizzie recognized a number of faces—Grigson, the Bingleys' butler from London; Mrs. Reed, the housekeeper; and Jane's lady's maid; and more than a few of the maids and footmen. Lizzie felt her smile falter as she moved past them—the stiff formality of the finer houses in London was not what she was accustomed to. At home, they had a maid and a cook who'd chat idly with Lizzie and occasionally shoo her along if they were busy.

But Jane was a Bingley now, with all the accoutrements of wealth to show for it.

"You brought many of your London staff with you," Lizzie remarked to Jane.

"We had to send for Mrs. Reed and a few others not long after we arrived," Jane said. "Charles's great-aunt had only one servant at the end, can you believe it?"

Lizzie could not—especially when she stepped inside the house. The entrance hall of Netherfield Park was even grander than the façade, if possible. It was all gleaming dark wood and polished marble, and Guy's toenails clicked daintily as he followed her into the house. There was a gently sloping grand staircase leading up from the ground floor to the first floor, wide enough that one could steer that hypothetical phaeton right into the house and up the stairs—that is, if horses could pull carriages up staircases.

Mrs. Bennet gasped, and the sound echoed. "Mr. Bingley, what a fine house! And to think this was in your family all this time and you never knew!" She shot Jane a conspiratorial wink, which Jane pretended not to see. "How fortuitous for you!"

"Mama, I hardly think you can call the death of Bingley's great-aunt fortuitous," Lizzie hissed.

"Oh, he knows what I mean," Mrs. Bennet said with a wave of her hand.

One thing Lizzie appreciated about her new brother-in-law was his ability to blithely ignore Mrs. Bennet's more impolite remarks. "I've always known of the estate, but had no reason to believe it would ever pass into my possession. The entail was broken ages ago, and it was never a guarantee that Great-Aunt

Honoria would leave it to me, although my father certainly hoped she would. He named Netherfield Shipping after the place."

"A bid for her good favor?" Darcy asked.

"Likely, although it didn't do him much good. We never had an invitation. I grew up hearing stories about how she'd married my great-uncle for his wealth, taken over the family home, and left us all out in the cold."

Bingley certainly didn't need the inheritance now. Although his family was of good standing, they'd fallen on hard times two generations previously. It wasn't until Bingley and his late father had built up Netherfield Shipping that they'd been able to restore their family to the upper echelons of society. Bingley had good manners, a good business (even better ever since Lizzie and Darcy had solved the small piracy problem that had been plaguing him more than a year earlier), and very favorable connections. He hadn't needed a family estate in the country, but two weeks before Jane and Bingley's wedding, he'd received word that Mrs. Honoria Bingley, the wife of his grandfather's brother, had passed away and bequeathed the entirety of her estate to the only living male Bingley heir.

Darcy had handled the legalities with Mrs. Bingley's solicitor, naturally, so Lizzie knew a bit more about the matter than she likely would have otherwise—there hadn't been very much money, but the true value had been Netherfield Park and its surrounding farms, which had been in the care of a steward for as long as anyone could remember while Netherfield Park sat closed up to all except its elderly mistress and a small handful of loyal servants whose numbers had dwindled to just one at the time of her death. Lizzie had expected a dilapidated old country manor house with drafty windows and soot-stained walls and perhaps mice. *Lots* of mice.

She hadn't expected vaulted ceilings and gilt-framed artwork.

"We had no idea what we were walking into when we arrived," Bingley continued, smiling fondly at Jane. "Not quite the honeymoon we'd imagined."

"Nonsense," Jane said with a faint flush as she smiled back at her new husband. "I didn't mind in the slightest."

Lizzie didn't know whether to grin or roll her eyes.

"The house was built in the sixteenth century," Bingley continued as he led them deeper into the echoing hall. "My great-grandfather constructed the west wing and made repairs to the central areas of the house, but I'm afraid the east wing suffered a fire some decades back and has fallen into disrepair—my great-aunt wasn't one for renovations, apparently. For everyone's safety, we've closed it off."

Lizzie couldn't help the arch of her brows at that. Jane caught her look and said, "Don't worry, it's not as though the entire wing is about to collapse."

"So you claim," a voice said, echoing through the hall. They all looked up to see Caroline Bingley floating down the grand staircase. The sun shone through the windows, casting a warm glow on her golden hair, and if Lizzie had been the betting type, she'd have put money on Caroline planning her entrance. "I can hear the entire house creaking throughout the night, as if it's going to tumble down with a stiff breeze."

No one laughed, which was just as well because judging by Caroline's sour expression, Lizzie didn't think she would take kindly to it. Bingley just shook his head good naturedly. "She's exaggerating, of course. There are a few odd creaks and moans, but it's nothing more than an old house settling. And I have a builder coming up from London to inspect the east wing and recommend the necessary repairs."

"Is my daughter safe here?" Mrs. Bennet asked, placing a hand on Jane's shoulder.

"Mama, it's safe as long as we don't go into the east wing!" Jane rushed to assure her. "We've been quite busy renovating the rest of the house. Caroline's help with the decorating has been invaluable, of course—you must see the paper she picked out for the drawing room. We've done the main rooms, and although we haven't gotten to the bedchambers yet, I think you'll be comfortable."

"Even if the décor is a bit baroque," Caroline added.

Jane winced, and Lizzie felt her protective instincts kick in. "That's all right. Baroque furniture never killed anyone," she said with false cheer.

"Is everything always so violent with you?" Caroline asked. "No one said anything about killing."

"Caroline," Bingley said reprovingly, and at the same time Mrs. Bennet laughed.

"Oh, don't mind Elizabeth. She's been involved in some rather violent business as of late, but that's all behind us now, isn't it?"

"Is it?" Caroline asked. "I've seen the papers."

So had Lizzie. In fact, she was convinced all of London had seen the papers. Although she wasn't able to publicly claim credit for solving Leticia Cavendish's murder, her name had been printed in the notice of her death, as she and Darcy had been the ones to discover her body. And then there had been the case that Lizzie had taken after that, which had resulted in a hostage crisis at the Pantheon. *Danger and scandal follow the young lady solicitor wherever she goes*, one rag had written.

Danger the ton might have forgiven. But scandal? Well, that was much harder to overlook.

"I don't know why everyone must make a simple case into a grand ordeal." Lizzie could feel her cheeks growing warm. "It isn't as though I go searching for danger."

"Well, you certainly don't do anything to discourage it," came Caroline's muttered remark, just loud enough that everyone could hear it.

Lizzie did not, as a general rule, assign much value to Caroline Bingley's opinions, but this remark cut deep. What did everyone expect—for her to give up her work and just sit idly at home because of some gossip?

Luckily for her, she could always count on her mother to interject with inane questions. "Jane, have you been able to find good tradesmen this far from London? If you need a drapier, I have a recommendation from Mrs. Smith—you don't want to use the one on Fulton Street!"

Jane led them all to the drawing room, and Charlotte fell back and took Lizzie's arm. Lizzie squeezed her best friend's hand. "I wish she'd find a husband already and torment someone else's family," Lizzie muttered, which was quite ungenerous of her and she knew it, but if one couldn't gripe about tedious people to one's best friend, then what was the point of friendship?

"I'm sure she feels just as trapped as you do," Charlotte said mildly. "After all, she swears she was within moments of a proposal when—"

"I know," Lizzie sighed. It had not been on purpose that Lizzie had spoiled Caroline's prospects with yet another suitor, but the other girl clearly wasn't ready to forgive Lizzie any time soon. Caroline had been in attendance at the Pantheon, and her suitor had abruptly left London following the resolution of the evening's excitement. There had been whispers that he'd been involved in the counterfeit art scheme Lizzie had helped her client uncover and he'd left town to avoid arrest. Lizzie was of the opinion that Caroline had dodged an unhappy marriage with an opportunist, but the other young lady clearly did not share that view.

"Ignore her," Charlotte advised. "Have you ever stayed somewhere so fine in all your life?"

"No," Lizzie admitted with a small smile. "Repairs and redecorating aside, it truly is very impressive."

"And can you just imagine how lovely the grounds are bound to be? We can go on long walks every day with Guy, and get far away from Caroline."

Guy's head tilted up when he heard his name in close conjunction with his most beloved word—*walk*. "All right, yes, you're right."

They were still lingering in the hall, and Darcy poked his head out of the drawing room. "Coming?"

Lizzie felt her smile slip as she looked at him. He'd been very quiet the entire carriage ride, and nearly impossible to read. In the last week, he'd made a habit of avoiding her gaze, but he didn't now. Lizzie stared into his eyes—eyes that made her feel deliciously light-headed and breathless when she recalled all their shared kisses, and the quiet moments when he'd drawn her close and she'd lost herself into the depths of his eyes . . .

But she wasn't thinking about that right now.

"Coming," she said shortly.

Darcy turned and went back into the drawing room without another word, and Lizzie didn't need to look at Charlotte to know that her friend was giving her a doleful look. "Oh, Lizzie. When are you going to put him out of his misery and forgive him already?"

"I don't know," she responded crisply. "I haven't decided yet."

TWO

In Which Darcy Plays the Part of Chimney Sweep with Disastrous Results

"SHE'S ANGRY," BINGLEY OBSERVED as he poured amber liquid into a cut crystal glass.

"Oh really? I hadn't noticed."

Darcy accepted the drink and barely gave the alcohol a swirl before taking a gulp. The whiskey slid across his tongue, smoother than silk. It was down his throat before he felt the burn, but he welcomed it.

Bingley didn't know the half of it.

His friend stared at him as he sat with the aftereffects of the alcohol. "You're being sarcastic. You're hardly ever sarcastic."

Darcy grimaced. Oh, the joys of long friendship—Bingley knew him almost better than he knew himself. "It'll blow over," he said, not sure whether he meant Lizzie's anger or his sarcasm.

They were dressed for dinner that evening, waiting for the rest of the house party to come down. The carriage with Mr. Bennet and the younger Bennet sisters had arrived with a predictable amount of carrying on, and they'd all made polite conversation in the drawing room while Lizzie had looked everywhere but at him until Jane rang for the housekeeper to show them all to their rooms. Bingley, of course, had missed none of it, and he doubted the rest of the party was oblivious to Lizzie's cold shoulder, either.

"Doesn't she understand this holiday is for her own safety?" Bingley asked.

Darcy thought of the (unfortunately, many) examples he had collected since he'd first become acquainted with Lizzie in which she had blithely thrown caution to the wind. "Yes. But while she's here, she can't be doing what she really wants."

And that was to find Lady Catherine. Darcy couldn't blame her—he wanted the woman found so she'd stop toying with all of them. But he also knew Lizzie. Neither caution nor relaxation were her strong suits. While whisking her away from London might have been the safest thing for her and her family, it was also the thing most likely to drive her—and by extension, him—mad.

"And your father?" Bingley asked. "Have you heard anything more from him?"

Darcy grimaced and took a sip. He reached into the inner pocket of his jacket and withdrew the travel-worn letter that had been sitting next to his heart all day. "He's responded about how I would expect," he said, and handed the letter to Bingley.

Charles Bingley was the only one he would trust with the letter. Not that he didn't trust Lizzie—but he didn't want her to ever read what his father had written about her. He looked away as Bingley opened the letter, the memory of his father's words echoing painfully in his head. *You've shamed me and the firm's name by taking up with that woman. I expect you to cut all ties with her and her father's business immediately.*

Bingley let out a low whistle.

"What part are you at?"

"The one where your father accuses you of debasing the entire legal profession."

Darcy finished his drink and got up to pour himself another. "Ah, that entire paragraph was so touching. Second only to the part where he wrote that Darcys are too good to dangle after some base bluestocking, and then said that Lizzie has likely set her cap on me."

Bingley's eyebrows went up as he read. "If there is any lady who is the least likely to ensnare a man into marriage, it is Miss Elizabeth Bennet."

"Try telling that to my father."

"What are you going to do?" Bingley asked, tossing the letter aside.

Darcy poured himself another splash of whiskey—but not too much. It wouldn't do to get sloppy, not with dinner ahead of them. "I can hardly tell him the truth."

"Which is?"

Darcy stared down into the amber liquid. It was easier to tell his drink than it was to face his best friend. "Which is that I would propose and marry her in a heartbeat if she'd have me."

"If she'd have you! What possible reason would she give for throwing you over?"

Darcy appreciated his friend's indignation on his behalf. It made him feel the slightest bit better. "I came close to asking," he admitted. "During the whole business with Tomlinson and that storehouse fire . . ."

His throat tightened when he thought about that early-morning carriage ride through London just three months earlier, when he had finally declared his intentions. He hadn't proposed, exactly, although he would have gladly, if that had been what she'd wanted. She'd asked for time, which he was glad to give. It would give him no pleasure to have her acquiesce to his proposal because she didn't want to disappoint him, or because she thought it expected of her.

"And why didn't you?" Bingley asked. "Was it Mrs. Bennet? I admit, she can be rather blunt and she has all the social graces of a canon, but—"

"No, it wasn't her mother. Lizzie said she wasn't ready, and I won't force the matter, even on the slim chance that it would placate my father."

"You're a brave man," Bingley said, with a small bit of admiration in his voice. "But your father . . ."

"He probably wouldn't accept her anyway. It's not just our association he objects to—it's *her*."

Edmund Darcy was an exacting man who expected his son to act rationally and to rarely show emotion. Growing up, Darcy had learned to hide everything from his father—his tears and sorrows, disappointments and flashes of anger. But he'd also learned to hide other things, too. Laughter and smiles, his triumphs when he succeeded at school, and the immense pride he felt watching Georgiana grow up to be as smart as she was beautiful. His father would have scoffed at all that emotion—feelings were weakness, and in order to succeed he must always come from a position of strength.

Darcy had spent so many years living up to his father's rigid expectations that he almost hadn't known what to do when he'd first encountered Lizzie and all her fiery passion and obvious emotion for her cases. But one thing was certain: He loved her, and he would not go back to pretending to be the cold, unfeeling automaton his father wanted. Nor could he pretend he didn't love Lizzie.

Which put them at an impasse—for now.

"Forget him," Darcy said, taking the letter back and stuffing it into his inner jacket pocket. "He's not here, and we have bigger problems."

Darcy could tell that Bingley wanted to say more on the subject, but he simply nodded. "Have you had any news?"

"No," Darcy said, and his frustration leaked into his tone. "I've seen neither hide nor hair of Graves since we decided to leave London. There have been no new letters. Lady Catherine could be anywhere by now."

"Well, she's not here at Netherfield," Bingley said, setting his glass down with a loud thunk. "And you all are safe to ramble the grounds as you please."

"Except for the east wing?" Darcy asked.

"Oh—yes. And on second thought, best to stay out of the barns as well. The stables weren't in terrible shape, but I fear that I'll be investing a bit more than expected in getting this place up to snuff. Say, would you mind walking the grounds with me tomorrow? It's not nearly as grand as Pemberley, but I'd love to get your advice . . ."

"Of course," Darcy said, for if there was one thing he knew aside from the law, it was how to manage an estate. "Don't take this the wrong way, but I suppose all these years, I thought of your great-aunt as playing a recluse in some old hunting lodge. I didn't expect . . . this."

He glanced about the dim study, which, despite having been very recently cleaned, smelled of musty books and showed signs of its age and disuse. But still, there was no mistaking that in its prime, the house had been quite impressive.

"Neither did I, to be perfectly frank. My father used to speak of the place, of course, and he'd send letters to Honoria every now and then, but they'd always be returned unopened. To this day, I haven't the faintest clue why she and my grandfather became estranged."

Darcy drained his glass. "Well, I suppose there's no use in dwelling on it. Not when you have a successful business, a wonderful wife, and now a proper estate."

But he must not have done a very good job at masking his jealousy, because Bingley said, "Don't be too quick to judge my life perfect. Caroline has been rattling about for weeks, growing more cross with each day. She's even more restless now that Jane and I are married, and while they get along well enough, she's made no secret of the fact that she wants to return to London as soon as possible."

Which would prove difficult if Bingley and Jane were to host them for the foreseeable future. Darcy felt properly chastised. "Forgive me, I appear to be in a rotten mood this evening. I'll blame it on the travel."

"There's nothing to forgive," Bingley told him, but he looked worried. "Will you be all right?"

His father had all but threatened disinheritance, Lady Catherine was out there somewhere, and Lizzie was angry with him. Of all his problems, the last one felt most significant. He lifted his empty glass to his lips, forgetting he'd already finished his drink. He hurriedly set it back down.

This did not have to be a miserable trip. He'd help Bingley with his estate, and he'd think of ways to placate his father. He couldn't do anything about Lady Catherine, but as for Lizzie . . .

He'd find a way to convince her to forgive him. He had to.

"Of course," he said. "Shall we go through?"

Not an hour later, Darcy was beginning to doubt his abilities.

The entire house party gathered in the drawing room before dinner, and Lizzie had yet to look at him once. She and Charlotte were sitting on a settee near the window, and Darcy sat in a nearby chair, hoping that he might be able to join their conversation, but despite a few sympathetic glances from Charlotte, Lizzie had steadfastly ignored him. Instead, Darcy was left to observe the others spread about the drawing room—Mrs. Bennet had engaged Bingley and Jane in an exhausting and animated discussion about the house's renovations and her opinions on particular design choices while the two youngest Bennet sisters cavorted about the room inspecting the various fixtures and objets d'art, whispering noisily to each other. Mary sat next to her mother, frowning with disapproval at talk of replacing the old furnishings, and Mr. Bennet was, unsurprisingly, reading a newspaper he'd brought with him from London. Caroline looked on from her position in a chair near the empty fireplace, bored. Darcy didn't even have Guy as a distraction—one of the maids had whisked him off to the kitchens, and the little dog had been more than happy to abandon his humans in favor of table scraps.

It was enough to make him wish he'd tossed back another drink.

When there was finally a lull in the conversation, Bingley stood and cleared his throat. "Excuse me, everyone. Might I have your attention briefly?"

Darcy tried to catch Lizzie's eye for a brief moment as she turned to look at Bingley, but her gaze slid right over him.

"I'm just so pleased that you've all joined us here at Netherfield Park. Jane and I hope that you will all feel very welcome here for many years to come. We want this estate to be a retreat from London life and a place to build many happy memories."

"I have a question," Lydia interrupted. "Kitty and I saw the ballroom—is there to be a ball while we're here?"

"Oh," Bingley said, looking to Jane. "Er—"

"Lydia, that's impolite," Lizzie chastised when it was clear that Mrs. Bennet was also eagerly waiting for a response to her youngest daughter's question.

"We haven't planned one," Jane said.

"Oh, but dear, you must consider it," Mrs. Bennet insisted. "It's your first summer in your new home. Surely there are enough families of good standing in the area to hold a simple ball?"

Darcy had not ever in his life known a ball to be "simple," but Mrs. Bennet looked at her new son-in-law expectantly.

"A ball? In the country?" Caroline scoffed. "Who will come, farmers and their sheep?"

"Sheep might make for more interesting conversationalists," Lizzie muttered, and Darcy bit his tongue to keep from laughing.

"There are a number of genteel families in the neighborhood," Jane said. "Not as many as in London, of course, but we shall not want for company here. It's only that with the repairs—"

"Do throw a ball, Jane!" Kitty implored. "*Please.*"

"You simply must—Jane, tell your husband he must!" Lydia looked as though she'd stamp her foot if she didn't get her own way.

"Perhaps we can discuss it?" Bingley said, posing the response as a question as he glanced to Jane. And Darcy knew that this was a fatal error, for the youngest Bennets took this as confirmation and began to squeal and clap their hands.

"We shall certainly discuss it," Jane said firmly, "but that doesn't mean—"

"We're going to a ball! We're going to a ball!" Lydia and Kitty chanted, and then Lydia broke off and said, "Mama, can we have new dresses?"

"Of course you shall have new dresses," Mrs. Bennet said. "I'm sure the modiste in the village won't be as fine as anything in London but should be quite serviceable."

Bingley seemed to realize the magnitude of his error just then, and looked wide-eyed over to Darcy. *Good luck*, Darcy mouthed.

"Girls, hush," Lizzie said. "Now is not the time—Bingley was in the middle of a speech."

The younger girls collapsed on a settee, giggling to each other, but they did quiet down.

"Hmm, they *can* listen," Caroline remarked. Lizzie shot her an open glare, one that Darcy was absolutely certain no one in the room had missed—except for maybe Mr. Bennet, who was already looking back toward his folded-up newspaper.

Bingley cleared his throat again. "Jane and I will discuss the matter of the ball. But in the meantime, I hope you'll be very comfortable here, and if there is anything you should want or need, you have only to ask . . ." He trailed off quickly, as if realizing he was opening himself up to more requests from Kitty and Lydia.

"It's cold in here," Caroline proclaimed. "Can't you ring for a maid to light a fire?"

"Caroline, it's June," Bingley said.

"And?" She glared at her brother and made a show of rubbing her arms. "I feel a draft."

"Of course," Jane said, nodding at the butler standing unobtrusively in the corner. "I'm terribly sorry, Caroline. And it may be summer, dear, but these old houses can be chilly in any season."

"Being a cold shrew must affect her temperature," Lizzie muttered, so quietly that only Charlotte and Darcy could hear. He let out a bark of laughter that he quickly smothered in a cough.

Lizzie looked in his direction, and for a moment he saw merriment dancing in her eyes. Hope fluttered in his chest, but then Caroline had to ruin the moment by addressing him directly. "Mr. Darcy, are you to stay the *entire* summer with us?"

He resisted the temptation to narrow his eyes at her in suspicion. "Yes."

Caroline arched one eyebrow. "Really? Isn't that an awful lot of time away from your precious work?"

"I can take the time," he said, although he really shouldn't. When his father found out that he'd left London for weeks to spend the season in the countryside, there would be hell to pay.

But what was his work to Lizzie's safety?

"How fortunate," Caroline said, settling herself into the chair by the empty fireplace. "I've often thought it must be tiring, working so much day in and day out."

"I don't find it tiring doing work I enjoy," Darcy said.

Caroline let out a brittle laugh. "And I've never found work to be something I enjoy doing."

"Perhaps that is because you don't work?" Lizzie suggested. "After all, one can hardly recognize the value of a thing they've never undertaken."

From the smug look on Caroline's face, this was exactly the sort of response she'd been hoping for. "Too true, Miss Bennet. I've never had to debase myself with anything so pedestrian as a *job*."

The air in the drawing room went still as a tense silence followed. Lizzie recovered from the shock first. "There's nothing debasing about honest work. We all must eat and have shelter and clothes on our backs. If we aren't laboring for those comforts ourselves, then I assure you that someone out there is. The only thing shameful about that is acting as though you're better than those who work hard for *your* comfort."

Lizzie's speech had the misfortune—or perhaps it was fortune, really—to be interrupted by the arrival of a housemaid carrying a bucket of hot coals from the kitchens. Everyone turned to look in her direction and she made a squeaking sound not unlike a mouse before dropping a sloppy curtsy to the assembled party.

Caroline sniffed and said, "Oh, good. It's gotten rather frosty in here."

The maid scurried to the fireplace, not looking at any of them, and Caroline stood, as if she didn't want to be too close to the actual labor of starting the fire she required. "Besides, I think you're mistaken, Miss Bennet."

Lizzie raised one eyebrow, and Darcy mentally begged her not to fall into Caroline's trap. "Oh? About what?"

"There is a difference between a job, and work. It is unseemly for a lady to hold a job, but work is unavoidable, even for members of the ton. Why, is it not work to find all your daughters good matches, Mrs. Bennet?"

Mrs. Bennet appeared surprised to be singled out in such a way, but it passed quickly. "Oh, a tremendous amount of work," she agreed eagerly. "Five daughters! One would be trouble enough, but you haven't the faintest clue the lengths I've gone to—"

"Exactly," Caroline said, neatly cutting her off. "But it is our duty, as ladies, to keep our husbands' homes and run households and raise children and see them properly settled in life. And there is nothing more sacred than a woman's role in the home."

Lizzie's mouth was a hard line, and Darcy didn't have to guess at what she was thinking—but surely whatever would come out of Lizzie's mouth would only fan the flames of this conversation, which is why he made the impulsive decision to cut in.

"You won't find me arguing that women don't work, even at running households, but I hardly think it fair to say that it's all women ought to do. Why not leave room for other occupations?"

"Surely you can't be advocating for women to find work outside the home, Mr. Darcy?" Caroline asked aghast. "It is one thing to take an interest, to dabble, but only until marriage."

Lizzie laughed, a sharp sound. "Caroline, you ask that question as though it's not something ladies do every day."

"Women," Caroline corrected. "Not *ladies*."

Darcy saw Lizzie's spine go rigid and Charlotte's expression become fixed. Of course Caroline would not consider the many young ladies who needed to work in order to keep themselves out of poverty, like Charlotte. She was an educated and well-mannered lady, but whatever her parents had left her when they died had not stretched into adulthood.

"I think men deserve a little competition," Bingley declared. His cheeks were pink, and Darcy knew what it must have cost his friend, who was normally very conflict-averse, to speak up against his sister. "After all, if not for Lizzie and Charlotte, our business would have been lost."

"Why does it always come back to that?" Caroline snapped. "I don't see why young ladies should be doing the jobs of men. You don't see gentlemen engaged in women's work."

"Perhaps they should," Lizzie said with a scoff. "I'd like to see a man make a loaf of bread or hem a dress before they tell me I can't negotiate a contract."

"You're full of the most absurd ideas," Caroline said, and then turned abruptly to the maid kneeling before the fireplace. "Speaking of work, where is the fire?"

"I'm sorry, miss!" the maid said in a small voice.

Darcy looked to see the girl desperately pumping the small bellows, trying to coax the stack of dry wood and kindling to catch from the coals brought up from the kitchen. But every time she managed to get the air flowing and the kindling to catch, the flames would fall down again, and smoke trailed past her, hanging in the drawing room. Darcy could see the girl's hands were shaking with every new attempt, and the attention from the party was not helping.

"Here," he said, standing to go by her side. "Allow me to assist."

"You can't be serious, Darcy!" Caroline scoffed.

And perhaps it was the drinks he'd downed on an empty stomach, but Darcy shot her a glare and said, "Why not? Can a man not do a woman's task?"

A snort of laughter from Lizzie galvanized him, even as Jane looked on with dismay and Bingley was rubbing his temples. "Darcy, I can ring for someone, you don't have to—" Jane began, but he waved off her protest.

"I know I don't have to, but I'd like to. I agree with Lizzie—I think men ought to know how to do as much as women. What if I were stranded somewhere with no help, and in danger of freezing to death unless I could light a fire?"

He looked down at the maid's handiwork and tried not to think about the fact that she had likely lit a hundred fires for every small fire he'd started when he wasn't inclined to ring for a servant. But Caroline had annoyed him so much, and the poor maid was practically quivering from fear, so he didn't regret stepping up.

"I can get it going with the bellows, sir," the maid said, so softly he almost couldn't hear, "but it won't keep."

"Well, that should be easy enough to solve. Is the damper open all the way?"

"I . . . I think so? I'm sorry, sir, but you see, I've never lit this fireplace before."

"Honestly, the ineptitude," Caroline huffed behind him.

"That's all right. It's an antique, this fireplace," Darcy said. "I've got one just like it at my estate, and they can be temperamental."

"Honestly, Darcy, I'll ring for Grigson," Jane said.

"No need." Darcy looked for the lever to control the damper. It was tucked unobtrusively below some of the more extravagant detailing of the mantel. He gave it an experimental nudge, but it didn't give. "You know, I don't think the damper is open."

"I'm sorry, sir," the maid said, stepping back. "I'm new here, and I thought—"

"Don't you worry," Darcy said cheerfully, gripping the level and giving it a pull. "It's just a matter of opening it up and—"

But the lever really didn't want to move, even when he put his back into it.

"Oh, Darcy, please don't tax yourself," Jane said.

But Darcy was determined, if for no other reason than it would annoy Caroline. "I've got it, thank you. I think just another . . . good . . . pull . . ."

With a metallic screech, the damper gave just a bit. He peered into the fireplace and up, and could see the damper had opened partway—perhaps a hand's width. It was probably not a wise idea to light a fire in a fireplace that hadn't been used in decades, much less one that clearly needed to be swept out. He squinted into the darkness—was it just that dark, or was there something blocking his view?

"Can you remove the coals?" he asked the maid. "I think there is something stuck in the chimney."

"Really, Mr. Darcy! A man of your station!" Mrs. Bennet sounded scandalized.

He cast a glance over his shoulder to the assembled party. The younger Bennet sisters were looking on in horror, Jane was biting her lip again, and Mr. Bennet had lowered his newspaper, deeming Darcy's actions at least marginally more interesting than whatever the paper had to say. But Darcy's gaze met Lizzie's, and she was staring straight at him with a mix of wonder and surprise and was that . . . a challenge in her eyes? She tilted her head and raised a brow.

Definitely a challenge.

"Oh no, I insist," he said, and allowed the maid to come forward and expertly sweep up the dying coals into a bucket so he could properly inspect the inside of the fireplace without getting burned. "After all, Bingley, I told you I'd be happy to lend a hand with the estate."

"Well, I didn't mean for you to sweep my chimneys for me," his friend said, sounding baffled.

"He's going to be covered in soot," Caroline said with disgust, but Darcy ignored her and stepped into the fireplace. It was so large that he only had to crouch a bit to look up at the damper. It had not escaped him that this was a rather foolish exhibition, but if it earned him Lizzie's attention, then it would be worth it.

The innards of the chimney were totally dark, and so the

only dim light he had to go on was in the drawing room itself. Gritting his teeth, he reached up into the meager opening, hoping he wasn't about to plunge his hand into a rat's nest. Or a bunch of bats—did bats live in chimneys? He didn't want to find out.

Darcy was expecting the worst, so he was surprised when his hand touched something firm, and covered in . . . cloth? Was there a wad of fabric stuffed into the flue? That seemed rather dangerous, and he was grateful all of a sudden that the maid hadn't gotten the fire to stay lit. The last thing they needed was to burn the place down. He felt around the blockage, trying to get a sense of the shape, but wasn't able to determine anything definitive, except that it appeared to be large. Growing confident, he pushed his entire arm into the opening.

"What is it?" Lizzie asked, and Darcy turned his head to find her lifting her skirts to step over the fender.

"Not sure," he grunted. "It's as if someone stuffed a large . . . something . . . up here."

The ladies in the room began to whisper, and Bingley came forward. "Don't trouble yourself, Darcy. I thought the chimneys were all swept last week, but we can call someone to take a look."

"No, I think I've got it," Darcy said. "The damper won't open because whatever it is is slumped down on it, but I'm going to push up and then Lizzie, pull on the damper lever."

Lizzie had already placed her hand on the lever. "All right, ready."

"One, two, three . . ." Darcy grunted as he pushed the object up. It was, he was certain now, heavier and bigger than he'd initially suspected. Cloth-wrapped, but something beneath his hand felt brittle and hard. It scraped up the inside of the flue reluctantly before stopping, but Lizzie managed to push the lever of the damper so the cover moved back, now unstuck. Darcy sneezed at the sudden swirl of old soot and dust, and lost his grip on the object. Only now that the damper was open, it was coming down the flue—right on top of him.

He jumped out of the way in time for the blockage to tumble down with a hard thud—but there was a hollow sound there, too, along with the ripping of old fabric. The Bennet sisters squealed and Caroline let out a small shriek of surprise as a cloud of gray dust billowed out from the fireplace, covering Darcy, Lizzie, the carpet, and the nearby furniture.

So much for showing up Caroline Bingley. She'd complain about the absolute mess he'd made for months. *Years.*

As the dust settled, Darcy could see the object that had fallen into the bare hearth was much larger than he had anticipated, about the size of a large dog. It was irregularly shaped and wrapped in a tattered brown cloth. It was, most certainly, not a rat's nest.

"That is not what I was expecting," he murmured, ignoring Caroline's cries about her sullied skirts.

"And what exactly were you expecting when you foolishly reached your hand into that flue?" Lizzie asked, coming closer to the object. It was the first time in days, Darcy realized, that she hadn't sounded annoyed with him—she was close to her old self again, almost teasing.

"Rats?" he asked.

She burst out laughing then, and the sound was so unexpected that he found himself grinning.

"Um, Darcy?" Bingley said.

Both he and Lizzie turned to look at Bingley, whose expression had gone ashen—and not just because he happened to be covered in a fine layer of grime. He was staring down at the floor.

The fraying cloth had come loose when the object had been dislodged from its unconventional resting place—tearing and falling aside to reveal something that Darcy could not, at first, fully register. It was a roundish object protruding from one end, brown and weathered and covered in more dust and debris. He took in every detail, slowly, his mind not coming up with the proper word for what he was seeing—at least, not until Caroline began to scream.

Darcy was staring into the sunken, empty eyes of a human skull.

THREE

In Which Lizzie and Darcy Make a Wager

OF ALL THE FOOLISH things Lizzie could imagine Darcy doing on this holiday, pulling a literal skeleton from the walls of Netherfield Park was the least of them.

Most of the ladies became hysterical, of course. Caroline, Kitty, and Lydia wouldn't stop screaming, and Mrs. Bennet had fallen into a swoon—a genuine one, probably, considering that she'd landed on the floor and not daintily on the settee or in someone's arms. Jane was trying fruitlessly to get her sisters to calm down, and Charlotte looked as though she'd seen a ghost. Mary sat in the corner, features drawn into a worried expression, and Mr. Bennet tossed his newspaper aside and came to stand next to Bingley.

But Lizzie was scarcely paying attention to anyone else. She looked straight at Darcy, whose mouth had fallen open with shock, and put her hands on her hips and said, "Well, this is a fine mess you've pulled down onto Jane's new carpet."

"I was trying to unblock the chimney!"

"And you've accomplished it," she said. "Shall we add chimney sweep to your list of credentials?"

"Lizzie, be serious. There's a dead body in the hearth."

She almost wanted to laugh then, but then remembered that she was cross with him.

"Is it really a dead body, sir?"

Lizzie had quite forgotten the maid, who had gone to cower behind a chair when the body had come tumbling down. Now she stepped forward timidly, scarcely able to look at the bundle.

Lizzie looked down at the skull, which she realized with fascinated horror still had a fair amount of dark hair attached to it. "It would appear so."

The maid began to tremble, and a strange hiccupping sob slipped out of her. "I can't—I can't be here!"

"I know it's upsetting," Lizzie said in her best soothing voice. "But—"

But . . . what? Lizzie hesitated on her next words. *He's long dead? You're safe? Whoever killed him and stuffed him up the chimney is very unlikely to still be lurking around?*

Lizzie didn't know nearly enough about the situation to be reassuring. All she knew was there was a *body*. In Jane's *drawing room*.

"Sarah, you're in shock," Jane said, stepping forward to place a hand on the maid's shoulder. "We all are. This is a dreadful thing, but I assure you, my sister is going to get to the bottom of this. Why don't you sit down?"

But Sarah was shaking her head vehemently. "I can't stay

here. I always thought it was merely stories, but I can't work in a cursed place!"

"Sarah, please," Jane tried again, but the maid shoved Jane's hand away and took off toward the door, throwing it open and racing out into the hallway. "Oh, heavens—someone ought to go after her!"

"I agree," Lizzie said. "I want to know what she meant by—"

Mr. Grigson burst into the room with an expression close to alarm. "I beg your pardon, sir," he said, addressing Bingley, "but I just saw Sarah leave the drawing room at a run, and she went straight out the front door. I can only imagine what might have caused her to do such a thing, and I can assure you—"

He stopped when he saw what was lying in the hearth, and went white.

"Mr. Grigson, don't you go running off, too," Lizzie said.

"I-I-I . . . I see," he said, although it was clear he did not. "Is that . . . ?"

"I'm afraid so," Bingley said, and then he turned to Lizzie and Darcy. "Whom does one call in a situation such as this? It seems as though it is much too late to call a doctor, but an undertaker does feel rather . . . preemptive, considering."

Bingley didn't say it, but Lizzie supposed he didn't have to. Everyone knew there was no innocent reason for a body to be stuffed up the chimney.

Lizzie looked at the body more closely and realized that what she was looking at was no mere skeleton with hair. While the shape of many of the bones was clearly visible, something like thin, brown leather stretched over the remains. Flesh, Lizzie realized. Or what was left of it. That explained then why there was still dark hair clinging to the skull, patchy and not very long, covering most of the head except where . . .

"Well, that's something," she muttered.

"What?" Darcy asked, pressing close behind her.

"I'm hardly an expert in anatomy, but what does that look like to you?"

Now Mr. Bennet and Bingley had joined in peering over her shoulder. It was her father who voiced what Lizzie had noticed. "Cracks."

"More than cracks," Darcy said. "The skull looks bashed in."

Bingley made a strange gasping noise and Lizzie looked up in alarm. Was he going to retch?

Mr. Bennet pulled his son-in-law away from the body and thumped him on the back. "Well, that settles it, then. A constable. Does this village happen to have one?"

"Yes, sir," Mr. Grigson said. "I'll call for him right away."

Lizzie's eyes met Darcy's, and for a moment she forgot about their animus. He had pulled a body from the flue, and its skull was cracked in. It could only point to one thing.

Murder.

But Lizzie's excitement was ruined by Caroline proclaiming, "I won't stay here! Not if there are skeletons and goodness knows what else!"

"Caroline," Bingley said with a heavy sigh.

"No, Charles! I mean it!"

"All right," Jane said, clapping her hands together sharply. "Now, we've all had quite a shock. I'll ring for tea, and we'll postpone dinner—"

Mrs. Bennet appeared to regain consciousness abruptly. "Jane, you can't expect us to take tea in the same room where a dead man lies!"

"Of course not, Mama—we can use the morning room for now. In fact, should we perhaps—"

"I have a question," Lydia interrupted. She had managed to calm herself far more quickly than Caroline, and she was peering toward the body with wide-eyed interest. "How do you know it's a man, Mama?"

Lizzie looked to her youngest sister. It was a good question, and it was always disarming when Lydia spoke sense.

"Because only men get murdered," Mrs. Bennet explained.

"Ah," Lydia said, nodding.

Lizzie rolled her eyes. "That's not true at all," she quickly corrected. "In my experience, women are murdered just as often as men. In fact, it's rather disconcerting, when you consider the numbers—"

"Oh, stop it, all of you!" Caroline snapped. "I don't want to spend another second more in this room, discussing murder! It's all you ever talk about!" She stomped out of the room, slamming the door behind her. She could be heard muttering to herself as she went down the hall.

"Oh dear," Lizzie said. "I do believe we might have driven Caroline to the brink."

Her words came out a bit less sympathetic than she meant them. "She'll recover," Jane said firmly. "We all will. Now, to the morning room. I'll call for tea."

She gave Lizzie a significant look as she corralled their younger sisters to help Mrs. Bennet to her feet and steered the rest of the ladies out of the room.

"I don't always talk about murder," Lizzie muttered when her sisters and mother were gone.

"Yes, you do," Darcy said.

"Even a little bit is more than your mother can manage," Mr. Bennet said.

"Well then, isn't it fortuitous for her that this body has clearly been dead for a good long while, and whoever is responsible is likely long gone?"

She knew that her father, Charlotte, and Darcy recognized her sarcasm for what it was, but Bingley, bless him, did not. "Er . . . no? Because wouldn't that make the killer all the more difficult for you to find?"

Lizzie turned to him. "Me? Oh, no."

Now Bingley looked truly confused, even more so than when the body had first appeared. "You aren't going to investigate this case?"

"That depends. I thought I wasn't allowed to investigate dangerous cases anymore." She looked at her father as she said this.

Mr. Bennet had the decency to look slightly abashed, but it gave Lizzie no satisfaction. She couldn't help but think of that fateful day when the last letter from Lady Catherine had arrived in the post. After she hadn't shown up to Lady Catherine's appointed meeting spot, Lizzie had known that the other lady wouldn't simply move on. And when she got the next letter, she wasn't going to hand it off, no—surely there would be some sort of clue in the letters, something Lizzie could use. So when the crisply folded note arrived, she'd actually been excited to break the seal right there in the front hall, pulse thundering in anticipation.

But it wasn't long before her insides had turned to ice at the words written inside.

She'd taken the note to her father and Darcy directly, of course. She might have been eager to solve the case, but she wasn't foolhardy. And she'd watched their faces sour with fear as they read the note.

My dear Miss Bennet,

I really thought better of you. Do you recall the first time we spoke, formally, in my carriage? You told me that you wish to be useful. I so admire usefulness in young ladies, especially ones such as yourself. You have talent and determination. Which is why I am so very disappointed that you chose not to keep our meeting.

I grow weary of being coy. You have proven yourself a keen solicitor, and I have a need for legal services. At one time I thought I might persuade you to see the wisdom of entering my employ, but your stubbornness has ensured that we must resort to unpleasantries. Allow me to be forthright: If you do not take my case, I will find Mr. Darcy first. He works such long hours at Pemberley, and as of late chooses to walk home rather than ride in his fine carriage—your influence, I presume? And if that does not convince you, then I'll come for your father next. Does he always walk home with his nose in a newspaper?

And lest you think I'll stop there, there are your younger sisters to consider—Mary, Kitty, and Lydia. Four is an awful lot of daughters to have still at home, I'm sure your mother would agree. How might she feel to have one or two fewer girls on the marriage mart? Why, if she were left with just you and no one else in the world, she'd have to depend on you to care for her in her old age—if losing her family wouldn't send her to an early grave.

Shall we try this again? You know the time and place already. I'll be waiting, three days hence.

—Lady Catherine de Bourgh

Lizzie had watched her father get to the end of the letter, hands shaking as he read. She hadn't had the heart to tell him, *I told you so*. But she was still surprised when he looked up and said, "We must leave."

"What do you mean, leave?"

But he had already moved to his desk and started riffling through his writing box. "That woman has been watching us. She knows our movements and our habits, and it's no longer safe. I will write to Jane and Bingley, and if that fails, your uncle Gardiner. We can all leave the day after tomorrow and be gone from London before this meeting."

"Get the girls away from London," Lizzie agreed. "Lydia and Kitty have far too much freedom here, and they aren't careful—"

"No, Lizzie. We are *all* leaving. Even you."

"Papa, I need to stay in London," she said, struggling to keep her voice measured. "You read the letter—she'll be back at the church three days from now, and if I go—"

"No!" Her father slapped the edge of the desk. "It's bad enough you're caught up with that woman, but you will not be touching this case. I'll write to Graves and inform him of our plans."

"Papa, be sensible! That didn't work the last time, and it won't work now. She's threatened your life—we can't just run! Tell him, Darcy!"

Darcy had remained silent as Mr. Bennet had gone about his preparations, and when Lizzie looked at him now, she realized he'd gone quite pale. The last time he'd looked like that was when he'd rushed to her side after Mr. Tomlinson had given her a rather nasty beating. "Lizzie," he said.

She felt an awful shock ripple through her as he looked at her with apprehension and fear. "No."

"I don't like it," he said, as if that excused his betrayal. "But I think your father is right."

"You want me to give up."

"No, I want you to be *safe*," Darcy said.

"I want you both to leave it alone," Mr. Bennet added.

"Papa!"

He didn't even look up from the letter he was composing. "Think of it not as giving up. Think of it as taking a holiday."

But Lizzie did not want a holiday. She wanted to face Lady Catherine. She wanted to look her directly in her cold, calculating eyes and hold her accountable for all the ruin she'd caused. She didn't want her to slip away like she had twice before.

"Go," she said. "But I won't leave."

"I'll come with you," Darcy said quickly, as if Lizzie would agree to this trip if he joined them.

Mr. Bennet had just nodded at him. "That would be fine."

"I don't agree—"

"You do not have to agree, but you will obey," her father said, in a tone so severe Lizzie nearly gasped. Her mild-mannered, book-loving father had never, ever spoken to her in such a way. "This is a matter for Graves, Elizabeth. Do not make me lock you in your bedchamber, because so help me, I will."

She had been too stunned—too *hurt*—to argue any further. And just like that, she had been overruled.

Now here she was at Netherfield Park, a most intriguing matter before her. And of course they expected her to begin investigating—it was what she did, after all. But if she was going to solve a case, she'd much rather put her efforts to solving something that actually mattered by finding Lady Catherine.

"But if not you . . . who?" Bingley asked.

Lizzie shrugged. "Perhaps Darcy is willing to look into the matter."

"Of course," Darcy said. "But Lizzie . . ."

She was doing her best not to look at her father, but she

heard him sigh. "Clearly the body is quite old. It hardly seems like a pressing—or dangerous—matter."

"I beg to differ!" Bingley exclaimed. "There is a dead body in my drawing room! Who is he? How did he get there? If we don't find answers, this could prove ruinous to our reputations."

Lizzie felt herself waver then. She hated the idea of Jane's reputation being sullied by her misfortune of marrying a man who happened to inherit an estate concealing a dead body. But she remained resolute. "I have a backlog of cases back in London that absolutely require my attention, so if anything, I should be seeing to those." She gave her father a sharp look, and then sat down on a nearby settee, not caring it was covered with dust—her own green skirts were sullied anyway. "I'm sorry, Bingley, but this matter would be better suited for the local constable."

She ignored the look her father gave her—part exasperation, part disappointment—and settled in to wait. She knew, on some level, that she was being petulant. And if this had been a recent crime, she would have immediately begun asking questions. But she couldn't help feeling a tiny bit of resentment toward the men in front of her, as much as she might love and care for them.

As the silence stretched on, though, Lizzie stared at the body and the tattered, stained cloth it was wrapped in, mulling over a hundred different possibilities. It was highly suspicious that someone should be placed in a chimney to begin with. It begged the question—why go to the trouble, when there were at least ten other ways to hide a body? No, you only chose the most difficult method if it was your only option. It was clever, but not practical. First of all, the body would have created a most horrendous stench in its early days of death. Second of all, the first time anyone went to use the fireplace, it would have been discovered. It didn't seem likely the body had been placed there recently, given the fragility of the bones and the soot streaks around the stained shroud. The shroud appeared mostly intact, suggesting that the soot had come from brushing up the inside of the chimney, not from catching fire. The fireplace, therefore, had likely not been used since the body was placed there . . . which suggested that Great-Aunt Honoria had not used the fireplace in years.

Had she known what it contained? And wouldn't she have noticed the stench?

Unless . . . she had been the one to place the body there to begin with.

Lizzie shuddered at the idea of sharing a roof with a decomposing corpse. The questions were like gnats—no matter how hard she tried to bat them away, they kept popping up.

From the hall, they heard the sound of a front door opening and Mr. Grigson's hushed, urgent tones. Bingley leapt up nervously. "That must be the constable!"

He rushed out of the room, and with a sigh, Mr. Bennet followed, leaving Lizzie and Darcy alone.

Alone, except for the deceased.

Darcy didn't waste a moment. "I know what you're doing."

"Oh?"

"You're being obstinate for the sake of being obstinate. It's not in your nature to let matters this serious fall to someone else." He stepped closer to her, so close that she could reach out and touch him. She might have, had she not been so thoroughly annoyed by the knowing look in his eye.

Instead, she stood, so he wasn't looking down at her from quite so great a height. Only now that she was able to look him in the eye without craning her neck, she found that they were perilously close. "Perhaps I'm turning over a new leaf," she said sweetly, trying to ignore the thumping of her heart.

Darcy rolled his eyes, but he said, "I know you, Elizabeth Bennet. If you're not on this case by the end of the night, then . . ."

"Then what?" she challenged.

He leaned in, so close she almost thought he would kiss her. "Then I'll pack up and go back to London first thing in the morning."

His familiar scent was tantalizing, and she found herself charmed by the mischievous look in his eyes, as if he knew that he'd walked her into a corner. For one breathtaking moment she wanted to forget all the reasons she was mad at him and kiss those smug lips. But then she rallied and took in a deep breath. By the time she let it out, her armor was back up.

"If that's the case, you might want to pack your bags."

FOUR

In Which Darcy Wins the Aforementioned Wager, Much to Lizzie's Annoyance

DARCY REALLY HAD THOUGHT for a moment that she was going to kiss him.

But then he'd seen a flash of determination in her eyes as she called his bluff, and he knew that he was foolish to think it would be that easy.

Lizzie whirled away from him just as the door opened behind him and Bingley and Mr. Bennet entered, followed by Grigson and a tall, lanky man of about thirty-five, who swaggered after them with distrustful eyes. Darcy hadn't given much thought to what sort of man the local constable might be, but if he had, he supposed he would have imagined a hard-working farmer type, with an earnest expression and a worried mouth, who would be shocked by the discovery of a body in the finest manor in the county but ultimately defer to the good judgment of the solicitors in attendance.

Darcy had a feeling this constable would not be such a man.

"Darcy, Miss Bennet, this is Mr. Oliver," Bingley said. "Mr. Oliver, my friend and solicitor Mr. Darcy, and Miss Bennet—"

"Where's this so-called body?" Mr. Oliver interrupted.

Darcy stood aside and pointed at the shrouded body on the hearth. "Right there."

Darcy could read the shock in the man's expression, although he seemed to be working hard to hide it beneath a tremendous scowl. If Darcy had to guess, he'd say Mr. Oliver likely hadn't fully believed there was a body in the house and had been upset to be called away from his evening. But as he came to a crouch beside the body, it became undeniable.

"Did you touch it?" he finally asked.

"Naturally," Darcy responded. "I had to, in order to pull it—him—down from the chimney. But no one has moved it since."

"And why would you pull him out of the chimney?" Mr. Oliver asked.

"It was blocked," he said. "We were trying to light a fire."

"And don't you have servants who will unblock chimneys for you?" he asked, a touch of sarcasm in his voice.

"My sister wanted to light a fire, you see," Bingley explained. "She said she felt a draft, even though none of us could, so we rang for a maid. And the maid was having trouble, and then Darcy stepped in, only he was having trouble, too, so he began to look up the flue, and well . . . here we are!"

Leave it to Bingley to fill the awkwardness with plenty of details.

"Is that so?" Mr. Oliver asked, looking between the gentlemen and Lizzie as if they were all guilty.

"Perhaps the means of discovery are not nearly as important as what follows?" Mr. Bennet suggested. "Identification and an inquest, perhaps?"

"It'll be a short inquest," Mr. Oliver said with a scoff. "Unless this bloke looks familiar to any of you?"

Beside Mr. Bennet, Lizzie rolled her eyes.

"No," Darcy said, resorting to the clipped tone he used when dealing with an unreasonable opposing counsel. "That's rather the point—we've only just arrived, and Mr. and Mrs. Bingley have been in residence for only a month. This fellow has clearly been dead for quite some time."

"Well, I don't have the first clue who it could be," Mr. Oliver said. "This place has been closed up for fifty years, and old Mrs. Bingley, God rest her soul, wasn't keen on visitors."

Now it was Darcy who wanted to roll his eyes. "I agree that fifty years is a rather long window of time for something like this to occur, but you're the local constable—you must know about the history of the village and the estate. Have there been any disappearances over the years?"

Mr. Oliver shook his head. "None that I'm aware of."

"Any strange rumors, or unknown guests in Netherfield Park that you can think of?" Mr. Bennet prompted.

Mr. Oliver straightened up and shoved his hands into his pockets somewhat defensively. "No."

"You're sure?"

"I've been the constable for fifteen years, and my father was constable before me. Don't you think I'd know?"

Damn. Darcy had been rather hopeful that the local constable would have at least something to go on. "Without an identity, the investigation will be more difficult," he said with a sigh.

"Perhaps he was a chimney sweep," Mr. Oliver suggested. "And he got stuck."

Lizzie actually snorted, and Darcy worked to keep his own expression neutral.

"Doubtful," Mr. Bennet pronounced. "Even if a chimney sweep had the misfortune of becoming stuck in this flue, he wouldn't have been left there."

"And he was wrapped in this," Darcy said, pointing at the tattered remains of the shroud. "Which implies he was dead before he was placed in the chimney."

"Placed," Mr. Oliver echoed. "Placed by whom? The old lady?"

"Isn't that the question?" Mr. Bennet said in a tone that was almost bemused.

Lizzie was pursing her lips in a manner that told Darcy she was trying to hold back what she really thought, but still she showed no signs of stepping in. He sighed. "A body, wrapped in a shroud, was placed in the flue. When we pulled it down, we observed that its skull was cracked. A logical conclusion can be drawn that the death was not natural, and therefore was purposefully obscured. Now, given the absence of any knowledge of a missing person, I suppose we'll have to go about this the old-fashioned way."

Mr. Oliver looked suspiciously. "And what's that?"

"An examination of the evidence, followed by questioning any potential witnesses," he said, darting a glance at Lizzie. But she was resolutely not meeting his gaze, as if she didn't want to be tempted by the tantalizing mystery before them.

"Fine by me," Mr. Oliver said with a shrug. "But whoever he is, he's not a villager, I can promise you that." He crossed his arms and looked at Darcy expectantly.

Darcy looked at Bingley, who looked at Mr. Bennet, who looked at Mr. Oliver, who continued to stare Darcy down. Darcy could practically feel the impatience radiating off Lizzie, but she didn't move, either.

"Oh, fine," he said, stepping forward.

Despite the fact that he'd been involved in at least three murder investigations in his short career, Darcy had never before had the chance to examine a body for evidence. He wasn't quite sure where to begin now. The face had been exposed by the shroud, which had been eaten away slowly by time, but the rest of the body was still wrapped. He reached for an edge of the tattered material and gently pulled; it was so fragile that it gave with little effort, tearing and disintegrating as he went. It felt both rigid and fragile, and Darcy had to suck in a deep breath to steady his roiling stomach—he was really regretting the whiskey now—when he realized that the source of the many stains on the cloth were likely bodily fluids, long since dried out.

Although no strong odor of putrefaction lingered, the body gave off the scent of a long-closed musty cellar. As Darcy carefully removed fraying pieces of the shroud, he noted what appeared to be remnants of a jacket, shirt, and trousers, although he didn't find any evidence of boots still on the body's feet.

"Given the clothing, I think we can assume this was the body of a male," Darcy said, wishing he could wipe his hands. "It's difficult to tell, but the clothes appear to be somewhat plain. So perhaps not a gentleman?"

"Or not a finely dressed one," Mr. Bennet pointed out. "Is there anything in his pockets?"

Darcy grimaced. It was a reasonable question, but he didn't relish the idea of peeling back the layers of cloth any further. Nonetheless, he gingerly began to search for pockets—or what might have once been pockets. The clothing was disintegrating on the body in a most unpleasant manner, and Darcy was beginning to think there was nothing there when he found an inner jacket pocket and felt something hard between the layers of fabric. "Something's here," he said.

When his fingertips touched it, he knew it was metal of some sort—it was cool and hard, with a raised imprint on a flat surface. A coin, he thought, even before he pulled it free. And he was right—it was a small silver coin.

The men and Lizzie crowded closer, hoping for a better look at the coin. "What mint is it?" Mr. Bennet asked.

"I don't know," he said honestly, holding it up for them all to see. Despite the grime that coated the coin, though, he could tell one thing right away: it was a hefty coin. Silver coins these days were hardly worth their weight, and they tended to be snatched up by collectors or those who'd melt them for their metal. But this one had the look of the genuine thing, which Darcy had only experienced in his father's coin collections.

Lizzie plucked the coin from his hand, and he let her, not trying to hide his satisfied grin—she wore a focused expression as she crossed the room to a nearby candelabra and held the coin under the light. "It's not British."

"Quite right," Mr. Bennet said. "Bingley, your knowledge of foreign currency is better than mine—what do you think?"

Darcy got to his feet as his friend leaned in, taking the coin from Lizzie. He flipped it from one side to another and said, "Spanish, I believe. The silver cross is unmistakable, and I think it says Hispania here—I'll ring for Grigson, and he can bring in some silver polish. Perhaps we can make out a date."

Lizzie, Bingley, and Mr. Bennet were bent over the coin, which is why they didn't see Mr. Oliver's expression change. But Darcy caught it—the man's suspicion morphed into wide-eyed shock. His hands clenched into sudden fists, which he shoved into his pockets as he darted a look to the dead body, then back at the coin.

"Hispania," Lizzie echoed. "So it's from one of the Spanish colonies?"

"Very likely," Bingley said. "The Spanish have been

plundering the Americas for silver and gold for hundreds of years. Here, I think this might be a year—a one and a seven, perhaps?"

"Seventeen something," Lizzie murmured, then looked back at the body. "I'd say it's more than likely this person has been in the chimney for at least twenty years."

"How do you figure?" Mr. Oliver asked, and Darcy noticed he was wearing a spectacular scowl once again, all traces of shock gone. But Darcy knew what he had seen.

"Because there's been a shortage of silver in England for as long as I've been alive," she said. "And anyone in recent possession of good silver like this would have either sold, traded, or melted it down."

Mr. Oliver didn't have a response to that. But it was just as well, for Lizzie was already beginning to pace.

"Of course, we cannot rule out the possibility that the body is not as old as that. We need to determine the date on the coin. That will give us a range from seventeen something to about . . . well, more than a year, I'd say."

"I don't know how fast a body might decay in the flue of a chimney," Mr. Bennet said, "but I would be shocked if that body wasn't at least five years dead."

"I shall write to Marianne Dashwood," Lizzie murmured. "Perhaps her Mr. Brandon will know . . . and oh! Bingley, how many of your aunt's former servants have stayed on?"

"She had just the one," Bingley said. "Great-Aunt Honoria didn't like people in the house, apparently."

And with a dead body in her drawing room, Darcy didn't think he could blame her.

"We shall need to speak with that person," Lizzie said, and Bingley nodded and went to the door, where Grigson was standing guard.

"Stop," Mr. Oliver barked, causing them all to turn. "What is the meaning of this?"

"Of what?" Bingley asked.

"This lady starts barking orders and you all jump? I'm the constable here."

Annoyance flashed across Lizzie's face, and Darcy almost felt sorry for Mr. Oliver. "Of course, Mr. Oliver. What would you have us do?"

The man looked to Bingley once more, almost as if he were expecting him to remark on Lizzie's sass, but when he didn't, Mr. Oliver straightened. "Speak with Sally Burton, then."

"Right," Lizzie said. "Thank you for your instruction."

Bingley continued to the door, and Lizzie caught Darcy's gaze. *Careful*, he wanted to warn her. Not because he didn't think she couldn't handle herself, but because she hadn't seen what he had. This constable knew something, and until Darcy had a better sense of what his stake in this case might be, it was in everyone's best interest to proceed with caution.

It didn't take long to fetch this maid. But when Grigson opened the door and announced, "Sally, sir," the young woman who appeared was not what Darcy had expected.

First of all, she appeared to be not much older than himself, perhaps in her early twenties. She had straw-blond hair and a long nose, and her green eyes were mistrustful as she entered the room. She was tall and quite slender, but her lean frame appeared strong—no doubt she had spent her entire life in service and had the physical stamina to show for it.

"Sir?" she asked as she stepped into the room. Her expression was distantly polite, but she did not look down or tremble at being summoned to her employer's drawing room. Darcy found this unusual. In big houses such as these, there was a strict pecking order, and housemaids fell somewhere near the bottom middle. Any maid in Pemberley would be quaking in her slippers to be summoned by his father.

"Hello, Sally," Bingley said. "So sorry to disturb you, but . . . well, you've been at Netherfield for a long time?"

How long could she possibly have been at Netherfield when she looked hardly older than he? But Sally nodded. "Aye, sir. I've been coming to Netherfield since I was a child."

"Right, well . . ." Bingley looked unsure of how to proceed. "There's no easy way to say this, so forgive me but . . . do you happen to know anything about a body in the flue?"

"Sir?" she asked.

Lizzie stood aside, and Sally's eyes widened when they fell upon the shrouded body. Her mouth dropped open in shock, and she seemed to sway slightly on her feet—Darcy wondered if she'd be the second person to faint this evening, but she managed to keep her balance.

"It appears that this fellow has spent a number of years in the flue of the drawing room fireplace," Lizzie said matter-of-factly. "And while we've determined that he hasn't been placed there recently, it does beg the question . . . how long has he been there, and why?"

Sally stared at the body for a long moment, so long that Darcy wondered if perhaps she hadn't heard Lizzie. Finally she tore her gaze away and said, "I don't know anything about that, miss."

"You grew up here?" Lizzie asked.

"My mother served Mrs. Bingley, and my grandparents before her. When she died, I took her place."

"Our condolences," Darcy said stiffly. "When was that?"

"Twelve years ago," Sally said.

Which would have made Sally perhaps eleven or twelve. Darcy supposed it was possible—girls as young as fourteen went into service all the time. Usually in much larger houses, with other servants and a housekeeper to watch over them. But if Bingley's aunt had trusted no one else . . .

"And in all that time, did Mrs. Bingley ever use the drawing room?" Lizzie asked.

"Never." Sally shook her head vehemently. "All the downstairs rooms were closed off. Mrs. Bingley only ever used the upstairs morning room. No one ever came in here, not until . . . well." Her gaze fell upon the body once more before she looked away. Unlike the other maid, she didn't appear to be frightened of it. Nor did she regard it with curiosity, exactly—it was as if the body were a dead rat she might encounter in the street.

Something unpleasant that one might look at in order to identify, and then not think anything more of it.

"He ought to be buried," Mr. Oliver said suddenly. "If you can lend me a cart and horse, I'll take him to Arthur Jones—he'd be the undertaker."

Bingley nodded his assent but then looked over his shoulder at Lizzie and Darcy. "I think that would be appropriate, that is . . . if you agree, Lizzie?"

"And why should it matter to her?" Mr. Oliver groused.

"Because," Lizzie said with a resigned sigh. She pointedly did not look in Darcy's direction. "It would appear that I am investigating a murder."

Darcy didn't even try to hide his smile.

FIVE

In Which Lizzie and Darcy Declare a Tentative Truce

DARCY HAD WON THEIR silly wager, but what of it? Lizzie couldn't have known how utterly incompetent the local constable would be.

Besides, having a new case gave her something to focus her thoughts upon. And this one would prove to be quite the challenge, for Lizzie had very little to go on aside from a tarnished silver coin, a window of opportunity decades wide, and a maid who didn't seem to know anything.

It was quite late by the time the body had been transported into the village under the grumpy Mr. Oliver's supervision, and given that it had been a very long day of travel already, Lizzie was fighting off yawns. When Jane had ventured downstairs to inform them that she'd send everyone to bed with supper trays and suggested they all get a good night's sleep, Lizzie had been all too happy to ignore Darcy's pointed looks that clearly communicated he wanted to talk, and headed straight to the opulent bedroom she'd been given for the duration of her stay. The body had spent a multitude of years in the chimney—one more night wouldn't severely impact their investigation.

Upstairs, a maid had deposited Guy into her bedchamber, and he greeted her enthusiastically. She managed a few quick bites of cold supper, tossing Guy the rest of her chicken, and had barely managed to wiggle out of her dress before falling fast asleep in the large four-poster bed, Guy curled up at her feet.

When Lizzie awoke the next morning, her mind was pleasantly swathed in the soft haze of sleep, and so she wasn't immediately alarmed to hear soft footsteps and the light sound of rustling fabric. Then there was a soft clunk of something heavy being set down, and the warm, reassuring weight of Guy's small body shifted as the dog jumped to his feet and barked once. Lizzie's eyes flew open as she remembered that she wasn't at home in Gracechurch Street. She was in Netherfield Park, and *there was someone in her room.*

She sat up suddenly, ready to scream, but just barely managed not to when she saw a young woman wearing a maid's uniform standing across the room. "Good morning, miss!" she said cheerily. "I'm sorry, I didn't mean to wake you both."

"Guy, sit," Lizzie croaked out, no longer quite so alarmed but still rather unsettled. The maid was about Lizzie's age, with auburn hair and fair, elfin features. She was short but quick on her feet. She bustled about the room as if it were entirely normal to be skulking about in someone's bedroom while they snoozed the morning away.

Then again, this was Netherfield Park—it probably *was* perfectly normal.

"Good . . . morning?" Lizzie added once Guy had scampered back and sat next to her, looking up at her for further instruction. The maid snapped open the drapes, letting in a cheery morning light. Lizzie squinted against it and rubbed her eyes. "What time is it?"

"Quarter past ten." The maid laughed at the shock on Lizzie's face. "But don't worry, no one else is up yet. After all that travel and last night's excitement, I can imagine you all needed a good lie-in."

Her face turned grave, and Lizzie tried not to shudder at the memory of the desiccated body. She reached out to pet Guy instead. "Does everyone downstairs . . . know?"

"About the body, miss? I'm afraid that's not a secret anyone could keep—Jimmy the stable boy saw Sarah running away from the estate like her skirts were on fire and came right in to report it to the rest of us, so we were all astir until Mr. Grigson came down and broke the news."

"It's a terrible thing," Lizzie said slowly, although the maid wasn't acting as though she was as traumatized as poor Sarah had been. That was . . . probably a good sign?

"Oh, just terrible," the maid agreed as she poured steaming water from a pitcher into the washstand. "Mrs. Reed cleaned the drawing room herself, along with Sally. She said it was because she trusted no one else to do it, but really the other maids are too afraid to go in there. I would have done it if ordered, but Mrs.

Reed really only needed one other person, and honestly? It gives me the shivers." She shuddered dramatically as if to prove her point.

"Did the other maid come back?" Lizzie asked. "Sarah? I'm afraid we gave her a real fright."

"No, miss, she didn't report for duty this morning. The others say she's not likely to, either. She's a real superstitious sort, and her mum was against her coming to work here to begin with. Jimmy says she holds her breath walking past the churchyard—can you fathom it? What does holding your breath do?"

"I don't know," Lizzie said, but the maid's mention of superstition shook something loose in Lizzie's memory. "But she said something peculiar last night. Something about a curse?"

"Aye," the maid said, nodding sagely. She turned her attention to a breakfast tray and began pouring tea. "The Netherfield curse. How do you take your tea?"

The Netherfield curse. The words sent a delicious shiver down Lizzie's spine. "What on earth is the Netherfield curse?"

"Milk?" the maid asked. "Sugar?"

"Milk," Lizzie said, getting to her feet and crossing the room to where the maid had the breakfast tray set out. Guy hopped down after her, sticking close to her heels. She felt a bit odd standing in nothing but a nightgown, hair a mess, while the other girl was dressed and not a single auburn hair out of place. "I'm sorry, can you tell me your name?"

"It's Agnes, miss."

"My thanks, Agnes," Lizzie said, taking the teacup from her. In Lizzie's limited experience, ladies' maids could be an excellent source of gossip, but Agnes seemed very keen. Likely whatever Lizzie revealed to her would be repeated downstairs, which wasn't entirely surprising. The discovery of the body last night was probably the most shocking thing to happen at Netherfield Park in decades. Lizzie could use the maid's apparent hunger for gossip . . . as long as she treaded lightly. "Now, what's this about a curse?"

Agnes began setting out breakfast. "I don't know the exact details, miss. I was hired on only last month, and didn't hear about it until my third day. But everyone in the village says the estate is cursed—those who spend a night under its roof are doomed to stay forever or die shortly upon leaving."

Lizzie accepted the porridge topped with clotted cream. "That sounds . . . well, rather severe. Who supposedly set this curse on Netherfield?"

"Old Mrs. Bingley. I don't understand why. I was going to ask, but then Mr. Grigson came along, and he won't tolerate gossip about the family."

"Nor should he," Lizzie said, offering Guy a slice of cold chicken from the plate Agnes had brought for him.

"Of course, miss," Agnes rushed to say. "I didn't mean to imply—"

"It's all right. I did ask, after all. And I don't blame anyone for being curious about a rumored curse. But tell me—do people actually believe in it?"

"I can't speak for everyone, miss, but Sarah and one of the footmen didn't show up this morning, and all the local help goes home at night."

"What do you mean, they go home at night?"

"They refuse to sleep under this roof. So even if we aren't finished until half past one, they still walk home, in the dark."

Interesting. Lizzie ate her porridge as she pondered this so-called curse. Clearly Sarah had been terrified last night, and in the moment Lizzie had chalked up her reaction to shock and fear. But if the local villagers really believed in a curse . . .

"Do you spend the night here, Agnes?"

"Aye, miss. Me and those that came up from London."

"And do you feel as though you're in danger?"

"No, miss. The only dangerous thing about this house is how many stairs there are between here and the kitchen—not that I'm complaining!"

Lizzie smiled. "Thank you, Agnes. If you hear anything more about the curse, please do tell me. I'm not sure if I believe in such things, but if other people do, that could prove useful."

"Useful in what way, miss?"

Lizzie took another bite of the delectable porridge as she considered her next words. When she swallowed, she said, "Useful in the sense that it might tell me something about who put that body in the flue in the first place. Oftentimes there is a glimmer of truth in the stories that people tell, no matter how far-fetched they sound."

"A glimmer of truth," Agnes repeated. "I like that. Now,

will you be wearing your green lawn or the blue muslin dress today?"

Lizzie blinked in surprise. "Oh, you don't need to—I mean, I am quite accustomed to dressing myself."

"Suit yourself, miss, but I have been instructed to act as your lady's maid while you're here," Agnes said, showing the first sign of uncertainty since Lizzie had opened her eyes and seen the girl in her room.

"Oh, well . . ." Lizzie didn't want her to get in trouble, even inadvertently. "The green lawn?"

Agnes smiled wide. "Excellent, miss."

A half hour later, Lizzie was washed and dressed, her hair set in an uncharacteristically fancy twist thanks to Agnes's adept fingers, and she was taking Guy, his belly full, on his first walk of the day in the Netherfield gardens. The sun was bright and the gardens verdant and fragrant, if slightly overgrown, and the countryside felt unnaturally quiet despite the twittering of birds and the rustle of the light breeze. It was peculiar being away from London—by half-past nine in the morning, Lizzie would have seen no fewer than a dozen people, but here she'd only seen Agnes. As she strolled up and down the garden path, letting Guy see to his morning business, she couldn't help but think that this sense of isolation did not bode well for this case.

"Lizzie!"

She turned at the sound of her name, only to find Darcy standing at the end of the long hedgerow, panting slightly.

"Wait for me!" he called, and jogged after her.

Guy, the little traitor, yipped in excitement when he saw Darcy and pulled at his leash to go meet him. Lizzie dropped the leash so the dog could run ahead, and Darcy dropped on one knee to pet him. Guy whined in happiness, then flopped over in the grass, exposing his belly to Darcy. Darcy obliged by giving his belly a good rub, and then had the audacity to look up at Lizzie and smile.

"Good morning," he said, unperturbed by her own lack of excitement at seeing him. "Sleep well?"

"Smugness is unbecoming," she said with a sniff.

Darcy gave Guy's belly one last rub before getting to his feet. "Here we are, all alone out in the countryside with nothing to occupy us . . . you'd be bored if you hadn't agreed to look into the case."

Normally Lizzie felt a thrill of delight whenever she realized that Darcy understood her. Now it was just irritating. "And whose fault is it that we are out in the middle of nowhere without any cases?"

"Lady Catherine's," he said, giving her a pointed look.

"Lady Catherine didn't drive us out of our home, and if we had just stayed—"

"Then we would have been risking certain danger to ourselves, if not your family."

It was a low blow, and she glared. "You think that I don't care for their safety? I wanted them to leave London—but me staying and finding a way to meet with her would have protected them. It would have protected *you*."

She felt a sudden pressure behind her eyes and realized with alarm that tears were building. She would not let them fall.

Darcy took a step forward, squaring off with her as if about to fight some absurdly close duel. "And who would have protected you?"

It was on the tip of her tongue to say that she didn't need protecting, but she managed to keep those words in. This was well-trod territory with them. Darcy thought she was reckless, and well . . . she had been, at times. But she hadn't gotten where she was—a solicitor, at last—by not taking risks. What was it he'd said to her, the last time she'd forged ahead without him? *I just want to be included.*

Well, so did she. And having him side with her father against her . . . she wasn't sure if she was ready to forgive that.

"Running away won't solve anything," she breathed. It wasn't fair, really, because his words had stirred something in her that she didn't want to face, and he was standing so close that she could inhale his scent.

"Don't think of it as running away," he said softly. "It's a strategic retreat."

This was the rather annoying thing about courting a fellow solicitor—Darcy always had a clever rebuttal for her every argument.

"Strategic? More like reactionary. There was nothing well-planned about our flight from London."

"I beg to differ—your mother told me in great detail all the planning that went into packing the eight trunks that came with us."

She smiled against her will. But she quickly righted her expression into something more stern. "Don't."

"Don't what? Joke? Make you laugh?"

He was so close—it would be nothing to close the gap between them, to tilt her chin up and press her lips to his . . . but no! She couldn't think about kissing Darcy when she was still so irritated with him.

Except . . . the fierceness of her anger was starting to feel less like a roaring fire and more like smoldering coals.

As if sensing the warring emotions within her, Darcy said, "I know you don't like it, but Lizzie—trust that Graves is doing his job. He has dozens of men on the case."

"That's just the thing," she said. "I'm not entirely sure I do trust Graves. He has his own agenda."

They didn't know much about him, other than that he worked for the Crown and had been pursuing Lady Catherine for many months. Of course, for a great number of those months he had known that she had escaped and hadn't deigned to tell Lizzie or Darcy, leaving them in danger of being targeted by her associates.

Darcy sighed. "I can't say I blame you—I can't bring myself to fully trust him, either. But he might want to catch her as much as you do. And the Dashwoods are utilizing their resources to try to flush her out."

"If I—"

"Lizzie." He took her by the shoulders. Lizzie felt the tension in them melt away at his touch. "There is no shame in letting others investigate if it is too dangerous for you to do so yourself."

"She's killed people, Darcy," Lizzie said. "Who's to say she won't kill again, or send someone else to murder another innocent? And what if it's Marianne this time, or—"

He drew her into an embrace, and she didn't fight it. "I know," he said. "But Abigail and Leticia and even Wickham—their deaths weren't your fault. They were hers. And until we have a more solid lead, Netherfield Park is the safest place for us all."

Lizzie didn't want to agree with him, but he presented a very persuasive case. Feelings churned inside her—guilt at leaving home, frustration at being forced to walk away from the case, and under it all, fear.

What would Lady Catherine do if Lizzie failed to meet her yet again?

Darcy released her. "Now, in the meantime—we have a new case."

Lizzie rolled her eyes. "Oh yes, a case that might predate us entirely, and in which there appears to be no living witness? What a scintillating mystery this will prove to be."

"Come now, you enjoy a challenge," Darcy said, and the only thing more annoying than his confidence was the fact that he was right.

"That constable didn't seem to be interested in the slightest that there is a dead body in his county!"

"About him . . ." Darcy's expression darkened for a moment,

and Lizzie felt her interest pique. "I wouldn't trust his disinterest entirely. While you all were examining the coin, I was looking at Mr. Oliver. When Bingley revealed that he thought it was a Spanish mint, Oliver looked . . . well, alarmed. I think he knows something he's not letting on."

Oh, well . . . she hadn't been expecting *that*. "You're certain?"

"Absolutely," Darcy assured her. "He seemed unsettled—and why would a Spanish coin unsettle him more than a body in the drawing room? When he insisted on transporting it to the undertaker, I almost wanted to protest, but I couldn't think of a single decent reason to stop it."

"Well, there's not much he can do with skeletal remains." Lizzie said. "But if he knows something he isn't inclined to share . . ."

"Then it might suggest there is someone else who might know a thing or two about this stranger?"

"Well, at the very least it's interesting," Lizzie said. She shared what the maid Agnes had told her about the Netherfield curse, and Darcy looked nearly as baffled as she felt.

"It seems rather ghoulish that people believe this place is cursed," he said. "There must be a story there."

"And perhaps it's tied to our dead man," Lizzie said. She couldn't help the twinge of excitement in her belly when she said that. She tried to ignore it. "All right, we need more information. There must be those who will be willing to talk to us."

"I'm glad you think so," Darcy said. "That's why I came to find you. Bingley wants to drive into the village to speak with the undertaker and vicar about putting the body to rest. I thought you might want to come along, make a few inquiries of your own?"

Lizzie was tempted to give in to childish refusal, but there was no denying it now—they had a case, and this case was sorely lacking in detail. Detail that could only be uncovered with a bit of sleuthing.

"Fine," she relented. "But just because we have a new case—flimsy as it might be—doesn't mean I'm abandoning the search for Lady Catherine."

Rather than appearing chastised, Darcy just smiled and took her arm.

"Of course not. I never would expect you to give up on anything quite so easily."

SIX

In Which Darcy Acquires a Lead of His Own

DARCY FELT THE CURIOUS prick of eyes upon them as soon as their small party stepped out of the carriage in the middle of Meryton's high street.

The village was both smaller and busier than Darcy had been expecting. As a market town, a number of shops lined the street, and the thoroughfare was busy with wagons and carts and plenty of pedestrians. Meryton boasted its own assembly halls, and on the outskirts of the village were barracks for the British Army. That said, Darcy was fairly certain he could have stood at the top of the street and looked all the way down to the end of the village and seen everything worth visiting in one glance.

"We're still causing a bit of a stir," Bingley muttered to him as he took Jane's hand and helped her down from the carriage. "Newly up from London, restoring the old estate, and all that."

"Of course," Darcy said, but the looks they garnered were not merely curiosity or excitement—there were wary glances and darting eyes. Darcy knew without hearing any of the whispers that the people of Meryton had heard about the dead man in the flue.

"All right, where is this haberdashery?" Lizzie asked as Darcy helped her out of the carriage. She sounded, unsurprisingly, cross. Darcy offered a hand to Charlotte, who emerged last from the carriage.

"There," Jane said, tilting her head ever so slightly to a small shop with a display of ribbons in its front window. "And the milliner is next door."

"How charming," Charlotte said, taking in the village. "Well, this should hardly take any time at all, should it?"

"No," Lizzie agreed. "But I fail to see how Meryton is so dangerous that I should require so much supervision."

Bingley raised his brows, and Darcy gave a slight shake of the head. "It would be highly improper for you to go with Charles and Darcy by yourself," Jane said, which had been her argument back at Netherfield when she insisted on accompanying them. She'd also invited Charlotte, and the other young lady had been quick to accept.

"I'm not making social calls," Lizzie reminded her. "This is business."

"And this isn't London. This is the country," Jane countered.

They'd made their plan in the carriage, and Darcy had been somewhat disappointed when Jane had insisted that Lizzie and Charlotte accompany her to the shops while Bingley and Darcy called on the vicar to discuss the dead man's burial. Darcy had looked to his friend, wondering if he had been privy to Jane's machinations, but Bingley looked just as surprised as Lizzie.

"Are you worried that I'll say something improper to a man of the cloth?" Lizzie had asked her sister, sounding irritated.

"No!" Jane insisted. "But this way we can all speak with more people about . . . the unpleasant discovery. You know how ladies love to gossip."

Lizzie didn't argue, although Darcy didn't miss her look of suspicion. Even so, he was surprised when she agreed, saying, "You can question the vicar without me, can't you?" He'd agreed, although the point wasn't that he needed her—he wanted her with him because he wanted her to stay invested in this case. But it seemed improper to argue when Jane was sitting across from him in the carriage, biting her bottom lip.

Now Bingley hovered next to his wife, looking uncertain. "Are you sure you'll be all right?" he asked. "Darcy and I would be glad to accompany you inside."

"It's Meryton, not Mayfair," Lizzie said, looking at her sister. "Right, Jane?"

"Right," Jane replied, although she looked uncertain.

"We'll be fine," Charlotte said firmly, taking Lizzie's arm, then Jane's. "Now, off you go. We'll reconvene in an hour and compare notes."

"Do be careful and try not to scandalize the villagers," Bingley said.

He meant it as a joke, but Jane merely winced. "No promises," Lizzie said as she was pulled in the direction of the haberdashery.

Darcy and Bingley continued on through the village. The church was at the end of the high street, on the edge of the village. It was a demure stone building with a single bell tower, a small rectory, and a carefully kept churchyard that wrapped around one side of the building and the back. The churchyard was full of modest stones arranged in tidy rows. Darcy wondered if the man from the flue had family buried there, a clan he belonged to and who would be glad of a resting place for their loved one.

Darcy followed Bingley to the door to the rectory, but before either of them could knock, it was opened by a gentleman far younger than Darcy had expected.

"Ah, Mr. Bingley," the man said. "I wondered whether I would see you today."

"Word has spread, I see," Bingley said grimly.

"Indeed it has. Well, come in."

Darcy sized him up while Bingley made the introductions. In Darcy's experience, vicars tended to be either elderly or boorish, but this vicar was neither. His name was Mr. Thomas, and he appeared to be in his mid- to late twenties, and he had curly brown hair and brown eyes that crinkled around the corners when he smiled. He greeted Darcy cordially, not appearing to be intimidated at all by the presence of a gentleman and a solicitor in his small study. If Darcy had to guess, he would have said that Mr. Thomas was likely the second or third son of a proper family short on assets.

"It's frightful business," Mr. Thomas said as he gestured for them to take a seat. "I heard an earful from Mrs. Jones—that's the undertaker's wife—but I'm not altogether clear on the details. She said that one of you pulled the body from the chimney?"

Bingley and Darcy exchanged glances before Darcy asked, "Does everyone in Meryton know what transpired last night?"

"Everyone in Meryton, and all the neighboring farms and estates, I'd wager," Mr. Thomas said with a pleasant smile. "It's the most exciting news we've had since Mr. Boynton's prize heifer had twin calves two springs ago."

Bingley laughed. "Surely you can't be serious!"

"Well, when your aunt passed and we heard that you intended to take up residence in Netherfield Park, that was probably a close second."

"It is nice to know where one ranks," Darcy remarked.

"Indeed," the vicar agreed. "Which is why you have to forgive my questions, and everyone else's curiosity. Mrs. Jones said it was impossible to tell who the body belonged to—was there any way of identifying him?"

"No," Darcy said, not willing to give away their only clue, the silver Spanish coin found in the man's jacket pocket. "The deterioration is . . . severe. It may be difficult, but it's imperative that we identify the man as soon as possible."

"How long do you believe he's been dead?"

"It's difficult to say," Darcy said with a quick glance at Bingley. "More than a handful of years, but beyond that I couldn't tell. However, given the circumstance, it's likely . . ."

"No, certain that he's been there since my aunt's time,"

Bingley confirmed with a sigh. "Although whether she was aware of his presence, we can't say."

Silence filled the small study for a long moment, and Darcy studied Mr. Thomas closely. He doubted that in all his liturgical training, the vicar had ever been instructed on how to respond to the news of a likely decades-old murder victim discovered in the house of one of his parishioners. He almost felt sorry for the man.

But Mr. Thomas seemed to take this news in stride. "I presume you'll want to arrange for a burial?"

"Yes, please," Bingley said. "A proper one, if we can. We may not know the fellow, but he doesn't deserve a pauper's grave. I want to see that he's laid to rest with a full service, even if only my wife and I are in attendance."

"I doubt you will be the only ones," Mr. Thomas said, but Darcy sensed approval in his tone. "I've already fielded a number of inquiries."

"Really?" Darcy asked. "By whom? People who might have known who the man was?"

Mr. Thomas shook his head. "Now, that I cannot say. No, the interest from the village is more . . . mundane, unfortunately."

"You mean there's been plenty of gossip," Darcy said bluntly.

The vicar winced. "It's difficult to overstate just how little excitement we get in Meryton."

Darcy couldn't help the sigh that escaped him. "I don't suppose you might have any idea who our dead man might be?"

"I'm afraid not. But if he's been dead a number of years, I'm not certain how much help I'd be anyway. I've only had the living here in Meryton for four years. Before me, Dr. Fellowes was here for, oh, I don't know, twenty-seven years? But he's passed on, unfortunately."

That was disappointing news, but if there was one thing Darcy had learned from Lizzie, it was to keep pressing. "You've never heard of any local man going missing, or stories of someone disappearing under mysterious circumstances? Or perhaps a newcomer to the village who left abruptly?"

"No, none of that, I'm sorry to say. People do leave, of course. They strike out for better farms, sometimes they join the military or navy, occasionally head off for work in London. But there's usually no mystery in that."

"Can you give us names?"

The vicar looked at Bingley. "I suppose, but no one comes to mind as someone who might be your dead man. You're very motivated to discover his identity?"

Darcy opened his mouth to say of course he was, a man had clearly been murdered and his body hidden away, but Bingley spoke first. "Well, it only seems right. And besides, there have been some rumors swirling about that I think Mrs. Bingley would prefer to be put to rest."

"The curse?" Mr. Thomas asked sympathetically.

Darcy lifted his brows in surprise. "You know about the curse?"

Mr. Thomas chuckled. "You spend enough time in Meryton, and someone will mention it. My parishioners may shy away from sharing their superstitious lore with me out of fear I'll keep them an extra hour in the pews on Sundays, but I'm afraid rumors of the curse on Netherfield Park are well-known."

"And what exactly does the curse say?" Darcy asked, leaning forward. He could imagine Lizzie doing the same thing. "We've heard bits here and there, but . . ."

"I don't know the exact details, I'm afraid," Mr. Thomas said, sounding truly regretful. "From what I gather, your great-aunt was at the center of it, Mr. Bingley. Something to do with why she hid herself away for so many decades. But I do know that in a small village where positions in service aren't easy to come by, most families won't send their youth to work for Netherfield Park if it means they must spend the night within the estate's gates."

"Oh, I gathered that much," Bingley said. "I had to bring most of my staff up from London, and my butler informed me I've lost two servants since yesterday."

"I'm sorry," Mr. Thomas said, "but I'm afraid this discovery won't help your home's reputation."

Darcy felt frustration well up inside him. There had to be a way to figure out who this man might be, short of questioning every single villager in Meryton. His gaze wandered the room, falling upon a very large Bible that sat open on a nearby table. The Darcy family Bible back at Pemberley was nearly as large, although certainly more ornate. It held the birth and death records of every Darcy going back to 1626 . . .

Birth records. Death records.

"Don't you keep records of all births and deaths?" Darcy asked.

"Of course," Mr. Thomas said. "But . . . you think that the man you found will be in the parish records?"

"Not his death, obviously," Darcy said. "But perhaps his birth, and if we cannot account for someone's death, then maybe that will give us a lead we need."

"But what if the man isn't from Meryton?"

Then this investigation would be at a dead end. But Darcy wasn't ready to think like that. He needed to have something to show Lizzie. With a new case at Netherfield to distract her, perhaps she would leave the issue of Lady Catherine well enough alone until Graves could make some headway. "We have to start somewhere. May I see them?"

"Well, I can show you what I have." Mr. Thomas rose and led him over to a shelf of simply bound ledgers and began to draw them out. "This is the latest register, started by my predecessor. Between us, Dr. Fellowes had an atrocious hand."

He handed the register to Darcy, who opened the book somewhere in the middle. The most recent entries were neat and orderly, recording names and dates, baptisms and burials. Darcy flipped back through the pages, watching as the years ticked back. Toward the front of the book, he encountered pages of uneven, hastily scrawled records. He squinted. "This is hardly legible!"

"It's quite awful," Mr. Thomas agreed. "Which is why I'm arranging for them to be reprinted at the Jeffries Print Shop. That's where the rest of the registers are, at the shop. Miss Clara Jeffries has been working on this task for . . . oh, a couple of months, perhaps?"

Darcy handed the book back to Mr. Thomas. "We need to see those records."

"Oh! Well . . . all right, I suppose. I think Clara is nearly done, but—"

"We can go there now and collect the registers," Darcy said eagerly, glancing at his friend. Bingley nodded, although he looked slightly confused by Darcy's rush.

"Well, I haven't settled up with Clara . . ."

"I can pay," Darcy offered. "For the printing of the registers. I'm happy to contribute to this endeavor if it means we might be able to inspect the records for any clue as to who the man might be."

Mr. Thomas thought about it for a long moment. "That is . . . very generous. I suppose it wouldn't hurt if you were to look through them."

Darcy intended to do far more than just look. "Finding what we need might take a while. Can we take the registers with us back to Netherfield to study them?"

The vicar's alarm was evident in his wide-eyed expression. "Take them back to Netherfield?"

"Just temporarily," Bingley assured him. "And we'd keep them very safe."

"And we'd only need the last . . . oh, eighty years or so? Perhaps one hundred, to be on the safe side?"

Mr. Thomas thought for a moment, and finally nodded his assent. "All right. I suppose the whole purpose of these records is to have them in case . . . well, not in case there is a murder victim we need to identify, but in case anyone comes along and wants to know the history of the village. But please be careful with them."

"Of course," Darcy said, eagerness thrumming through him. It was not a very exciting lead, but at least he wouldn't be returning to Lizzie empty-handed. "Thank you. Do you mind if we go now?"

"I make my rounds to the farms north of the village today," Mr. Thomas said. "And if I don't leave soon, I'll never be back before dark. But I'll write you a note to take Miss Jeffries, saying that I give my permission for you to take the registers."

"Thank you," Darcy said, reaching out to shake the vicar's hand. "Thank you very much!"

Bingley and Mr. Thomas then discussed the final details of the dead man's burial, setting a date for a service two days from then. Mr. Thomas wrote a quick note on a slip of paper and folded it tightly, writing *Miss Clara Jeffries* on the outside before handing it to Darcy, and the two took their leave.

"He's an agreeable one," Bingley said. "It's rather nice having some youthful energy in the parish. And his sermons don't put me to sleep, either."

"While I'm happy for you on that count, for once I wish we'd encountered an old, stodgy vicar," Darcy said, following Bingley to the carriage. "Someone with a long memory for every mundane detail about his parish who could say, 'Oh, you found a body in your chimney? It must be old Jimmy Hackett—we always wondered what happened to him!' "

Bingley snorted. "And have your mystery solved in a moment? Now where's the fun in that?"

SEVEN

In Which Lizzie Extends a Rather Impulsive Invitation

JANE WAS ACTING ODD.

Normally, Lizzie's older sister was sweet and easygoing, and she very rarely made demands. Which was why Lizzie was so perplexed when Jane had not only insisted upon accompanying them into the village along with Charlotte but had also proposed a last-minute change of plans. Arguing for propriety was one thing, but trying to direct the course of the investigation . . .

Something was amiss.

"Jane, is everything all right?"

"Everything is fine," she said. "Now, once we are inside, please don't make any overt mentions of murder, dead bodies, or any other indelicate topics. Do remember to hold your shoulders back and smile."

She sounded so much like their mother in that moment that Lizzie nearly stumbled. "Might I remind you that we are looking into a suspicious death, and I only agreed to come with you rather than go to the vicar because you said that ladies have the best gossip!"

"Hush!" Jane said, already reaching for the door.

Lizzie had little time to do anything but cast a puzzled look at Charlotte, who appeared as baffled as she, before a bell tinkled overhead, drawing the gaze of every lady within the small shop, including two women behind the counter wearing green aprons.

"Good day!" Jane squeaked.

Lizzie stared at her sister. Jane never *squeaked*.

No one spoke immediately—in fact, Lizzie got the sense that there had been conversation just a moment ago, but now it was quickly hushed upon their arrival. The moment stretched out into awkwardness until finally one of the green-aproned ladies said, "Good day, Mrs. Bingley."

But that was it. No follow-up questions, no offers of help locating buttons or a bolt of silk. Not even a banal comment upon the fine weather they were having! Lizzie eyed the other women of the shop with suspicion and realized they were doing the same.

So the news had spread.

Next to her, Jane shifted uncomfortably, and Lizzie remembered her sister's orders. Well, if she couldn't ask questions directly, she could play the part of visiting sister, and perhaps pry information out of the ladies that way.

"What a charming shop!" Lizzie exclaimed. "Jane, you described it so perfectly in your letters, I feel like I've been here before."

The shop was, in fact, nothing special. It contained the requisite ribbons and silks, buttons and needles, and bolts of fabric alongside yarn and other various notions. Compared to the haberdashery that the Bennet ladies frequented in London, this one was rather small. But Lizzie noted the way the two women behind the counter—likely the proprietors—seemed to take her comment with matching smiles. They had the same dark hair streaked with gray, and shrewd eyes, and Lizzie guessed they must be sisters.

"Is there anything I can help you find, miss?" the younger-looking one asked. Her face was framed by curls while her sister favored a more severe style with little embellishments.

"Hair ribbons," Lizzie said. "Mrs. Bingley told me you had a lovely selection?"

"Of course," she said.

Lizzie stepped forward, dragging Charlotte along, and pretended to admire the small selection of ribbons, using this as an opportunity to survey the rest of the women. There were about eight shoppers in total, all women ranging in age from a young teenage girl about Lydia's age to a woman older than her mother. And every single one of them was doing their very best to study Jane, Lizzie, and Charlotte without appearing to care about them.

Lizzie let out a tiny sigh. Oh, how she loathed society's games.

Jane approached a lady only a little older than themselves. "Miss Nelson, how lovely to see you again."

Miss Nelson actually jumped, dropping the card of lace she'd been inspecting. She rushed to pick it up, and then when she had straightened back up said, "Mrs. Bingley! Hello!" as if she hadn't seen Jane come in just moment earlier.

Lizzie felt her hands tighten into fists.

"How is your family?" Jane asked.

"Well," Miss Nelson said. "And how is . . ."

The words seemed to die in her throat and she cast a nervous glance around the shop, as if hoping for someone to rescue her. Lizzie abandoned the ribbons and stepped around the display. "Hello," she said. "I'm Miss Elizabeth Bennet, Jane's sister from London. And this is our dear friend, Miss Lucas."

"A pleasure to meet you," Miss Nelson said, although her expression seemed to say that this was not the distraction she had been looking for.

Lizzie affected a voice not unlike Lydia's—breathy and overly enthusiastic. "We've been dying to visit, ever since Jane left us to marry Mr. Bingley. And everything about Meryton and the countryside is just so charming. Wouldn't you agree, Charlotte?"

"Absolutely darling," Charlotte added in a very impressive impersonation of a London lady's drawl.

"It is so wonderful to meet one of Jane's new friends," Lizzie continued, having the distinct pleasure of watching Miss Nelson's eyes widen in surprise.

"Oh, well . . . I don't . . . I mean, the pleasure is all mine?"

"You must come to tea while we're here—mustn't she, Jane?"

"Of course," Jane said, and it almost pained her to hear how eager her sister sounded. "You and your mother would be very welcome, Miss Nelson."

"That's very kind," a flustered Miss Nelson responded. "But I just . . . well, you see, I'm not sure if I'll be able to because . . . because . . . I fear . . . my mother would not allow it!"

And with that, Miss Nelson fled from the shop, the little bell tinkling sadly behind her.

Lizzie turned to face her sister. Jane had gone very, very pale, and her mouth had fallen open in shock.

"Is it true, then?" asked a woman with strawberry-blond curls. She abandoned the bolt of linen she'd been inspecting. "We heard that a body was discovered in your drawing room, and there can be no other reason why Mrs. Nelson wouldn't allow Sophie to call."

Her cheeks turned pink as soon as she said the words, as if she didn't quite believe her own audacity, but this was exactly what Lizzie had been hoping for.

"It's true, unfortunately," she said gravely. "Some poor soul was stuck in the flue. It's quite upsetting, of course. Mr. Bingley is making burial arrangements with the vicar."

"Who was it?" another woman asked, this one a tall, thin lady wearing a pink lawn dress.

"We don't know," Lizzie said. "I'm afraid he's been gone too long to tell. But . . ."

"But what?" the lady in pink asked.

"Oh, Jane, I hope I'm not overstepping?" Lizzie asked, fluttering her eyelashes at her sister, who stared back at her in wide-eyed shock. "It's just that Mr. Bingley would very much like to learn his identity. He feels awfully sorry for what happened. What if the man had a family?"

The other ladies murmured in sympathy, and Lizzie heard one remark: "Can you imagine?"

Jane didn't seem to have caught on to Lizzie's scheme, but Charlotte was nodding in sympathy. "The poor family," she said.

"Would any of you happen to know who it might be?" Lizzie asked.

"We've been racking our memories all morning," said the lady with the strawberry-blond hair. "But no one has the faintest clue!"

"All the caretakers over the years are accounted for," added the woman in pink. "And the previous Mrs. Bingley didn't accept visitors."

"It's a waste if you ask me," said strawberry curls. "My gran used to tell me stories about all the parties at Netherfield when she was a girl—the ballroom was the most beautiful room she'd ever seen."

"How'd he die?" asked the teenage girl, drawing gasps from those around her.

"Gwen!" her mother scolded, but Lizzie noted that none of the other ladies looked away. They stared at Lizzie expectantly.

"That's the mystery," Lizzie said, shaking her head sadly. "We have no way of telling whether it was a tragic accident or—"

"Nonsense!" said a woman by the button displays. She jutted

her chin out defiantly. "My John heard it from Mr. Jones that the man's skull was cracked—his death was no accident!"

The solicitor in Lizzie wanted to point out that a cracked skull did not preclude an accident, but she knew that semantics would only be wasted on this audience. "Accidental or not, it is tragic. If only we knew the circumstances . . ."

"This is proof," the defiant woman said. "Proof that Netherfield Park is cursed, just as we all thought!"

There it was. Lizzie tried not to smile in victory.

"There's no such thing as curses and you know it, Julia Watkins," the woman in pink said primly.

"Then what do you call the streak of misfortune that befalls everyone who spends one night under that roof?" Mrs. Watkins asked.

"We don't have to listen to this nonsense," said the mother of the teenage girl, but her daughter was listening with rapt attention, and she herself made no move to leave.

"Misfortune?" said the lady in pink. "The previous Mrs. Bingley was an eccentric, but any rumors of a curse—"

"Her husband was thrown from his horse!"

"A tragedy—"

"And then all her servants took ill!"

"Coincidence—"

"And she let no one into the manor for decades, just her caretakers!" Mrs. Watkins was getting worked up, and now she turned to Jane. "Forgive me, Mrs. Bingley, but you see—that manor has history. And all these years no one knew what your husband's great-aunt was up to, despite many offers of help and company, and now to hear there was a body hidden in the walls . . ."

"I—" Jane looked uncertain, and cast a desperate glance at Lizzie.

"Scandalous," whispered strawberry curls.

Jane seemed to crumple. Before she could respond, the bell tinkled once more, and everyone turned to see a formidable woman enter the shop. She was not tall, but she held her head high and her silk dress was very fine—as fine as anything Lizzie would see at a tea party in London. Immediately, she noticed how every other lady in the shop seemed to bow their head slightly toward her . . . even Jane.

"Good day," the newcomer said frostily, gaze landing upon Lizzie and Charlotte with sharp curiosity. Lizzie stared back. This woman reminded her uncomfortably of Lady Catherine—self-assured of her own importance and power, expecting everyone else to acknowledge it. But Lizzie refused to pay deference.

"Good day, Mrs. Fitzgerald," Jane said finally, stepping forward. "How lovely to see you again. May I introduce my sister, Miss Elizabeth Bennet?"

Mrs. Fitzgerald's gaze swept from Lizzie to Jane, her stony expression unmoving. After a very long pause, she stepped neatly around Lizzie and Jane, brushing right past Charlotte, and went to the counter as if she hadn't heard Jane's greeting. "Miss Brewster, I've come for the brocade I ordered."

"Of course, Mrs. Fitzgerald," said the sister behind the counter, hurrying to retrieve the order.

Jane stood frozen in the center of the shop, her pale face drawn. Lizzie had never seen anyone cut Jane. Jane! Her sister, who was the sweetest, most sensitive—

Jane turned on her heel and nearly ran out the door.

By the time Lizzie and Charlotte caught up with her, she was five storefronts away, wiping furiously at her eyes. "Jane!" Lizzie called. "Wait for us!"

Jane whirled around to face her. "Why did you bring it up? I told you not to!"

Lizzie stopped, shocked. "Jane. Everyone knew. It was obvious. Not saying anything—"

"Would have been the best thing! These are ladies, not common men or criminals! I know you deal with that sort quite a bit, but I would have thought you'd have the sense to not be so scandalous in a haberdashery!"

Charlotte pulled them away and down a quiet alley between two buildings, where there was no one but a stray cat lounging in the sun. "Jane, what's the matter?" Lizzie demanded. "You were acting odd in there, even before I brought up the death. And who was the awful lady?"

"Josephine Fitzgerald," Jane said miserably. "And she's the most influential woman in the county. Everyone takes their cue from her. She's terribly proper—and judgmental. She invited me for tea when we first arrived, but she's not once returned the call!"

Oh, that was bad form. "And do you think it's because she resents you, or because of these nasty rumors about the estate being cursed?" Lizzie asked.

"I don't know!" Jane threw up her arms. "But after that cut direct, we might as well pack up and go home to London, except . . ."

Except they probably shouldn't go back to London, because Lady Catherine had threatened nearly everyone Lizzie loved. Strangely, she hadn't targeted Bingley or Jane in her letter, probably because they had already left London by the time it arrived. Which suggested that Papa had been right, and that getting away from London had likely been the safest bet for them all.

Lizzie hated it when Papa was right.

"I'm sorry, Jane," Charlotte said, rubbing her arm. "I know it's little comfort now, but ladies like that—they're not worth socializing with, if that's how they treat others. You'll make some true friends."

"Everyone in the village is terrified of her. Even if they were inclined to befriend me, none of them will take that first step because they fear Mrs. Fitzgerald. She saw Mrs. Watkins laughing in the street last week and disinvited her from weekly tea because she thought it improper behavior!"

Things were making more sense to Lizzie now. "And this is why you didn't want me to be seen unchaperoned with Bingley and Darcy, and why you wanted to come with me into the village? To ensure I didn't embarrass you?"

"Lizzie, I . . ." But Jane didn't have anything else to say to that.

The implication of Jane's actions settled on her, and it did not feel good. Lizzie knew she was unconventional and that she pushed social boundaries. But Jane was not like her. And Jane loved her, she knew, but sometimes she repaid Jane's care and support by making her life more difficult.

Lizzie sighed. She didn't have it in her to be angry at Jane. Anger could be useful—it could propel her forward, inspire her to fight injustice, and give her strength when she needed it. But anger could also be exhausting, especially when directed at those she loved. She thought of Darcy, of her father. They loved her, even when she was stubborn and wrong. And Jane loved her, too, even when she proved to be embarrassing.

"I'm sorry," she said to her sister. "The last thing I wanted was to make things more difficult for you."

Jane just shook her head. "I didn't want to tell you how bad things were before you arrived—everyone acts as though it's not just Netherfield that's cursed, but us as well. And the body will not help with that perception. You have no idea how lonely I've been since we arrived!"

Lizzie and Charlotte encircled Jane in a hug, and Lizzie felt her heart breaking for her sister. How dare the ladies of this county treat Jane poorly because of what—some rumor of a curse? Well, Lizzie didn't believe in curses.

"We'll prove them wrong," Lizzie said. "They'll eat their words before the month is out."

"At this stage, I'd settle for someone returning a call," Jane said wistfully. "Perhaps if I could convince them all to come to tea at once, they would see that there is no dark force lurking in the halls and it's just a normal house, with nothing to fear!"

Lizzie went still, Jane's words tumbling around in her mind.

"What is it?" Charlotte asked.

"Jane," Lizzie said. "Do you trust me?"

"Of course," Jane said. "You know I was being silly earlier when I was telling you what to say and what not to say, you're actually very good at making conversation, but why—"

"Come on," Lizzie said, turning back toward the high street. She had Jane's hand in hers, and took Charlotte's arm in her other, pulling them after her.

"Lizzie, where are we going?"

But Jane didn't press when she saw Lizzie's destination—the haberdashery. She tried to slow her pace, but Lizzie pulled her along, bursting into the shop with such force that the small bell above the door clanged against the wall.

Every woman in the shop turned to look at them, including Mrs. Fitzgerald.

"Hello again," Lizzie said. "We've come back to say that Jane has decided to throw a ball at Netherfield Park, one week hence, and you're all invited. I know there have been some silly rumors about a curse, and while yes, we have had some misfortunes in the house as of late, the Bingleys are looking forward to putting all that behind them and celebrating an evening with new friends and neighbors."

Lizzie paused. The ladies seemed stunned at her unconventional announcement, but the teenage girl looked rather thrilled by the prospect. Mrs. Watkins was wide-eyed with shock, but then . . . she grinned.

Lizzie bit back her own smile. "Expect your formal invitations to arrive tomorrow," she said, then turned and swept Jane and Charlotte out of the shop once more.

"Lizzie!" Jane hissed. "What on earth have you done?"

"You said that not a single one of them would come on their own . . . but they might come if they all know that someone else will be there. And you heard the way Mrs. Watkins spoke about Netherfield—she wants to see your ballroom."

"You do realize that this could backfire entirely if no one comes?" Charlotte asked.

"They wouldn't dare," Lizzie said. "One or two might be rude to Jane, and Mrs. Fitzgerald might be bold enough to give you the cut direct in the village, but they won't all be able to turn down an invitation to a ball—it would be unspeakably rude. No, they'll come because they'll believe they must, and then once they arrive at Netherfield, they'll see it's just a house. You'll win them over, Jane. A ball really does solve everything—I can't believe I'm saying that."

"Neither can I," Jane said, sounding stunned.

"Mrs. Bennet will be delighted," Charlotte observed.

They all had a laugh at that, and then Jane clenched Lizzie's arm. "You said it would be in a week!"

"Oh, I did, didn't I? That's very soon?"

"That's nearly impossible! We've only just finished the first stage of renovations. I haven't touched the ballroom—the floors will need waxing, and the chandeliers haven't been polished in an age. I'll have to place an order with the grocer tomorrow, and write the invitations out tonight, and see about flowers and candles and menus and serving staff . . ."

"Make a list," Lizzie said. "And put Kitty and Lydia to work."

"There was a dead man in my drawing room last night! Now I'm to throw a ball that won't embarrass me in a week's time, and you want me to have *Lydia and Kitty* help?"

"Don't worry," Lizzie said, wrapping an arm around her sister. "The dead man should be buried by then."

EIGHT

In Which Lizzie and Darcy Learn the Origin of the Netherfield Curse

DARCY WAS EXCITED ABOUT his lead, meager as it might be. Solving mysteries could be tedious—following an endless string of leads in the hope of uncovering a vital detail took determination and persistence—but he was looking forward to calling on Miss Jeffries. So he was rather taken back when they rejoined the ladies and the first thing Jane said was, "I must return home."

"Is everything all right?" Bingley asked her, concerned.

"No," Jane said peevishly, casting a look at Lizzie. "It appears I am to throw a ball."

Darcy turned to Lizzie and raised an eyebrow. She looked somewhat sheepish.

"A ball?" Bingley echoed. "I thought you didn't—"

"I'll explain on the way," Jane said, moving toward the carriage. The others made to follow her, but Darcy did not.

"Wait a moment," he said. "What about the print shop?"

“What print shop?” Lizzie asked.

“I got a lead on our dead man,” Darcy explained. “Not a name, so don’t get too excited, but the vicar said we could look through the parish registers . . .”

“I’m sorry,” Bingley said, already helping Jane into the carriage. “But . . .”

“Go,” Lizzie said. “We can walk back to Netherfield when we’re done.”

“Would you like my assistance, Jane?” Charlotte asked.

“Not at the moment, thank you,” she said. “And Lizzie . . . thank you. I think.”

“Walk?” Darcy echoed as Bingley joined Jane in the carriage and it pulled away, leaving him with Lizzie and Charlotte.

“Oh, don’t give me that—you walk the distance easily back home. It just appears farther because we’re in the countryside,” Lizzie said. “Now, where are these registers, and what did the vicar say?”

Darcy summarized his visit with Mr. Thomas. In the telling, his lead didn’t appear to be all that thrilling. A village this size, and how many people were born or buried in any given month? Year? It seemed silly now to think they might find their dead man this way. And that was supposing he had been from the county and not someone passing through.

But Lizzie was not as doubtful as he might have expected, and even Charlotte nodded in approval when Darcy told them about the agreement he’d struck with the vicar. “It will be a fair amount of research," Charlotte said, "but it's better than what we accomplished."

"Oh?" Darcy looked to Lizzie.

"Well, we might not have any solid leads," Lizzie said, "but I feel as though I've learned a fair amount about the people of Meryton this morning."

She told him about their encounter with the ladies in the haberdashery, and the rumors that swirled around Netherfield Park. By the time she finished recounting her impromptu announcement of a ball to be held at Netherfield, Darcy was beginning to understand why Jane was somewhat frantic to get back to the estate.

"How will a ball solve the issue of Jane's ostracization?" he asked. "If they think the estate is cursed—which is absurd—then why would they come to a ball?"

"For the spectacle," Charlotte explained. "The one thing society enjoys above all is a diversion."

"And if it's bound to end in scandal, all the better," Lizzie added. "None of them will miss it, not even Mrs. Fitzgerald. I'm certain of it!"

"And how do we ensure it doesn't end in scandal?"

Lizzie looked at him as though he were very silly indeed. "By solving the mystery of this dead man's identity and proving that whatever the cause, it's not something anyone needs to worry about now. Once everyone realizes that there is no curse, then Jane can get on with charming them."

Darcy didn't say what he was thinking, which was that if the ladies of Meryton had rejected Jane over something as trivial as rumors about a house she'd inherited, then they likely weren't worth knowing. He did not pretend to understand why ladies cared so much about such connections, but he knew they did—and he could tell that seeing Jane vindicated was important to Lizzie.

The Jeffries Print Shop was on the opposite end of the high street from the church, in a small storefront with rather dusty windows. A new-looking sign hung above the door, painted green with gold lettering, incongruous with the tired appearance of the building. But when Darcy held open the door for the ladies and they stepped inside, they found it quite busy indeed.

The air in the shop was warm but not oppressively so, and it smelled of ink, dust, and oil. Two men labored in the back of the shop on a printing press, not even bothering to look up from their work. A small breeze drifted into the shop with their arrival, rustling newly printed papers hung on lines that zigzagged through the shop. A young lady stood amid the pages, hanging new sheets as they were printed.

"Oh, hello," she said, turning to greet them. "Can I help you?"

"I hope so," Lizzie said, smiling. "We're told that you are in possession of the parish registers?"

It was a curious thing—the young lady's polite smile seemed to freeze, and something more guarded took its place. "Really? Who told you that?"

"Mr. Thomas," Darcy said, withdrawing the letter of

introduction the vicar had written. "I'm Mr. Darcy, and this is Miss Bennet and Miss Lucas. We're staying at Netherfield Park—Miss Bennet is Mrs. Bingley's sister."

"Oh," said the young lady, looking to the men running the press. One of them nodded at her and she left them to their work and approached the trio. "This wouldn't have something to do with the body that was discovered there last night, would it?"

"Does the entire village know about it, then?" Lizzie asked.

"Afraid so," said the young lady cheerfully. "I'm Miss Clara Jeffries, the owner of this establishment."

"Owner!" Lizzie exclaimed.

Miss Jeffries raised her chin a hair. "Yes, owner. My grandfather established the business, and I took it on when my father passed."

"That's wonderful," Lizzie said. "I mean, about owning the business—not about your father's death. My condolences."

Darcy regarded the young lady, who didn't look to be that much older than they. It must take a fair amount of fortitude to run a business like this, especially in a small village such as Meryton. And to do it as a young, unmarried lady must be all the more challenging.

"Miss Jeffries, we were told that you were in the process of printing copies of the parish registers for Mr. Thomas. It's imperative that we inspect them, and we've gotten Mr. Thomas's permission. He wrote a note for you." Darcy handed her the note and watched as she took it and read it.

Miss Jeffries didn't scowl exactly, but her brow furrowed

and the lines only deepened as she read. When she finished, she looked up and said, "I'm afraid I've gotten behind on this project—we've received an order for sheet music from a publisher in London. I haven't finished printing the new one."

"That's all right," Darcy said. "We can take the handwritten registers and muddle through ourselves."

But Miss Jeffries shook her head. "Mr. Thomas's note says that you're allowed the ones that have been printed, if you pay for the printing costs. But I'm afraid I need the originals if I am to finish the job in a timely manner."

Darcy didn't want to be perceived as forceful, but this was the only decent lead they had, especially since Lizzie hadn't gotten anywhere with the ladies of the village. "Can we—"

"It's all right," Lizzie said sweetly. "We can come back, if that would be easier for you?"

"I can deliver them," she offered, and Darcy thought that was surprisingly generous, until she added, "If you're willing to pay for the printing costs up front, of course."

"Of course," Darcy echoed. Investigations often had a common language, and it was money. "I'm happy to settle things right now, if you wish."

Miss Jeffries didn't even try to hide her pleasure. "Thank you, sir. That will be fifteen shillings."

He began to withdraw his purse, and she added, "Each."

He hesitated, astounded at the cost. Fifteen shillings *apiece*? Why, they'd better be leatherbound and gilded. He'd bought two volumes of Plutarch's biographies just before leaving London, and those had only been thirteen shillings for the two. But Miss Jeffries was watching him, and the expression on her face suggested she knew exactly what he was thinking.

"How many volumes?" he asked her.

"Three."

Darcy counted out the coins, and Miss Jeffries swiped them up quickly. "I'll just write you a receipt," she said sweetly, and turned to disappear into the back of the shop.

Charlotte leaned in and whispered to Lizzie and Darcy, "Printing an entire bound book must be an expensive endeavor—but the cost does seem rather steep."

"Miss Jeffries is a keen businesswoman," Darcy muttered in a low tone.

"Printing is costly," Lizzie said. "She might have made the original offer to lend credence to her business. It's difficult to be taken seriously as a woman."

Before they could speculate further, Miss Jeffries returned with a slip of paper in her hand and presented it to Darcy. "I'll work on finishing them up as soon as possible," she promised.

"When might that be?" Darcy asked.

"Another day or two at least. I'm not a binder, but if you want them covered it'll be another day or so—"

"No need! We'll take them unbound."

"We so appreciate the amount of work you must put into this project," Lizzie added.

"Of course," she said. "I'll bring them around to Netherfield

Park when they're complete. How are you enjoying your stay there?"

The way she asked the question made the back of Darcy's neck prickle.

"Last night's excitement notwithstanding, we are liking it very much," Lizzie said.

"You three are braver than I," Miss Jeffries said.

"Oh, do you believe in the so-called curse as well?" Darcy asked.

"I do, sir."

Lizzie stepped on his foot. "Please disregard Mr. Darcy," Lizzie said. "He's naturally a skeptic."

"Hmph. If that's the case, perhaps you ought to ask more questions before being too quick to judge."

Touché. "My apologies, Miss Jeffries. I meant no offense."

"If I may," Lizzie said. "Perhaps you could tell us about the origins of the curse? We've only heard snippets here and there."

Miss Jeffries looked uncertain for a moment, and Darcy found himself thinking that after all the coin he'd just handed out, the very least she could do was throw in a story for free. He tried to school his features into a politely neutral expression as she studied the three of them. Something seemed to war within her. "Well, it's said that if you spend a night in Netherfield Park, you're destined to never leave."

When she didn't continue, he said, "No offense intended, Miss Jeffries, but clearly that is not true. The three of us spent the night at Netherfield just last night, and we're here now. Mr.

and Mrs. Bingley have been there a month, and they were just in the village with us."

Miss Jeffries merely rolled her eyes. "Aye, and are you going back to Netherfield tonight?"

"Yes," Darcy responded.

"Well then." Miss Jeffries said this as if it made sense. It did not.

"But what exactly does it mean?" Lizzie pressed. "If you stay too many nights under that roof, you'll be trapped there forever, like some kind of very well-appointed and luxurious prison?"

"There's no special force that holds anyone there," Miss Jeffries was quick to point out. "More like . . . bad things happen to anyone who does leave. And if you do leave, then death follows shortly after."

It sounded ridiculous, except Miss Jeffries was very serious. Darcy felt his legal instincts take over. "And what proof do you have of this?"

Miss Jeffries sighed. "None that you'll believe, I'm sure. But it all goes back to the late Mr. Geoffrey Bingley, when he was a young man some sixty years ago. He was known to be an adventurer. He and his younger brother, Francis, left home at a young age and commissioned a ship to take them abroad. They were gone for years, leaving their elderly parents behind with nary a word except for the stray letter here and there. Until one day when Geoffrey and Francis's father died. It took months, but eventually they returned from across the ocean and Geoffrey brought with him a young wife."

"Honoria?" Lizzie asked.

"Yes. And she brought with her a fortune, too—which was helpful, because the estate and farms had fallen on hard times. Their father hadn't been a particularly attentive landlord. Or so the story goes."

This was not an unsurprising tale. Darcy knew plenty of young gentlemen even now who shirked their duties to their estates, spending money like it was water, only to find that money did not in fact grow in fields—it required a bit more work and cultivation than that. He even knew of a few such gentlemen who'd married their way out of such money troubles. "So Honoria's money restored Netherfield Park."

"Yes, and soon after, Geoffrey and Francis's mother died," Miss Jeffries said. "And the brothers grew restless again."

"And then what?" Darcy asked, now more intrigued. As Bingley's oldest friend, he had a sense of the family's history, but he'd not heard the story from this angle.

"Honoria held the purse strings, and she didn't want her husband to leave. But she had no qualms about Francis setting sail. She gave him the money he needed, and he left—but she refused to give Geoffrey the same. He became enraged, and so she hid her fortune somewhere in Netherfield Park."

"Clever," Lizzie said admiringly.

"How does one just hide an entire fortune?" Darcy asked. "How much was it?"

"It's said she brought trunks of silver with her when she married, and she hid whatever remained after restoring the estate."

How perfectly vague, Darcy thought. It sounded like a rumor, but . . .

He looked at Lizzie and Charlotte, and knew they were thinking the same thing. *Silver.*

Was that a coincidence?

"What happened after she hid her fortune?" Lizzie asked. "I take it Geoffrey wasn't pleased?"

"No, miss, he was not. He had no choice but to stay. He was quite angry with his wife, and rumor was they slept in separate wings of the house. But one day, they had a spectacular shouting match, and Geoffrey threatened to burn down the house around them unless Honoria revealed where the money was hidden."

"The east wing," Lizzie said.

Miss Jeffries nodded. "He lit it on fire. But luckily for everyone, it was contained before it could spread to the rest of the house—a miracle, really. The staff saved the house."

"And Geoffrey?" Darcy asked.

"He survived, too. But he was angry—he'd thought that would work. He left in the night. But they found him the next morning when his horse came back to the stables. He was lying on the ground a stone's throw from the gates. The consensus was he'd been thrown."

This was starting to sound like something from a gothic suspense novel—and not a good one. "So it was a terrible tragedy," Darcy said, sounding doubtful even to himself. But . . . what if Geoffrey Bingley was their dead man?

Lizzie shook her head, as if reading his mind. "There must

have been a burial—for someone of his status, half the village would have been in attendance. Besides, why entomb her husband in the drawing room flue?"

"So he'd never leave?" Charlotte suggested.

It was quite a macabre thought, but Miss Jeffries said, "Miss Bennet is right—Mr. Bingley is buried in the family plot. But the story doesn't end there. The next day, Geoffrey's former valet left to find work elsewhere. He drowned crossing a river in the next county. And one of the maids gave her notice so that she could marry a farmer, but shortly after, she fell sick and died."

"That's awful," Lizzie said. "But—"

"I'm not finished," Miss Jeffries said. "A footman enlisted and was killed when his musket backfired during training. Not long after that, the butler dropped dead in the lane while walking to the village. And a groom was stung by a bee and swelled up until he could no longer breathe!"

"Oh, well . . . that is . . . a lot of tragedy," Lizzie said, sounding uncertain.

Darcy was not so convinced. "That doesn't mean Netherfield is cursed. My own estate has experienced its fair share of misfortune—it's very sad, but that is life, I'm afraid."

"Just wait," Miss Jeffries said. "About a year after Geoffrey died, smallpox struck. It killed every single person in the house—everyone except the housekeeper."

"Oh," Lizzie said.

"Aye. She lived in a cottage not very far from the house with her husband. She was the only one spared, because she didn't spend her nights under a cursed roof."

Darcy knew Lizzie well enough to know she wouldn't accept this faulty logic, but she didn't argue. "Well . . . how fortunate for her?"

"It was the old vicar who put it together," Miss Jeffries said. "On account of him having to preside over so many funerals. He said the common thread between them all was that they laid their heads down under that roof after Geoffrey died, and it was all on account of Honoria. Her presence—or her silver—cursed the house."

Charlotte's lips pursed in disapproval, and Lizzie's expression clouded over. "And why was he so quick to blame her? Why not Geoffrey or Francis for leaving? Or why not blame their parents for neglecting the estate to begin with?"

"Because it's easier to blame the outsider," Charlotte said before Miss Jeffries could reply. "Isn't it?"

Miss Jeffries had the decency to look chastised. "I didn't mean to imply—"

"No, but the entire village has, haven't they?" Lizzie asked. "They all blame Honoria for the curse?"

Miss Jeffries neither confirmed nor denied it, but Darcy suspected he knew the answer. Of course they'd blame the recluse, the woman who'd come from away with her wealth, and then denied sharing it with her husband.

"What about Francis?" Lizzie asked. "Did he not return when his brother died?"

"Bingley's grandfather died at sea," Darcy said, able to fill in this bit of the story. "He left behind his pregnant wife at a port town, and his grandmother brought up his father with help from her family, and then Bingley's father founded Netherfield Shipping before he died."

Miss Jeffries nodded. "Aye, Francis had passed by that point, and Honoria inherited it all. Everyone wondered whether she'd remarry, but after the smallpox outbreak, she rarely left the estate. No one wanted to work there. Honoria rarely had visitors, and if she did, they all left before sundown."

"What a lonely life," Charlotte said, profound sadness in her voice.

"She was a nice lady," Miss Jeffries added. "She sent Sally down to buy books and sheet music, and Sally would say that Mrs. Bingley always sent her regards."

"Sally," Lizzie repeated. "Of course—but she's far too young to be the housekeeper. Her grandmother?"

Miss Jeffries nodded. "That position has been passed down in her family, and she's the third generation to work at Netherfield."

"That is a very tragic story," Darcy said. "And I can see why rumors of a curse have grown. However—"

"However," Lizzie interrupted, "a curse is not proof of anything. And we still don't know who the dead man might be."

"And that's why you want the registers?" Miss Jeffries asked.

"It's a lead," Darcy said.

"It's likely too late anyway," she said in a dark tone.

Despite his pragmatism, a shiver ran down his spine. "Because you believe that we'll all perish in the near future?"

"No, because I heard what Mrs. Jones was saying about the body when Mr. Oliver brought it to her husband—the man was unrecognizable."

Oh. Darcy felt a flash of embarrassment for getting caught up in talk of curses.

"However," Miss Jeffries continued, "it may just be a story to you, but we've seen what happens, haven't we? My gran warned me to never stay in the manor after dark, and I'm not about to disobey her now, God rest her soul."

"Those deaths sounded awful," Lizzie said, sounding sympathetic. "But they happened nearly fifty years ago. No one has died recently."

"Well, I suppose that for the last fifty years no one has visited Netherfield Park to put the theory to the test." Miss Jeffries looked at the three of them, and added, "Until now."

NINE

In Which Lizzie and Charlotte Find Themselves in a Precarious Position

WHEN LIZZIE, DARCY, AND Charlotte returned to Netherfield Park, they found the family parlor in chaos.

The party was not quite ready to set foot in the drawing room once more, despite its thorough cleaning. Jane and Mrs. Bennet were arguing about menus, and Caroline sat close to them in an overstuffed chair, looking put out as she made the occasional interjection. Lydia and Kitty were shouting about dresses and decorations with Guy in between them, and Mary was hiding in the corner, book in hand. Bingley stood in the middle of the room, trying to intercede between Caroline and his wife.

Mr. Bennet, Lizzie was unsurprised to see, was nowhere to be found. "What's going on?"

"Lizzie!" came at least three shouts, and then Mrs. Bennet pulled her into the fray. "Come, Lizzie, tell your sister that she needs to invite the Hamiltons and Gardiners to her ball."

"Mama, it's next week! They can't possibly come in time. And besides, we have nowhere to put them up!"

"In a house this size? Nonsense!"

"Not all the rooms are ready for guests!"

"I think it's a terrible idea," Caroline said. "A ball in a week's time? It can't be done."

"It is an awfully tight timeline, Jane—are you sure you can't put it off until later in the month?" Mrs. Bennet asked. "That way the Gardiners at least could join."

Jane gave Lizzie a look that clearly said, *This is all your fault.* Lizzie smiled weakly and mouthed, *Sorry.* Although, announcing the ball in front of all those snobby women had felt good in the moment. "It'll happen in a week because that's what we told Mrs. Fitzgerald."

"Jane, are there to be any young, eligible gentlemen at this ball?" Lydia demanded.

"Why? You're too young to court," Mary said.

"Am not! Mama, tell her—"

"Now, Mary, I would be happy to see any of my girls settled! Although it would be nice if proper birth order could be considered." Mrs. Bennet said this with a significant glance to Darcy, who made a great show of studying the wallpaper.

"I intend on being next, before even Lizzie. And then I shall be addressed as Mrs. and Lizzie will have to follow after me into every room," Lydia said, flouncing over to Lizzie.

Lizzie scowled and picked up Guy. "Being married doesn't make you more important than anyone else."

"It would make me more important than you," Lydia said. "Socially, anyway."

"Oh, stop it, you two!"

Lydia and Lizzie turned to look at Jane, Lizzie's mouth dropping open in shock. Jane never raised her voice at her, but now she stared at them with a cross expression. "Lydia, enough taunting. There shall be a few gentlemen and—"

"A few?" Lydia screeched. "Jane! Surely you know more than a *few*—"

"I said enough!"

Lizzie sat down, cowed by her older sister's firm tone. Even Lydia stayed quiet, shocked as well.

"I've decided not to invite the Gardiners or Hamiltons, Mama. This shall be a small, intimate affair for our closest neighbors. No overnight guests."

Across the room, Lizzie, Charlotte, and Darcy exchanged glances, and she knew they were all thinking the same thing: if most people believed in the curse, they'd likely not stay anyway.

"It'll hardly be a ball, then," Caroline said. "Why bother?"

"Because we have a duty to cultivate a genial relationship with our new neighbors, especially given the tragedy that we've uncovered here," Bingley said, coming to stand by Jane. "We ought to show them that Netherfield Park is turning over a new leaf."

A fresh start in the country was exactly what Lizzie wanted for her sister. "I think that's an excellent idea," she said. "Jane,

I know you'll be able to pull off the most splendid ball—party? Ball."

"We'll open the ballroom," Jane said with a sigh, and Lydia and Kitty squealed. "But it shall be a small affair!"

"If you say so, dear," Mrs. Bennet said doubtfully.

"Did you discover anything of interest in the village?" Bingley asked Lizzie, Darcy, and Charlotte in a clear ploy to change the subject.

Lizzie looked back at Darcy, unsure of where to start. What they had learned was very interesting indeed, but she wasn't sure quite how to break it to Bingley. Luckily for her, Darcy stepped up. "How much do you know about Honoria Bingley?" he asked his friend.

This was not what Bingley had been expecting. "Not much, admittedly. My great-uncle married her abroad and brought her back here, and then he died shortly after. My father never even met her."

"Right, well, word in the village is that she is the reason Netherfield is cursed."

Lizzie winced. She might have delivered that news a bit more gently.

Bingley looked puzzled. "Please explain."

Lizzie and Darcy did so quickly, with a clarifying point here and there from Charlotte. When they were done, the entire room was blessedly silent before Caroline crossed her arms and said, "*Of course* this place is cursed."

Bingley reached into his pocket and withdrew something. Lizzie recognized it as the silver coin they'd recovered from the dead man's pocket, now polished. "This silver—it could be from Honoria's fortune?"

Darcy reached out a hand for the coin, and Bingley gave it to him. "It could be."

Lizzie leaned in to look at it. Now that untold years' worth of grime—and other things Lizzie did not want to think about—had been cleaned away, Lizzie could see that one side boasted a shield topped with a crown, and a year: 1731. On the opposite side was a cross surrounded by filigree, and HISPANIARVM was etched above it. Charlotte leaned in to examine the coin alongside Lizzie and then gasped.

"What is it?" Lizzie asked her.

"I've done some reading," Charlotte said slowly. "About the history of the West Indies."

A flush crept across her cheeks, as if she were embarrassed to admit that she was curious about her mother's homeland. Charlotte didn't talk about her mother very often. Lizzie knew that her parents' marriage had been rather scandalous at the time. Her mother was from the West Indies and her father had been a British merchant. They'd spent their time mostly outside of England, away from wagging tongues, but when their untimely deaths had left Charlotte orphaned as an infant, she was sent to London, where she grew up under the guardianship of her father's business partner.

"What have you learned?" Darcy asked.

"The Spanish conquered much of the Americas," she said. "And they stole gold and silver and whatever else was valuable. They made coins, like this one, stamped for the Spanish king. And they sent them back to Spain in great fleets. But . . . one fleet was almost entirely lost. It was caught in a hurricane, and most of the ships sank. Thousands and thousands of coins were lost to the ocean. This was in 1733, but the coins that were lost were the 1731 mint."

Lizzie did the mental math—that was roughly eighty years ago. But Honoria would have come to Netherfield Park only fifty years earlier. "Were the coins ever recovered?"

"Many were," Charlotte said. "But there were many that weren't. Treasure hunters and pirates have been searching the waters for them for years."

"So, which was Honoria?" Bingley wondered. "Heiress or scavenger?"

"Both," Charlotte said, earning her a look of surprise from those gathered. "The silver was stolen from rightful citizens of the land by the Spanish."

"No wonder everyone thinks it's cursed," muttered Darcy.

"What a bunch of nonsense," Caroline said, crossing her arms. "Rumors from a backward village don't mean anything! They're jealous of the Bingley family wealth."

"It looks so small," Lydia said. "Are you sure it's worth much?"

"Honestly, Lydia," Mary said, voice dripping with condescension. "It's solid silver in an age of silver shortages! If Bingley has a mountain of them somewhere in this house, then he has . . . well, not a small fortune. A very, very large fortune."

"If your great-aunt had that much silver, then why didn't she use any of it to fix the roof or decorate the rooms?" Lydia demanded.

"Lydia!" Mary and Lizzie both reprimanded.

"What?"

"I'm sure she had her reasons," Lizzie said doubtfully. But she couldn't help but wonder whether that reason was connected to the dead man in the flue. It would be impossible to open the house to builders, servants, and guests while concealing a body.

"We should look for it!" Lydia said.

"I don't know if that's a good idea," Lizzie began to say.

"Why not?" Bingley asked, looking to Jane. "We know this old house has more than a few secrets."

"It might be an interesting diversion," Jane said, surprising Lizzie. But then, her eyes kept straying to the stack of invitations she was penning, and Lizzie imagined her sister was desperate for a bit of peace.

Lydia clapped her hands in delight. "I already know how I shall spend my share! Kitty, come on—let's start in the ballroom!"

"What?" Bingley said. "Girls, come back here! We ought to lay down a few ground rules!" He turned and said, "The rest of you, pair up. And the east wing is still out of bounds!"

Bingley disappeared after the younger girls, followed by Mrs. Bennet, who was calling, "Girls, don't break anything!"

"Darcy, be a darling and accompany me to the portrait

gallery?" Caroline asked. "After all, if dear old Aunt Honoria was going to hide something valuable, why not hide it among the valuables?"

Darcy glanced stiffly at Lizzie, and she knew he was hoping she'd rescue him. However, she simply smiled and said, "What a clever idea, Caroline."

Caroline harrumphed and dragged a reluctant Darcy after her. Lizzie turned to Charlotte. "Partners?" she asked.

"Of course," said her friend.

They left Mary with Jane, as neither of them showed much interest in searching, and headed upstairs, Guy trotting after them. There, they were presented with a series of options. To the left was the west wing, a long hallway of guest rooms that eventually turned a corner to the family wing, where Jane and Bingley's private rooms could be found. Most of the party was staying down this hall. Straight ahead was another hall of more guest rooms, and this was where Darcy, as the lone bachelor, was staying. To the right was the door to the east wing, locked tight. Lizzie and Charlotte chose to go straight down the hall, past Darcy's bedroom chamber, and began opening doors along the very long corridor.

"This feels like snooping," Charlotte said in a hushed tone as they crept into a bedroom, Guy leading the way. His nose worked double time sniffing across dusty carpets. White sheets covered the furniture, making Lizzie think of funeral shrouds.

"Be honest—haven't you ever longed to go snooping through a grand house like this, to uncover all its secrets?"

Charlotte laughed. "I don't know about uncovering secrets," she admitted. "But sometimes I do wonder what might be in other people's wardrobes."

Lizzie grinned as she drew back a dusty sheet. "Why don't you look?"

Charlotte opened the cantankerous old walnut wardrobe, whose unoiled hinges screeched. They both winced and froze, as if waiting for someone to catch them, then dissolved into giggles with Guy pressing up against Lizzie's side eagerly to see what all the fuss was about. "Nothing but dust," Charlotte said with disappointment.

"Oh, well," Lizzie said. "There's more where that came from, I bet."

They moved methodically down one side of the hall and then the other, checking old fussy sitting rooms and dusty bedchambers that had long since seen proper daylight. Guy ran circles in his excitement, sniffing away and sneezing quite often. Lizzie checked every drawer and cabinet, and Charlotte opened up every wardrobe. They were all empty save for a smaller room toward the back of the house, overlooking a corner of the gardens. The wardrobe there held a collection of stiff old dresses, the fabric discolored with time. Lizzie and Charlotte exclaimed over the old mantuas and the open skirts, the yellowing lace and the fraying ribbons.

"Do you suppose these belonged to Bingley's great-aunt?" Charlotte asked.

"They must have. Look at the style—my father has a portrait

of my grandmother in a dress like this, and she would have been of the same era as Honoria." Lizzie looked around the small bedchamber. The bed was small, with a worn mattress stripped down to the ticking, and the furnishings weren't ornate, but they were solidly made. "This must have been her room . . . but why would she choose this one, when there are larger and better-appointed rooms?"

"Perhaps she had bad memories elsewhere in the house, and this room suited her better?" Charlotte suggested, gently pushing the dresses back into the wardrobe and shutting it.

Lizzie and Charlotte spent a quarter of an hour in that room, searching for false bottoms in drawers or hidden cubbies or shelves. They even lifted the mattress and rolled back the rugs, searching for loose floorboards, much to Guy's consternation. Lizzie got up the courage to peer up the flue of the fireplace but found nothing.

"I don't think there's anything here," Charlotte concluded. "And there's not much in the way of personal effects, either. Whoever cleaned up after she died might have moved the treasure."

"I suppose you're right," she said. One more thing to ask Sally about.

They reluctantly left Honoria's room and continued down the hallway that stretched along the back of the house. Here, there were fewer chambers, but a slightly uneven seam in the wall caught Lizzie's notice. She ran her fingers along the seam and the panel of the wall, searching . . . click!

The wall swung inward, revealing a dark, dusty corridor.

"Charlotte, look! A secret passageway!"

"I'm sure it's hardly a secret," Charlotte said, peering into the darkness. "It's likely a passageway for servants to get from one end of the house to the other without having to run into guests or the family."

Lizzie didn't care—her heart was pounding with excitement. "Come on!"

Guy followed Lizzie as she took a few steps into the passageway, but Charlotte hesitated. "Are you sure we should go in there?"

Of course Lizzie was certain—this was far more interesting than a half-empty room full of dust. "We'll leave the door open for light," she said. "And only go in a bit of the way. Far enough to get a sense for where it leads. We can always turn around and fetch Bingley."

"All right," Charlotte said uncertainly, stepping into the corridor after her. The old wood creaked under their feet, and the corridor itself was rather cramped—only large enough that two people could pass each other if they turned themselves sideways—but the ceilings were tall. Guy forged ahead, not seeming to care that it was growing darker with each step.

"Lizzie, perhaps we ought to come back with a lantern," Charlotte said.

Lizzie brushed away a cobweb she'd walked straight into and was glad that Charlotte couldn't see what she was doing. "I just want to see how far it goes. Surely it will come out somewhere."

"I know, but it's getting difficult to see."

"Just a little farther down," Lizzie said.

But very quickly, she realized, there was a wall before her. A dead end. "Oh, drat."

"What is it?" Charlotte asked, her voice high with apprehension.

"Dead end. Don't worry, we'll just turn around."

Lizzie turned to face her friend, who was backlit by the light all the way at the end, where the door stood open. "Sorry, Charlotte, I didn't mean to—"

BAM!

They were plunged into darkness and Charlotte screamed. Lizzie jumped but managed not to make a noise, even as she felt fear claw its way up her throat.

"Lizzie!"

"I'm here," Lizzie said, trying to keep calm in the sudden darkness. She reached out and felt Charlotte's arm. At her touch, Charlotte clasped Lizzie's hand tightly. "It's all right. A draft probably slammed that door shut on us."

"The door opened into the corridor," Charlotte whispered. "And I don't feel a draft."

Charlotte was right, of course—the only thing Lizzie felt now was the stuffy, closed-in air, Charlotte's desperate grasp on her hand, and Guy pressing against her skirts.

"Well, one never knows with these old houses," she said with far more confidence than she felt. "Turn around and start walking toward the door. I'll be right here behind you. Guy, come."

Slowly, they began to move back toward the door. "You're

doing brilliantly," Lizzie encouraged Charlotte. "And Guy, what a good dog you are."

It seemed to take an age, but they finally reached the end of the corridor, and now that Lizzie's eyes had adjusted, she could see a faint line of gray light where the seam of the door was. She could hear Charlotte feeling around for the knob.

"Lizzie, I don't know how to open it," she whispered.

"Try pulling?"

"I am!"

"Here, let me." Lizzie brushed past Charlotte and felt her way down the door. She could feel the seam of the jamb, and a groove where she supposed one might grip the door, but neither pushing nor pulling yielded any results—it was stuck. Or locked. A shiver traveled down her spine when she thought about the way the door had slammed suddenly. She didn't recall seeing movement around the door before it closed, but perhaps . . .

No, she wasn't going to think about the possibility that someone had trapped them here on purpose.

"Lizzie," Charlotte said in a voice that sounded perilously like a whimper.

"I know. I'm sorry," Lizzie said. Her friend was no coward, but she also vastly preferred office work and research to going down strange corridors and exploring unknown spaces. "Look, there has to be another way out. They wouldn't have built a corridor to nothing. Let's keep looking."

"Perhaps we bang on the door and hope someone will come to our rescue?"

"That's not a terrible idea," Lizzie said. "But it could be hours before they realize we're missing. I haven't heard anyone else in quite a while."

Charlotte sighed. "Are you sure you can find another way out?"

"Of course," Lizzie said confidently. "Put a hand on my shoulder. Guy, with me."

Lizzie turned once more and moved slowly back down the corridor, reaching in every direction. The sound of Guy's small steps beside her was a reassuring presence in the dark, and hearing Charlotte's quick breaths grounded her. Lizzie wasn't sure how many steps she'd gone when she sensed that Guy was no longer right beside her—he was simply gone. He hadn't pushed ahead of her, she was fairly certain. "Guy?" she said, and reached out and felt along the wall and gasped when she felt the rough walls give way to nothing.

"What?" Charlotte asked, barely containing her panic.

"There's another corridor, to the left," Lizzie said. "We missed it in the dark."

"Lizzie, I don't like this!"

"I know, but this has to be a way out. Trust me."

Lizzie pulled Charlotte to the left, and she could hear Guy just ahead of her, leading the way. Lizzie took tentative steps forward, sweeping her arm left and right as she went. Charlotte clung to her shoulders, barely a step behind her. They made their way like this for what felt like a few hundred more steps, turning left then and right again. Lizzie lost all sense of direction, and there was a part of her that began to worry that they truly would be lost in the bowels of Netherfield Park, never to be heard from or seen again. She felt vaguely glad that Darcy was not here—he was utterly useless in dark, enclosed spaces and would be panicking even more than Charlotte.

Darcy. She could just imagine what he'd say when she saw him next. *You found a secret corridor and just went down it? With no lantern? Do you not value your life?*

At the final turn—to the left—Lizzie blinked. "Charlotte, can you see that?"

"I can't see anything, Lizzie!"

"No, but . . . I swear it's lighter in here. I think there must be a way out up ahead."

"Oh, thank God," Charlotte breathed.

Lizzie was sure of it now. She still couldn't see much, but the corridor seemed to take on an amorphous shape before her eyes rather than just an endless stretch of black. And the more steps they took, the more defined the space became. Finally, her eyes adjusted, and she saw the shape of a door standing ajar.

"Charlotte, look!" Lizzie said. "We're almost out."

They picked up the pace, even Guy, and Lizzie could now make out the cream-colored shape of him before her. They came to the end of the enclosed space and burst into a lonely hallway with grimy windows overlooking the forest that enveloped Netherfield Park.

"Never. Again." Charlotte held a hand to her chest and shook her head. "Elizabeth Bennet, you're far too adventurous for your own good."

"So everyone tells me," Lizzie said, laughing. "Look—you're covered in dust!"

"Look at yourself! You have cobwebs in your hair!"

"Nothing a bath won't fix," Lizzie said with a laugh. She looked down and showered Guy with pats. He was similarly grimy. "I think you also have earned a bath, sir."

They were so giddy at finally finding their way out, Lizzie didn't think about where they were until Charlotte grew serious as she gazed out the window. "Lizzie, are we in the east wing?"

All laughter dried on Lizzie's lips as she gazed out the windows. "Oh. I think so."

She walked up to a window and ran a finger across a pane and inspected the pad of her finger. It was dark. Soot. The plaster walls around her were not just darkened with time—they were damaged and smoke-stained, and extensively cracked in more than a few places. Above her, giant chunks of plaster had fallen from the ceiling, revealing the laths beneath them. The air was stale and still, and every stray creak of the floorboard beneath her put Lizzie on edge.

"How have we come all the way to the opposite end of the house?" Charlotte asked, panic back in her voice. "I thought Bingley said the east wing was closed off!"

"It is, but he must not know about the servant corridors," Lizzie said, looking back at where they'd emerged. She wasn't eager to revisit it without light.

"How do we get out?" Charlotte asked. "We can't go back the way we came."

Lizzie thought for a moment. They could try to find their way to the original door and pound on it until someone came and rescued them. But that could be hours from now. Or . . .

She looked up and down the hallway, which stretched to either side for at least twenty paces. She peered out the window and oriented herself toward the front of the house. If they could make their way, carefully, to the front of the house, they'd find the door that separated this wing from the rest of the house. They could knock on that until someone heard, and considering the door to the east wing was very close to the landing where they'd begun their journey, it was far more likely that someone would hear and open the door for them.

It would also mean they wouldn't have to wander around through the dark again.

"We'll move very carefully to the center of the house," Lizzie decided.

"Is it safe?"

"Well . . . plaster damage aside, these floors and walls look solid enough," Lizzie said. "Bingley just said the wing wasn't entirely suitable for guests, but I doubt that means we'll fall through."

"All right," Charlotte agreed. "Anything but going back the way we came."

They crept down the hall the way they'd moved through the servant corridor—Guy in front, Lizzie in the middle, and Charlotte bringing up the rear. Lizzie couldn't help but let her gaze wander as they carefully stepped down the creaking hallway—this part of the house was not as evenly proportioned as the west and central wings. Alcoves and strange corners hid doorways into rooms she desperately wanted to explore, and streaks of soot and warped wood finish betrayed the fire that had occurred decades earlier. Lizzie was beginning to doubt the treasure actually existed. If Honoria had access to a pile of silver, why hide it when her home desperately needed repairs?

Lizzie and Charlotte followed a strange, angling passage that led them past empty rooms with damaged or destroyed furnishings boasting heavy layers of gray dust that covered what appeared to be more black soot. Lizzie got the impression that they were headed toward where the fire had been the worst. But very soon, they came to a turn, and when Lizzie peered out the nearest window, she saw with relief that it overlooked the front of the house. "We're back to the front," she said. "Which means that door at the end of this hall is probably our way out," she told Charlotte. "See, that wasn't so bad. We'll be out in just a—AH!"

A shriek of surprise ripped out of Lizzie as she felt her right foot plunge through the floor and into nothingness. She fell forward, catching herself on her hands, and tried to dislodge her right leg, but it was caught between splintered floorboards at the knee, and fiery pain ripped through her. Charlotte shrieked when Lizzie went down, somehow managing to throw herself to the left, away from where the floor had given way.

"Lizzie!"

"Don't come any closer!" Lizzie ordered. It was the strangest thing, but Lizzie could feel the floorboards beneath her groaning. She couldn't see or feel anything beneath her right foot—it was dangling in the liminal space between floor and ceiling . . . and then a terrifying thought occurred to her: What if there was no ceiling below her? What if the plaster had all fallen, and the laths were rotted away, and nothing else was between here and the floor below but these rotting floorboards? She closed her eyes. The ceilings were nearly fifteen feet downstairs! Would a fall from that height kill her?

Very probable.

"Lizzie," Charlotte said again, and Lizzie came back to herself. Guy was standing before her, licking her face very earnestly, and her best friend was huddled on the floor two paces away.

"I'm all right," Lizzie said, which was true enough for now. "But I want you to crawl on your hands and knees toward the door. Carefully."

"What about you?"

"I'm stuck. I need you to get help."

"I can't leave you!"

"You have to, Charlotte."

Charlotte crawled forward hesitantly. "Don't get too close to me," Lizzie warned. "And call Guy."

"Here, Guy," Charlotte said in a thin, scared voice. The dog looked between the two ladies, uncertain. But he did as he was bidden and followed Charlotte. Lizzie watched with her heart in her throat as her best friend and dog made the long, slow, perilous journey down the rest of the hall. At every groan and creak, Lizzie had to grit her teeth and pray that Charlotte wouldn't fall through as well. Finally, she made it to the door and twisted at the knob desperately. "It's locked!" she cried.

"Bang on it!" Lizzie called back. "Someone will hear."

Charlotte began knocking and banging, and then after a moment she started yelling, too. "Help! Can someone help? We're in the east wing! Please, help!"

"Good, keep going!" Lizzie encouraged.

Her muscles were starting to burn. Her right leg was outstretched, sunk into the floor to the knee, and her left leg was folded under her. She had thrown her torso and arms down on the floor, too afraid to sit up and try to yank her leg loose because if she shifted her weight toward the rotting boards, she feared she'd fall all the way through. Now she dared to wiggle her right leg a little bit, and the groaning of the floorboard beneath her made her go still.

"Someone's coming!" Charlotte shouted. "Hold on, Lizzie."

"I've no intention of going anywhere," she assured Charlotte, and then the most beautiful sound in the world floated her way: a key scraping the inside of the lock.

The door separating the east wing from the rest of the house swung open, revealing Mr. Grigson. "Miss Lucas?"

"Miss Bennet is stuck and needs help!" Charlotte shouted.

"Don't come any closer!" Lizzie warned the butler, who was a very tall and somewhat stout man. "Get Mr. Darcy. And tell him to bring some rope."

The butler disappeared without another word—he really deserved a raise and a lengthy holiday considering all he'd put up with lately—and Charlotte stood on the other side of the door, waiting and worrying while Guy barked in excitement. Lizzie could hear shouts and various cries of alarm, but hardly five minutes had gone by before Darcy appeared in the doorway.

"Lizzie!" he shouted.

The anguish on Darcy's face sent her stomach plummeting—so much so that she dug her nails into the floorboards, certain she'd started to slip. But at the same time, she felt her breath become more even at the sight of him. Darcy was here. She was going to be all right.

"Hello," she said in a surprisingly weak voice. "I seem to have taken a wrong turn."

"Save your breath, and don't move," he ordered.

A crowd of footmen and various members of the house party had gathered beyond the door, and Lizzie couldn't tell exactly what they were up to. Minutes seemed to drag by, and then when she looked up again, she saw Darcy carefully making his way toward her, a length of rope wrapped around his torso and another one in hand.

"Don't come too close," she warned. "I don't want you to fall."

Darcy ignored her, dropping to his knees and crawling when he was within ten paces. The floors creaked ominously beneath them, but he didn't hesitate. When he was close enough to reach her, he said, "Push yourself up with your arms. I'm going to secure the rope around your waist."

Lizzie did as she was told, very carefully easing herself up on her elbows, trying to ignore the creaking of the rotten boards, hyperaware of even the slightest give beneath her. "I didn't mean to come to the east wing," she said. "Charlotte and I found a corridor, and then we got lost, and we couldn't go back, and so ended up moving forward and—"

"Explain when you're safe," Darcy whispered, brushing his lips against her right ear as he carefully worked to tie the rope snugly around her waist. Lizzie shivered. It had been days since she'd last felt his lips. She'd missed them. Something about dangling so close to peril made her feel rather silly for the cold shoulder she'd been giving him these past few days.

"All right," she said, when he confirmed the rope was tied securely around her and anchored properly. "You might want to move back a bit."

Using her arms, Lizzie slowly pushed herself back toward where her leg had fallen through. There wasn't just creaking or groaning wood—there was an ominous ticking sound that raked her spine with panic. Lizzie pulled her right leg up from the jagged hole it had fallen through and had almost succeeded in getting free when her ankle caught on something sharp—the splintered edge of the floorboard she'd broken through. She hissed with pain.

"Lizzie!" Darcy cried out in panic, and started to crawl to her.

"Stay back!" she shouted, and she tried again, this time kicking the ragged edge of floorboard to the side. She lost her slipper, but then she was free, and she pushed herself up on her good foot, her entire leg screaming in pain but holding her weight. Lizzie launched herself forward, falling into Darcy's arms as the floorboards that had held her just a moment before broke. A cascade of falling wood echoed from behind her as Darcy propelled Lizzie down the hall, half carrying and half dragging her to safety.

When they crossed the threshold into the central part of the house, Darcy slowly relaxed his death grip on her, but Lizzie dug her fingers into his arm, swaying. After the excitement and fear had washed over her, she just felt weak. She wasn't certain what had scared her more—the fact that she'd almost fallen through to the ground floor, or the wild, desperate look on Darcy's face when he'd thought she was going to fall through.

"I'm sorry," she whispered.

"I know," he said, wrapping her into a hug. His lips found her ear once more, and he whispered, "Me too."

TEN

In Which Lizzie Makes a Midnight Discovery

LIZZIE AND CHARLOTTE'S FORAY into the forbidden east wing of Netherfield Park put an end to their short-lived (and probably ill-advised) treasure hunt. No one had turned up much of anything, anyway: Caroline had grown bored of the picture gallery after half an hour, Kitty and Lydia and Mrs. Bennet had prowled around the ballroom, billiards room, and the drawing rooms and found nothing of note, and when questioned, Bingley sheepishly admitted to half-heartedly searching the library and study before giving up as well. It seemed that Lizzie and Charlotte were the only ones to have found anything interesting, and that something interesting had nearly gotten Lizzie killed.

Bingley and Jane were horrified when Charlotte and Lizzie recounted their discovery of the servants' passage, and their entrapment within the dark hallways. Lizzie had even led them to the back corridor to show them the secret door and how they'd gotten trapped, but when they'd arrived, Lizzie was perplexed to find the door swung open easily. She even stepped within the passageway and closed the door after her to see whether it stuck, but she was able to open it without issue.

"It must have been panic," Bingley told her when she opened the door, bewildered. "You were in the dark, so you weren't able to get the door to unlatch."

If he had been anyone else, Lizzie would have informed him that she'd been held at gunpoint, chased by various villains, and been caught in a number of dangerous locales that she was not meant to be in, and she'd never panicked. But since he was Bingley, and he meant no harm, she bit her lip and just shook her head at the door.

It had been jammed. Or locked. It hadn't opened for them. And now it was open.

Which begged the question: Had someone closed the door after them, forcing them to forge ahead to the east wing?

But who? And *why*?

After baths for Lizzie, Charlotte, and Guy, the rest of the day passed with little excitement and much fussing over Lizzie's scraped leg and torn dress. By the time it was late enough to retire, she was actually glad to say her good-nights and whisk Guy upstairs with her, where the featherdown bed awaited her. She undressed without calling for Agnes, leaving her clothes tossed over the wardrobe door, and pulled on a nightdress and fell into bed. Guy pressed his small, warm body alongside the back of her legs, and within seconds Lizzie was drifting away.

Lizzie startled awake suddenly some hours later. She wasn't certain what had awoken her, and the unfamiliar bed and utter darkness of the room were disorienting. She lay very still, straining for any sound or hint at what could have roused her, her body coming to full alertness.

She heard nothing for what felt like an impossibly long time, and then she realized she could no longer feel Guy curled against her legs, as was his habit each night. His absence made her heartbeat slam even harder, and then she heard a small, snuffling sound, followed by a piteous whine.

"Guy?" Lizzie whispered, sitting up. Heavens, it was dark. Had she left the drapes closed tightly against the night, or had Agnes come in after she'd fallen asleep to draw them? The idea of someone, even a lady's maid, coming into the room while she slept made her uneasy.

Guy whined once more, and Lizzie threw back the covers, wincing as she bent her right knee. It was bruised and sore and boasted a few scrapes, but it held her weight and was only a little stiff. Feeling her way around the room, she managed to make it to a window, where she drew back one heavy velvet panel. It was as she suspected—still the dead of night, but clear, and she could see a waxing gibbous moon and a field of sparkling stars in the sky. She turned into her dark bedroom and made her way to the door, where she could make out the pale shape of Guy. His eyes glinted in the scant light, and she knew he was looking up at her expectantly. Lizzie groaned. "You have to go out? Can't it wait till morning?"

Guy's whine informed her that it could not.

She sighed, knowing better than to tempt fate. The last

thing she needed was for Guy to ruin the carpet and give Mrs. Bennet more ammunition for her argument that the dog was ill-mannered. It would not be fair to him. Or to Jane's carpet.

Lizzie managed to find her dressing gown and slippers in the dark, and she fumbled for Guy's leash. She eased the bedroom door open and peeked out into the hall. It was dark and shadowy, but there was a bit of moonlight illuminating the space. Not wanting Guy to run off, she picked up the dog and carried him down the hall, walking carefully so as not to wake anyone. They made it down the stairs and across the marbled hall straight for the door. It took Lizzie a moment to figure out how to unlock it, and then she carefully slipped out into the night.

She took Guy down the steps and to the left, where the drive curved toward the stables. The last thing she needed was for her dog to make a mess on the pristine front lawn for some poor gardener to discover in the morning. "Come along, Guy," Lizzie whispered, shivering in the cool night. "The quicker you see to business, the quicker we can be back to bed."

Unfortunately for Lizzie, Guy was rather picky when it came to the exact spot in which he deigned to relieve himself. In London, she always attributed his reluctance to the fact that he had very little nature that hadn't been trod on by at least a hundred other souls to sniff out. But here they were, out in the countryside, surrounded by plenty of barely touched green, and her dog was still taking his sweet time.

Lizzie sighed and drew her dressing gown around her even tighter.

She stood there long enough to grow chilled and to feel the weight of sleep drag on her, but finally Guy saw to his business. Lizzie sighed in relief and patted him on the head. "Good boy," she told him. "I'm sorry I gave you such a hard time about coming out at night. Let's get back to bed."

But when she turned to face the house, something caught her eye. She stopped. Watched.

Candlelight flickered in the windows on the first floor. It was not very strong, but this late at night, with nothing to light up the countryside but the moon and stars, it was starkly noticeable. It was a single candle, if Lizzie had to guess, and it seemed to be bobbing ever so slightly, as if someone were carrying it from room to room. Lizzie tilted her head back and squinted into the darkness, and then realization cut through her exhaustion.

Someone was in the east wing.

She watched, even as questions flooded through her. Who would be on the first floor of the east wing after Lizzie had very nearly fallen to her death just that afternoon? And why were they there in the middle of the night?

She tried to recall her own walk through the wing. Were they walking the halls, or in one of the many rooms that overlooked the forest? Finally, one window seemed to grow brighter and the movement stopped. Whoever was there had paused. Lizzie counted the shining black windows—it was the fifth window from the southeast corner.

Suddenly, Guy let out a single high-pitched bark—his *Let's move along now, if you please* bark. Lizzie jumped, and then looked down at her dog, who was looking up at her impatiently. He barked once more.

"Shh!" She picked up the dog, startling him into silence, and dodged behind a row of nearby hedges. In the daylight, she surely wouldn't have been able to hide from whoever was positioned in a first-floor window—their vantage point would be too great. But she hoped that the darkness would prove to be her friend, and that whoever it was would not be able to pick her out of the shadows if she was mostly obscured.

"Good boy, Guy," Lizzie whispered as she petted the dog. "That's a very good boy. Be quiet for me, hmm?"

Guy let out a very ungentlemanly grunt and settled happily in her arms. She whispered to him a moment more, then she dared to peek up, carefully lifting her face.

The candle flickered in full view of the fifth window on the first floor, and a figure stood framed in the glass, looking down. For a fleeting moment, Lizzie wondered whether she was hiding from the ghost of Honoria Bingley. Then she got ahold of herself.

This was no ghost. It was a woman.

Lizzie had a hard time making out her face, but she was reasonably certain she hadn't been spotted—the woman seemed to be looking left and right, as if searching for the source of the noise. Lizzie strained her eyes, trying to make out more detail. The woman's hair was tied back, but her figure was cast in shadow, and it was impossible to discern features from this distance and in such poor light until . . . the woman turned away, and candlelight glinted off her white-gold hair.

Lizzie gasped. It was Sally.

Sally moved quickly, not lingering. The light retreated and then appeared again in the sixth window, although this time not as bright—she wasn't as near to the window. After a moment, the candlelight withdrew again and bobbed into the seventh window, then the eighth. She was moving away, toward the back of the house.

Lizzie stood and jogged back to the front door. It swung open on silent, well-oiled hinges, and Lizzie shut and locked it behind her. Scarcely daring to breathe, she ran up the stairs, still carrying a squirming Guy. She hesitated a brief moment at the top of the stairs, and then crept very softly to the door to the east wing. With a shaking hand she reached for the knob and ever-so-gently tried to turn it.

Locked.

For a moment she wondered if she'd imagined it all—but no. As Lizzie had discovered, there was more than one way into the east wing. But why was Sally there in the dark? Surely that was madness.

Lizzie was tempted to turn right and knock on Darcy's door. She wanted to tell him what she had seen, and then . . . what? Wait for Sally to emerge from the hidden corridor and confront her? But then sense prevailed. If she did that, there was a good chance they'd wake someone else. It wouldn't do for her to get caught out of her bed in the middle of the night, in the presence of an unmarried gentleman. Although her mother would surely be overjoyed at the swift wedding that would have to follow.

She went straight back to her room, setting Guy on the bed and jumping under the covers after kicking off her slippers and dropping her dressing gown. She shivered, despite the warmth of the bed, and tried to think up all the reasons why Sally might be creeping through the east wing. Was she looking for something? Inspecting the floors? Seeing if Lizzie and Charlotte had disturbed something?

What else was Netherfield Park hiding?

In the morning, Lizzie managed to rouse herself before Agnes came bustling in, bringing in a wave of cheerfulness.

"Good morning, miss!" she said, clearly surprised to find Lizzie already awake sitting near the window and looking out onto the dewy lawn. Guy was still tired from his midnight adventure and lay sprawled across the bed, but he jumped up and let out a single yip when Agnes entered.

"Good morning," Lizzie said. "How are you today?"

"Me, miss? I should be asking you that question."

"Why can't we ask it of each other?"

"Well, because you're . . ." Agnes looked unsure for the first time since Lizzie met her. "You're a guest, and I'm a maid."

"We're both human beings with manners," Lizzie pointed out.

"Very well. I am well, and you?"

"Quite well," Lizzie said, although it wasn't exactly true. She was still thinking about the previous day's events, and what she had seen last night.

"And did you sleep well?"

"I did," Lizzie said. Another lie. She'd fallen asleep quickly enough, but it had been a light, restless sleep that had left her a bit weary this morning. "And you?"

"Yes," she said, seemingly embarrassed.

"And how is the household this morning? We haven't lost anyone else since yesterday, have we?"

"Well . . ." Agnes poured water into the washbasin, avoiding Lizzie's questioning look. "Jenny Hollister didn't come in today, but she could just be sick. And Danny, the youngest footman, also didn't turn up this morning, but his mum never liked the idea of him going into service. Wanted him to stay home and help tend the farm."

"Oh dear," Lizzie said. "But you believe they left because of the curse."

"Mr. Grigson has banned all talk of it, miss," Agnes said nervously.

Lizzie didn't want to force the girl into disobeying the butler, but she had rather hoped to get some information from her. "Well, what is said in here stays between the two of us. But does everyone believe the curse is real?"

Agnes shrugged. "I don't know, miss. I don't hold much with talk of curses. But everyone from Meryton certainly thinks it's real."

"And what about Sally?" Lizzie asked, trying to sound casual as she stood and began flipping through the dresses hanging in the wardrobe.

"Sally? The head housemaid? I reckon she believes in it more than any of us. She's the one who told Jenny that if she doesn't feel safe, it would be best for her to leave."

Now that was interesting. Lizzie decided to feign ignorance as she asked, "Sally was the only one who was here when Honoria Bingley was still alive, isn't that right?"

"Yes, miss," Agnes said, her voice dropping a notch. "She grew up in this house, but she doesn't like to talk about it. She's the last to leave each night, and she reminds Mr. Grigson to lock up after her. I don't think he likes being told what to do by a housemaid very much."

"Hmm" was all Lizzie said, because secretly her mind was spinning. She had seen Sally in the window in the east wing last night, hadn't she? Or had the light and her own exhaustion been playing tricks on her eyes? But her white-blond hair was unmistakable, and Lizzie didn't recall seeing any other servant with hair the same hue when they'd all lined up before Netherfield Park on the day of their arrival. "Does she often stay late?"

"Later now, since you all arrived. She doesn't like that, and she insists that she and all the locals need to be gone by midnight each night. Mr. Grigson and she are already rowing about what to do the night of the ball."

Lizzie winced. She hadn't thought of that—London balls went until dawn, although she doubted that would be the case for Jane's country ball. But still, the staff would be expected to stay very late.

"And do you share the others' concerns about staying overnight, Agnes?"

"I don't have anywhere else to go, miss. I came from an estate near Ware when I heard that Mr. Bingley was hiring a household staff. And I sleep like a babe, too."

"Glad to hear it," Lizzie said, reaching for the breakfast plate. "Hopefully Sally will make an exception for herself and all the local servants for Jane's party. My sister is very much looking forward to it."

"I think she might come around, miss. Mr. Grigson pointed out that they won't be sleeping, they'll be working. But she's still uneasy. Truth is, I wonder if she's less worried about the curse than she is about leaving her grandparents alone at night."

Lizzie's head jerked up. Her mouth was full of toast, and she swallowed quickly. "Her grandparents?"

"She lives with them in the caretaker's cottage on the edge of the grounds," Agnes said, then tilted her head to the side. "Or at least, I think so. One of the scullery maids was whispering about her, but Cook told her to get back to work, so I didn't hear the entire story."

"Her grandmother who was the housekeeper before?" Lizzie asked.

"Aye, miss. And her grandad was the groundskeeper. But they're in no fit state now, that's for certain."

In all the commotion of discovering the dead man, Lizzie

hadn't actually asked whether the caretakers of the estate from Honoria's days were still alive. Jane had said that only one servant remained after Honoria's death, so she had simply assumed they had passed. And Sally . . . Sally had been careful not to bring them up. Lizzie had made an error in assuming that they were no longer among the living, like Honoria Bingley herself.

But they were alive.

Lizzie stuffed the rest of the toast into her mouth and placed a small plate with Guy's breakfast on the floor, which was enough to rouse him from the bed. By the time she finished chewing, she was already reaching for the wardrobe. "Agnes, I've just remembered that I promised Mr. Darcy I would speak with him this morning."

"All right," the maid said, clearly baffled by Lizzie's sudden change in topic. "Let me help you dress, at least."

"I'm all right," Lizzie said, stepping behind a screen and tearing off her nightgown. "I'm terribly late."

"They're just now serving breakfast, so I'm sure Mr. Darcy isn't even awake yet."

"No, Darcy is very prompt," Lizzie assured her, working the ties of her dress.

"Let me at least set your hair for you!"

Lizzie emerged from behind the screen a moment later. "It's all right, I'll pin it up. Can you hand me those stockings?"

Agnes watched in vague disapproval as Lizzie made short order of readying herself for the day, clearly not up to the maid's standards. When she was finally presentable, Agnes gave her a begrudging nod, then withdrew something from her apron pocket. "Before you go running off, miss, you've had two letters. They came in this morning's post."

Lizzie took the letters from her, barely glancing at them. "Thank you! Guy, come."

Lizzie snatched the leash from the side table as the dog trotted after her and she hurried out into the hall. A lead! It was wonderful to have a new lead. And to have a lead in the form of people who might have been alive when their dead man was placed in that flue . . . well, that was a break Lizzie hadn't been expecting!

She was halfway down the stairs before she thought to look at the letters in her hand. The top one was from Marianne Dashwood, and she tore it open, eager for news from home.

Dear Lizzie,

We've no signs of Lady Catherine de Bourgh. There, I've gotten that out of the way—I know it is the first question on your mind. Graves and I have had a few meetings, and despite what you may think of him, I do believe he's working very hard to find her. I've also had a few meetings with Fred—when he's not working at his apprenticeship, he goes around asking his friends for help. And Henry—you don't need to worry about him! He wants to help as well, of course, so Fred has taken him under his wing. But we're keeping a close eye on him. I have a few more leads to chase down, none of which I want to put to pen and paper in case this letter is waylaid, but have faith, dear Lizzie. We'll bring her to justice and welcome you home soon enough.

In the meantime, Elinor wishes to share some less pressing news from London . . .

The rest of the letter was in Elinor's hand, sharing news of mutual friends and court cases, which Lizzie skimmed. No signs of Lady Catherine! How was the woman able to emerge to send threatening letters, only to disappear into nothingness? It was maddening!

Lizzie got to the bottom of the stairs and made a note to write the Dashwoods back to thank them and to share news of the case at Netherfield. Perhaps Marianne could ask her Dr. Brandon about the body they'd found and offer a few helpful hints for her investigation here . . .

Lizzie went very still. She'd refolded the Dashwoods' letter and finally glanced at the second letter. It was a small letter with crisp corners, addressed to Miss Elizabeth Bennet, Netherfield Park, Hertfordshire. But that's not what made her heart leap.

It was written in Lady Catherine's hand.

ELEVEN

In Which Lizzie and Darcy Conceal and Uncover Various Secrets

"FANCY A TURN ABOUT the gardens?"

Darcy couldn't help but jump slightly at the sound of Lizzie's voice, sudden and close to his ear. He turned in his seat at the breakfast table to find her standing behind him, hair slightly in disarray.

"Now?" he asked, glancing sadly back at his half-eaten breakfast.

"Guy needs his morning constitutional."

He glanced down at the dog, who was sitting rather patiently at the end of his leash. Then he got a good look at Lizzie. She was smiling, but her expression was strained. She was very purposefully not looking at Mr. Bennet, who was reading his paper. *You're up to something*, he thought, but he couldn't help the slow smile that spread across his face. "All right."

Mr. Bennet finally looked up from his newspaper—delayed

from London by a day—and said, "Lizzie, dear, let Darcy at least finish his breakfast."

"It's all right. I was nearly done anyway," he said, stuffing one more bite of sausage in his mouth before wiping at his face with a napkin.

"I want to escape before Mama comes down," Lizzie said, so convincingly that Darcy didn't doubt her—but he also doubted that was her *only* reason for haste.

"All right, but try not to wander into unsafe areas today." Mr. Bennet picked up his paper and grumbled, "I thought I was removing you from danger when we retired here."

Lizzie's expression turned strained for a moment, and Darcy stood. "Don't worry, I'll accompany her wherever she needs to go, Mr. Bennet."

He might have thought his chivalrous words would win him some favor, but Lizzie just scowled at him and turned on her heel.

He really couldn't say the right thing at all.

"Lizzie, wait," he called out as he chased her down the hall. Good lord, but she moved quickly—even Guy was trotting to keep pace with her. "I thought we were going to go for a walk, not a run. I've just eaten."

She slowed down, but just a smidge. "I wish you wouldn't do that."

"Do what?" he asked, catching up with her as they reached the door.

"*I'll accompany her wherever she needs to go*," Lizzie repeated in a falsetto that Darcy would have found insulting from anyone else. As it stood, he tried not to laugh. Lizzie caught the humor on his face and her scowl deepened. "Don't."

She stormed outside, and Darcy scrambled to follow her. "What am I supposed to say to your father—that I won't look out for you?"

"I don't need looking after. I'm perfectly capable."

"I know that," Darcy protested. "He's just worried about you. Lady Catherine—"

"This isn't about her!"

Darcy reached out to gently grab Lizzie's arm. "Lizzie. Talk to me. What's the matter?"

"Is this how it's always going to be?" she asked. "And I don't just mean in regard to Lady Catherine, but every time there's danger or concern, will you always default to my father? Override my wishes?"

Darcy was perplexed. "You know I respect you," he said. "And anything I do, I do because I care about you, and I want to ensure that you're safe."

"I don't need you to protect me," she said, glowering. "I need you to listen to me."

Darcy opened his mouth to say that he was listening, and besides, he could listen to her and protect her at the same time. But something in her look stilled his tongue, and he closed his mouth. "All right," he said. "I'm listening."

Lizzie exhaled. "Do you trust me?"

He looked into her eyes. What he wanted to say was that

he never distrusted her, even when her plans appeared reckless in the moment. Agreeing with her father that they all ought to depart London had never been about distrusting Lizzie but about fearing Lady Catherine and her threats.

"Yes," he said.

She nodded, then pulled him around to the east side of the manor, Guy trotting alongside them. When they were far enough away from where any passersby might happen upon them, Lizzie withdrew something from her pocket. "I need you to promise you won't overreact," she said.

Darcy had a sick feeling in the pit of his stomach as he reached for the letter in her hand. He knew before seeing the address whom it must be from, but when he opened the letter, the confirmation sent his world spinning.

My dear Miss Bennet,

I confess, I did not take you for a lady who runs away from a challenge. You disappoint me. Were my threats against your family a step too far? I truly do not wish to go to such lengths. I don't enjoy hurting others, and I find it very difficult.

Darcy scoffed. *Try telling that to Wickham*, he thought.

But you see, Elizabeth—I can call you Elizabeth, can't I? I feel as though after all we've been through, we are intimately acquainted—I'll be direct. You owe me. My insurance dealings as they pertained to Netherfield Shipping were quite valuable, and when you interrupted them, it left me in a very vulnerable position. And I believe I have you to thank for the Royal Navy's sudden fixation on me. My plans to reestablish business interests in England have been yet again thwarted by you, and I am vexed—do you think it is easy to smuggle goods between England and France? I find my freedom threatened by a myriad of legal issues, and you, Elizabeth, are to blame. Just know that I won't hesitate to call in my debt, whether you're in London or Hertfordshire or Ireland or the Americas.

I will send further instructions.

Cordially,

Lady Catherine de Bourgh

"Well?" Lizzie asked after he'd finished.

He swallowed and found his mouth was completely dry. "I think you've made her very mad."

Lizzie actually laughed as she took the letter back. "Is that all you have to say?"

"I think we ought to tell your—"

"Absolutely not." The look she gave him was severe. "If my father were to see this, he'd have us all in carriages before luncheon. No. We cannot keep retreating—you saw what she wrote."

Darcy closed his eyes and took a deep breath. "How did this letter arrive?"

"The maid said it came via the post—I also received a letter from the Dashwoods."

"How did she know we're here? And so quickly—she must have known the day we left London. But who—"

"I don't know!"

Darcy tried to collect his thoughts. "What *do* we know?"

"She's good at recruiting allies," Lizzie said. "Think of Collins, Wickham, Tomlinson . . . She always has someone working for her."

"And those people have managed to get exceedingly close to you. To us," Darcy added. "So it stands to reason that someone back home could have let it slip."

"I think that's the most likely answer," Lizzie said grimly.

That was what worried Darcy. "Did the Dashwoods have any news?"

"None. Marianne has a few more leads, but . . ."

Darcy looked at the letter once more. "She might not even be in London anymore. She could be on her way here."

"If she was ever in London to begin with," Lizzie said.

"What do you mean?"

"It's just a thought I've had . . . she has so many people who've gotten close to us, perhaps she doesn't need to be in London at all."

That was an unpleasant thought.

"Either way, we have an advantage," Lizzie said, taking his hand in hers. "Look at this place—an estate surrounded by acres of forest and field, where outsiders will stick out like a sore thumb. She can't sneak up on us here, like in London."

"Promise me you won't do anything reckless," he said. "No going off on your own."

She didn't roll her eyes. "I promise."

As for what to do next . . . "It says she'll send further instructions."

"I know," Lizzie said. "Which is why I think we keep this to ourselves and wait until we have something concrete to take action on. She hasn't made good on any of her threats yet, but she might if we run again. She knows where we are, which means she must know my family is here. I want to wait and see what she says."

Darcy didn't like it, and he couldn't pretend otherwise. But Lizzie had a point—they'd already antagonized Lady Catherine by leaving London, and he didn't want to think what might happen if they continued to test her. At the same time, he shuddered to imagine what Mr. Bennet might say if he found out that they'd kept this information from him. He'd be disappointed, to be sure . . . but would he be angry?

Would he be angry enough to separate them?

"We could always go to Pemberley," he said, almost hopefully.

Lizzie surprised him by smiling. "Looking for any excuse to whisk me away to your ancestral home?"

"Any excuse to keep you safe," he said, reaching up to cup her cheek.

Lizzie turned into his touch, kissing his palm. "I don't want to run, not yet."

Darcy wanted to protest, but her question minutes earlier rang in his ears. *Do you trust me?*

"Fine," he said. "We wait. But please, no wandering off alone, and you must tell me—or someone—if you leave the estate."

"All right," she said, and he was taken aback by how quickly she agreed—and then he saw her victorious little smile. This was what she'd wanted all along. Oh, Elizabeth Bennet would be the death of him.

"We should probably stay close to the estate then, just in case—"

"Actually," Lizzie said. "I have something I need to tell you."

Oh no. "What is it?"

"It's about the case. And you have to promise you won't be upset . . ."

The previous evening, Darcy and Bingley had spent two hours in Bingley's study, going over the estate's ledgers and familiarizing themselves with the property and its tenants so that Darcy could advise Bingley on how to best bring the estate into a new era. One aspect of their evening had included inspecting a map of the main property and surrounding farms, which included labels of all buildings. So when Lizzie had told him about how she'd taken Guy out the night before—alone—and had seen Sally in the window, and then explained the conversation she'd had with her lady's maid, and *then* expressed her intent to find Sally's grandparents, Darcy was fortunate enough to have a general sense of where their cottage was located.

It was a twenty-minute walk to said cottage, which was

tucked into a small valley on the way to the village. Naturally, Lizzie had insisted they walk, and Darcy hadn't argued. He was too busy berating himself for not thinking to ask whether Sally had any living relatives who also had access to Netherfield Park.

"Careless," he muttered as they turned from the country lane to a smaller track leading toward the cottage. It was what his father would have said if he'd been there. It was what he always said when Darcy missed something important.

"Maybe," Lizzie said, "but I think we were purposefully misled. I keep thinking back about it now, and Sally was careful to not refer to her grandparents in the present tense. Almost as if she wanted us to believe they were no longer with us."

"And I suppose she did that because she wanted us to *not* do what we're about to?"

"Very likely," Lizzie said cheerfully. The cottage was in sight, and although Darcy couldn't see any activity around it, it looked far from neglected.

"What is our plan?"

Lizzie bit her lip. "We're outsiders here. I don't think we'll be able to fool any locals into telling us what we want to know, so . . ."

"So we'll just have to rely on our natural charms," he deadpanned.

Lizzie let out a snort. "You can be almost charming when you put your mind to it."

"Which is more effort than I am typically inclined to expend, but today I shall make an exception."

The Burtons' cottage was a small, one-story stone home surrounded by a stone fence that enclosed a tidy, well-kept garden. Darcy caught sight of an old woman sitting on a bench under a nearby tree. She held a piece of knitting, and she didn't seem to notice as they approached.

"Hello?" Lizzie called out. "Good morning, madam."

The woman looked up slowly and blinked at them in surprise. Then her face broke out into a happy smile. "Oh, hello!"

Darcy couldn't help the small bow that his deeply instilled manners prompted. "Good day, madam."

The old lady laughed, sounding delighted. "My, aren't you handsome?"

"Uh . . ." Darcy did not know how to respond to that. Then he realized that she was talking to Guy, who had approached the woman and sat at her feet, looking up with mournful brown eyes. Darcy cleared his throat in embarrassment.

Lizzie, however, grinned. "He is, isn't he?"

The woman set aside her knitting and offered a hand to Guy, who sniffed it and then happily allowed her to pet him. "Is he yours?" the lady asked.

"He is indeed, although I like to think I am his as much as he's mine."

Guy flopped onto the ground, exposing his pink belly for scritches. The woman chuckled and complied. "Hello, handsome. Aren't you a handsome one?" When she looked up, she said to Lizzie, "Hold on to the handsome ones, miss." Then her gaze slid to Darcy, and she added, "But only if their hearts are true."

Lizzie laughed. "Thank you for the advice. Are you Mrs. Burton?"

The woman didn't respond, but neither did she refute Lizzie. She gave Guy another pat.

"I'm Miss Elizabeth Bennet, and this is Mr. Fitzwilliam Darcy."

At that, Mrs. Burton looked up, something like alarm in her eyes. "Oh my! A lady and gentleman come to visit, and I've made no preparations!" She made to stand, slowly, and Darcy winced at her pained movements—it appeared as though her joints troubled her.

"Oh, no—please stay seated," he said, taking Mrs. Burton's hand and guiding her back down to her seat. "We don't wish to inconvenience you."

"It's no trouble," she insisted, but she didn't try to rise again. "But where is Amy? She really ought to be seeing to you."

Darcy exchanged a puzzled look with Lizzie, who kept her smile gentle and polite, but didn't seem to know who Amy was, either. "We're quite all right as we are, Mrs. Burton," Darcy said. "But thank you for your concern."

Mrs. Burton smiled and Lizzie continued. "I'm afraid the reason for our visit is a little unconventional, Mrs. Burton. As we mentioned, we're staying at Netherfield Park. My sister is Mrs. Bingley."

Almost instantly, the good humor drained from the woman's face. "You're staying at Netherfield Park?"

"Yes," Lizzie continued brightly. "We've only recently arrived, but—"

The woman's wrinkled hands grabbed at Lizzie's. "You must not stay there. Did your sister not warn you? *No one* is to stay there."

The forcefulness of her words gave Darcy pause. He did not believe for a solitary moment that Netherfield Park was actually cursed, but the vehemence in Mrs. Burton's voice was real. Was she . . . scared?

"May I ask why?" Lizzie asked gently.

But Mrs. Burton didn't answer. She looked about the garden as if searching for someone. "Where is that girl?"

Lizzie was undeterred. "Mrs. Burton, I don't know whether you've heard the dreadful news, but something was discovered at Netherfield Park this week."

The old woman went very still, and she didn't meet Lizzie's gaze. "Oh?"

"A body was found," Lizzie said. "Stuffed into the chimney."

The old woman's laugh was worn and cracked but contained genuine mirth. "You're having me on."

"I'm telling the truth, Mrs. Burton."

The woman looked at Darcy. "She's lost all sense. A body? In a chimney?"

"I'm afraid she's right," Darcy told her gravely, and watched as confusion fell over Mrs. Burton's face like a heavy veil.

"A body in the chimney," she repeated. "But no, that's not right."

"Who're you?"

A newcomer's voice, rough and hostile, cut through the

garden. Lizzie and Darcy turned to see an elderly man in a patched jacket with a slight stoop to his shoulders hurrying toward them with as much haste as the carved cane he leaned on allowed. As he drew closer, Darcy was surprised to find the man taller than he, despite the slump to his posture. In his prime, the newcomer had likely cut an imposing figure. Now time and age seemed to weigh him down.

"Mr. Darcy," Darcy said. "And my companion, Miss Bennet."

"Yes?" the man said, eyeing them with suspicion. "What is it you want?"

"Mr. Burton, I presume?" Lizzie asked. "As I was just telling your wife, we are staying—"

"Allan, where's Amy?"

Lizzie stopped, startled by Mrs. Burton's interruption. Mr. Burton, however, did not look surprised. In fact, he looked weary.

"She'll be along soon, dove."

"Oh. All right." Mrs. Burton sat back down and picked up her knitting.

Lizzie continued. "As I was saying, we're part of the party come to stay at Netherfield Park. I understand that you and Mrs. Burton were the caretakers for the previous Mrs. Bingley for many years. We were wondering if we could ask you some questions."

Darcy watched Mr. Burton closely. The man seemed to be weighing the request, and it was clearly not one he wanted to grant. But eventually he nodded and said, "Wait here."

He went over to his wife and took her by the hand. "Let's get you inside, dove."

"Oh, is it time for luncheon?"

Lizzie glanced at Darcy, confused. It was not yet mid-morning.

"Mm-hmm, and Amy has something lovely prepared."

"Oh, wonderful. Amy's a marvel in the kitchen." She turned to Lizzie and Darcy. "Would you two like to join us?"

"How kind of you, Mrs. Burton," Darcy said quickly, "but I am afraid we can't. Thank you for the offer."

Mr. Burton led her into the cottage and Lizzie hissed, "What did you say that for?"

"Because I don't think there's anyone named Amy in that cottage preparing a luncheon. I think Mrs. Burton's memory is addled."

"Oh," Lizzie said, taking that in. "Oh. How can you be sure?"

Darcy picked up the bit of knitting that she had left behind on the bench. The ball of yarn had rolled into the grass. "I don't mean to be impolite, but does this look like . . . anything to you?"

"Normally, I'd make a remark about men and their inability to identify women's handiwork, but in this instance, you are correct." Lizzie plucked the knitted article from his hands. It was a lopsided rectangle with bumpy rows of purls and dropped stitches, and the stitches alternated between too tight and overly slack.

"Just so you know, Mrs. Greenfield, the housekeeper at Pemberley, taught me how to knit," Darcy informed her defensively.

He had the pleasure of watching her jaw drop. "Now you're having me on."

Before Darcy could defend his knitting abilities, Mr. Burton returned, and he was back to looking aggravated. "Now, I don't know what it is you want—"

Darcy held his hands up in a placating gesture. "We mean no harm, sir."

"You're from Netherfield," he said, his voice dripping with disdain.

"Indeed. Mrs. Bingley is my sister," Lizzie explained. "And we heard that you were the caretakers of the estate for many years. I'm sure by now you've heard of our, uh, rather unpleasant discovery?"

Mr. Burton nodded. "Aye. But we don't know anything about that."

"You never had any hint that there might be something—someone—dead within Netherfield Park?" Darcy asked. It wasn't as though he disbelieved the man entirely, but if the unidentified man had died during Mr. Burton's tenure, the smell alone . . .

"No," he said sharply.

"When was the last time the drawing room fireplace was swept?" Lizzie asked quickly, her tone slightly more placating.

The man let out a snort. "When did Mr. Geoffrey Bingley die? Probably a fair bit before then."

"Really?" Darcy asked. "You didn't once order a chimney sweep or light a fire in the room for the last . . . forty years?"

"Mrs. Bingley, God rest her soul, was an eccentric. Too much loss."

"What do you mean?" Lizzie asked.

"She withdrew into herself, after Mr. Geoffrey died. Didn't want to replace the staff—not that anyone blamed her at first, of course. It was a tragedy watching them all die, one by one. It could have been us. Susannah and me, we were just married. She stayed home the day the housekeeper fell sick with smallpox—she had burned her hand the day before, and the doctor wanted her to rest. The next day, word had spread. We didn't dare approach the estate, until there was no one left alive in that house but Mrs. Bingley."

"How awful," Lizzie murmured, and Darcy repressed a shudder.

"And after that?" Darcy prompted. "You never moved into the manor house?"

Mr. Burton shook his head. "This is our home. I told Mrs. Bingley she'd have to hire someone else to stay the night if she wanted that. Otherwise, we'd come home at the end of each day."

"But in almost fifty years, you never once spent the night?" Lizzie asked.

Mr. Burton gave her a sharp look, as if he knew what she was really asking. "No. And I know the rumors, too. I'm a god-fearing man, young lady. I don't hold with any nonsense about curses. Mrs. Bingley herself never wanted anyone to stay."

That seemed particularly odd to Darcy—he didn't know a single well-bred lady who lived alone, without servants. He thought of the army of servants and the paid companion at Pemberley, all to keep Georgiana supervised and occupied during their father's absence. "You didn't think that odd?"

"It's not for me to say, sir."

"In all that time, Mr. Burton, you wouldn't have any idea of who might have been in the chimney, or how they might have ended up there?" Lizzie asked.

"Of course not. We were just as shocked as anyone when we heard."

It was clear to Darcy that Mr. Burton would not be offering any speculation. "But it seems likely, does it not, that if someone was killed at Netherfield and their body hidden within the house, that it would have occurred during the period of time when the only occupants of the house were Mrs. Bingley and occasionally your family?"

Mr. Burton's eyes narrowed. "What are you implying, sir?"

"He's not implying anything," Lizzie rushed to say. "But if there is anything you can share that might shed some light—"

"I'm sorry, no." The man glared. "I'd like you both to leave now."

Lizzie tried once more. "Mr. Burton, please understand—he was a *person*. If you lost a loved one with no explanation, wouldn't you want someone to find out the truth about what happened to them?"

Darcy watched Mr. Burton's face—he was not taken in by Lizzie's emotional entreaties. A bushy gray eyebrow rose, and he said, "And you, a stranger to Netherfield and this county, are just the person to right this wrong?"

"Why not?" Lizzie asked. "My sister is the new mistress of Netherfield Park, and this discovery certainly hasn't done any favors for her reputation."

Mr. Burton let out a small guffaw. "Aye, that's the most honest thing you've said to me yet, Miss Bennet."

"Both reasons can be true, though," Lizzie argued. "I can want to both help my sister and find the truth."

"A word of advice, Miss Bennet? Let it lie. Bad things have happened at Netherfield Park. Mrs. Bingley was unhappy there, and her husband and his family before her. If you care for your sister, then encourage her to go back to London. Now, good day."

He turned and walked back to the cottage as fast as his two legs and cane would take him, leaving Lizzie, Darcy, and Guy standing in the garden. But Darcy had one last question he couldn't let rest. "Mr. Burton?" he called. "Who is Amy?"

The old man stopped. He turned slightly. "Sally's mother," he said gruffly.

"Oh," Lizzie said. "And she—"

"She's dead," he said abruptly. "Died of a fever, although those fools in the village will probably tell you the Netherfield curse got to her, too."

And with that, he walked into the cottage and slammed the door behind him.

Darcy looked down at Lizzie. "What do you think?"

"I think," she said slowly, thoughtfully, "that I can't believe you know how to knit."

"After all that, my knitting abilities are what you've focused on?"

"That," she said, "and the Burtons are most definitely hiding something."

TWELVE

In Which Lizzie and Darcy Take an Unplanned Detour

LIZZIE STOOD AT THE corner where the path to the Burtons' cottage diverted from the lane, uncertain. She felt as though they were dancing around the edge of something, but she didn't know what.

"Are you all right?" Darcy asked.

She nodded, although she didn't feel particularly confident. "How can a dead man appear out of nowhere, and no one has any idea as to who he might be?"

"It's possible that they truly don't know," he suggested, although he didn't sound convinced himself. "Fifty years is a long time."

Lizzie nodded, but she wasn't entirely convinced. Unless the body had been placed in the flue during the time when all the household staff had fallen sick but before the Burtons had returned to work . . . But how long did a body smell? She would put the question to Marianne Dashwood in a letter as soon as they returned to Netherfield, and hoped she would receive a quick response.

"I know you're not about to give up," Darcy said, nudging her arm. She looked up at him and gave him a look, and he grinned. "Why don't we walk into the village? We're already halfway there. We can see if Miss Jeffries has made any progress on those registers."

"All right," she agreed, "although I am not sure she's the type to take well to being pressured."

"I paid her fifteen shillings apiece for those registers—she should feel pressured," Darcy grumbled, making Lizzie laugh.

It was a lovely morning for a walk—bright and cloudless but not too warm. Guy happily trotted along, although he wanted to stop and sniff every five or six paces, which meant their progress was not quick. As they walked, Lizzie realized that in her anger toward Darcy and her father as they'd left London, and then in the excitement over a new case, she and Darcy hadn't really talked in days.

"How is your sister?" she asked, causing Darcy to turn to her in surprise. "I never did ask—did you tell her about leaving London?"

"I did," he said. "Hopefully she'll have gotten the letter by now."

"And did you tell her the reason for our leaving?"

He nodded. "I don't keep secrets from Georgie. Sometimes I may downplay certain dangers, to keep her from worrying, but . . . I don't lie to her. She deserves that, at least."

"Of course," Lizzie said. "I'm glad you told her. She's a

delightful girl. I can't imagine how difficult this last year has been for you, being apart."

He sighed. "Yes, but I imagine she'll be back in London for the season—she's old enough now to make her debut."

Lizzie looked up at him. "She will? Is your father . . ."

Darcy's expression was stony. Lizzie knew this expression—it was the one he wore when he was upset but trying not to show it. Unfortunately for him, looking like a severe marble sculpture gave him away. "I've had word from him, yes." Darcy's voice was clipped. "He's on his way back to England. I don't know exactly when his ship will dock but . . . soon."

"Darcy," Lizzie breathed. The subject of his father was a sore one. When they'd first met, the senior Mr. Darcy had been a distant figure to her, but Lizzie had gotten the distinct impression that he did not approve of Darcy's association with her. Darcy had assured her he was glad enough to have another solved case in the books, and even grateful that their investigation had proved what a scoundrel Wickham could be. Lizzie had suspected him of exaggerating but had said nothing.

When Darcy's father had announced his prolonged business trip to the continent, Darcy had been upset—but Lizzie knew it was less about his father's absence and more about his insistence on sending Georgiana to the countryside with no company except a paid companion. And she knew that his father hadn't been pleased by how their case with Jack Mullins had turned out, although she had hoped he'd at least recognize that their efforts had uncovered a mole in Mr. Tomlinson.

Judging by Darcy's expression now, she doubted his father had voiced his admiration for a job well done.

"Please don't worry," Darcy said, which was what he always did when the subject of his father was brought up.

"You're clearly upset. Has your father said anything about . . ." She wanted to say *us* but chose the safer route and finished with, "Lady Catherine?"

Darcy grimaced. "Not in as many words."

Ah. Lizzie feared that meant he'd had plenty to say about her and their prolonged partnership, then.

"But this is a good thing," Lizzie said, attempting to put on a brave face, though she did not in fact think that Darcy's father's return portended much of anything good. "Georgiana will be back in London soon enough, and surely having her close by will be an improvement for you both."

He smiled a little at that. "She's been awfully bored at Pemberley. She claims the lady's companion is terrible company, always complaining of a headache or finding some excuse to abandon her duties. Georgiana is hoping Father will sack her as soon as he returns."

"Oh dear," Lizzie said, unable to help feeling a pang of sympathy for the lady's companion. The position was reserved for gentlemen's daughters who had little money and no marriage prospects on the horizon as a way of earning a respectable income. It did not sound like a pleasant living to Lizzie, but there weren't exactly many respectable positions open to ladies who must work.

Lizzie was about to further inquire about Georgiana when Darcy stopped. "Isn't that Sally up ahead?"

It didn't take Lizzie very long to see whom Darcy was referring to. They were approaching the outskirts of the village now, and some distance ahead of them in the field to their right, a distant figure of a woman, tall and slender with white-blond hair, walked toward the village.

"I believe so," Lizzie said, shading her eyes to look out. "Do you think she's coming from Netherfield? Why not use the lane?"

"Perhaps she knows a shortcut through the woods?" Darcy suggested.

Instinct took over, and Lizzie picked up her pace, dragging Darcy and Guy along with her. "Come on. I want to see where she goes."

"Lizzie! We can't just . . ."

"Follow her? Of course we can! If she's just going to the shops, then all right. But if she goes anywhere else or sees anyone else, I want to know."

"All right," Darcy grumbled as he increased his pace to keep up with Lizzie. "But this isn't London—there is considerably less coverage to tail someone in a village like Meryton. You'd better start thinking up your cover story should we get caught."

"When have I ever not had a cover story prepared?"

Darcy muttered something incoherent but followed.

The path Sally was on appeared to run somewhat parallel to the lane, although it was separated by some distance and the length of a stone wall. Lizzie kept an eye on Sally as she approached the edge of the village, but the other young lady's path did not take her to the high street—instead, she skirted around a row of gardens, heading to the north side of the village. "Interesting," Lizzie said. "So she's *not* running an errand for the household."

"We don't know that for certain—she's just not going straight into the village," Darcy corrected. "Let's let her get ahead a bit and then follow."

Lizzie fidgeted but waited until Sally was a good distance away and in danger of slipping out of sight before she and Darcy left the lane and strode through the long grass of the hayfield that separated them from the worn footpath Sally took, Guy trailing them. Right before it entered the village proper, it branched off, running alongside the back of many of the cottages and buildings. That was the direction where Sally had disappeared. "I can't see her anymore," Lizzie said in a low tone.

"She can't have gone too far. Come on." Darcy took her arm, and they picked up the pace. The path curved to the left, leading to the north side of the village before meeting the high street as it led out of the village. Lizzie and Darcy halted, looking around for Sally.

"She could be anywhere," Lizzie murmured. On this end of the village were mostly cottages, a farrier, and what appeared to be a smithy. There were some people out and about, and a few men at work, but no sign of the tall, blond young woman they'd been tailing. Disappointment plummeted in Lizzie's stomach.

“There,” Darcy said suddenly, looking to the right. “The churchyard.”

Lizzie spotted a flash of white-blond hair as it disappeared around the corner of the church. Wordlessly, Lizzie and Darcy took off for the church, briskly but not so quickly as to draw attention. Guy kept up beside them, his small pink tongue hanging out as he panted lightly. The poor dog would deserve a bowl of water and a nap after this.

As they approached, the front of the church faced them, with the entrance to the vicarage on the right. To the left was a gate to the stone fence that enclosed the churchyard, Sally’s apparent destination. Darcy pulled Lizzie to the right, giving the vicarage entrance a wide berth to avoid being spotted by Mr. Thomas, and they slunk along the tree line toward the churchyard, where a good number of headstones in varying sizes and conditions stood. They ducked low, making certain to keep out of sight behind the stone wall.

Sally stood near a modest stone, looking down silently. Lizzie and Darcy didn’t dare get closer. As the seconds passed into minutes, Lizzie’s racing pulse slowed, and she began to feel a bit ridiculous. They had trailed Sally on nothing more than a hunch and followed her to a churchyard, where she appeared to be paying her respects. Perhaps to her mother, Amy? It felt intrusive, watching what was surely a private moment. She bit her lip and glanced at Darcy, who also looked chagrined.

“Perhaps we should go,” Lizzie whispered.

Darcy nodded, and Lizzie began to slowly make her way

back in the direction from which they'd come when Darcy's hand shot out and stopped her. He nodded toward Sally.

Her back turned, and now she was looking toward the front of the churchyard, where someone new was approaching. Lizzie ducked back out of sight and was surprised to find that the newcomer was someone she recognized.

Clara Jeffries.

The two young women greeted each other and exchanged words. Lizzie could make out the sound of their voices but not what they were saying.

"Do you think this is a planned meeting?" Darcy whispered.

"I can't tell."

Sally's back was to them, and she held herself almost rigidly. Even from a distance, Lizzie could make out Clara's expression, which wasn't exactly warm. No, it looked . . . worried. She gestured with her hands, and Sally stepped closer and seemed to shush her. Clara's face went still as she listened to whatever Sally had to say, and then she nodded once, quickly. Sally withdrew something from the pocket of her dress and Lizzie squinted. It appeared to be a small purse or pouch of some kind. She handed it over to Clara, quickly and unobtrusively, and Clara tucked the pouch into her basket without looking at it. They exchanged a few more words, and then Clara abruptly turned and left.

Lizzie looked at Darcy and found his eyes widened with surprise. What had they just witnessed?

Sally waited a little while longer, turning back to look down at the headstone she stood before. Lizzie and Darcy went still so as not to draw attention. Luckily for them, Guy was happy to lie in the tall grass behind a rather large bush, tongue lolling, and didn't seem at all perturbed by his humans' strange antics. After nearly two minutes had passed, Sally straightened her shoulders and turned her back on them and the headstone once more and made her way out of the churchyard.

"What do you suppose that was about?" Darcy whispered.

Lizzie shook her head. "I'm amending my earlier opinion—that had to have been planned. But a churchyard is a strange meeting place, wouldn't you agree?"

"For most people, yes . . . but you have to admit, it's a clever place to go if you don't want to be disturbed."

"Only the dead as witness," Lizzie murmured, and then had to suppress a shiver despite the heat of the morning. She was allowing herself to jump to dramatic conclusions. Certainly there could be a reasonable explanation for what had just occurred . . .

"Do we think that Miss Jeffries has anything to do with our mystery at Netherfield?" Lizzie asked.

"They're both hardly older than we are," Darcy said. "Assuming that it would take more than several years at least for a body to reach that advanced stage of decomposition, they would have been, what? Fourteen, fifteen when the man was killed? Younger?"

"Maybe they weren't involved, but they know who he was."

"Maybe," Darcy allowed. "Or maybe this is just a very

strange meeting place for some perfectly acceptable business. We can't say without knowing more."

But how? Lizzie didn't think Sally was the type to take kindly to questioning about her whereabouts, and Miss Jeffries . . . well, she hadn't seemed inclined to trust them the day before, but she had told them all about the curse's origin. Perhaps she would be the weaker link.

Lizzie, Darcy, and Guy waited until Sally slipped out of sight around the side of the church, and then made their own way back around the vicarage toward the lane. The more she thought about it, the odder it appeared. If Sally was engaged on some legitimate business with Miss Jeffries, why not go to her shop? And that handover—it had looked like Sally was paying Miss Jeffries. But why? Was Miss Jeffries . . . blackmailing Sally?

As they skirted the vicarage yard and came closer to the front of the church, Darcy held out his hand and Lizzie halted, ears pricking up. Someone was speaking.

"—think I don't know that you're hiding something!"

"I can assure you, I haven't the faintest idea what you're referring to."

"Don't get wise with me," the deeper voice growled. "I know you understand what I'm talking about."

Lizzie tightened her hold on Guy's leash and nodded at Darcy. Together, they crept forward and peeked around the corner of the church. Sally stood near the entrance of the churchyard, where she appeared to have been waylaid by none other than the constable, Mr. Oliver. He stood blocking her way on the small path that led back to the lane, arms crossed.

"I'm afraid you must be mistaken," she said, and took a step forward. When Mr. Oliver didn't budge, she sidestepped him, but Mr. Oliver grabbed her arm and dragged her back, jerking her none too gently. Lizzie gasped, and Darcy's hand tightened around her elbow.

"Quit playing innocent, because I know you're not. You and I both know what's hidden in that great big house, and I want a cut."

"Unhand me!" Sally ordered.

But Mr. Oliver only twisted Sally's arm, causing her to cry out. "I won't tell you again—"

Lizzie couldn't stand it any longer. She stepped around the corner of the church and walked briskly toward them, Darcy hurrying after her with a whispered, "Lizzie!"

"Hello!" she called loudly, infusing extra cheer in her voice. She waved at Sally and Mr. Oliver, an overly exaggerated motion that likely looked as silly as she felt, but her abrupt appearance did the trick of surprising Mr. Oliver. Sally yanked herself out of his grasp and took two large steps back. "Mr. Oliver, Sally. What a lovely surprise running into you both here."

Lizzie hadn't really given much thought to what she would do after that—her main priority had been to get that odious constable to let go of Sally. Now that that was accomplished, she pasted on a smile and acted oblivious to Mr. Oliver's glare.

"What do you want?" he demanded.

"I apologize if I'm interrupting" She looked significantly

at Sally, but the young woman didn't meet Lizzie's gaze. "Mr. Darcy and I were out for a stroll with Guy when we spotted you from around the corner."

"All of Netherfield Park, and you choose to take a turn around the village?" Mr. Oliver asked.

"The dog enjoys a long walk," Darcy said.

"How fortunate we ran into you," Lizzie continued. "Have you been able to learn anything more about the possible identity of the body we discovered?"

Mr. Oliver's scowl deepened. "No. Seems unlikely, given how much time has passed. Honoria Bingley took that secret to her grave."

"Perhaps." Lizzie said, side-eyeing Sally, who wore a stoic expression. "But as we've discovered, some things don't stay buried."

An oddly menacing smile slowly stretched across Mr. Oliver's face, putting her on edge. "You're right about that, Miss Bennet. Secrets have a way of coming to light, don't they?"

He seemed to direct this question to Sally, who steadfastly ignored him. Lizzie considered the two of them—there was something Mr. Oliver wanted from Sally, that was clear, but she remained stoic.

An awkward pause ensued, and Darcy cleared his throat. "Will you be at the burial service tomorrow, Mr. Oliver?"

"Aye," the man said gruffly. He looked between Sally and Lizzie and Darcy, then tipped his hat. "Good day."

The three of them watched him follow the lane north, away

from the village, and disappear among the trees that hugged the road. As soon as he was out of sight, Lizzie turned to Sally. "Are you all right?"

"Fine, thank you," Sally said, her voice clipped. "I ought to be getting on."

"What did he mean, secrets have a way of coming to light?" Lizzie asked, causing Sally to stop abruptly and turn back to look at her.

"I don't know, miss. Why don't you ask him?"

Whereas Clara Jeffries had been brimming with information once they'd gotten her talking, Sally was a locked box, unyielding and reluctant to give anything up. Now was the time for Lizzie to show a little bit of her hand—not too much, but enough to see if Sally could be rattled into revealing anything more.

"I heard Mr. Oliver speaking, before we interrupted," Lizzie said, trying to sound casual. "He mentioned something hidden in the house, and wanting a cut?"

Sally, to her credit, hardly blinked. "I wouldn't put much stock in Mr. Oliver, miss. He might be the parish constable, but he's hardly a reliable man."

"I thought he said he'd been constable for fifteen years, and his father was constable before him," Darcy said.

"That doesn't mean anything. Just because *you're* a solicitor doesn't make you a good one. Anyone can be a solicitor."

Lizzie chose to ignore both the slight and the fact that it wasn't true that just anyone could become a solicitor. "Are you saying he takes after his father?"

"Oh, I wouldn't know about that. I never met the man—it's been Tom Oliver for as long as I can remember. No one else wants the job. But if you're waiting on him to solve the mystery of your dead man, you might be waiting until kingdom come. The man can't even figure out where Mr. Rowan's cows keep wandering off to."

Lizzie regarded Sally, realizing how neatly she'd sidestepped Lizzie question about Mr. Oliver's comments—she hadn't denied, but she'd downplayed and changed the subject expertly. It made Lizzie decide to change course.

"We've been hearing a good number of rumors about Netherfield Park."

Sally stayed cool. "I imagine you have." She wasn't going to make this easy for Lizzie, that was certain.

"The most interesting bit of news was the rumored Netherfield treasure."

Sally let out an abrupt snort of laughter. "Of course."

"You don't believe there's any truth to it?"

Sally shook her head. "It's all talk. The people of this village cannot fathom why Mrs. Bingley would prefer to be left alone in her house all those years, so they gossip. They assume the only reason a lady like her would hide away is if she had something to hide, like a dragon guarding her hoard." Sally's derisive tone communicated clearly how she felt about these rumors.

"But you knew differently?" Lizzie asked.

"Mrs. Bingley was lonely," Sally said bluntly. "The loneliest person I ever met. She couldn't let herself live, too grief-stricken by all she'd lost. If she could have gotten on alone, she would have—but she needed my grandparents, and then my mother, and then me."

Pain flashed across her face, but only for a moment. Lizzie wondered how close Sally had been to Honoria—had she confided in Sally?

"Perhaps she didn't have a fortune hidden," Lizzie said, "but surely a man doesn't end up in the flue of her drawing room fireplace without her knowing."

"I told you, I don't know anything about that," Sally said, but she didn't sound angry—she sounded *bored*.

"Not even a theory?" Lizzie asked.

Sally regarded her a long moment, then said, "I think you're looking in the wrong direction, Miss Bennet. If it were me, I'd be asking different questions."

"What sorts of questions?"

"If everyone in this village believes there's a treasure in Netherfield, perhaps it might be best to consider what *they* might do with that information. What sorts of boundaries they might be willing to cross."

And on that note, Sally sauntered off, leaving Lizzie with quite a bit to think about.

THIRTEEN

In Which Lizzie Takes a Swing and Misses

THE JEFFRIES PRINT SHOP was locked, with no sign of Miss Jeffries, and so Lizzie and Darcy returned to Netherfield Park, where a new horror awaited them: a garden party.

It was Jane's idea of a distraction. "The maids need to do a thorough clean, and they can barely manage it with us all coming and going," she whispered to Lizzie as she attempted to corral everyone outside. "Besides, Lydia and Kitty are growing so restless I fear they may start jumping on the furniture."

Which was how they found themselves in the back gardens, sitting under the shade of a large tent, enjoying a cold luncheon spread that could have fed a small army. Everyone had been coaxed outside, even Mr. Bennet, who squinted against the sunlight as he read his book. It was a lovely way to spend an afternoon, out of doors, and Guy was happily running through the grass, but Lizzie was just wondering how soon she could sneak off to write to the Dashwoods when Lydia said, "What's that?"

She turned to see Bingley standing before what looked like a set of lawn games, and groaned softly. Charlotte shot her a pitying look.

"This is a pall-mall set," Bingley announced, pulling out a series of wooden mallets all painted with different colored stripes. "And today I am going to teach you all how to play."

"Is it difficult?" Kitty asked.

"I don't know if I like sports," Lydia said doubtfully.

"No, it's not difficult," Bingley said. "And all of the ton plays this game at their house parties, so it's a good one to learn."

That was all the convincing Kitty and Lydia needed, and even Mary set aside her book, intrigued. Bingley looked past them to where Charlotte, Lizzie, and Caroline were sitting in the shade. "Come on, you can't just sit there!" Bingley called. "Come pick your mallets, ladies."

Lizzie glanced at her parents. Her father was reading, and her mother was dozing off in her chair. "I think I am all right, thank you."

"Are you afraid to lose?" Darcy asked, arching a brow. He ambled over to Bingley, who handed him a green-painted mallet.

"It doesn't look very difficult," Lizzie pointed out.

"Then why don't you come show us how it's done?" Darcy loosened his cravat and took a few practice swings.

Nearby, Caroline let out a small scoff from under her bountifully decorated bonnet. "Unseemly," she muttered.

"Come along, Caroline," Bingley called. "You too. You can even play with the pink mallet."

Lizzie was shocked when Caroline stood. "Of course I will. The pink one is mine."

"Come along, Lizzie," Charlotte said, getting to her feet. "It wouldn't do to be unsporting."

"Oh no, it wouldn't do at all," Lizzie said as she followed Charlotte and accepted a yellow mallet. If Caroline could play, then Lizzie could certainly learn. It was clear that this was a familiar game with Bingley, Caroline, and Darcy, and she did her best to pay attention as Bingley explained the rules—the wickets that were arranged about the grass, and the goal of whacking the ball through the wickets with their mallets in as few hits as possible . . . but one had to follow an order.

"Charles always makes it harder by putting the wickets as far apart as he can manage," Caroline said.

"Not harder," Bingley said, pointing at the various wickets in the distance. "More interesting."

"So you say," Darcy said, lining up his mallet to take the first swing. With a great thwack, the ball soared through the air and bounced a bit on the springy green grass, just short of the wicket.

"Lucky shot!" Bingley cried, and gestured for Jane to go next.

They all took turns—Jane's falling a bit short, for she was hesitant to hit the ball as hard, Caroline's ball landing rather close to Darcy's, and Kitty and Lydia taking a few wayward swings before each managing to hit their balls in the direction of the wicket. Mary hit the farthest shot, overshooting the wicket by a good ten paces, but Bingley assured her that was just fine. Bingley himself then took a shot that nudged Darcy's ball closer to the wicket, and a confusing conversation ensued about the rules for hitting another person's ball, and finally it was Lizzie's turn.

She'd watched all the others go before her, and they had made it seem easy. Therefore, she made the mistake of assuming there was no strategy or form to hitting her ball with her mallet, but when the wooden head caught the side of the ball, the force of her exuberant swing sent her ball soaring . . . all the way over to the right. Quite far from the first wicket.

"Oh, drat," she muttered. She turned to look at Bingley, who was struggling to suppress a laugh. "What now?"

"After Charlotte swings, you go to your ball, and you try to get the ball closer to the wicket in your next turn," Darcy said, not even bothering to hide his amusement.

Charlotte took her turn, and Lizzie wasn't certain whether she'd accidentally hit her ball off to the right as well or if she'd done it out of solidarity, but on the next round, they both ended up on the far right of the lawn, watching as everyone else (much closer to the wicket) took their turns.

Lizzie was, by nature, somewhat competitive. She liked having goals, and she liked them even more when she knew that someone else was also striving for the same thing . . . and there was motive for her to accomplish it first. This drive, however, did not extend to yard games. It was just hitting a ball with a stick! Under the sun! And soon everyone was spread out across the great lawn, so it was impossible to hold a conversation—the others had to shout at them when it was their turn as they advanced across the green space toward the next wickets.

"This is driving you mad, isn't it?" Charlotte asked as they both managed to (finally) nudge their balls through the first wicket. The others cheered from the third (and in Darcy's case, fourth) wicket, and Lizzie waved at them.

"What is even the point of a house party," she whispered, "unless it is to torture your guests with tiresome activities and take bets on who will leave first?"

"I believe the point is to socialize, but in a different setting," Charlotte replied with a laugh.

"I can socialize perfectly well back home," Lizzie grumbled, but she didn't have it in her to be truly grumpy. After all, Jane appeared to be smiling, and their younger sisters were entertained. Caroline wasn't complaining for once, and it was nice to see Bingley and Darcy ribbing each other as they continually knocked their balls into each other—Lizzie couldn't deduce whether that was part of the game or just how Bingley and Darcy played it.

"You are like your father," Charlotte said. "You love the work, so it's difficult to be away."

Lizzie looked over her shoulder to the tent where her parents sat. "I suppose."

"Have you forgiven him yet?"

Lizzie looked in surprise at Charlotte. "Pardon?"

"You can tell me if I am overstepping," her friend said, "but you seem to have made your peace with Darcy. However, you've hardly spoken to your father since you arrived."

Lizzie sighed. Charlotte was right, of course. "I just . . . hate it when he makes decisions that concern me without consulting me."

"I know. But he loves you. And he wants you to be safe. Well, as safe as you can be while still investigating various suspicious deaths." Charlotte nudged her, her smile teasing.

Lizzie strained to return it. Charlotte didn't know about the letter from Lady Catherine that Lizzie had received that morning . . . or the promise she'd extracted from Darcy to keep it secret for now. But she looked out across the lawn. Her sisters were happy and safe. Her dog was running across the grass, tongue lolling, and Darcy was chasing him. Her mother was napping in the shade of her married daughter's country estate, which was quite possibly the pinnacle of all her hopes and dreams these past twenty years.

"You're right," Lizzie said reluctantly, thinking for the first time that maybe it was a good thing they'd left London after all, despite Lady Catherine's note.

"Did you learn anything of interest this morning?"

Lizzie caught Charlotte up on their visit to the Burtons and the strange encounter between Sally and Miss Jeffries in the graveyard, and then Mr. Oliver's confrontation. She finished with Sally's parting words, and Charlotte's expression turned thoughtful.

"What an interesting question," she said. "What if the man from the fireplace wasn't a guest or servant but a thief?"

"Someone from the village who wanted the Netherfield treasure?" Lizzie asked.

"Or any of the many other valuables in the estate. Think about it—even if there wasn't a pile of silver somewhere in the house, those walls still hold a great number of easily pawnable objects."

Charlotte wasn't wrong—crystalware, the tea sets, the art, the many figurines and collectibles. Where had they all been while Honoria Bingley lived out the last fifty years—tucked away, or in plain sight, under a layer of dust?

"But the fact that he was discovered with a silver coin in his pocket suggests that he did discover *some* silver," Lizzie said slowly. "Unless it was planted."

"And why would it have been planted?"

"Any number of reasons. Someone wanted to frame him. Or perhaps make it only appear as though he were a burglar." Lizzie sighed. "Oh, it's useless speculating. The Burtons claim to know nothing, and Mr. Oliver says no one he can think of has gone missing. Yet they antagonize each other in broad daylight."

Beyond them, Bingley let out an enormous whoop of victory as he knocked Darcy's ball farther away from the wicket, and his own landed quite near. Darcy grimaced, and Caroline rolled her eyes at the display, but Bingley's good cheer was infectious. He turned to them and shouted, "Ladies, you're up next!"

Lizzie found her ball and measured the distance between where it lay nestled in the grass and the next wicket. She took a swing, sending her ball (and a clod of grass) flying. It landed nowhere near her target.

She shrugged and turned to Charlotte. "I hope you have better luck than I did."

Charlotte sent her ball toward the wicket with an easy swing, and she allowed herself a small smile in triumph when it landed closer than Lizzie's. "The question I find most intriguing is, what does Sally Burton know?"

"There's something about her," Lizzie said as they ambled toward their balls. "She's so cool and collected every time we speak. Not at all what I'd expect from a housemaid who has just discovered the remains of a man in the house she practically grew up in. That would rattle most people."

"Do we think she was involved or just knows something?"

Lizzie shook her head. "I would be shocked if she were involved. I think she's too young. But then again, I suppose anything is possible. No, it seems more likely that her grandparents know what happened, and she knows what they know, and she's keeping the family secret. To what end, though?"

"There's no statute of limitations on murder," Charlotte muttered.

"Which implies she's protecting someone, or something."

"Her grandparents?"

Lizzie thought about the elderly couple she'd met that morning—it hardly seemed possible that either of them could be capable of causing a death, but they hadn't always been elderly. And they likely knew more about Honoria Bingley's secrets than anyone else. What if they were paid to keep quiet about . . . well, whatever they knew?

But if they did have any amount of the Netherfield treasure, why was Sally working as a housemaid still?

"Ladies!" Bingley called out, sounding winded. "Your turn again!"

"I don't think they're paying attention, Charles," Caroline said.

"Come on, Lizzie," Lydia whined.

"All right, all right," she said. "Where's my ball?"

"Isn't it back there?" Caroline asked.

Lizzie turned and looked about in the grass for the wooden ball but didn't immediately see it. She looked back in the direction of her last swing. She had hit the ball this way, and it had landed . . . where, exactly? She was loath to admit it, but Caroline was right—she hadn't been paying very good attention. "I seem to have misplaced it!" she called to the rest of them, eliciting a round of groans.

Fortunately, Lizzie was saved from having to continue her losing streak by Guy yipping in excitement. When she turned toward the house, she saw Mr. Grigson leading two newcomers toward them across the lawn. The game was quickly abandoned as Bingley and Jane strode forward to offer greetings, and Lizzie saw with some surprise that one of their guests was none other than Miss Jeffries, who was accompanied by a young gentleman in all black, wearing a vicar's collar—so this must be the young new vicar.

"Thomas!" Bingley called out in his overly familiar way, confirming Lizzie's hunch about the man's identity. "And Miss Jeffries. What a lovely surprise."

"I'm sorry for dropping by unannounced," said Miss Jeffries, although as her eyes took in the scene before them, she didn't appear to be the least bit sorry.

"Nonsense, you're very welcome," Jane said, brushing frantically at her flyaway hairs. "Please excuse our casual appearance—you've caught us in the middle of a game."

"Thank you, Mrs. Bingley," Mr. Thomas said, giving her a slight bow. "I was walking home on my rounds, and I encountered Miss Jeffries on her way to Netherfield, so I offered to accompany her."

Darcy joined them, wiping at the light sheen of sweat on his brow, and Bingley and Jane made official introductions. Lizzie studied Miss Jeffries as they went through the social niceties. She looked much the same as she had earlier that morning in the graveyard, only now she was smiling, and instead of a basket on her arm, she held a satchel.

"You've brought the registers?" Darcy inquired.

"Indeed, Mr. Darcy. All three of them, and I've sewn them in cardboard so that they're easier to read. Mr. Thomas made me aware of your eagerness."

Lizzie couldn't quite tell whether that was meant as a reprimand of some sort, but Mr. Thomas said, "Whatever we can do to help clear up this terrible business. I know I speak for the entire county when I say how glad we are that you've taken up residence at Netherfield, and I am only sorry that certain . . . ah, unpleasantness . . . has disrupted your stay."

Bingley smiled gratefully. "Well, we are certainly happy to

be here. And as for any unpleasantness, as you put it . . . Darcy and Miss Bennet have untangled more than a few such cases in their time, and I have no doubt they'll prevail yet again. Please, come inside."

Bingley ushered their guests into the house, and Lizzie, Darcy, and Charlotte followed. The study was darkened and the air a bit stuffy. Bingley called for refreshments, and Miss Jeffries set the satchel on Bingley's desk and withdrew three volumes, bound in cheap cardboard.

"Here we are," she said, and though she smiled, Lizzie sensed there was something stiff about her features. She had assumed that Miss Jeffries's hesitation the previous day had been on account of her not being acquainted with them before they'd come into her shop. But now that she was here, Lizzie couldn't shake the feeling that Miss Jeffries didn't want to hand over these registers.

But why?

"They go back to 1689," Mr. Thomas said. "Or at least, these volumes do. I took the liberty of assuming the earlier volumes would be less relevant to your interests."

"It's highly unlikely the remains have been in the flue that long," Lizzie confirmed. "They showed no sign of smoke or fire damage, and we presume that the fireplace was in use prior to Honoria's arrival."

Darcy reached for the nearest book and withdrew a penknife from his pocket, sliding it between the pages and slicing them open. When he opened the book, the spine creaked in that delicious, new book way, smelling of ink and paper and promise and . . . well, maybe Lizzie was getting carried away.

"I'm not sure how useful these will be in helping you identify your dead man," Mr. Thomas said. "And Dr. Fellowes used shorthand at times—I confess I've had trouble translating it, although I wrote down what bits I have been able to discern."

Mr. Thomas handed them a quarto sheet with neat, even handwriting. Lizzie took it and immediately showed it to Charlotte. "Thank you, sir. And this is incredibly helpful. Miss Lucas is our legal secretary at Longbourn and Sons, and if there's anyone who can help us make sense of it all, it's she. She's brilliant."

"She exaggerates," Charlotte said quietly.

"I do not. More than one case has depended on her thorough notes and her knack for remembering details in records."

Mr. Thomas looked surprised but also intrigued. "You work as a legal secretary, Miss Lucas?"

"Yes," she said, but tentatively. Lizzie also waited to hear what the vicar's next words would be—not all gentlemen approved of a lady with a career.

But Mr. Thomas looked impressed. "That is not easy work. I confess sometimes I get overwhelmed with all my correspondence, and I am just a country vicar. You must be very organized and astute to work in a legal firm."

Now Charlotte blushed lightly. "I've found that a good management system is essential."

"Ah. Can you offer me any advice, then, as a professional?"

Charlotte hesitated, and Lizzie looked at Mr. Thomas in

surprise. He was regarding her friend with curiosity and . . . admiration? She had to bite back a grin.

Was Mr. Thomas flirting with Charlotte?

"Well," Charlotte began, "I devised a system of ordering all incoming correspondence by priority . . ."

While Charlotte detailed her organizational efforts to a charmingly receptive Mr. Thomas, Miss Jeffries turned to Lizzie. "Mr. Thomas tells me you work as a solicitor, Miss Bennet."

"Yes," Lizzie confirmed, surprised that Miss Jeffries was bringing it up. Most of polite society tended to ignore that aspect of her life. "Back in London."

"How intriguing. That must be a very difficult job."

"No more difficult than running a print shop all on your own," Lizzie pointed out.

Miss Jeffries simply smiled. "It is my passion, and my father's business before me. I could no sooner abandon it than I could renounce my own name."

"I feel quite the same," Lizzie said, and found herself studying the other young lady. "But at least I have my father as my mentor—tell me, is it very difficult running the shop alone? The presses are mammoth."

"Well, that is why I hire journeymen," Miss Jeffries said, and then leaned forward and whispered conspiratorially, "although I do know how the machines work."

Lizzie laughed politely at her joke. "I never doubted you did."

"Well, you'd be the first to say so," Miss Jeffries said. "When my father died, his competitors descended upon Meryton like wolves, wanting to purchase the presses at a good price. They thought they could trick me into selling below value."

"But you saw right through them?" she asked.

"I knew that the print shop would be more valuable in my own hands," she said, her smile only a little coy. But then her expression softened, and she added, "Unfortunately, it really does take two people to operate the presses, and I can't do it all. It took me time to find journeymen willing to work for a woman."

Lizzie thought that under different circumstances, if she didn't suspect Clara Jeffries of hiding something, she might enjoy the other young lady's company very much. They could trade stories of what it was like to be a woman in a man's world. "So the journeymen operate the presses, and you run the business side of things?"

Miss Jeffries nodded. "I handle all the correspondence between writers and artists and publishers, as well as with our suppliers and our customers. I set most of the pages we prepare for printing, and I manage quite a few of the deliveries."

Lizzie saw her opening and realized she might not get one quite like it. "You must be running all around the countryside, then! In fact—did I spot you this morning?"

Miss Jeffries tilted her head quizzically, and Lizzie added, "By the church, just north of the village. Mr. Darcy and I were walking the dog. I could have sworn I saw you."

But Miss Jeffries just shook her head. "Sorry, no—it must have been someone else."

Her tone was light and courteous, and Lizzie waited a beat

to see if she'd add anything else. Liars tended to overexplain, rush to fill in details. But Miss Jeffries stayed perfectly pleasant and unbothered, and if not for the fact that Lizzie had seen her with her own two eyes in the churchyard with Sally Burton, she might have believed her.

Oh, Miss Jeffries was good.

"My mistake," Lizzie said lightly, shaking her head. "It must have been someone who looked like you. I'm unfamiliar with the village, after all."

But Miss Jeffries didn't pick up the conversational thread after that. In fact, she stood, signaling her intent to depart, and forcing Mr. Thomas to wrap up his conversation with Charlotte. Lizzie accompanied them outside to see them off, along with Bingley.

"Very pleasant neighbors," Bingley said as soon as they were out of earshot. "I must make sure Jane's invited them to our ball next week."

"Very pleasant indeed," Lizzie agreed, but she wasn't thinking about Mr. Thomas.

She was thinking about how Miss Jeffries had so coolly lied to her face, and how she might have squandered her one chance to question the other young lady and still feign polite manners.

She was thinking that Miss Jeffries was more than a liar—she was a keeper of secrets.

FOURTEEN

In Which Lizzie and Darcy Cause a Scene

"AND THEN NEXT SPRING, we'll have someone out to inspect the roof. Darcy, are you listening?"

"Hmm?" Darcy said, looking up. "The roof, yes."

Bingley gave him a look. "Yes, what about the roof?"

"It's . . . a roof. Very solid. Keeps the rain out."

"No, it doesn't—that's the point. It leaks. Badly. The attic after a rainstorm looks like a bazaar that sells nothing but pots and buckets."

Darcy winced. He really hadn't been paying attention. "I'm sorry. I got a little distracted. But yes, the roof—if it's that bad, then I think getting it repaired sooner rather than later is wise. You can't properly begin to address the damage from within until the exterior is secured."

The two of them were outside, standing in the drive and looking above at the east wing. From outside, no one could tell there was any fire damage, but Darcy still shuddered when he thought of seeing Lizzie on the floor, her leg caught and the wood around her groaning. Bingley had asked him to come outside to survey the exterior of the house before the party left for the burial service in the village.

"I don't know," Bingley said, rubbing his chin. "I thought I was lucky to inherit this place—it was always a secret hope of my father's, you know. He felt as though our branch had been ousted from our ancestral seat. But now that it's mine . . ."

"Ownership is a curse as much as it is a blessing," Darcy said.

"Yes, exactly." He sighed, then tilted his head back. "And the facade—look at the stone and how it's been eaten away. How long before it all comes tumbling down around us?"

"It won't happen today," Darcy assured him, clapping his hand on his friend's shoulder.

They were interrupted by the sound of a loud voice shouting "Oy!" followed by the crunching of gravel and the creak of a carriage. Darcy startled, turning quickly to see the carriages being brought around. The groom blanched to see them standing there. "My apologies, Mr. Bingley," he said, drawing the carriage up short. "It's just that Arrow here has been acting a bit restless. He takes a firm hand sometimes."

"It's all right," Bingley said. "We'll be there in a minute, thank you."

The groom urged the horses forward to park closer to the entrance, and Bingley turned to Darcy. "Are you all right? You're awfully jumpy today."

"I slept terribly," Darcy said, which wasn't a lie—it just wasn't the reason for his jumpiness.

"Is there anything—"

Darcy shook his head. "Just my own thoughts keeping me awake."

"The case?"

Darcy nodded, but it wasn't quite the truth.

Something Darcy had never admitted to anyone, not even Lizzie, was that Lady Catherine *scared* him. It wasn't just that she was a criminal—although that was the major concern—but that she'd proven herself willing to go to extreme lengths. And she had tracked them here, to Netherfield, which suggested she was not far off. With the chaos of preparations for the ball underway, who was to say she couldn't just slip into Netherfield Park and find Lizzie? And then what? Maybe she wouldn't kill Lizzie . . . but what sort of havoc would she wreak in pursuit of what she wanted?

Bingley attempted a change of subject. "Have you discovered anything useful in the registers yet?"

"No," Darcy said, feeling the weight of that word. "Not yet, anyway. But we've only had a few hours with them, and there's still plenty more to read. Mr. Thomas was right—Dr. Fellowes used shorthand indiscriminately. There's a great deal to decipher still."

"I have faith in you," Bingley said.

The two rounded the corner toward the front of the manor where the carriages sat waiting, one of the horses stomping very irritably. Lizzie, Charlotte, and Caroline were already outside while Mr. Bennet stood in the doorway, calling, "We mustn't be late, dears!" to the Bennet women still somewhere within the house.

Sally stood not too far from the assembled party, Guy's leash in hand. Darcy gave her a small nod, which she returned stoically. Darcy wasn't quite sure what to make of her—was she so stern because she was looking out for her grandparents? Or was she keeping secrets, as Lizzie suspected?

He went to stand next to Lizzie, who was wearing a navy blue dress that looked overly warm for the beautiful summer weather. "You look lovely," he said in a low voice.

"Thank you," she said, smoothing her hand across the skirt. "Jane lent it to me. I am afraid I didn't bring anything appropriate for a funeral. It's not black, though."

"No one will fault you for that," he said.

"I suppose," Lizzie said. "Even so, it feels disrespectful somehow . . ."

Darcy suddenly felt a flurry of tiny sharp pains on his head and face. As he looked at Lizzie, a handful of small stones bounced off the shoulder of her navy dress. He looked up to see where they were coming from, and some base instinct took over. He shoved Lizzie aside, and just in time, too—he'd no sooner jumped back himself when a large, heavy object whooshed through the air, slamming into the gravel where he'd been standing only moments earlier.

Everyone cried out, and the horses spooked. The impatient one—Arrow—bolted against his harness, causing the three others to shriek in surprise. The carriage lurched ominously as the groom struggled to gain control of the animals. Mrs. Bennet, who'd been inside, came rushing out. "What's going on?"

Darcy found Lizzie first, standing only a stone's throw away, her expression white and shocked. Charlotte clutched her arm, and they both looked down at the object that had very nearly smashed into Darcy's skull: a large hunk of masonry that appeared to have fallen from the house. The stone was crumbling and well-worn, and it would have been about the size of Darcy's head, if it were still intact. But the impact had broken it into three larger pieces and many smaller chunks, which now lay strewn about the gravel at their feet and left no doubt as to what it might have done to their own heads, if not for Darcy's quick action.

"Is everyone all right?" Bingley asked, rushing forward, panic in his eyes. "Is anyone hurt?"

"No," Darcy said, feeling rather faint nonetheless. "We moved just in time."

"The curse," a voice said. They turned to find a footman, pale as a sheet, standing in front of the open door of one of the carriages. He was staring at the hunk of stone. "It's the curse."

"Don't be absurd, James," Mr. Grigson said, striding forward to take charge. "It's an accident, nothing more. We shall clean this up, sir."

Mr. Grigson leaned forward, and Darcy could tell he was whispering a scolding in the footman's ear. The young man didn't seem to care—he looked frightened.

"Mr. Bingley, are you sure my daughter is safe here?"

Lizzie hastened to answer before Bingley. "The curse is only for people who try to leave, Mama. We aren't going anywhere—just to the church."

Mrs. Bennet stared at the chunk of masonry, and uncertainty seemed to waver on her face. But then Mr. Bennet came up from behind her and said, "Old houses need repair. Now, we mustn't be late."

"Don't tell me you're believing in curses now," Darcy said to Lizzie, coming to take her arm. There was no reason for him to do so, except that he needed to touch her, feel the warmth of her skin and remind himself that she was alive and unharmed.

Lizzie tucked her arm into the crook of his elbow, and he wished they could go one step further and he could wrap her up in his arms and never let go. "Of course not. But . . ."

He followed her gaze upward, craning his neck to see if he could spot where the stone had fallen from. On the second floor, there was a steady row of windows framed by the stone facade of the manor, and one appeared to be missing a chunk. He squinted. Was there . . . movement behind that window? Darcy took a step back, but nothing changed, except for the reflection of light against the glass. He shook his head. It was a trick of the light.

"Are you all right?" Lizzie whispered to Darcy.

"Just thought I saw something," he murmured. He gazed up at the window, wondering if he had simply imagined movement.

"I don't see anything," Lizzie said, and before he could reply, they were distracted by the footman declaring, "I'm sorry, sir, I can't stay here. There's no saying who could be next! I'll send back the livery!"

Darcy and Lizzie turned in time to see the footman backing away from the house, as if afraid it would attack.

"James!" Mr. Grigson shouted. "Come back here at once!"

"I'm sorry!" he repeated, but he turned and began to run down the drive.

Mr. Grigson turned to Bingley, flustered. "Sir, I don't know what has gotten into the boy."

The same thing that had gotten to each and every servant who'd left, Darcy thought. He had sympathy for Mr. Grigson. It was difficult running anything—from a household to a business—when you could not rely on your staff. His father had taught him that. He still thought the curse was a load of nonsense—two accidents since they had arrived didn't mean there was a curse. It just meant the house was old and needed many repairs. No one had died.

He looked up and thought, *Yet*.

"Don't worry, Grigson," Jane said, coming up to place a hand on Lizzie's shoulder. "We've all had a fright, and perhaps James will see sense when he's calmed down. Please send someone to check on the window to ensure it's stable."

"That's the east wing, ma'am," Mr. Grigson said. "I'm not sure—"

"Oh," Jane said, looking up. "Of course it is. In that case, leave it until the builder arrives from London. He should be here in a fortnight, but we'll write and see if he can come sooner."

"Everyone, please step away," Bingley said, and he and Jane began ushering the party into the waiting carriages.

Darcy saw that Lizzie, Charlotte, and Mary made it into the nearest carriage and then looked up once more. The window glass reflected the sunny day, and no movement could be detected. He hadn't imagined it, had he?

He brought his gaze downward and spotted Sally Burton, all but forgotten off to the side, holding Guy's leash. She wasn't looking at any of them. Her hand shielded her eyes, and her gaze was tilted upward.

Given that no one had laid claim to the body of the unknown man, it was rather surprising to find his funeral nearly as well-attended as an Easter service.

Bingley was shown directly to the very front pew, along with the rest of his guests, and so Darcy and Lizzie were unable to get a decent view of the attendees during the service. Mr. Thomas's service was respectful, but understandably short, given that virtually nothing was known about the man.

"Although his name goes unspoken, we mourn nonetheless," he said, his strong voice reaching all the way to the back of the church, "as we mourn all loss of life. My prayer is that whoever this man may be, his loved ones might find comfort in the Lord."

The mention of the man's loved ones had Darcy wishing he could turn to survey the church, peering into faces. Had the man had any loved ones? Were they in attendance? And if so, why not come forward?

The service concluded with a graveside liturgy. The funeral-goers processed outside, where it was sunny and cheerful, a contrast to the somber funeral service. Lizzie and Darcy held back once they were out of doors, as if by some unspoken agreement, and watched as the attendees drifted to the freshly dug gravesite. Darcy tried to catalog each and every face that passed, but very few of them beyond Clara Jeffries, who nodded at them as she passed, were recognizable to him. No one seemed overly distraught or upset, so unless they were very good actors, it didn't seem that there were any mourners in the crowd who'd known the man personally.

In the distance, they could hear Mr. Thomas's voice rise, and Darcy turned and raised a brow to Lizzie. But she wasn't paying any attention—she was looking past the gathered attendees, toward the edge of the churchyard. He followed her gaze and saw Mr. Oliver leaning on the stone wall, hands shoved into his pockets, glaring at the gathering. Darcy was fairly certain he'd not been inside the church.

"He looks displeased," Darcy whispered. "Does he not think the man worthy of a good Christian burial?"

"Good question. Shall we ask?"

"Lizzie. It's a funeral."

"I think Mr. Oliver appreciates a direct approach."

Darcy had to work at not sighing. Lizzie had told him yesterday of her attempt at questioning Miss Jeffries—and how Miss

Jeffries had boldly lied to Lizzie's face. He knew that Lizzie was growing more frustrated. But approaching Mr. Oliver right now didn't feel strategic—it felt desperate.

The man himself looked about, and noticed Lizzie and Darcy, their heads bent in whispered conversation, looking right at him. He sneered.

Lizzie shook free of Darcy's grasp and began to march over to him.

All Darcy could do was follow.

"Oh, here they come," Mr. Oliver said as they grew close. "The fancy solicitors from London. Have you cracked the mystery yet, then?"

Lizzie stopped short a few paces away, as if not wanting to get too close. And after a moment, Darcy could see why—he could smell the alcohol on Mr. Oliver, even from this distance.

"Good day, Mr. Oliver," Lizzie said. She was speaking in a low tone, so as not to disrupt Mr. Thomas's final words over the plain pine box.

The man ignored her niceties. "What do you want?"

"The truth," she said, and Darcy's heart twinged. She was so earnest in her pursuit of a case. He couldn't help but love her for it. "No one seems to have come forward to claim any knowledge of the poor man."

"Why would they?" he asked. "They all know where he died. Either Honoria Bingley killed him herself, or the Burtons did it. They had to know—" He stopped and burped. Yes, he was most certainly drunk.

Even though Bingley, and not his great-aunt, was Darcy's client, he couldn't help but ask, "What proof do you have?"

"Proof? I've common sense, lad. Don't tell me that there's any way neither of them knew what was in that flue."

It was difficult to argue with Mr. Oliver on this point when he and Lizzie struggled with the same question. "Is that what you discussed with Sally Burton yesterday?"

"Sally's just like them," Mr. Oliver hissed, leaning in closer. Darcy instinctively stepped forward to shield Lizzie, but she stayed him with a hand on his arm and did not back down. "She lies and covers things up."

"What things?" Darcy had to admire the steadiness in Lizzie's voice.

"The Burtons know exactly where the treasure is. And they've been stealing from the Bingleys for years!"

His voice rose with the accusation, and at least half of the funeral attendees turned to look at them. Darcy winced when he saw Bingley's questioning look, but when he turned back to Lizzie, she just looked thoughtful. "What an interesting theory, Mr. Oliver," she said. "But again, I'll ask, where is your evidence?"

"I don't need proof. I know it to be true!"

"Unfortunately, the law would disagree with you," Darcy said, "and making a false accusation could lead to charges of slander."

"Solicitors!" Mr. Oliver spat. "Always hiding behind your fancy words. Do you think I give a damn?"

He pushed past them both, stumbling a little as he did so,

and went barreling toward the open grave. The pine box had been lowered into the hole, and Mr. Thomas appeared to have finished the final prayer as people began to disperse—but not with much haste. It seemed they anticipated some sort of scandalous display, and Darcy could tell that Mr. Oliver intended to fulfill their expectations.

"Bingley!" the man shouted.

Darcy went after the constable, hoping to intervene. Bingley looked up in surprise from where he'd been speaking with Jane and an unfamiliar couple of about thirty or thirty-five. "Please excuse me," he said to them, and turned. "Mr. Oliver, what can I do for you?"

"That man just lowered into the ground was found on your estate," Oliver said, jabbing his hand toward Bingley. "His head was bashed in, and he'd been left to rot. Your great-aunt lived in that house for fifty years, and you're telling me she didn't know she had a dead man in her drawing room all that time?"

"I—I can't say," Bingley said. His wide eyes found Darcy's, and Darcy shook his head. *Say nothing more*, he thought.

"Oh, you can't say, can you? What *can* you say about his death?"

"Mr. Oliver, please," Mr. Thomas interceded. "We are on church grounds."

"I know that! And isn't it a sin to lie in church?"

"It's a sin to lie at all," Mr. Thomas said patiently. "Now why don't we—"

"You hear that? It's a sin to lie! So why don't you tell everyone what your family did!"

"Mr. Oliver, I have no knowledge of what transpired before—"

"Someone killed that man, and the options are limited. Your great-aunt, or the caretakers of Netherfield. Allan Burton was a strong man in his day. You're telling me that he didn't know? That none of them knew?"

Darcy stepped between them. "Mr. Oliver, this is neither the time nor the place for such discussions. Mr. Bingley has no knowledge of what may or may not have occurred in Netherfield Park before he inherited the estate. Any questions about what might have happened ought to be directed to the parties who know—"

"Oh, I asked Allan Burton—he denies all knowledge. Everyone here—you all deny it! You all lie, lie, lie—" Mr. Oliver belched, stopping his parade of words.

It was Lizzie who asked the next question. "Mr. Oliver, you seem highly impassioned—do you know who the man is?"

He was sweating profusely, and his cheeks were reddened. The man swung his glare at Lizzie. "No! But I'm the constable, aren't I? And I know how this village is—how you all are!" He turned around, pointing wildly at the crowd. Not a single person was rushing away. They were all too entertained by the spectacle unfolding. "But when I uncover the truth, you'll all be sorry!"

"Mr. Oliver, I cannot have you threatening others in this churchyard," Mr. Thomas said, stepping in "Let me accompany you home, and—"

"He needs to pay!"

Mr. Oliver pointed at Bingley, and for a chilling moment

Darcy thought he meant that Bingley ought to pay for the crime committed against the unidentified man. From the way Bingley's face went ashen, Bingley clearly thought the same thing. But then Mr. Oliver added, "For a stone. A man died in his manor, and he gets a pauper's grave!"

Darcy hadn't noticed this beforehand, but the grave that had just been dug was in a nondescript row toward the back of the churchyard. The row was marked only by a series of weather-worn crosses, not stones. Apparently, Bingley had paid for the burial service, but not for a choice spot among the other well-to-do deceased of Meryton.

"Of course," Bingley agreed quickly. "Mr. Thomas, I am glad to pay for a stone as well—"

"That's right, toss your money at the problem!"

"Sir, I don't know what you want from me," Bingley said, starting to sound heated himself. This was unusual, for Bingley had the patience of most saints.

"I don't think a churchyard is the appropriate place to discuss this," Darcy said severely, stepping between them. "And Mr. Oliver is in no state to—"

"Don't you tell me what state I'm in!" Mr. Oliver shouted. "He needs to pay! I want to be assured, as constable of this parish, that he pays!"

"Perhaps we ought to step into the rectory, and—"

"Gentlemen, there is no need!" Mr. Thomas said, raising his voice. They all turned to look at him. "There's no need for Mr. Bingley to pay for a stone."

"Why not?" Lizzie asked.

"Because this morning when I stepped out of the rectory, I found a coin purse with enough funds to cover the man's burial and a stone," Mr. Thomas said. "There was a note with it that said, 'For today.' "

"You didn't think to mention this until now?" Darcy asked.

"I was going to tell you all after the service." Mr. Thomas sounded thoroughly irritated. "Not like this. Mr. Bingley, given the generosity of this anonymous donor, I am happy to return your funds. What was left is more than sufficient for today's service, burial, and yes, Mr. Oliver, a proper stone."

"Keep the money," Bingley said, sounding resigned. "Help another family with it."

"Aye, that's right—you've got money to spare, don't you?"

"Mr. Oliver—" Darcy started to say, but was shocked when Mr. Thomas interrupted them.

"Enough! We have just buried a man. You disrespect the souls who have been laid to rest here by carrying on this way. Now go home, all of you. Mr. Oliver, I will call on you later this week to consult about what sort of stone you think is proper, but I will hear no more about it today."

Mr. Thomas's voice had iron in it now. Mr. Oliver glared at the vicar, then spat at Bingley's and Jane's feet, drawing shocked gasps from the crowd. He stormed off, pushing past those unfortunate enough to be standing in his way.

It was Jane who asked, "Should someone see that he makes it home all right?"

Beside him, Lizzie let out a small snort. Darcy pressed his mouth shut.

"I'll call on him later," said Mr. Thomas with a sigh. "Now, everyone, go home."

The crowd began to disperse, the Netherfield party along with them. Up ahead, Darcy could hear Mrs. Bennet muttering not quite under her breath about the rudeness of some people as she shooed her youngest daughters along. Darcy leaned in to Lizzie and whispered, "Well? I imagine that was not the outcome you were hoping for."

"Is it just me, or does he seem far more invested in this matter than he ought to be?" Lizzie asked.

"Perhaps it's jealousy," Darcy said. Mr. Oliver's constant references to the treasure seemed to be a sticking point—and money could turn people sour. "If he thinks they might have killed to protect a fortune, perhaps that would explain the force of his ire."

"I don't think we'll get any more out of him, even sober, unless we stumble upon new information," Lizzie murmured.

"Oh? What do you propose?"

"I have to find a way to convince Sally to talk. Not only that, I have to find a way to convince her to tell us something *true*." Lizzie paused, then added, "And I can't make any missteps."

"Right," Darcy said, thinking of the stubborn set of Sally's jaw every time they'd spoken to her. "Sounds simple enough."

FIFTEEN

In Which Lizzie Finds a Clue and Loses Something Invaluable

UNFORTUNATELY FOR LIZZIE, FINDING an approach to questioning Sally Burton would likely be easier than finding a time in which to do it. Time before the ball was running out, and Jane was leaning on Lizzie to help her with all the added duties involved with the preparations—the increase in correspondence, overseeing the airing out and cleaning of many rooms, designing the menu and having to redesign it once more when the Meryton market could not supply all their desired food items on such short notice, and endless lists.

So many lists.

In between the many preparations and Darcy's assistance to Bingley, Lizzie, Darcy, and Charlotte spent as much time with the registers as possible. They decided to divvy up the work: Darcy would take the oldest register, Lizzie the second oldest, and Charlotte would read the newest. Without something specific to look for, the work was slow going, but they managed to meet in the library two days before the ball, while Jane consulted with the housekeeper to go over the final details and Bingley caught up on correspondence with his overseas trade partners.

"Well," Lizzie said, sitting down at a table next to Charlotte. "Have we found anything interesting?"

"If I have, I didn't recognize it as significant," Darcy said.

"I've uncovered many interesting things," Charlotte said. "However, any relevance to the case at hand remains unclear."

Lizzie tried to withhold a sigh. Research was an essential part of any solicitor's career, of course. Reading her father's legal books was what had first piqued her interest in the law, after all. But as she grew older, she found herself more drawn to people and cases than to theory and history—although Mr. Bennet had certainly made sure she had a strong foundation in both. She knew that with a case as old as this, and with few witnesses, the historical record could prove invaluable. But it was difficult to give these registers her total focus when Sally Burton was somewhere in this house, likely concealing secrets, and she could just divulge them . . . if Lizzie could find a way to persuade her.

"Lizzie?" Darcy asked.

"Oh, it was the usual ebb and flow of baptisms and burials, livened up by a handful of marriages each year and the occasional note about the weather or crop yield. There was a span of three pages devoted to every young man in the county who went to fight in America and who did and didn't come back, but all of them were accounted for." Lizzie grimaced at the memory of all the names listed as dead. "Eventually, anyway."

"I read in mine that Dr. Fellowes used to pay regular visits to Honoria," Charlotte said, holding up the register that covered the last thirty-five years.

"Really?" Lizzie asked. "What did they talk about?"

"Now, that he doesn't say. See, he made record of the date and the people he visited. He visited her at least twice a month, starting . . ." Charlotte flipped through the book, and Lizzie noted that she'd cut several lengths of string and used them to mark her place. "Here. Twenty-three years ago this August."

"Why?" Darcy asked. Then he looked at Lizzie. "He didn't say anything about visiting her in your volume?"

"No. He received the living here about five years before Honoria married Geoffrey. He mentions her arrival to Netherfield, and the first time she comes to church with the family—there's a rather unkind remark about how worried he was that she'd be Catholic on account of her 'Spanish blood' but she appears to be satisfactorily Anglican. And then that's it, really, until . . . well, the deaths. Everything we've heard about the so-called curse is corroborated in here." Lizzie paged through the book, having memorized the page numbers. "After that, Honoria is mentioned only very occasionally."

"What about you, Darcy?" Charlotte asked.

"I'm afraid my volume is even drier than yours. The vicar before Fellowes was a man named Owens, and his records are perfectly perfunctory, but hardly interesting. I think it likely that he predates our case."

"So much for that," Lizzie muttered.

“Come now, we’re not giving up.” Darcy closed his book and then reached for a quarto sheet, pen, and ink. “Just because we didn’t stumble upon something obvious doesn’t mean that all hope is lost. Perhaps we begin to make our own list of all the men who were born, say, at the beginning of your book, Lizzie, and then we make a list of all the burials, and cross-reference the two and track down whomever we can’t account for.”

Lizzie felt her eyes widen. “Darcy, that could take . . . days. Weeks, even. We don’t have that kind of time!”

“Don’t we?” Charlotte asked, looking between the two of them. “I thought we were here until Jane and Bingley return to London for the season?”

“Of course,” Lizzie said quickly, “but we can’t just let the mystery drag on forever! Jane’s reputation—”

“It is unfair how Jane has been treated,” Charlotte interrupted gently, “but that is not for you to fix. And we all hope that the ball will help matters on that front. What’s the rush?”

The rush, of course, was Lady Catherine. As soon as this mystery was solved, Lizzie would go back to London. She hoped she could do so after the ball, for she didn’t want to test Lady Catherine’s patience a third time.

Lizzie sighed. “Never mind, then. We make lists and cross-reference. But before we do that, is there anything else of interest that either of you found?”

Darcy shook his head, and Charlotte looked mildly suspicious, but she did not press Lizzie. “I found record of Sally Burton’s baptism.” She turned to another string-marked page and turned the book around before sliding it over to Lizzie. Darcy leaned in as well.

Lizzie skimmed the page until she found the entry that Charlotte was tapping with her index finger. *Sally Ann Burton, baptized this day, the twenty-second of March*, it read.

"Interesting," Lizzie said, unsure why this was noteworthy.

"Keep reading," Charlotte instructed.

"Daughter of Amy Burton," Darcy said. He frowned. "No father?"

"None mentioned," Charlotte said.

Now that was . . . intriguing. "Did he die?" Lizzie asked. "But he must have, if Dr. Fellowes didn't make any record of him at the baptism."

"There's no record of burying any Burton," Charlotte said. "I would have remembered the name."

"No," Lizzie said, feeling faint with excitement. "But I read about a Burton!"

She flipped through her own book, trying to remember where she had seen it—somewhere around the middle? She found the page she was looking for. It was before all the awful records of the war in America, around the same time her father had been born, but only a few years after the first mention of Honoria Bingley coming from across the sea as a new bride. *There.*

Amy Elizabeth Burton, born the second of September to Allan and Susannah Burton.

"I'm a fool," Lizzie said, showing Charlotte and Darcy. "She's a Burton not by her father's line, but her mother's. Of course she is! How could I have overlooked this?"

"Do you think this means her mother . . . never married?" Charlotte whispered the last part.

Darcy let out a low whistle. "That had to be quite the scandal."

"You don't recall anything about Amy ever marrying?" Lizzie asked Charlotte.

She shook her head. "No. And if Sally was christened Burton . . ."

"Foolish," Lizzie repeated. "I'm not asking the right questions. I keep looking around and assuming things are as I see them, and not thinking about what is missing."

"Do you think our dead man could be . . ." Darcy almost looked afraid to say it.

"Well, that would certainly explain why Sally and her grandparents are so tight-lipped," Charlotte said. "But it doesn't explain why he ended up in the flue in the first place."

"I could think of more than a few reasons." Lizzie didn't voice them—she knew that Darcy and Charlotte, having worked in the law, were all too aware of the various ways husbands or lovers could mistreat those they professed to love. Perhaps Sally's father ended up in the flue because he was a bad man.

"It's as good a theory as any," Darcy said. "But not one we can prove exactly."

"What are you going to do next?" Charlotte asked Lizzie. "It's not quite the irrefutable proof we were hoping for."

"No, but it is something," Lizzie said, thinking. Sally Burton was all stoic expressions and withering looks. Lizzie could not simply approach her and chip away at her reticence to reveal the truth with cleverly placed questions. No, if Sally had been hiding something as big as a dead body for years, something that could potentially be the murder of her own *father*, then she would not fold quite so easily.

Just then, a gong sounded, interrupting her stream of thought. She sighed. "Let's pick this up after tea—Charlotte, I think we ought to go over the register again. Say, two years prior to Sally's birth to the time that Amy passed away. Perhaps there is something that didn't seem significant the first time around that will stand out once more."

They all agreed and headed for the dining room, where they were the last to arrive. Lizzie took a seat next to Kitty, right across from Caroline, and Charlotte sat on her other side. Lydia was speaking as they arrived, so caught up in what she was saying that she paid them no mind. "Mr. Chatsworth was really very charming. Wouldn't you agree, Mama?"

"Very charming," their mother said, nodding vigorously. "Courteous, and very handsome."

"And he said he'd love to introduce us to his companions, a Mr. Dalton and a Mr. Hartman," Lydia continued. "Jane, can you please, please, please invite them to the ball?"

"We ought to be calling it a party, not a ball," Caroline groused.

"Jane is opening the ballroom. Therefore, it is a ball!" Lydia protested.

"I don't know, Lydia," Jane said. "I've not met these gentlemen and—"

"But I have! And they know Bingley—Bingley, can't you invite them for propriety's sake?"

"I'm sorry, who are we talking about?" Lizzie asked.

Mary spoke up. "Mama took us into town to visit the haberdashery, and we met an officer along the way. Lydia dropped a handkerchief, and he returned it."

Lizzie coughed around a sip of her tea. "I beg your pardon, you went where?"

"Don't be so dour, Lizzie. You and Darcy went into the village on your own," Kitty said.

"Excuse me, you did what?" Mrs. Bennet asked, eyes pinning Lizzie in place.

"For our case!" Lizzie protested. She turned to her father. "Papa, are you sure it's a good idea—"

"Papa was with us, Lizzie," Lydia said, a note of smugness in her voice. "Well, he was buying a newspaper at the time, but it was all perfectly proper. Romantic, even. Mr. Chatsworth ran after us in the street, and he said, 'Excuse me, miss, I don't wish to be so forward, but I would hate it if you took one step more without realizing that you've dropped this,' and then he held up my handkerchief—the one embroidered with roses, and the pink edging?—and it was very neatly folded and you just know he must have done that himself because I'm sure when I dropped it, it wasn't folded at all . . ."

As Lydia prattled on, Lizzie looked across the table and

to the left at Darcy. He stared back, looking concerned. It wasn't just the impropriety of Lydia meeting officers in the village—Lizzie wasn't naive enough to think that her mother would curb such behavior, although she had hoped her father would show a bit better judgment. It was that her parents and sisters had left the safety of Netherfield and she hadn't known it.

And they didn't know Lady Catherine was close by.

Lizzie lost her appetite entirely. This was the cost of keeping secrets, she realized. Her sisters thought they could do what she did because she hadn't told them the danger.

When Lizzie tuned back in, Lydia was saying, "—and I just think it would be nice to have a few more young men to dance with, Jane!"

"Perhaps we should not invite people to Jane's party for her?" Lizzie suggested.

"Mr. Thomas is coming," Jane pointed out. "I'm sure he'll be a willing dance partner."

Lydia let out a dismissive huff. "He's hardly a catch!"

Next to her, Charlotte stilled. Lizzie looked at Jane, who simply smiled in Lizzie and Charlotte's direction and said, "Well, you would be wrong about that. I happen to think Mr. Thomas is perfectly agreeable. Besides, he's the second son of a baron."

Lizzie pressed her lips together as the conversation continued, with Lydia and Kitty recounting every detail of their encounter with Mr. Chatsworth, with commentary from Mrs.

Bennet, and then moving on to who had confirmed their attendance for the ball. Almost everyone on Jane's list of guests had responded favorably, including the Fitzgeralds. Lizzie couldn't help but smile at that.

At least one thing was going right.

"Just think, this could be the night that changes everything," Kitty said with a wistful sigh.

"It's just a country ball," Caroline complained. "Hardly the event of the season."

"A young lady's imagination is very rapid," Mr. Bennet observed. He spoke so rarely at meals that everyone turned to look at him as he added, "It jumps from admiration to love, and from love to matrimony in an instant."

Charlotte and Lizzie stifled laughter as Mrs. Bennet voiced her offense at her husband's observation. Lizzie felt Darcy's gaze upon her. He was watching her with an intensity that made her heart race slightly, even though she was seated. They had not discussed marriage directly. Lizzie had told him of her need for more time and was relieved when Darcy had seemed unbothered. Now she felt her resolve to wait waver—if she poked at it, there was some give.

Was she . . . was she contemplating marriage?

She tore her gaze away from Darcy's, wondering whether anyone noticed the heat rising in her cheeks.

As they finished their tea, something else occurred to Lizzie. "Kitty, Lydia—if you all went to the village this morning, then where is Guy?"

"Hmm?" Lydia asked.

"Guy," Lizzie repeated. "You said you were taking him for a walk after breakfast. Where is he?"

"Oh," Lydia said. "We did walk him. But then we went into the village."

"And where did you leave him?" Lizzie could feel her irritation growing, along with a tiny bud of concern.

"You passed him off to a maid," Mary said. "Remember?"

"Why would I remember something as trivial as that?"

"I don't know, probably because you have nothing but trivial thoughts in that head of yours?"

"Mama! Mary said—"

"Girls," came Mr. Bennet's stern voice. "Not at your sister's table."

"Well, this is unacceptable. If you're going to take responsibility for him, you can't just fob him off on the nearest maid whenever you grow bored."

"We were going into the village, and Mama said—"

"Then you should have brought him back to me or Darcy!"

"I'll ring for someone to bring him up," Jane said hastily. "He's likely down in the kitchens."

Mr. Grigson came and promised to fetch the dog at once, which mollified Lizzie somewhat. However, the butler returned quickly, wearing a serious expression. "I apologize, madam," he said to Jane. "But we've been unable to locate the dog. He's not belowstairs, and none of the staff I've spoken with have seen him since shortly after breakfast."

Panic shot through Lizzie and she stood. "What about the maid Lydia said she gave him to? Do you know who it was?"

"Where are you going, Elizabeth?" Mrs. Bennet demanded.

"To find my dog!"

"The maid in question was Agnes," Mr. Grigson said. "And she said she placed him in the servants' sitting room, but he's no longer there."

Darcy joined Lizzie. "Don't worry, we'll find him."

Lizzie was already walking out of the room. She raced upstairs to her bedroom in case someone had put the dog there. "Guy?" she called out as she opened her door, Darcy on her heels. "Guy, come here, boy!"

But her room was empty.

"I'll check mine," Darcy said, taking off in the other direction. Lizzie followed, and stood in the doorway of Darcy's room as he searched, but it was abundantly clear that the dog wasn't there, either.

Lizzie clenched her fists. "Where could he have gotten off to?"

"He's likely sleeping in some comfortable corner somewhere," Darcy said, coming to place a hand on her shoulder. "Don't worry."

Normally, Darcy's touch would have brought her some comfort, but panic was rising up in her. "We need to search the house and the grounds. Darcy, what if someone let him out and he's outside, wandering around, completely lost?"

"We'll find him," Darcy repeated. "Come on."

Downstairs, Bingley was waiting outside the dining room. "Any luck?"

Darcy shook his head, and in short order, Bingley and Mr. Grigson began to arrange an organized search. The gardener and groom and two footmen were sent outside to search the grounds while inside three housemaids were appointed to search the downstairs rooms. Mr. Grigson informed them the kitchen staff was searching the lower level, and he instructed several maids and valets to go upstairs and begin searching room by room.

But Lizzie couldn't sit still. The more time that passed, the tighter her chest felt. She knew that with more than twenty people searching, they were likely to find him. But a darker worry overshadowed everything, and she pulled Darcy into the foyer and halfway up the stairs, where no one could eavesdrop on their conversation. "I can't shake this feeling. What if *she* took him?"

Lizzie could tell by the pained expression on his face that Darcy had been contemplating this as well. "If she did, I'll wring her neck myself."

"I'm so stupid," she said. "I'm everything that anyone has ever accused me of—headstrong and unreasonable and foolish and naive—"

"Where is this coming from?" Darcy asked, sounding alarmed. "Lizzie, you're not—"

"I am! Because she wrote me a threatening letter saying what exactly she'd do if I didn't show up at the appointed time and place to do as she wants, and I ignored it, and then when she figured out where we'd gone and sent another note, I ignored it! And I asked you to ignore it, and I put my family at risk, and now Guy is missing!"

"Stop," Darcy told her, so sternly that it startled her. "First of all, we don't know whether she is even involved—"

"How could she not be? She—"

"And second of all, you're not to blame. Besides, her last letter said to await her instruction, did it not? So why take Guy? Why not send instructions?"

"To get me to do what she wants," Lizzie said miserably. "And Darcy, I know he's just a dog, but—" Her voice broke.

"I know," he said. "But it does us no good getting ourselves worked up. Let's go downstairs and see if anyone has found anything. Perhaps . . ."

"Perhaps what?"

"Perhaps, if it is she—and I am not saying it is—then there is another letter with her demands."

Rather than scaring her—Lizzie was already terrified—that prospect strengthened her resolve. They'd turned to head back down the stairs when something made Lizzie stop suddenly.

"What's the matter?" Darcy asked.

"Shh! Do you hear that?"

Darcy went still as well, listening. The house was quiet and absorbed sound surprisingly well. They could hear distant voices downstairs, but then . . .

A very distant, sad yip.

"Guy!" Darcy's eyes lit up as he looked around. "Where is he?"

"I don't know!" Lizzie clutched at his hand as hope surged through her. "Guy! Here, boy!"

They went quiet and waited. But then . . . yes, another sad yip.

"Where's it coming from?" Darcy asked as he climbed the rest of the stairs.

"I can't tell!"

He was barking now, she was sure of it, but she couldn't trace the source. Mr. Grigson came down the guest hall after hearing the commotion. "Have you found him, miss?"

"No, but listen!" Lizzie tilted her head and . . . there it was again. "Did you hear that?"

"Yes," the butler confirmed, sounding relieved.

"Where is he?" Darcy asked. "Somewhere upstairs, but . . ."

Mr. Grigson walked to the door on Lizzie's right and pressed an ear against it. Lizzie stared at him, uncomprehending, and then the butler said, "Call him again, miss."

"GUY!" both Lizzie and Darcy shouted, drawing the others from downstairs in the marble foyer, where their voices echoed.

Lizzie closed her eyes and concentrated. There it was—Guy's distinctive yip. She opened her eyes just as Mr. Grigson straightened up, a grim expression painted across his face.

She knew it without him having to say a word.

Guy was somewhere in the east wing.

SIXTEEN

In Which Lizzie Questions Her Prime Suspect

THE KEY WAS FETCHED and the door to the east wing was opened, but no one could agree on who was to cross the threshold.

Lizzie wanted to run toward the sound of Guy's barking, but her memory of falling through the floor was too fresh. She could see the splintered floorboards from where she stood and recalled the terror she'd felt as she realized that the only thing between her and a potentially fatal fall was a bunch of rotting wood.

A small crowd gathered, including Jane, Charlotte, and half a dozen servants. They all took turns calling for Guy, but no matter how much they shouted and cajoled, the dog never sounded as if he were coming any closer. After nearly twenty minutes of this, his barks subsided into unhappy whines and cries that pierced Lizzie's heart. "What if he's stuck? Or hurt? He clearly can't just *come.* I have to go retrieve him."

"You're not going back in there," Darcy said, eyeing the floor as if plotting his own path.

"Neither are you! You're more likely to fall through the floor than I!"

"If I may, sir." They all looked to find Mr. Grigson at Jane's elbow. "I took the liberty of fetching Sally. Of everyone below-stairs, she knows the house best."

Sally stepped forward, wearing a grim look and her dark blue maid's uniform with a starched apron. She looked at the floor of the east wing and grimaced. "It's not safe to enter here. Right where Miss Bennet fell through earlier this week, and beyond the corner of that hall, that's where the fire burned the hottest. It's the most unstable part of the east wing."

"Then we go through a different way," Lizzie said. "Charlotte and I accessed the east wing through a service corridor by accident, and that seemed sound."

Sally nodded. "More sound than this hall. But still risky once you reach the east wing."

"We have to try," Lizzie said. She didn't care if she had to charge through all these people; she wasn't going to leave Guy. She stared into the other young woman's blue eyes. "Will you help me?"

"Lizzie," Jane whispered, but seemed unable to finish her thought.

To the others, it might have sounded like a selfish request on Lizzie's behalf. What reason would a servant have to put her safety at risk for Lizzie's dog? But Lizzie knew something the others did not: she had seen Sally in the east wing on her second night in Netherfield.

If anyone could help her, it was Sally. Lizzie poured every bit of meaning into her stare as she waited for Sally to respond.

"All right," the other girl said, her expression betraying nothing.

Lizzie sagged in relief. "Thank you."

"But you'll have to come with me," Sally said.

"I'll do it," Darcy rushed to say.

"No, it should be Miss Bennet. She's lighter than you. That will be to our advantage."

"Wait a moment." Jane held up a hand. "Sally, how do you know it's safe?"

"I grew up exploring this house," she said, shrugging. "I've been in the east wing many times."

"Let's go," Lizzie said to Sally.

"Lizzie," Darcy said, a pleading note in his voice.

She turned to face him. There was a sort of desperation in his eyes, not unlike there had been back in London when Lady Catherine's threatening final letter had come through. Lizzie knew that he was scared for her, and that he just wanted her to be safe. But unlike in London, now she reached out to take his hands and acknowledge his fear rather than brushing it to the side.

"I can do this," she said. "I have to."

He looked deep into her eyes and there was a moment when Lizzie felt as though everything and everyone had dropped away. She saw how he didn't like this plan one bit. And she knew that his protests weren't because he wanted to control her or limit her, but because he wanted her to be safe. But this world wasn't safe, and Lizzie had never been one to back down from a challenge. She knew Darcy understood that, but he needed a moment to accept it. Finally, he nodded. "Be careful."

And even though the hardest part was yet to begin, Lizzie felt relief course over her. "Always," she promised, squeezing his hands. He clung to her as if afraid to let go but released her after a moment more.

There was little discussion to be had after that. Everyone followed Sally down the hall to the back of the house, where Lizzie and Charlotte had found the service corridor. The door swung open on silent hinges. Lizzie shivered now to remember it shutting, locking them both in the dark passageway with no light.

"Will you stay here?" Lizzie asked Darcy. "Hold the door open until we come out?"

She didn't need to voice her fears to him—she was sure he could see them written on her face as plain as day. "Of course," he said, sounding a bit gruff. "But if you don't come back in a timely manner, I'm coming after you, structural integrity be damned."

His gaze slid toward Sally, and although it was fleeting, Lizzie saw the mistrust there.

"No one is getting hurt, do you understand?" Jane said. "Be careful, the both of you. Lizzie, if you don't come back in one piece, I will never hear the end of it from Mama. Or Papa, for that matter."

Sally seemed unimpressed by these theatrics. She waited just inside the corridor, a lamp in one hand. Lizzie squeezed Darcy's hand reassuringly, offered a weak smile to her sister, and turned to follow Sally into the darkened passageway.

They didn't speak, the only sound being the creak of the floorboards beneath their feet and the sound of Lizzie's breath in her ears. It was much different, walking down the service corridor with a lamp illuminating what had been mystery the last time Lizzie was here. The walls were not plastered, and the floors were rough-hewn boards. There was an expected amount of dust, but not nearly as much grime as Lizzie might have expected. Sally led with quick, quiet confidence, and in the light Lizzie noticed what she hadn't before—doors, designed to lie flush against the walls.

"Where do these doors lead?" Lizzie asked, breaking the silence.

"Other rooms," Sally said. "Don't worry, none that any of you are staying in. The west wing doesn't have the secrets the east wing does."

"Why is that?"

"I certainly wasn't privy to those decisions," she said. "Perhaps the previous generations of Bingleys didn't care for secret passageways leading into their bedchambers while they slept at night."

"Well, when you put it like that," Lizzie muttered. But she could have sworn she saw Sally glance back with a wry half smile in the sliding shadows. "Do you explore the east wing often?"

Sally snorted. "No, miss."

Something about the way Sally said "miss" felt mocking to Lizzie, but she chose to ignore it. "No? Not even to check to make sure that there are no trespassers?"

Sally was silent for so long, Lizzie was sure she'd offended her, which, given the dangerous situation Sally was leading her into, was probably not very wise.

"Not in several months," she said finally. "Not since Mrs. Bingley died."

It was not much, but it was a crack. Lizzie felt a surge of victory. She wanted to ask her about the other night but decided not to press too hard.

"What was the previous Mrs. Bingley like?"

"What do you mean?" Sally's voice was cautious, but not entirely defensive.

"Well, I hardly know anything about her at all. Was she short, tall? Was she sickly, or was she hale? Did she enjoy walking, or was she confined to her chambers most of the day?"

Sally slowed, and Lizzie thought for a moment that she wouldn't answer. But finally she said, "She was medium-height. She had silver hair she almost always wore in a braid, like a girl. She was kind, but she was sad. She was terribly lonely."

This was not the first time Lizzie had heard of Honoria Bingley's apparent loneliness. "If she was so lonely, then why—"

"Why was she a recluse?" Sally cut her off, as if she'd heard the question before. "Because this village wasn't very nice to her when she arrived, and they were even more terrible to her when her husband died."

Lizzie hadn't always been mindful of such things, but she knew how awful people could be to those who were different from them—those with different physical characteristics, or those who came from beyond England's shores. Charlotte had stories, and Lizzie had seen it in the Mullins case. "Did she ever think of going back?"

Sally scoffed. "Nothing for her to go back to. She lost her entire family before she was twenty-five."

Now, that was a detail Lizzie hadn't heard yet. "What happened?"

Sally stopped. Lizzie realized they'd reached the end of the service corridor and were standing before the entrance to the hall in the east wing overlooking the woods. Sally set the lamp on the floor and turned to face Lizzie. "She was the daughter of a Spaniard and an Englishwoman, as you might have heard. She was born in the colonies. Her entire family—father, mother, sisters—died of cholera not long after she came of age. She was left with a fortune in silver, but she had no one. Then, as she told it, a handsome Englishman and his brother came to her island, and she fell in love with him because of the stories he told about his family estate back home—how idyllic it was, the perfect place to grow up, how he dreamed of going home to the green fields of England and restoring his family home. And to a girl with no family and no attachment to her current home but an awful lot of money, well . . . you can't be surprised about what happened next."

Lizzie nodded. "She married him."

"Exactly. And he brought her here, where she thought she'd

finally have a home and family. Only he didn't want anything to do with her, not really. He wanted her silver to make the repairs and keep up the estate so his parents would stop writing and begging him to come home to do his duty, and then he wanted the rest for his adventuring while she stayed and kept a home. And when she put her foot down, well, he died. Then everyone else in the house got sick and died, exactly like her parents and sisters. She spent the rest of her life believing *she* was cursed."

Lizzie felt like wilting under Sally's directness. She had nearly forgotten one of the trickiest things about any case—there were two sides to every story. And in this telling, Lizzie was starting to feel as though Honoria Bingley was less eccentric and more downtrodden than Lizzie had ever entertained.

"I'm sorry," Lizzie said finally. "No one deserves to feel as though they're at fault for all the misfortunes in their life."

Sally huffed but said nothing more on the subject. She turned and stepped out into the main corridor of the east wing. "Come along."

"Is it safe?"

"If you follow me, and step where I step. Now, call your dog."

Lizzie gingerly stepped onto the moth-bitten, soot-stained carpet precisely where Sally had and shouted, "Guy? Guy, here boy!"

She paused to listen, and when she didn't hear anything right away, she called again. This time, she heard a sad little yip, somewhere to her left and . . . above?"

"I know where he is," Sally said darkly. "Come on."

Lizzie followed the young woman, listening for ominous

creaking or the sound of boards splintering. Nothing happened, however, as Sally led them down the hall in the opposite direction from where she and Charlotte had gone the other day. When they reached the end of the hall, Sally slid open a concealed door, revealing service stairs that went up. Guy's barking sounded much closer. "Guy!" Lizzie called out. "Guy, we're coming, boy!"

"Careful—"

Sally's warning came too late—Lizzie placed her weight on one step and heard a groan followed by a snap, then felt the board give way under her foot. She leapt to the next step, bracing her hands against the walls of the narrow stairs. The stairs were so steep she nearly lost her balance, but Sally grabbed her forearm, steadying her. There was strength in Sally's calloused hands. "Are you all right?"

Lizzie nodded. "Thank you."

Sally released her. "Come on, he's close."

The second floor was not nearly as nice as the first. The floors were bare and the walls were a simple whitewashed plaster, and the ceilings weren't as tall as they were on the ground and first floors. Sally noticed Lizzie taking it all in and said, "This used to be the servant wing. But no one has lived here for a very long time."

Lizzie shivered, thinking of all the poor servants who'd taken sick and died, never to be replaced. There was something unnerving about the empty hall, with its diffused light. "Is the floor stable up here? Did the fire . . ."

"I wouldn't go farther down that hall, but he should be—"

Sally reached for the closest door on the right, and it opened soundlessly. A small cream-colored bundle barreled into Lizzie's ankles. "Guy!"

The dog made pathetic whimpering noises, and his entire body wiggled with excitement to be reunited with Lizzie. He jumped up, scrambling at her knees, and she bent down and swooped him up. "Oh, I'm so sorry, boy. How on earth did you get up here?"

"That is the question, isn't it?"

Lizzie turned to look at Sally. The other young lady was regarding her with a strange expression—half wonder, quarter confusion, and a quarter . . . suspicion? "What is it?"

"You've been here before," she said. No, she didn't just say it—she accused Lizzie. "Haven't you?"

"What?" Lizzie shook her head. "Charlotte and I were here in the east wing, yes, but that was an accident. I found the service corridor and wanted to see where it led. The door shut on us, so we had to find another way through. But we didn't come up here."

Sally took a step forward, and for one heart-stopping moment Lizzie was afraid of her. What was she accusing Lizzie of, exactly? What was she going to do next?

But Sally stepped around her, and into the room Guy had been closed into.

The implication of that settled around Lizzie—Guy had been behind that door. But how? Unless . . . someone had deliberately shut him in there.

She followed Sally, holding Guy. The room was a large, open space. An ancient cradle sat in the corner, as well as miniature beds with musty, moth-eaten bedding. Old, broken toys were piled in a heap, and there was a single rocking chair poised tilted to look out the windows. They offered a view of the front lawn, sloping down toward the magnificent gates.

"A nursery?" she asked. "All the way up here, with the servants' quarters?"

"It was the servants' nursery," Sally said, voice sounding strangely hollow. "In a different time, I might have grown up in this room."

Sally's words reminded Lizzie of what she and Darcy and Charlotte had uncovered that morning, about Sally's father—or lack of evidence of one. Something about this room had rattled Sally.

Lizzie had no sooner realized this than she noticed something else: The room itself wasn't covered in dust and grime. The bedding in the corner didn't look at all inviting, but the floor was swept clean, and as she took a few timid steps to the fireplace, she saw the mantel had been recently dusted. There was no sign of fire damage, either. Almost as if the whitewashed walls had been scrubbed clean of whatever smoke damage or soot might have reached this far.

"Sally," Lizzie said in a voice that sounded more confident than she felt, "what is significant about this room?"

She didn't think the other young woman would answer, but Sally responded as if in a trance. "I would find her here, often.

Rocking in that chair, staring out the window. An entire manor full of luxurious rooms and the most comfortable seats you could imagine, but she'd come to this room."

"Why?"

Sally went to the window. "That was the other thing—she wanted a child, but Mr. Bingley never gave her one before . . . well. I think she liked the simplicity of this room—it's not as nice as the nursery in the west wing, but the view out the window is better."

"Do you keep this room clean? In her memory?"

Seeing Sally in the window late at night suddenly made a lot more sense if Sally made regular visits to the east wing to this very room for . . . sentimental reasons? Lizzie shook her head. Why risk the danger for sentimentality?

Sally still hadn't answered, so Lizzie decided to take a gamble. "I saw you in the east wing. Four nights ago. When I took Guy out at night, I could see a candle in the east wing, going from room to room."

Sally's head snapped back. "You saw that?"

"Yes." Lizzie swallowed hard. "It was you, wasn't it?" She didn't like how her voice came out with a slight squeak.

Sally sighed, and in that one defeated sound, Lizzie knew she was right.

"Why?" Lizzie asked. "It's so dangerous! I—"

"Your story about the service door closing and not reopening for you didn't sit well with me. There is a way to latch the door so it won't open from the inside, but one can't deploy it from inside the corridor."

"Someone intentionally locked us in," Lizzie said, adjusting her grip on Guy. She had already suspected as much, but it still unsettled her to hear her theory confirmed. "Why?

"I'm hoping you can tell me."

"I haven't the faintest idea!"

But of course, she was thinking about Lady Catherine. Lady Catherine, who'd threatened Lizzie in London and who knew she was at Netherfield Park. Lady Catherine, who was as wily as they come and had gotten the jump on her multiple times.

Could she be here, in Netherfield Park? But how?

"I tried to get away all day to check the east wing," Sally admitted. "But with so many people in the house, and a house-keeper always wanting to know what I am up to, it was impossible. So I left that night, but waited until Mr. Grigson had gone to bed, and then I came back."

"How did you get in?" Lizzie asked.

Sally rolled her eyes. "I have a key. No one asked for it back after Mrs. Bingley died."

"So you came in and went into the east wing and had a look around? In the dark? You could have fallen. Or set the house on fire again."

"Do give me a little more credit than that. But yes, I had to see if there were signs of the house being disturbed."

"And were there?" Lizzie could scarcely breathe.

"It was too difficult to say," Sally said. "But I'm certain of it now."

"How?"

"Apart from the fact that your dog was in a closed room on the second floor? This."

Sally stood before the window, which was framed with shelves and boasted a window seat beneath the ledge that Lizzie would have coveted, under different circumstances. Lizzie looked down to see what Sally was indicating.

A large chunk of stone was missing from the outside facade, right below the windowsill. Lizzie could see a crack between the window frame and the stone wall, the summer sun slipping in. Scrape marks on the surrounding stone and splinters from the frame betrayed that the damage had been intentional.

Lizzie looked down.

Below them was the edge of the drive, where she and Darcy had stood just three days earlier, moments before a chunk of masonry had nearly caved in their skulls.

"Oh." Lizzie said, feeling faint. "Darcy was right."

"About what?"

"He said . . ." Lizzie swallowed, her mouth dry all of a sudden. She wished he were there. "He said he saw movement in the window, but he thought it was a trick of the light. If someone was here, and they purposefully loosened the stone . . ."

She relived the moment of the accident—no, not an accident. Darcy's hard shove and the rain of debris, and the sharp thud of the masonry making impact with the ground. "This is all my fault."

Sally looked at her with genuine surprise. "What are you talking about?"

But Lizzie couldn't—didn't—have the time to explain Lady Catherine and her letters. "Do you have any idea who has been coming up here?"

"No," she said. "But I don't think it's one of your lot. Whoever it was, they were able to move very carefully. And they know a bit more about this house than I would have thought."

Something in Sally's tone made Lizzie pause. "What do you mean? What's significant about this room, other than Honoria liking it?"

Sally closed her eyes. When her response came, it was so quiet that Lizzie almost didn't hear it. "Because . . . this is where she hid her silver."

Before Lizzie had a chance to react, Sally nudged her away from the window seat and knelt before it. Reaching under the tip of the seat, she felt round for something. Lizzie heard the soft snick of a latch, and then the top of the seat swung open on hidden hinges that were as silent as a secret. Lizzie gasped and stepped forward, looking down into the dark hiding space.

Sally made a surprised noise. "Now, that's not what I expected."

SEVENTEEN

In Which Darcy Receives Some Unsolicited Advice

DARCY WATCHED LIZZIE DISAPPEAR into the dark tunnel of the service corridor and had to fight against the urge to follow her. He knew she'd keep her wits about her, but it was Sally he didn't trust. He hoped that whatever secrets she might be keeping, she'd guide both Lizzie and Guy back to safety.

"She'll be all right," Jane said, coming to stand next to him. The servants had dispersed to call off the search for Guy, leaving him with Jane and Charlotte. "She's obstinate, but she's not reckless."

Darcy raised an eyebrow. Even Charlotte looked doubtful.

"All right, she's not as reckless as she used to be," Jane clarified. "I believe you're a good influence on her."

Darcy let out a small half laugh. "I dare you to tell her that."

Jane didn't laugh like he'd hoped she would. "I know my sister. Loving her often means standing in the background, fretting as she goes about her mad plans. But Lizzie . . . she cares for you."

"And I for her," Darcy said awkwardly. He hoped Jane would leave it at that—it was bad enough that his own sister routinely hassled him into revealing his feelings, and now Jane was doing it, too?

Alas, Jane had a gleam in her eye awfully similar to the one Lizzie got when she was about to argue a case. "Good. Although her moods may run toward extremes, she usually sees reason. She just sometimes needs to be . . ." She glanced at Charlotte.

"Nudged?" Charlotte supplied.

"Exactly."

Darcy looked between them in confusion. "I beg your pardon?"

"What Jane means to say is . . . Lizzie knows her own mind, but she can get caught up in the moment. Sometimes she needs extra time to think about her next steps, and when she does, she is open to advice."

Now Darcy was really confused. "Is this about leaving London? Because we've discussed it already. She was upset when I agreed with Mr. Bennet rather than siding with her, but she knows that it was only because I wanted to ensure her safety."

The ladies exchanged looks. Then Jane said, "Well, that's very good. But we were thinking more along the lines of your . . . future."

"Together," Charlotte added.

"Marriage," Jane clarified, as if it wasn't obvious.

"My future marriage with Lizzie?" Darcy repeated. Even just saying the words caused a warmth to spread in his chest. Marriage. To *Lizzie*. He could only be so lucky. Then the implication of their words sank in. "Wait—do you think that she needs to be convinced to marry me?"

"No!" Charlotte exclaimed.

"Well," Jane said, looking at Charlotte, "maybe a little?"

Darcy could feel that warmth in his chest rising to his face, only now it wasn't so pleasant—in fact, it was deeply humiliating. "Oh."

"Don't fret. We can help," Jane said, placing her hands on her hips. She was looking at him as if he were a pile of correspondence or a list of menu options. Something to be tackled, checked off her to-do list. *Convince Lizzie to accept Darcy's marriage proposal.*

"Has she—" He cleared his throat. "Has she said something lately?"

Charlotte shook her head. "But we want you to know that you shouldn't be afraid of proposing, because we will be there with encouragement."

"I'm prepared to convince her this is the best opportunity for her future," Jane agreed.

Darcy blinked. Wait. "When I . . . but I'm not proposing!"

Jane's expression went from anxious to affronted in an instant. "What? Why not?"

This was all wrong. Nothing he was saying was making proper sense because the last topic of conversation he'd ever expected to have with Charlotte and Jane was how to propose. "Because she told me not to!"

"I beg your pardon?"

He raked his fingers through his hair. "She didn't tell you?"

"Apparently not," Charlotte remarked.

Jane appeared shocked. "She really doesn't want to marry you?"

"Well, I hope that's not the case." He coughed. Gods, this was mortifying! "I told her . . . I told her I cared for her and . . . I'd follow her to the ends of the earth. There was a metaphor in there about sailing—"

"Sailing?" Jane asked, baffled.

"We were rather exhausted and somewhat traumatized at the time. But yes, I gave her a speech about how I wanted to be there for her, forever. And she told me she wasn't ready."

A pause followed. Then Jane asked, "And when did she say she'd be ready?"

"I don't know. We didn't discuss timelines."

"Oh, for goodness' sake! I'll talk to her."

"Please don't," he begged.

"I have to. I have to talk to her and explain that she cannot drag her feet on this for the rest of time—"

"I'll wait," Darcy said simply. With those two words, he felt more sure than he'd had about anything in his entire life. "For as long as it takes, I'll wait."

"Jane," Charlotte said.

Jane took a deep breath and seemed to collect herself. "I'm sorry, Darcy—forgive me."

"There's nothing to forgive," he said, although he was still rather perplexed and embarrassed.

"It's just that . . . I thought the reason you hadn't proposed was that you didn't think she'd say yes. Or because she'd given you an indication that it wasn't what she wanted. When I know that she loves you very much."

His embarrassment was a well—a deep, bottomless well, but hearing from Jane that Lizzie returned his affections . . . well, it was like finding the most magnificent treasure in those murky depths. "Oh, well . . . ahem. You have no idea how much I would love to propose. But I won't until she's ready."

"How very noble of you," Jane said somewhat begrudgingly. "And exactly how long ago did she say she wasn't ready?"

"All right, Jane," Charlotte said, taking her arm. "Let it rest! You know Lizzie. Everything will be done in her own time."

Jane looked unabashedly at Darcy. "It's just . . . she's my sister."

"I, too, have a sister."

"Then you understand that I'd do anything for her. I just want her to be happy."

He nodded. He did understand. And Jane's words brought to mind Georgiana, unhappily stuck at Pemberley for nearly a year. He hadn't visited her, first because he had been too busy at the firm, keeping up with the work his father expected of him. Then because he'd been too afraid to stray from Lizzie because of the threat of Lady Catherine. Guilt gnawed at him. At least Georgiana was safe, far away from this madness, but seeing how fiercely protective Jane was of Lizzie left Darcy feeling as though he hadn't done enough for her.

"I don't suppose there's any chance that we can keep this

little conversation among the three of us?" Jane asked. "I feel a bit foolish, assuming the worst."

"It's understandable," Darcy said. "If a gentleman were as close to Georgiana as I am to Lizzie, well . . . I would be expecting a proposal as well."

"She's worked hard for her position," Jane said. "I want her to be happy. Preferably, with you."

It wasn't as though Jane's words didn't make him glad, but . . . "Why me?"

"Because you see her for who she is," Jane said simply. "Capable and smart. And you let her be her own person. She doesn't have to prove herself with you, and it's when she's trying to prove herself that she takes the most risks."

Darcy couldn't respond, for he was suddenly overcome with emotion. "I . . . thank you."

"You're welcome," she said, leaning against the wall. "That said, if Papa finds out about this . . ."

"If Papa finds out about what?"

The three of them turned to find Lydia at the end of the hall, ambling toward them with a smile like the cat who'd caught the canary. "Have you found Guy? Why are you all standing around?"

"Not yet," Jane said with a sigh. "Lizzie's gone to fetch him."

Lydia looked pointedly into the dark service corridor. "In there?"

"Yes."

"Where does it lead?" Lydia tried to cross the threshold into the corridor, but Darcy put up an arm to block her.

"It's not safe."

"But if Lizzie is in there—"

"Lizzie and one of the maids went in. She'll be back soon."

"Why won't you tell me where it goes?" She crossed her arms. "I'm not a child!"

"To the rest of the house," Jane replied.

"You mean the east wing?"

Jane hesitated. "Yes, but—"

"Your husband said the east wing was off-limits!"

"It is," Jane said severely.

"Is this how you and Lizzie ended up in the east wing the other day?" Lydia looked at Charlotte, then back at Darcy when no one answered. He wouldn't have been surprised if she stomped her foot. "Why is it that no one ever lets me do anything interesting?"

"It's not very interesting. It's dusty," Charlotte said. "I had cobwebs in my hair."

"Papa wouldn't like it."

Darcy didn't trust her sly tone. And neither, it seemed, did Jane. "Lydia."

"I heard you say not to tell Papa—"

"Yes, because he'd only worry."

"Well, it is dangerous . . ."

Jane sighed. "What do you want?"

Lydia was smug, and Darcy thought that Lizzie wasn't the only Bennet sister who knew how to bend a conversation to her will. But Lydia was determined to use her skills for her own self-interest. "I want you to invite the officers billeted at Meryton to the ball so we'll have someone to dance with beside your husband and *Mr. Darcy.*" She spoke his name like an insult.

"I'm right here," Darcy muttered.

"*Fine,*" Jane said. "But don't blame me if they don't come on such late notice."

"Yes!" Lydia squealed, tackling Jane in a hug. "Thank you, Janie! You won't regret it!"

"I doubt that," Jane said, but she accepted Lydia's affection nonetheless. "But you have to be on your absolute best behavior. No carousing, no dancing without introductions, no hysterics—"

Lydia ignored her. "I have to tell Kitty! And Mary owes me a shilling—she bet me that I wouldn't get you to relent!"

Before Lydia could run off, a scuffling sound emerged from the dark corridor. Darcy turned. "Lizzie?" he called out.

"We're coming!" came her voice from a distance. There was a tiny bit of light far within the corridor, and it grew as she approached. "I've got Guy!"

Darcy felt himself sag in relief. "And Sally?"

"She's here, too! We're all right!"

Darcy and the others crowded around the entrance to the corridor. Soon, they could make out the shape of the two ladies and Guy loping alongside them. Guy ran straight to Darcy, and he scooped up the small dog. "Where did you run off to? Don't do that to us again!"

"He's fine," Lizzie told him, and he didn't care about their audience—he wrapped his other arm around her, too. "And we are perfectly all right. No falling through rotting floorboards."

"Just the one on the stairs," Sally said.

"What?" Darcy and Jane said in unison.

"It was a small stair board. I didn't even fall!"

Darcy was so relieved to see Lizzie—a bit dusty and smiling widely, blessedly not hurt—that he hadn't noticed the leather satchel she was carrying until now. "What's that?"

Lizzie let out a satisfied little *hmph*. "This? Well . . ."

She opened the flap of the satchel and held it out for them all to see.

Darcy nearly dropped Guy, he was so surprised. Inside the satchel was a pile of coins. Not just any coins—silver coins. Silver Spanish coins. They were nestled heavily in the bottom of the stiff leather satchel, which appeared to have been battered by use and age.

"Is that the Netherfield treasure?" Lydia demanded. "Jane, you're rich!"

"Where did you find this?" Darcy asked.

"On the second floor of the east wing, in a room that appeared to be a nursery. They were hidden in a window seat. And coincidentally, Guy just happened to be trapped in the same room."

"Trapped?" Darcy echoed. "How did he get up there?"

"That's the question, isn't it?" Lizzie asked, scratching the dog's ears. Guy was squirming in Darcy's arms but seemed all too happy to be at eye level with them for once.

"Oh my," Jane whispered. "Lizzie, I think we ought to find Charles."

"I agree," Darcy said, closing the door to the service corridor behind them. He looked at Sally, who had hung back, silent. "Will you come as well?"

She nodded but said nothing else. He gave Lizzie a questioning look, but she shook her head slightly in a way that he knew meant *Later.*

The whole party made their way downstairs, where they found Bingley and Mr. Bennet coming back inside. They were in conversation, and both looked worried. Their expressions cleared somewhat when they spotted Guy trotting down the stairs, tongue lolling. "Oh, thank goodness you found him!" Bingley exclaimed. "Is everyone all right?"

"We're fine," Lizzie said.

"That's not all they found!" Lydia added.

Jane placed a hand on her youngest sister's shoulder. "Let's all retire to the study," she said firmly, and Bingley and Mr. Bennet exchanged looks before following.

Once the door was shut behind them, Lizzie upended the contents of the satchel on Bingley's desk. Silver coins tumbled out in a heavy, clinking rain.

Bingley's eyes went wide. "Is that—what on earth?"

"The rumors are true," Lizzie said. "The Netherfield treasure."

Bingley and Darcy each picked up a silver coin. They had genuine heft and Spanish markings. Unlike the one that had been recovered from the body in the flue, these weren't tarnished beyond recognition, although a small layer of dark discoloration covered them all. Darcy flipped his over and looked for a date, which he was able to make out easily: 1731.

Charlotte also reached for a coin. "They're the same mint."

"And they were hidden in the house this entire time?" Jane asked.

"I haven't seen such a pristine specimen in years," Mr. Bennet mused. "If the Crown had known your great-aunt was sitting on a stash like this, they might have solved the silver shortage."

"I had no idea," Bingley said, baffled. "Nowhere in any of the paperwork did her solicitor even suggest that she had all that hidden away."

"What are you going to buy with it?" Lydia demanded. "A new gig and horses to match? A hundred silk dresses for Jane? A new town house?"

Darcy and Bingley exchanged glances. To Lydia, for whom money was something distant and nebulous, this seemed like a life-changing fortune. And, for some people, it would be. But a pile of silver coins was only a small sliver of the wealth someone like Bingley possessed. It would pay for the needed repairs, to be certain, but it would run out. He wondered whether this was the reason the house was such a trap—perhaps Honoria Bingley had been unwilling to spend the last of her nest egg.

"We aren't spending it," Jane said firmly. "We don't know where it came from, or to whom it really belongs."

"If it was hidden within the house, and Bingley now owns the house, doesn't that make it his?" Lydia asked.

"Technically, yes," Darcy said.

"But if it was ill-gotten, then there are certain liabilities," Mr. Bennet added.

"How did you find it?" Bingley asked. "I can't believe Honoria had it stashed away all this time."

Lizzie glanced behind her, and Darcy turned to see her looking at Sally. Sally, whom he had almost forgotten about. "I didn't find it," Lizzie said. "Sally did."

Sally held her head up high. "It was just a lucky guess."

Darcy glanced quickly at Lizzie and saw her tilt her head in surprise. Clearly that was not what Lizzie had expected her to say.

"A lucky guess?" Bingley echoed. "You knew about the coins? Why didn't you say?"

"You never asked," Sally countered. "How was I supposed to know she didn't leave some kind of directive in her will?"

"Guy was locked in the room where it was hidden," Lizzie added, her voice sounding strained.

"Guy was locked in a room?" Darcy repeated.

"And in that room was the same window where the masonry fell from the other day, nearly killing us. There were marks around where it came loose, which suggests to both me and Sally that the masonry was purposefully damaged."

Darcy gaped at her. Too many of the week's unfortunate circumstances were lining up in an alarming pattern, one that he couldn't voice.

"I had nothing to do with that," Sally emphasized.

"I know you didn't," Darcy said. "You were outside with us. And I saw movement in the window moments after it happened."

"Do we think that the same person who took Guy and displaced the masonry also killed the man in the flue?" Bingley asked, sounding confused.

Darcy looked at Lizzie and knew what she was thinking: Lady Catherine had made threats. And yet . . . could it really be she? And if she could snatch Guy, why not Lizzie?

"Why not steal the coins, then?" Sally asked, surprising them all. "It seems like a rather large coincidence. Presumably this trespasser knew the room was important—why not take the silver and be gone?"

"Perhaps they didn't know?" Lizzie suggested. "I'd have never thought to check the window seat if I hadn't seen you open it."

"Wait a moment," Mr. Bennet said suddenly. "You mean to tell me that *you* went into the east wing?"

Darcy saw Lizzie wince. "Yes, Papa."

"The very same east wing that is expressly forbidden, and that you nearly died exploring? What were you thinking?"

Mr. Bennet was not a man prone to outbursts or bouts of anger. But now he was positively glowering . . . at Darcy. "How could you let her go there again?" he demanded. "After watching her nearly fall to her death! Have you no sense?"

"I—" Darcy started to say but was cut off.

"Papa, it's not his fault!" Lizzie stepped between them. "It was my choice, and Sally guided me."

This seemed to make Mr. Bennet even angrier at Darcy. "Why didn't you go?"

"Sally advised that—"

"Sally is a housemaid! You could have overruled her!"

"Sir, I don't like it any more than you do, but Sally was the best person to guide Lizzie, and Lizzie is slighter than I."

"You shouldn't have let it happen! Are you this careless with your own sister, Darcy?"

"Papa!" Lizzie admonished.

Darcy went still. It was a low blow, bringing his sister into this. Especially since Mr. Bennet knew exactly what foolish lengths Darcy would go to—and had—to protect his little sister's honor.

"Darcy doesn't have any say over my behavior any more than you do," Lizzie said. "So if you're going to be angry with someone, be angry with me."

"Oh, I am," Mr. Bennet said. "How could you be so reckless? What would I say to your mother if you had fallen and broken your neck?"

"Tell her I was stubborn and incorrigible and I wouldn't listen to reason—she'd believe it. But if you're more concerned with appearances and propriety than about what I want or how I conduct my investigations, then I don't care to take your counsel on this matter!"

Mr. Bennet stood still, looking absolutely stricken. "That's not fair," he said, swallowing hard. He seemed to regain some of his strength after a moment, then said, "I care about you. And I don't want you to be hurt or killed because you insist upon poking at every single mystery you run across. There are dangerous people in this world, and they won't care that you're a lady!"

Darcy knew that Mr. Bennet was no longer talking about Lizzie's trips to the east wing.

"Do you think that being a lady isn't dangerous?" she demanded. "Safety is an illusion, Papa. If I am going to risk my life and reputation, I'd rather it be in the pursuit of what I'm passionate about!"

Mr. Bennet seemed to wilt. "I just want you to be safe."

"You can't protect me forever, Papa."

"But that's my job," he said, and his voice broke. No one else in the room moved, and Lizzie bit her lip. Then, Mr. Bennet seemed to collect himself. "If something were to happen to you, your mother would not be able to bear it," he said finally. Then he added, much softer, "And neither would I."

And with that, he swept from the room. Darcy could plainly read the anguish on Lizzie's face. She didn't want to hurt her family or friends, he knew. But chasing after mysteries was as much a part of her as her green eyes and her love of debate, and Darcy knew she'd never back away from what she truly believed was right.

Lydia was the one to break the silence that followed. She turned to Jane and said, "You'll still invite the officers to the ball, won't you?"

EIGHTEEN

In Which Lizzie and Darcy Strike an Unexpected Bargain

***IF SOMETHING WERE TO** happen to you, your mother would not be able to bear it. And neither would I.*

Mr. Bennet's words echoed in Lizzie's ears long after he'd left the study, attempting to hide the pain that was so apparent in his eyes. Lizzie had never wanted to be the cause of her father's heartbreak—she was the one he smiled at with pride. And while she was no stranger to her mother's disappointment concerning her marriage prospects, she didn't want to hurt her, either.

And yet, she couldn't shake this case.

Nothing about the discovery of the coins had made much sense to Lizzie. Who would take her dog and lure her into a very specific room in the east wing? And to what end? Lizzie would have suspected Sally herself, if the other girl had not appeared to be genuinely spooked by the whole ordeal. Lizzie realized now that Sally had expected the coins to have been stolen . . . which meant that Mr. Oliver was right about one thing: at least one of the Burtons knew about them. She thought of that day in the churchyard, witnessing Clara Jeffries receiving a small bundle from Sally.

Was Sally toying with them all?

The following morning found Lizzie and Charlotte with Jane in the ballroom while Darcy walked Guy, overseeing the final cleaning before the servants began decorating. The ball was only a day away, and a small furrow appeared to have taken up residence between Jane's brows as she directed servants and answered last-minute questions. Nonetheless, when the Fitzgeralds had sent a letter confirming their attendance, Jane had broken into a genuine smile and Lizzie had been glad for her. After all, wasn't this what Jane had always wanted—a husband who loved her, a home of her own, and a place in society?

She likely could have done without the dead body in her drawing room, but life wasn't always what you expected.

"What do you think?" Jane asked Lizzie and Charlotte as she surveyed the ballroom, empty save the footmen who were presently bringing in chairs and a few chaises from lesser-used rooms. "Chairs along all four walls, or just the two? Or three—we can leave the back wall clear? And should we have potted plants? I feel as though all the London balls have a garden inside."

"Chairs against three walls—no one wants to sit so near the musicians. You can't carry on a conversation that close to the music," Lizzie said.

"You're right, of course," Jane muttered. "Mr. Grigson, just the three walls!"

"Of course, madam," Mr. Grigson said, and began to direct the footmen accordingly.

"It's impressive," Charlotte reassured her. "Can you just imagine the parties that were held here?"

"There must have been plenty when it was first built, to justify the expense of this room," Jane said. "The frescoes aren't in terrible shape, but I wanted to replace the drapes before we entertained."

Lizzie didn't think anything in the ballroom looked shabby—not with its gleaming wooden floors and high ceiling, the tall windows framed by sumptuous (albeit faded) velvet drapes, and the crowning jewel, of course: the enormous crystal chandelier that hung in the middle of the room. It was three tiers, with the widest ring of crystals at the top, tapering into a tip upon which hung the largest crystal Lizzie had ever seen. It was capable of holding a small fortune in candles, and although it was unlit now, it sparkled in the morning sun. Lizzie could only imagine how stunning it would be when the candles were aglow and the room was full of people and music.

"No one will notice the drapes, and the frescoes will pale in comparison to the chandelier," she reassured her sister.

Jane followed Lizzie's gaze upward. "Oh, that will need to be polished and fitted with new candles. I do hope Mrs. Reed received our order from the candlemaker."

"Would you like me to polish the chandelier next, ma'am?" Lizzie turned to find Agnes, holding a bucket and mop. In the wake of losing local help, all of the servants in the Bingleys' service had been deployed to prepare for the ball. The maid's red hair was slightly disheveled, and there were two high pink spots her cheeks. Despite her recent exertion, she looked cheerful. "'Tis no trouble."

"Yes, please," Jane said, "but do catch your breath first, Agnes. It won't do to have anyone fainting."

"Of course, ma'am. Thank you for your concern. I'm quite all right."

"Get one of the footmen to help," Jane said, already turning to see if she could spot someone ready for the next task.

"Excuse me, Mrs. Bingley!" Sally had been polishing a set of silver candelabras in the corner, and now she marched over to Jane. "I really ought to take care of dusting the chandelier myself. She's old and finicky, and I'm familiar with the mechanism for lowering her down within reach."

"I don't mind," Agnes began to say, but Sally cut her off.

"I insist. I don't want anyone getting hurt." Her words were heavy with meaning.

"Neither do I," Jane said. "Thank you, Sally. Agnes, can you find Mrs. Reed and see if she needs assistance airing out the lounge? I want to set up card tables in there for the gentlemen."

"Yes, Mrs. Bingley," Agnes said, darting a final glance up at the chandelier before heading out of the room.

"I'll see to the chandelier next, madam," Sally said.

"Thank you, Sally," Jane said.

Sally went back to polishing the candelabras, and Lizzie's gaze lingered on her a few moments longer. Despite yesterday's revelations, she wasn't about to try to press information out of Sally again quite so soon. The coins were locked away in Bingley's strongbox, and he and Darcy were making inquiries about moving them to a safer location in London, but such preparations had to be carefully made.

The ladies were interrupted from their inspection of the ballroom by the sound of distant knocking. Jane stopped and cocked her head, listening. "Is that the front door? I'm not expecting anyone, and if someone is calling today, of all days—"

"I'm terribly sorry, madam," Mr. Grigson said, turning on his heel and walking out of the room at a brisk pace. It was the closest Lizzie had seen the butler look to frazzled. Charlotte trailed after him.

"I'm a monster," Jane whispered. "Even Mr. Grigson jumps when I speak."

"What? No." Lizzie nudged her sister so she was facing her. "Tensions are a little . . . high. But they always are before big events. Mr. Grigson just wants to see you happy. We all do."

Jane bit her lip, and for a moment, Lizzie thought she was about to cry. "I am starting to think this was a very silly idea."

"Of course it was," Lizzie said with a straight expression. "I was the one who came up with it and announced it to half of Meryton society without consulting you."

Jane smiled at that. "Yes, please no more rash invitations on my behalf. My nerves can't take it."

"Now you're starting to sound like Mama," Lizzie said, which made Jane pull a face.

"Lizzie, Jane," Charlotte said from the door to the ballroom. "I think you might want to come here."

They both turned, and that's when Lizzie registered raised voices from down the hall and in the foyer. Curious, the Bennet sisters walked to the foyer, where they found Clara Jeffries standing just inside the door.

The young lady was panting heavily, and her hair was in disarray. Her shoulders sagged, and she held her right side, as if it pained her. "You must fetch her," she was saying. "It's urgent."

"If you're here to call on a servant, then I must ask you to knock at the kitchen door," Mr. Grigson said stiffly. He looked up at the sound of their footsteps. "Mrs. Bingley! I do apologize about this—"

"It's all right, Mr. Grigson," Jane said. "Fetch her some water, please."

"Miss Jeffries, did you run here?" Lizzie asked.

"Yes," she said, straightening up. "Mrs. Bingley, please, you must call for Sally Burton. It's urgent."

"What is the matter?" Lizzie asked. She felt her pulse pick up. "Did something happen?"

"She has to come quick, before it's too late!"

"I'll go fetch her," Charlotte said, and spun on her heels.

Jane guided Miss Jeffries to a chair against the wall of the foyer, and Lizzie followed. "Take a deep breath and tell me what happened."

"It's her grandparents," Miss Jeffries said.

Lizzie went still with dread. "Oh no. Did something happen to her grandmother?"

"No—I mean, yes. But not just her. The both of them. Mr. Layne is in Meryton today!"

"Who's he?"

"The justice of the peace," Jane said. "He lives on the other side of Kimpton but comes to Meryton once a week to hear complaints. Charles knows him, and I've meant to have him to dinner but—oh, never mind. Miss Jeffries, what do the Burtons have to do with Mr. Layne?"

Lizzie's sense of dread returned, and she wasn't at all surprised when Miss Jeffries said, "Mr. Oliver has set out for the Burton cottage. Word is he intends to bring Sally's grandparents before Mr. Layne on the accusation that they were involved in the murder of the man here at Netherfield!"

Lizzie heard the clatter of something falling behind her. She turned to find Sally standing at the other end of the foyer, feather duster at her feet. "What?" she demanded.

"Sally, I'm sorry—I doubted I could stop him, so I ran here as fast as I could!"

"I must go," Sally said, and without further ado, she took off through the front door at a run.

"Sally!" Mr. Grigson shouted after her, but it was no use. He turned back to the ladies and muttered, "If one more maid flees this house through the front door . . ."

"Find Darcy and tell him to come!" Lizzie said to her sister and Charlotte. "I'm going with her."

Lizzie didn't wait for a response. She picked up her skirts and ran after Sally. The other girl had covered a surprising distance in just a few moments.

"What are you doing?" Sally demanded when she took note of Lizzie following.

"If Mr. Oliver has evidence against your grandparents, I want to hear it."

"I'm not going to slow down for you," Sally warned. She was not quite running anymore, but she was moving much faster than a brisk walk.

"I wouldn't expect you to."

The village was two miles away, too far to run the entire way in their long skirts, but Lizzie had to concentrate to keep up with Sally's grueling pace, and it wasn't long before sweat began to pour down her back and the sides of her face. Her shin hadn't been injured very badly when her leg fell through the floorboards in the east wing, but it wasn't long before she felt the scrape and the soreness in her every step as she trailed just a bit behind Sally, unwilling to let her get too far ahead. Sally led her off the estate grounds through a track in the woods, which fed directly into the path that ran parallel to the lane, the same one Lizzie and Darcy had spotted her on just a few days earlier.

All the while, questions swirled. Had Mr. Oliver uncovered new evidence? Everything he had now was circumstantial . . . but people had been known to hang for less. When they were more than halfway there and Lizzie's feet were screaming in protest, she heard the familiar rumble of a gig not too far away.

She turned and saw a carriage with Bingley's crest rolling down the lane toward them from the direction of Netherfield. "Sally, look," she said, pointing at the carriage. "Come on."

Sally shook her head, not wanting to deviate from her path, but Lizzie surged forward to take her by the arm and dragged her to the lane. "It'll be faster this way, trust me. Besides, you don't want to arrive so out of breath that you can barely speak."

The carriage rolled to an abrupt stop in the lane, and Sally relented. They cut through the long grass, and the carriage door was flung open. Darcy leaned out and simply offered a hand, and Lizzie felt a pang of love for him just then that was altogether inappropriate considering the urgency of the situation.

"You're a savior," she said with a sigh, allowing Sally to go first. He simply shook his head, but there was a small smile there, too, as he pulled her in next, and she found that Charlotte and Miss Jeffries were already inside, Guy perched on Charlotte's lap.

The carriage lurched into motion the moment Darcy closed the door after himself. He and Lizzie sat across from the other ladies. "What do we know?" he asked them.

"Mr. Oliver intends to bring Sally's grandparents before Mr. Layne," Miss Jeffries said. "He wants to formally accuse them of murdering that man and putting him in a flue at Netherfield Park."

"They didn't do it," Sally said fiercely. "He has no right—"

"He has every right, I'm afraid," Darcy said. Sally leveled a fierce glare at him and opened her mouth, but Lizzie interrupted.

"What he means to say is that as constable, Mr. Oliver has the right to bring anyone he thinks has committed a crime to a justice of the peace. But a justice of the peace is very unlikely to make a decision in a matter of murder."

"Really?" Sally asked, sounding hopeful.

Lizzie cringed and said, "That is to say, if Mr. Layne believes the accusation has merit, he won't decide on it himself. He's likely to refer the case to the court of assizes."

"What's that?"

"A higher court that is in session twice a year, in Hertford."

"Hertford!" Miss Jeffries exclaimed.

"Twice a year?" Sally repeated. She looked between them all. "And what will happen to my grandparents until then?"

"Jail," Darcy said grimly. Lizzie bit her lip. For all she badgered Darcy about his bluntness when dealing with clients, she wasn't certain there was a softer way to say this. "All accused will be housed in the nearest jail until the next session can be called."

Sally's distress settled into something harder, more steely. Her blue eyes flashed dangerously. "My grandparents can't go to jail."

Lizzie had had the misfortune of seeing the inside of Newgate, and on this point she agreed with Sally. Elderly, confused Mrs. Burton would not do well in such an environment. "We'll do all we can to prevent that."

Darcy cleared his throat. "Well."

She looked at him, raising her eyebrows.

"Lizzie," he muttered.

"What?"

He darted a look at Sally, who was glaring at him, and then said to Lizzie, "We cannot promise to keep her grandparents out of jail if they *are* guilty."

"They aren't!" Sally protested.

Lizzie bit her lip as she considered. Solicitors represented guilty people all the time. In fact, Lizzie estimated that the solicitors of Pemberley & Associates represented many less-than-scrupulous clients simply because they could afford to pay for the service. Lizzie herself had been hired by Jack Mullins, who had revealed himself to be not so truthful about his motivations. Lizzie didn't like making a habit of this practice—helping people avoid the consequences of their own bad behavior because they had money left a sour taste in her mouth.

But this felt different somehow. Sally's fierceness held a ring of truth.

"Sally, look at me," Lizzie said. The other girl pinned her in place with defiant blue eyes. "I can likely talk the justice of peace out of pursuing this case with your grandparents. But if I do, you need to tell me what you know. The entire truth, so no one else gets hurt. I promise that we will help in whatever way we can, no matter how bad it may be."

"Lizzie," Darcy said, but Lizzie didn't tear her gaze away from Sally. The other girl was clearly weighing something. Her jaw was clenched, and she was breathing heavily.

"Why?" Sally demanded. "Why would you help me?"

It was a fair question. A dozen answers flitted through

Lizzie's mind, but she discarded each and every one, settling on something that she felt Sally would understand. "You helped me find my dog. I think I owe you this."

Sally nodded. "Fine. But save them first."

The carriage slowed, and Lizzie peeked out the window and saw that they were pulling into Meryton. The driver directed the carriage to the assembly hall and came to a stop. Sally was the first one out, and Miss Jeffries followed, along with Charlotte and Guy. Darcy held Lizzie back a moment. "How do you intend to exonerate the Burtons from the charges?" he hissed.

Lizzie squared her shoulders. "I don't know."

"You don't know! Lizzie—"

"Come along!" Sally called.

Lizzie squeezed Darcy's hand quickly. "Don't worry. I'll come up with something."

She said the words with far more confidence than she felt as she followed the other ladies into the assembly hall. Lizzie took note of the dark wood of the floors and walls, and the long benches that had been set up in the center of the room before focusing on a man sitting at the head of the gathering, where a table and a single straight-backed chair had been set up for him.

Mr. Layne, the justice of the peace, was a man in his early forties with thinning blond hair and a harried expression. He glanced up when the party entered the assembly room and took note of the murmuring that followed. Lizzie guessed that there were about thirty people in the audience, including Mr. Thomas, and to the right of the table stood Mr. and Mrs. Burton, along with Mr. Oliver, whose mouth turned down into a sour expression when he saw them.

"All those wishing to bring forward grievances must take a seat and wait their turn," said Mr. Layne.

"Begging your pardon, sir," Lizzie said, throwing her voice so it rang out throughout the hall. "But we are here on behalf of the Burtons."

"You heard the man," Mr. Oliver spat out. "Take a seat and wait your turn."

Lizzie strode forward, ignoring the new round of whispers that went through the assembled audience. "I do apologize for my tardiness," she said, addressing Mr. Layne politely. "We came as soon as we heard."

"She can't be speaking right now," Mr. Oliver said, taking a step toward Lizzie.

Mr. Layne held up a hand. "What is your purpose, Miss . . ."

"Bennet," Lizzie said. "I am a solicitor at Longbourn and Sons in London, sir. I am here to speak on the behalf of Mr. and Mrs. Burton."

Mr. Layne sat up straighter. "Is this true?" he asked the couple.

Sally had rushed forward to join her grandparents and had an arm around her grandmother, whose agitation seemed to lessen now that Sally was present. Sally whispered something to her grandfather, and he said, "Yes, sir."

Mr. Layne turned to look at Lizzie. "Well, Miss Bennet? What is it that you have to say?"

Lizzie took a steadying breath. She'd argued cases in court before—important cases. Bingley had been accused of murder, and she'd helped secure his freedom. But in that scenario, she'd known exactly who the killer was and had all the evidence in her arsenal to prove it. Now she had little more than her wits. "May I ask what the charges are?"

Mr. Layne raised his eyebrows. "Mr. Oliver has accused Mr. and Mrs. Burton of murder, and of concealing a death."

Lizzie did some quick calculations. The charge for concealing a death was not nearly as serious as murder, which was a hanging offense. "And what evidence has Mr. Oliver presented to indicate that Mr. and Mrs. Burton are responsible for these crimes?"

"You know very well what I—"

"Mr. Oliver," Mr. Layne interrupted. "You speak out of turn."

The man shut his mouth, but Lizzie could see a large vein bulging in his neck. What was behind this rage?

"Mr. Oliver accuses the Burtons on the grounds that they were the caretakers at Netherfield Park these last fifty years, and they were responsible for the upkeep of the house and its security. A man whose body showed signs of being purposefully killed was found concealed on the property."

Lizzie pressed her lips together so as not to smile. "I see," she said. "And since when has proximity to a crime been grounds for guilt?"

"I beg your pardon, Miss Bennet?"

Lizzie stepped toward the Burtons. "Sir, I will not argue the facts that you have stated—Mr. and Mrs. Burton have been the caretakers of Netherfield Park for many decades. They are the only ones among us who had regular access to the estate. But Mrs. Honoria Bingley also lived on the estate."

"Are you implying that the late Mrs. Bingley is responsible for the murder of the man discovered in Netherfield?" Mr. Layne asked, which elicited shocked murmuring from the onlookers.

"I'm simply pointing out that Mr. and Mrs. Burton were not the only ones who could have put the body in the flue."

"You think an elderly lady such as Mrs. Bingley was responsible?" Mr. Oliver demanded.

"Well, I wouldn't presume to think that she was elderly when the death occurred. The body was in an advanced stage of decomposition." She looked at Mr. Oliver. "It could have been placed in that flue when Mrs. Bingley was younger. It could have been placed there before she arrived. It could have been placed there sometime within the last decade." She paused and then leveled her gaze back to Mr. Layne. "The point is, no one can say with any certainty when the murder occurred and who was around to conceal it. There is no evidence showing that the people standing before you are guilty."

"They've been in that house—"

"So if a crime is committed in a house, is a servant liable simply because they happened to be there?"

Mr. Oliver was turning red. "Of course not, but—"

"Exactly. Furthermore, is it not true, Mr. Burton, that you and your wife did not spend your nights in Netherfield Park?"

Mr. Burton seemed surprised to suddenly be addressed, but at Mr. Layne's nod, he swallowed and answered. "Yes, miss. We never spent a night in that house. Not in nearly fifty years of service."

"And why is that?" Mr. Layne asked, sounding genuinely curious.

"Mrs. Bingley believed that bad things come to anyone who spends a night under that roof."

Lizzie was not immune to the foreboding of those words, even if she didn't believe in the curse. She felt a shiver run down her spine as the audience nodded and someone said, "That's right."

Lizzie knew she could use this to her advantage. "Ask anyone in this village, and they'll tell you all about the so-called Netherfield curse. I've heard more than a few stories myself. No one in this village would risk spending a night there if Mr. Burton himself would not. I wager that for as many hours as he spent on the grounds and within the walls, he also spent the same amount, if not more, away from Netherfield Park."

"They're responsible," Mr. Oliver began to shout. "They're the most likely—"

"Are they responsible because you think they're the most likely suspects, or because you have proof, Mr. Oliver?" Lizzie looked the man in the eye. "Because for a charge as serious as murder, I for one would like to see some proof."

The gathered crowd began to murmur, the sound of their voices rising behind her. Lizzie knew that the tide had been turned. She turned to Mr. Layne, for it was his judgment now that mattered. He was considering her carefully, and Lizzie forced herself not to twitch. She breathed slowly and began to count the tapestries that hung behind him, trying to keep her nerves steady.

"As would I," Mr. Layne said finally. "Oliver, what proof do you have?"

"They were there—"

"Means are hardly solid evidence—"

"Thank you, Miss Bennet," Mr. Layne interrupted. "I'll ask the questions now. Mr. Oliver?"

"There was a coin found on the body. A coin that came from Netherfield Park."

Now it wasn't even whispers that erupted, but a cacophony of voices and questions. Mr. Layne began banging on the table before him for order.

"The coin proves nothing," Lizzie said.

"It proves that the Netherfield treasure is real!" Mr. Oliver commanded the audience's entire attention. "We all know the rumors, and we've all seen evidence of Mrs. Bingley's peculiar ways. She hid a fortune in that house, and do you truly believe that the Burtons wouldn't know? They killed the man to hide the truth!"

He pointed dramatically at the Burtons. Sally was glaring at Mr. Oliver, and Mrs. Burton didn't appear to understand what was going on. "Is he talking about the silver?"

"Granny, hush," Sally said. "It's all a misunderstanding."

But Mr. Layne had heard her, and now he turned the questions on to her. "Mrs. Burton, do you have a response to the accusation that you knew of a fortune hidden in Netherfield Park, and you and your husband killed a man to keep the secret?"

Lizzie gritted her teeth. That was an awfully leading question, and one that no judge or magistrate in London would be so sloppy as to ask . . . but this was not London, and she didn't want to risk Mr. Layne's ire by objecting.

Mrs. Burton looked at Sally. "What is he talking about, Amy?"

"Granny, it's me, Sally. Remember?" When Mrs. Burton didn't respond, Sally implored Mr. Layne, "Please, she's confused. She thinks I'm my mother. She doesn't know—"

"Answer the question, Mrs. Burton," Mr. Layne said.

The entire room was looking at Mrs. Burton, who suddenly seemed very small and old. She felt the weight of their gaze upon them, and her mouth wobbled. "I don't like this," she said, looking at her husband. "Allan, I don't like this!"

"Answer the question!" Mr. Oliver shouted, banging his fist on the table.

Mrs. Burton visibly recoiled from his outburst, but then something in her seemed to want to fight back. She stood up straight and glowered at him. "Don't you raise your voice at me, George Oliver! I know what you're about, sneaking around at all hours! Do you think I haven't noticed?"

Lizzie glanced at Charlotte and Darcy in confusion—she'd thought Mr. Oliver's given name was Tom, not George.

"Leave her alone!" called someone from among the spectators. "She's addled—she thinks Tom is his father!"

There were a few calls of agreement, but before Mr. Layne could call for order, Mrs. Burton continued. "Don't think I don't know what you get up to after dark! Allan and I have seen you, and we've told Mrs. Bingley."

Real fear flashed in Mr. Oliver's face, but it was replaced in an instant by fury. "You shut your mouth, you old crone. If you don't admit to what you did, I'll—"

He charged forward as if to grab the elderly woman, and Lizzie was too slow to react. Sally pulled her grandmother back, and Mr. Burton stepped forward to try to protect his wife, but he was not able to move his cane quickly enough and stumbled slightly. Lizzie opened her mouth to cry out, but then Darcy was there, shoving himself between Mr. Oliver and the Burtons. In a very handy move, he blocked Mr. Oliver's raised fists and landed a blow to the man's stomach. Mr. Oliver doubled over, looking like a sack that had been emptied unceremoniously. As he bent over, something he'd been clutching in his fist fell to the ground with a loud, solid *plink*.

It rolled, coming to a stop right before Lizzie's feet. She bent down and picked it up.

It was a gleaming silver coin.

NINETEEN

In Which Lizzie and Darcy Hear Sally Burton's Testimony

DARCY HAD WATCHED THE proceedings warily, ready to spring into action when needed. Lizzie was doing a fair job with her argument, so he wasn't worried about her—it was Mr. Oliver he didn't trust.

The man had seemed erratic and agitated from the moment they'd made their unceremonious entrance. He'd blustered and pounded, but he also kept shoving his hands into his pockets, and it was obvious to anyone looking at him that he kept clenching his fists.

Darcy didn't trust him to hold his temper, not for a single moment.

And his suspicion was warranted. When he saw the constable make as if to strike Mrs. Burton, he launched into action. Within seconds of Darcy hitting Mr. Oliver, a number of men from the audience raced forward, most running to restrain Mr. Oliver, though a few positioned themselves at Darcy's side, holding his arms lest he take another swing at Mr. Oliver. Darcy didn't try to shake them off. He had no intention of hitting anyone else—not unless it was in defense.

"Order! I demand order!" Mr. Layne shouted. He'd jumped to his feet and was pounding on the table. "Mr. Oliver, if you do not hold your temper, I will have you restrained!"

Mr. Oliver stopped struggling, but he was breathing heavily. His eyes darted around wildly. "Where is it?" he asked.

Darcy didn't know what he was talking about at first, until he looked over to Lizzie. She was standing several paces away, bending down to pick up something that had fallen on the floor, a peculiar expression on her face. "This?" she asked, holding up the object.

"Give it back! That's mine!" Mr. Oliver attempted to lunge toward her but was held back.

"What is it, Miss Bennet?" Mr. Layne asked.

Lizzie approached Mr. Layne. She dropped the object into his palm, although Darcy noticed she appeared reluctant to do so.

"A Spanish cob," Mr. Layne said, turning the coin over. "Genuine silver, if I'm not mistaken, 1731 mint."

Darcy let out an incredulous breath. "Exactly like the one found on the body, then."

Mr. Layne turned to look at him. "Sir?"

"I pulled it out of the dead man's pocket myself," Darcy told him. "I'm Mr. Darcy, Mr. Bingley's solicitor. You can ask him; he kept the coin. And not only that, but an entire cache of silver coins—Spanish, that exact mint—was discovered hidden away in Netherfield Park recently. So the question becomes: How did that one come to Mr. Oliver's possession?"

Murmurs burst forth once again, and Darcy heard someone say, "So it's true, the Netherfield treasure is real?" before Mr. Layne turned and smacked the table behind him.

"Order!" When the room quieted, he turned to Mr. Oliver. "Well?"

All Darcy could see in Mr. Oliver's face was unchecked fury, directed at Lizzie. Darcy tensed, anticipating needing to shake off the men holding on to him in order to leap between Mr. Oliver and Lizzie. But it was Mrs. Burton who replied.

"He stole it!" she accused. "I knew he would. Always skulking about the grounds and dropping by unannounced. I told Mrs. Bingley, he may be a constable, but I don't trust him one bit. He beats his son, and I've always said that you can't trust a man who will treat his horse better than his own son."

Mrs. Burton finished her little speech with a smug smile. Mr. Oliver shook his head. "I don't have a son, you mad old—"

"She means your father," Mr. Burton said. "Your father was always stopping by the estate, trying to call on Mrs. Bingley. She told us to turn him away, but he kept insisting on checking up after her, to ensure she was fit to be living alone in that great house."

Mrs. Burton looked very confused all of a sudden. "His father?" she asked.

"Yes, Granny—that's Tom Oliver, not George Oliver." Sally

patted her grandmother on the back. "His son, Tom, is the constable now."

"Oh, he's grown up," Mrs. Burton said in a not-so-quiet voice to her granddaughter. "I thought he was that criminal George."

Mr. Burton clasped his wife's hands and said quickly, "Susannah, darling, this isn't the best place—"

"I told Amy he was no good, too. She was too good for him. Oh, it breaks my heart, Allan. Why didn't she listen to us?"

Darcy didn't understand at first. He thought Mrs. Burton was speaking nonsense once more, but Sally's sharp intake of breath and her whispered, "Granny!" said otherwise. He looked to Lizzie and saw that her eyes were narrowed as she looked back and forth between Sally . . . and Mr. Oliver?

Understanding began to dawn.

"What's she talking about? What do you know?" Mr. Oliver struggled against the men restraining him, managing to break free of one of them. He lunged forward. "You know something! What did you do?"

The men holding on to Darcy abandoned him to insert themselves between Mr. Oliver and the Burtons. Mrs. Burton cried out in alarm, and Darcy took this opportunity to join Lizzie's side, shaking out his hands. It had been a long time since he'd hit anyone outside the boxing ring, and fortunately no one called for him to be restrained once more, although Mr. Layne did shout for someone to bring a rope.

"I expect all of you to conduct yourselves with decorum!" he shouted at the room, which was filled with shouts from the audience. "Mr. Oliver, there will be no more outbursts from you!"

Mr. Oliver didn't stop struggling until the rope was fetched and he was restrained. Mrs. Burton began to cry, and her family tried to comfort her as best they could. In all the commotion, Darcy looked down at Lizzie. "What are you thinking?"

"I have a theory of what might have happened," she whispered. "But I'm not sure if he'll be all that cooperative. Follow my lead?"

"Always," Darcy said.

She cleared her throat when Mr. Oliver was finally tied up and swearing up a storm. "Mr. Oliver. How long has it been since you last saw your father?"

The man simply glared at her. "I won't answer any of your questions!"

"Now we really are getting rather far afield," Mr. Layne said.

"Sir, I must ask that you allow the question," Darcy said. "Mr. Oliver is the one who has accused the Burtons and brought us all together today. The least he can do is answer Miss Bennet."

The justice of the peace sighed. "Answer them, Mr. Oliver."

Something seemed to break in his expression, and Darcy recognized the anger for what it truly was—a mask for grief. "Twenty-two years ago," he said, voice rasping. "It'll be twenty-three years in November that he last walked out the door to patrol and never returned home."

How had they missed that? He glanced behind him toward

Charlotte, who sat in a chair next to Mr. Thomas, holding Guy. Her forehead was creased, and he knew she was thinking about the parish registers, which hadn't mentioned Mr. George Oliver disappearing from the village more than twenty years earlier. Perhaps his disappearance wouldn't have warranted a mention in the registers—it wouldn't do for vicars to be perceived as gossiping—but if he had left behind a child, surely there would have been record of a parish family taking him in, and funds from the church to support him?

"I see," Lizzie said, her voice soft and sympathetic. "And is it your belief that the body we discovered in the flue is that of your father?"

Darcy had foreseen where Lizzie was going, but her question still drew gasps.

Tears streamed down Mr. Oliver's face even as he glared at her. "I knew it the moment I saw the coin. They killed him! They killed him, and I won't let them get away with it!"

Everyone was in an uproar, shouting questions and chattering at a louder and louder volume. The justice of the peace banged ineffectually at the table, and it wasn't until Mr. Thomas got up and went to the front of the room and placed two fingers between his lips, letting out a piercing whistle, that everyone fell into silence once more.

"Thank you," Darcy said. "Now, Mr. Oliver—"

"I don't know what he's talking about!" Mr. Burton said, stepping forward to address Mr. Layne. "Honestly, sir—we had no idea there was a body in the flue, let alone that it was George

Oliver. We all thought he'd taken off, abandoned his child—he was prone to drink . . ."

" 'Tis true!" someone from the crowd added.

"And he did beat that boy," added another.

"I heard he went to debtor's prison."

"He owed me!"

"And me!"

"QUIET!" Mr. Layne shouted. The crowd hushed, and Darcy had the feeling that whatever had led Mr. Layne to becoming justice of the peace, he deeply regretted it. "Mr. Burton, I appreciate that you and your wife have proclaimed your innocence, but I find this difficult to believe. If George Oliver did in fact lurk about Netherfield Park with the intent of—what, robbing the place?—then how did he end up dead in a flue?"

"I swear on my life, I don't know," Mr. Burton said, eyes wide with panic.

"Well, I'm afraid that's just not good enough—"

"Mr. Layne, if I may," Lizzie said. "I believe I might have a satisfactory answer for you."

The man rubbed his temples. "Oh, by all means, Miss Bennet," he said sarcastically.

"Mr. Burton, your wife mentioned that George Oliver visited Netherfield Park often, calling in on Mrs. Bingley."

The old man was trembling just slightly, but he nodded. "Yes."

"And you suspected he was after something of value?"

"Didn't know it for certain," Mr. Burton said. "But that was our suspicion."

"And . . ." Lizzie paused, and Darcy knew she was choosing her words carefully. "Did he show interest in your daughter, Amy?"

Mr. Burton didn't answer the question, but Darcy could read all the answer they needed in his eyes.

"He used her," Mrs. Burton said. "I told her, 'Don't trust that one, my girl. He's slippery and not good to the child he has. He just wants a mother to manage his boy.' But he could work the old charm when he had a mind. And Amy, she liked the idea of being someone's wife, of a life in the village. She never wanted to be in service."

Darcy noted that Sally stood beside her grandmother, her expression stony. She didn't appear shocked or dismayed by this revelation . . . which meant that she'd likely known that George Oliver and her mother had carried on a relationship. Darcy thought back to the day before, when they'd pored over the registers . . . how long ago exactly was Sally's baptism?

"What happened?" Mr. Layne asked. "If he courted your daughter, and you weren't pleased about it, and he ended up dead—"

"I tried to pay him off, all right?" Mr. Burton shouted. "I knew he wasn't good for my Amy, and I knew he didn't really care for her. He was using her, just as he was attempting to ingratiate himself with Mrs. Bingley. We all knew the stories about Mrs. Bingley's silver. Only, Susannah and I actually knew where she kept it. So I took some of it—yes, I stole it!—and I gave it to George Oliver and said, 'Here, take what you came for and go.

Don't ever come back here.' And as far as I knew, he did—he just didn't take his boy with him, either."

The room was shocked into silence by Mr. Burton's confession, but Mr. Layne was unconvinced. "So how did George Oliver end up dead?"

"I don't know," the old man replied, his voice breaking. "But you have to believe me—I only stole what I did to protect my family from that snake of a man."

"You killed him! You're a liar, and I've always known it!" Mr. Oliver struggled against his restraints, shouting. "I'll make sure you hang!"

"I'm afraid this case is out of my hands," Mr. Layne began to say. "For matters of murder, I must refer this to—"

"No!" Sally said sharply, stepping forward. "My grandparents didn't kill George Oliver. They never knew the truth of what happened that night."

"And you do?" Mr. Layne asked doubtfully. "You're hardly more than twenty yourself—"

"I'm twenty-two. And while I might not have witnessed what happened, I know. I'm the only person alive who knows." Sally swallowed hard, and Darcy saw for the first time a crack in the young woman's careful mask of stoic indifference. "Mrs. Bingley told me everything before she died."

"And why would she do that?" Mr. Layne asked.

"Because she thought I ought to know what happened to my father."

Of all the revelations that morning, this one stunned the

audience into silence. Sally did not cry or become overwrought, but Darcy could see her chin tremble slightly as she turned to her grandparents. "I'm sorry I didn't tell you."

"You knew?" her grandfather asked, incredulous. "But how?"

"Gran," Sally said with a sigh. "She slipped up one day and mentioned how he tried to court Mum. I asked Mrs. Bingley about it, and . . ."

"Sally," Lizzie said gently, "the only way to clear your grandparents' names is if you tell us what you know."

Sally nodded, and when she first spoke, her sentences came haltingly. "Mrs. Bingley said it was late. George would come in the late evening, when my grandparents had left and only my mother remained."

Sally did not elaborate on what George Oliver and Amy Burton did during those late-night visits, but one could make the appropriate assumptions.

"But this night, Mrs. Bingley thought she heard someone else rattling around in the house, and she went to find my mother. Together they found George in the drawing room. Mrs. Bingley kept the silver close back then, locked in a box in the fireplace. He was plundering it."

"And then what happened, Sally?"

"I don't know exactly, but Mrs. Bingley said an argument broke out. George raised his hand to my mother, and Mrs. Bingley said she reacted without thinking. She grabbed the fire poker and hit him over the head."

Sally didn't elaborate, and Darcy cleared his throat. "That is consistent with what we observed of the body, Mr. Layne."

"I see," said the justice of the peace. "And then what did they do with the body?"

"They hid him," Sally said. "In the fireplace. Mrs. Bingley said my mother was distraught. She wanted to tell her parents the truth. But Mrs. Bingley thought the more people who knew, the more likely it was that my mother would get in trouble, on account of George being the constable. She was also worried that the vicar at the time thought her mad—he'd been poking about the place, and she knew if the crime was discovered, it would be bad for everyone. If Honoria was tried for murder, she couldn't employ my family, and Mum might have been accused as well. They decided to hide the body because they could hardly dig a hole anywhere in the park without my grandfather noticing—he was the groundskeeper, after all. So they wrapped George Oliver in one of the sheets covering the furniture, and they found a way to push him up into the chimney."

"But what about the smell?" Mr. Layne asked.

"There was a smell, all right," Mr. Burton cut in. "The winter before Sally came. Amy said she'd seen rats, and she put out poison for them. Whenever we'd smell anything unpleasant, Amy would say it was the poison doing its job, and she'd go find the corpses and dispose of them."

"And did Mrs. Bingley ever express remorse for what she'd done?" Mr. Layne asked Sally, and Darcy held in a scoff. After everything Sally had just revealed, *that* was what he chose to ask?

"Honestly, no," Sally said. "She only told me because I asked; otherwise I think she would have taken it to her grave. She also told me where to find the coins she'd hidden after that night. She said she'd taken back what Mr. Oliver had stolen, but I suppose she must have missed one in his pocket—and I suspect she never had any idea that my grandparents had attempted to bribe George to go away."

She said this last sentence with a glance to Mr. Oliver. *Her brother*, Darcy thought. Tom Oliver stared back at her in shock.

"And Mr. Oliver," Lizzie said. "How is it that this coin came into your possession?"

Mr. Oliver stared at it, as if he didn't fully understand the question. Mr. Layne cleared his throat. "Answer the question, Mr. Oliver."

"My . . . my father gave it to me. He said we'd be rich. He just needed . . . time." Mr. Oliver swallowed hard. "He gave me one of the coins and said he had to fetch the rest. Only, he never came back. And I spent years—two decades!—thinking he'd left me! All because your mother—"

"That's enough, Mr. Oliver," Mr. Layne said.

Lizzie spoke up next. "Sir, in light of what has been revealed here today, I must ask that you release the Burtons. It is clear now that Mr. and Mrs. Burton had no idea what occurred in the house all those years ago, and the two people responsible for Mr. George Oliver's death and concealing his body are dead themselves."

"I don't believe them," Mr. Oliver said. "They say it was rats, but if they knew my father had left—"

Emotion caught in Mr. Oliver's throat, and Darcy felt a wave of pity for the man, who must not have been more than thirteen years old on the night that his father had gone out into the dark to claim a fortune, only to never return.

Do we ever stop yearning for our fathers' approval? he wondered. *Even when they aren't much of a father to begin with?* One thing was clear to him: even if George Oliver hadn't been much of a father, Honoria Bingley wasn't the only one who'd been robbed that night.

"Sir, we cannot hold the Burtons liable for a crime they were not reasonably aware of," Darcy said. "The burden of providing proof that they had knowledge of their daughter's crime and covered it up would fall upon the accuser, and Mr. Oliver has yet to produce a single shred of evidence—"

"Yes, yes," Mr. Layne said with a heavy sigh. "I am aware of the duties of my office, Mr. Darcy, despite not being a London solicitor."

Darcy didn't envy the decision before the justice of the peace. Lizzie had made a convincing argument for releasing the Burtons, but Mr. Layne was charged with dispatching justice in this parish, and failure to hold someone accountable for a crime could have unforeseen consequences. He looked at Lizzie. She was staring at Mr. Layne, shoulders thrown back and head held high. He knew she was likely mentally composing a counterargument to a counterargument, preparing for the worst.

Finally, Mr. Layne spoke. "I'm inclined to agree with Miss Bennet."

Mr. Oliver growled with anger and tried to push against the men holding him in place. The gathered villagers broke into applause, and Darcy noticed that Mr. Layne appeared relieved at the approval of the audience.

"They're liars!" Mr. Oliver shouted. That sobered the crowd, and Mr. Oliver continued. "How will you rest at night, knowing they live among us? Don't come crying to me when they've wronged you—you've been warned!"

Sally's magnificent scowl did little to soften the harshness of Mr. Oliver's accusation. "I've done more for this village than you and *your* father ever have," she said, the emphasis of her words leaving Darcy with no doubt as to what she thought of George Oliver. "And these people—they won't forget that."

With that, Sally ushered her grandparents out of the assembly rooms, followed closely by Lizzie and a stream of villagers. Darcy lingered, for he had an unanswered question of his own. He approached Mr. Oliver, who was glaring at him with pure hatred in his eyes. Darcy knew that he and Lizzie had made another enemy today. Before Mr. Layne could order Mr. Oliver unbound, Darcy leaned down and looked into the older man's eyes. "Have you made unlawful entry into Netherfield Park recently?"

Mr. Oliver spat at his feet. "Why don't you and that scheming shrew of yours go to hell?"

Darcy felt his fist curl, but he showed no other reaction. "Answer me honestly, or I'll bring my own complaint before Mr. Layne right now—have you trespassed onto Netherfield Park?"

"I'm not telling you a goddamn—"

Darcy straightened. "Mr. Layne?"

"No. I only went that night, when . . . when he was discovered . . ."

Darcy stared at him, considering. "All right," he said finally. He withdrew a pocketknife from his jacket pocket and saw Mr. Oliver's eyes widen. But he didn't struggle when Darcy grabbed his bound hands and cut through with the knife. Mr. Oliver made to walk away, but Darcy snagged his sleeve. "Wait," he said.

He withdrew his card from Pemberley & Associates, and held it out to the other man. "Take it."

"What am I supposed to do with this?"

"Go to the address on the card. Ask for Mr. Edwards. Tell him I sent you. If you leave Meryton and promise never to come back, I'll pay for you to start a new life somewhere else."

"Why would you do that?"

Darcy ignored the question. "Nothing extravagant, mind you. But a fresh start somewhere where no one knows your name—or your father's. You'll be required to sign an agreement saying you won't ask for more money, and you'll never come back to Meryton or have contact with Sally and her family ever again, do you understand?"

Mr. Oliver simply pocketed the card and walked away.

"The offer is only good for a week!" Darcy called out. The other man ignored him, and Darcy sighed, already mentally composing the letter he'd have to send Edwards back in the London office. He wasn't sure Mr. Oliver would take him up on it, but he supposed after everything that had been revealed today, Sally and her grandparents deserved to live in the village without worrying about him wanting retribution.

With a nod to the justice of the peace, Darcy went outside and looked about for Lizzie. He spotted her standing by the carriage that had brought them to Meryton, speaking in a hushed tone to Sally and her grandparents as she gestured for them to step inside. Sally seemed reluctant at first, but whatever Lizzie had said must have convinced her, for she finally nodded and helped her grandparents into the carriage. Miss Jeffries got in with them as well, and Lizzie instructed the driver to take off.

"It looks like we're walking back to Netherfield," Charlotte said.

Darcy turned to find her standing near the door, holding Guy's leash. Mr. Thomas stood next to her. "That's all right," Darcy said. "I think I'll need a walk after all that excitement."

"That was rather shocking," Mr. Thomas confessed. "Of course, I never knew Amy Burton, but I did not expect . . . well."

"Nor did I," Darcy said. "And I doubt that we'd have been able to put any of it together if not for the coin."

"I feel awful. I didn't even think of Tom Oliver's father when you came to the vicarage to ask about missing persons."

Both Charlotte and Darcy turned to look at Mr. Thomas. "Oh?" Charlotte asked.

"I'd heard rumors that he ran off," Mr. Thomas said. "But it was so long ago, and I think I'd only heard it once from Miss Brewster and . . . well, she does like to gossip. But I never questioned it because Dr. Fellowes recorded the event in his register."

"He did?" Darcy asked. He flicked his gaze to Charlotte, who looked equally surprised. "I don't recall reading that part."

"I'm fairly positive he did," Mr. Thomas said. "I seem to remember an entry about the boy—Tom, of course—being put in care of another parish family on account of his father being unable to care for him and leaving the county."

"I must have missed that," Charlotte muttered.

"Oh, well. I suppose we know the truth of it now."

"Yes," Darcy said, watching as Lizzie slowly walked toward them. She looked tired, but when she saw the three of them standing together, she offered up a small smile and leaned down to pet Guy.

"I'm having them taken home, and I told the driver to go on to Netherfield. Hello, Mr. Thomas."

"A job well done, Miss Bennet," he said. "The both of you, really. With all that sorted, perhaps you've now lifted the so-called Netherfield curse."

Charlotte laughed softly, and even Lizzie smiled. "Perhaps," she said. "I suppose we shall see how well-attended Jane's ball is tomorrow night. I hope we'll see you there?"

Mr. Thomas assured her they would, and the conversation

shifted to lighter topics, but Darcy couldn't smile or participate. It was true, the dead man's identity had been revealed and a great deal about Netherfield's past had been explained, but Mr. Thomas's words grated at him.

The curse allegedly targeted anyone that spent a night beneath Netherfield's roof, and while Darcy was of the opinion that it was and always had been rumor and exaggeration, likely encouraged by Honoria Bingley to keep prying eyes away from Netherfield, the strange occurrences and accidents of the last week bothered him.

They'd solved the mystery of the dead man in the flue, but their questions were far from answered.

TWENTY

In Which Lizzie and Darcy Attend a Ball, with Detrimental Results

"THERE," SAID AGNES, SLIDING the last pin into Lizzie's hair. "What do you think, miss?"

"I think you're a miracle worker," Lizzie murmured as she peered into the mirror. Her normally plain appearance seemed somehow elegant thanks to the coiffure that Agnes had carefully pinned into place. "You must teach me how to do that."

"It's no trouble. The trick is twisting the hair here, and then sliding two pins crossways . . ."

She'd already lost Lizzie, but she nodded—gently, so as not to loosen her hair, although Agnes had secured it very well—and couldn't help the soft smile that played across her lips when she took in her own reflection. Unless Jane did her hair, Lizzie's style ran toward practical and simple. She didn't dare let her mother or sisters anywhere near her with an implement that had to sit near a hot fire, either. But Agnes had wielded her papillote iron with great aplomb, creating a soft halo of curls that seemed to transform her into someone who looked more grown. Sophisticated. *Beautiful.*

"So you like it, miss?"

"Oh, Agnes, I love it," she said, resisting the urge to pat the curls gently. "Thank you."

The maid smiled and began to briskly set to rights the various tools and supplies she'd used for Lizzie's coiffure. "And are you hoping to catch the eye of anyone in particular tonight?"

Lizzie laughed. "I think I'll leave the officers for my sisters to pursue."

"And what about Mr. Darcy, will he fill your dance card?"

"I think I can manage to wrangle a dance or two from him," Lizzie said, smiling.

"May I ask you something, miss?"

"Certainly," Lizzie said. Anyone who'd made her feel as pretty as she did now had earned a forward question or two.

"Are you and Mr. Darcy attached?"

"Not officially, no," Lizzie said carefully, uncertain of the maid's reason for asking.

"But unofficially?"

Lizzie winked at Agnes through the mirror. The maid simply shook her head. "I knew it. Do you think he'll ask for your hand soon?"

At that question, Lizzie felt her smile falter. "Oh, I don't know. All in good time."

The idea of marriage used to frighten Lizzie—it had felt too much like giving up her freedom, sacrificing everything she'd worked for. Even now she could imagine what the gossips would say. *You know she used to fancy herself a solicitor? Well, she married and came to her senses.* Even though Darcy understood that she wasn't going to give up her career for any reason, not even marriage, she still had a hard time imagining what a future where she was both married and a solicitor even looked like. And then there was the not-so-small matter of his father's disapproval . . .

That was hardly a romantic thought.

"Perhaps he'll be so moved by the sight of you tonight, he'll propose on the spot!" Agnes continued, oblivious to Lizzie's inner turmoil. "The ballroom is a sight to behold!"

"I can't wait to see it," Lizzie said, choosing to ignore Agnes's comment about proposals. She stood and allowed Agnes to help her carefully into her dress. "You all worked so very hard to pull this off. And this ball is very important to my sister."

"She invited unmarried gentlemen," Agnes pointed out, tightening the laces of Lizzie's dress. "It will be a success for that fact alone."

Lizzie giggled at that and then turned to get a look at herself in the mirror. She was wearing a white dress with delicate pink-and-green embroidery, and her cheeks had a natural flush to them. Agnes fussed with her skirts. "There," she said, straightening her hem. "Now, if you need me, I'll be downstairs, serving. I ought to hurry down, in fact."

"You're serving?" Lizzie asked in surprise. "I thought the valets would be doing that."

"Well, yes—that is to say, the two valets that are left," Agnes said. "The maids are helping out."

Lizzie sighed. She had hoped, perhaps naively, that solving the mystery of the body in the flue would debunk the myth of the curse, and the servants who'd quit would come back. Alas, that had yet to happen.

"Will there be enough of you tonight?" Lizzie asked.

"Oh, please don't worry about us, miss. The London staff are all hard workers, and I won't go anywhere."

"Thank goodness for that," Lizzie said. "If only the rest of them had your sense."

Agnes bobbed a quick curtsy and slipped out of the room while Lizzie surveyed the chamber, finding Guy sprawled across her bed. She went over to rub his belly, which was quite full, thanks to his friends in the kitchen. "You be good," she told him. "Don't go off anywhere with anyone."

She didn't relish the idea of leaving Guy alone, but Jane had given her a key to the room, and this was the safest place for him, short of bringing him with her to the ball. A sense of unease still hung over her when she thought about all the strange occurrences she couldn't yet explain.

"Tomorrow," she whispered to herself. "Tomorrow you must come clean to Papa about Lady Catherine."

But for now, she had a ball to attend.

She locked the door behind her, slipped the key into the pocket of her dress, and hurried toward the sound of voices and music that floated up from below. At the top of the stairs stood a tall, sharply cut figure in evening wear. As she approached, he turned, and Lizzie smiled to see Darcy. He took her in and laid his right hand over his heart, as if the sight of her were too much for him. "Mr. Darcy," she said, dipping into a small curtsy.

"Miss Bennet," he said with a bow. "You look . . . stunning."

Her smile grew as his words sent a thrill down her spine. "And you look quite handsome yourself. What are you doing up here?"

"Waiting to escort you, of course," he said, offering her his arm.

"How chivalrous," she said, taking it. "And that has nothing to do with the fact that you don't want to face all those people on your own?"

He grimaced. "I believe every eligible young lady in the county is here."

"Darcy, you've faced down murderers and thieves and villains of all sorts, but you're afraid of young ladies?"

"Terrified," he confirmed. He leaned in closer and whispered into her ear, "And even more intimidated by their mothers."

Lizzie laughed, leaning into Darcy. She wanted to enjoy tonight—for all of the things that she and Darcy had seen and undergone together, they'd never been to a ball together. And maybe she was a little romantic after all, or maybe it was the flickering of hundreds of candles in the foyer below and the strain of music from the ballroom, but she felt lighter than she had in days. Weeks. Then she looked into Darcy's eyes and realized no, it wasn't the setting—it was he. Darcy was the one who made her feel as though she didn't have to fight to prove herself. He saw her exactly as she was, and he made her laugh, and he was always there.

"What are you thinking right now?" he whispered.

That I want you to kiss me, she thought. *And never stop.*

But before she could say anything reckless, a door slammed somewhere behind them. She and Darcy startled, and Lizzie took a half step back, turning to see Caroline coming around the corner, dressed in an exquisite peacock-blue dress and looking extremely annoyed.

"Well, are we going down or not?" she demanded.

Lizzie tilted her head to Darcy, and he sighed and offered an arm to each of them. "Be nice," he reminded Caroline as they glided down the stairs.

"Darcy, the sooner Charles and Jane give up on trying to impress these country bumpkins, the sooner I get back to London," she muttered under her breath. "I don't give one fig about being *nice*."

"Eloquent as always, Caroline," Lizzie said.

"Don't pretend you're any happier here than I, Lizzie Bennet," Caroline said as they reached the bottom of the stairs. "I know you're just dying to go home."

Then she extricated herself from Darcy and glided away, slipping between guests as she made her way to the ballroom.

"I've a new theory," Lizzie whispered. "Do we think that Caroline is perpetuating the rumors about this place being cursed in order to get herself back to London faster?"

"Don't give her any ideas," Darcy said.

They made their way through the foyer, where Jane and Bingley stood greeting guests as they arrived, and to the ballroom, which was down a short hall to the left of the front door. The room seemed to glow from the hall, and when Lizzie and Darcy stepped into the space, Lizzie caught her breath.

The ballroom had been transformed.

The wood floors were polished to a high gleam, and gone was the musty smell of air being shut up for too long. Lively musicians played along the far wall, and everywhere Lizzie looked, the people of Meryton were chattering animatedly. Above them all, the giant chandelier cast a brilliant, shining light down on the guests from dozens of lit candles. The overall effect was cheerful and inviting, with an undercurrent of excitement.

Lizzie spotted the ladies from the haberdashery, including Mrs. Fitzgerald and two tall, wide-eyed young women who could only be her daughters. Clara Jeffries stood near the edge of the dance floor, staring up at the chandelier. And Mr. Thomas was deep in conversation with Charlotte, who looked especially lovely in a saffron-colored dress. Lizzie smiled and nudged Darcy. "Look," she whispered, nodding in their direction. "Mr. Thomas seems quite taken with Charlotte."

"Taken?" Darcy repeated. "You mean . . ."

"Perhaps. She deserves someone nice, don't you think? And he seems nice."

"Mr. Thomas, though?" Darcy asked.

"Do you think her not good enough for him?" Lizzie felt her voice rise in defensiveness, but she didn't care.

"On the contrary—I wonder if he is good enough for her."

"Well said," Lizzie said. Then she spotted another familiar figure—her mother, headed straight toward her.

"Quick, ask me to dance," she murmured.

"Lizzie, I don't—"

"It's either that or talk to my mother!"

Darcy didn't hesitate. "May I have this dance?"

"You may."

Lizzie placed her hand in his and he swept her out onto the ballroom floor so they could join the country dance that was just beginning. Lizzie caught a glimpse of her mother's exasperation before she was pulled into the movements.

Darcy stood across from her, watching the leading couple, waiting for their turn to take the next steps. How serious he looked! If she did not know him, she'd have thought him very unpleasant indeed. He seemed intent on completing the dance in utter silence, so when he drew close to her again, she remarked, "There are a great many more people here than I thought there would be."

"Indeed," he replied.

She cast a small, surreptitious look about the room. There were a good number of red-coated officers in attendance. "I imagine Lydia and Kitty are over the moon to have so many opportunities to dance."

"I imagine so."

Now she had to work at not rolling her eyes. "It's your turn to say something now, Darcy. I made a remark about the dance and the number of couples, now you may say something perhaps about the room."

"The room is . . . very large," he allowed.

"If that is all you have, perhaps we'd better remain silent."

"Is it a rule that we must speak while dancing?"

"One must speak a little, you know. It would look odd spending the next half hour together, totally silent. People might think that you don't like me very much."

He waited to deliver his reply until they stepped together in close proximity and he was obliged to take her hand. "They would be very wrong," he murmured.

Lizzie's cheeks flushed, and she bit her bottom lip to keep from grinning outright. Darcy's intense gaze followed her as she glided across the ballroom, stepping apart from him and crossing other couples, but always coming back. His touch scorched her skin, and the rest of the ballroom seemed to drop away. Perhaps people imagined they were courting, and wondered as Agnes had when he'd ask her to marry him. But to think of Darcy as merely her suitor . . . no, he was more, so much more. He was her partner in detection and the first person she wanted to tell when there was a new development in a case. He looked out for her safety and protected her—even if she didn't want to admit she needed protecting. And he listened to her and never walked away, even when she was being truly obstinate. She had known for a while now that she loved him, but now as they danced together, she knew with a startling clarity: She was in love with him, and she wanted to do this—dance with him and solve mysteries with him, tease him and argue with him—for the rest of her days.

The music came to an end and Lizzie stood there, staring at him, while the other couples clapped and conversation picked up around him. It was in that weakened state that her mother pounced.

"Elizabeth! I was waiting for you to come down and you were late, but never mind. I've been having Jane introduce me to as many people as possible, and have you seen how many young gentlemen are here? Officers, Lizzie!"

"I—" Lizzie started to say, but her mother continued.

"Now, you cannot dance with one gentleman all evening. Mr. Darcy, I know you don't mean to commandeer my daughter when there have been no intentions stated between you two?"

Lizzie wanted to shout, stomp her foot at the idea of Darcy asking another young lady to dance, but this was a ball. It was what was done. They could get away with one more dance, perhaps. But three dances and Mrs. Bennet would resume talking about an engagement.

Was it wrong that Lizzie almost didn't mind, if it meant she got to keep holding on to Darcy's hand?

"Of course not," Darcy said, releasing Lizzie. She missed the warmth of his touch immediately. "Although I hope you'll save another dance for me later, Miss Bennet."

"Later," Mrs. Bennet said, pulling Lizzie away. "Now come along, I've got at least three officers I can introduce you to . . ."

Lizzie was dragged unwillingly across the room, where she

was introduced to a number of people whose names she promptly forgot. Her renown in Meryton for saving the Burtons from jail had spread, and she found herself nodding politely as many people gave her their opinions on the Burtons' innocence or guilt. However, when an officer by the name of Mr. Spotswold remarked that a lady couldn't possibly understand the complexities of criminal law, Lizzie didn't even feel like putting him in his place. Instead, she plastered on a fake smile and said, "Excuse me, I'm afraid I'm feeling faint."

She pulled away from the cluster of conversation and began weaving aimlessly through the crowd, ignoring her mother hissing her name behind her. Everything felt warm and close, and she wanted to look for Darcy. She wanted to be back on the dance floor with him. Or even better, on the outskirts of the room, away from the press of bodies.

Instead, she found herself nearly in the center, at the edge of the dance floor. A pocket of space allowed her a moment to pause and think about her next steps as she watched the minuet. She spotted Jane and Bingley, and Charlotte dancing with Mr. Thomas. Darcy was dancing with Clara Jeffries, and Lydia was grinning as she danced opposite a red-coated young man who looked as though he was having trouble keeping up with her.

"It's gauche, is it not?" came a voice to her left, and she turned to find Caroline standing not three feet away, also watching the dancers.

Irritation flared up in her and Lizzie couldn't help the words that spilled out. "It is not, and you know it. Besides, I seem to recall a similar dance at a ball where you danced quite happily with a certain red-haired gentleman."

"The same dance you followed me to?" Caroline asked. "Because you thought that I'd framed my own brother for murdering my sister's husband?"

"Well, I didn't know you very well then."

Caroline did the unthinkable: She *laughed*. "And you know me so much better now?"

"Well enough to say that you'd never hurt your brother," Lizzie admitted. She paused, and then realized that perhaps half the chilliness between her and Caroline was her fault. After all, she'd never made much of an attempt at smoothing things over with her following that incident. She'd been too consumed with the case and all that she'd learned that night—the night she'd met Lady Catherine for the first time. "I won't apologize for what I did—I was simply following my instincts and eliminating suspects. But I recognize now that doing so was . . . well. What I'm trying to say is, if I caused any difficulties in your life because of what I did, I am sorry for *that*."

Caroline raised a single brow. "Are you?"

Goodness, why couldn't she just accept an apology? Lizzie was tempted to throw up her hands and walk away. But she couldn't—Jane was married to Bingley now, which meant that Caroline, for better or worse, was Lizzie's relation, too.

"Yes," Lizzie said. "Whatever happened to your dance partner, anyway?"

“That’s none of your concern,” Caroline replied tartly.

So much for extending an olive branch.

Lizzie turned back to the dancers. Even with the officers, there were still far more ladies than gentlemen in attendance, and many of them milled about, chattering and watching the dancing. Around the perimeter of the room, servants moved unobtrusively, serving drinks, picking up glasses, and fetching fans. The mood was excited and happy, and Lizzie saw Jane’s smiling face flash by. The ball was a success.

“It’s a nice ball,” Caroline said suddenly. “Jane managed to pull it off.”

Lizzie glanced at Caroline, shocked. “She did, didn’t she?”

“She’s very good at these sorts of things. Planning events, making people feel welcome. I am glad that she married my brother, despite whatever else—”

But Lizzie never got to hear what Caroline was going to say next, because an ominous creaking sound made her look up. Standing as they were in the center of the ballroom, the enormous chandelier was directly overhead. It swayed gently, and she felt something sting her arm. She looked down—candle wax.

She didn’t understand, just then. Not until another creak sounded, so loud that almost everyone could hear it above the music, and a ripple of gasps broke out around the room. And then the candles in the chandelier began to tip and snuff out, their hot wax falling like scalding rain and causing several ladies to shriek in shock and pain. Lizzie heard Caroline shout

"Look out!" and felt a hard, sharp shove to her ribs. The push knocked the air out of her lungs and sent her flying across the floor, where she tripped over her own skirts and fell to the ground . . .

Just as the great chandelier came crashing down on the spot where she had been standing.

TWENTY-ONE

In Which Lizzie and Darcy Come Clean

SCREAMS RIPPED THROUGH THE ballroom as Darcy dropped Miss Jeffries's hand and ran from the dance floor toward where he'd seen Lizzie just moments earlier. People were scattering every which way, and Darcy had to shove his way through, not caring who he bumped into. All he cared about was Lizzie. Lizzie, who'd been standing beneath the chandelier. Lizzie, whom he could no longer see.

"Lizzie!" he shouted. Most of the candles had been extinguished in the fall, leaving the room suddenly much dimmer than it had been only moments earlier. Candle smoke wafted in the air lazily as Darcy searched. "Lizzie!"

"Here," came her voice, and he spun around to find her on the floor just beyond the chandelier, hem ripped and skirts splattered with candle wax.

He strode over to her and fell to his knees. "Oh, thank God!"

"She pushed me," Lizzie sputtered. "I bet she's been wanting to do that for a year at least, but she didn't have to . . ."

Lizzie's voice trailed off as she looked beyond him, and Darcy turned to see what had caused the color to drain from Lizzie's face. She scrambled to her feet and ran to where the chandelier had fallen. It lay like a felled beast in the middle of the ballroom, and beneath it was a pile of peacock blue . . .

Caroline.

"Help!" Lizzie yelled. "Someone call for a doctor!"

Caroline was beneath the chandelier. The outer edge of the behemoth had knocked her flat. Blood pooled underneath her, soaking into the brilliant blue of her gown. Lizzie's hand went to her neck and horror overtook Darcy. He felt as though he were watching the scene from outside his body, as if it were a dream. But then Lizzie turned and said, "I think she's breathing—Darcy, help me get her out from under this thing!"

He lurched into action, reaching for the frame. He lifted it a few inches, wincing at the musical clink of all the crystals sliding about. It was enough for Lizzie to drag Caroline out from under the weight of the felled chandelier. She ripped at the hem of her already torn dress for a wad of fabric to stop the bleeding—Darcy could see now the terrible gash on the side of Caroline's head, turning her blond hair dark red. But Lizzie's bandage wasn't enough. He dropped the chandelier with a loud *thunk* and shrugged off his jacket. "Here," he said, wadding it up and handing it to Lizzie.

"Caroline!"

Darcy looked up to find Bingley running toward them, panic

on his face. He dropped to his knees and reached out to his sister. "No, no, no—Caroline, can you hear me?"

Behind Bingley, Jane appeared. Her hands flew to her mouth when she saw the amount of blood on the ballroom floor, and she turned and ran for help.

All around them, guests were fleeing. A few lingered, watching wide-eyed in shock, but then the whispers started up. Darcy heard more than one person say the word *curse*, and he shuddered. This was the third accident to befall their party since they'd arrived at Netherfield Park.

Either he'd have to start believing in curses, or someone in the house wished them ill.

"She's breathing," Lizzie assured a panicked Bingley. "Let's get her up."

Darcy and Bingley lifted Caroline and Lizzie held Darcy's jacket to the wound on her head. They carefully maneuvered around the spilled candles and stray crystals that had broken off from the chandelier, out of the ballroom and into the foyer, where guests were pouring out the door. They headed for the stairs, and Charlotte ran up to join them. "Mr. Thomas has gone on his horse to fetch the doctor," she said. "And I ran to the kitchens and told Sally to bring up bandages and hot water."

They got Caroline to her bedroom and into bed, and Jane came up with bandages herself. "The guests?" Bingley asked her.

"Forget the guests," Jane said. "They're all running home as fast as they can, convinced that this place is well and truly cursed. How is she?"

"Alive," Lizzie said, looking up to meet Darcy's eyes. He could hear the words she didn't want to say: *For now.*

While the ladies tended to Caroline's wound, Bingley paced and Darcy stood next to him, feeling utterly useless. It seemed to take an age for the doctor to arrive, and Caroline neither stirred nor woke as they waited. Her breathing had settled into a shallow rhythm, but it was a rhythm nonetheless. Sally eventually brought in hot water, and her eyes widened at the sight of all the blood. Not long after, the men were shooed out so the ladies could change Caroline's blood-soaked dress into a fresh nightdress.

"I can't lose her," Bingley whispered as they stood out in the hall.

"You won't," Darcy said, clapping a hand on his friend's shoulder. Of course, he had no way of knowing that for certain. But what else was he supposed to say?

"This place is a death trap," Bingley muttered. "Curse or no curse, I think we all ought to leave and not come back until I've had every bit of it inspected. I suppose one should never look a gift horse in the mouth, but I am starting to wish Honoria had never left it to us."

"Gentlemen." Darcy and Bingley turned to find Mr. Bennet striding toward them. He wore a serious expression, which was not unusual for him, but there was something about this particular look, and his purposeful march, that made the hair on the back of Darcy's neck stand up. "How is she?"

"Alive for now," Bingley said. "We're waiting for the doctor."

Mr. Bennet nodded gravely. Then he said, "There's something you ought to come see."

He led them downstairs. The foyer was empty, the last of the guests having fled into the night, and the double doors leading into the ballroom were thrown open to reveal the chandelier at the center of the room, tilted over on the floor. Caroline's blood stained the parquet, and small crystals were scattered about. Around the ballroom, empty glasses were abandoned and chairs were tipped over. But Mr. Bennet didn't point to the wreckage in the room—instead, he led them to the side of the room, where, concealed by a velvet drape, the crank to the chandelier protruded from the wall.

"Look at this," he said.

Darcy saw instantly what he was referring to: One end of a tattered rope hung limply from the crank. Darcy stepped forward and took a closer look, picking up the broken end. He spent a long, silent moment staring at it.

"This rope was cut," he said. The end was not frayed or torn, like it would be if the rope had simply given out or the weight of the chandelier had been wearing on the fibers over time. The cut was clean. The type of cut that had been done with a knife.

"I believe so, yes," Mr. Bennet said tersely.

"But what . . . how . . ." Bingley appeared incapable of speech, so great was his shock. "Why would anyone do this?"

"That's precisely what I would like to know." Darcy had never heard Mr. Bennet speak in such a foreboding manner, and it caused a shiver of apprehension to run through him. He stared at Darcy, as if he could guess at the secret he was keeping.

"Mr. Bennet," Darcy said. "I can explain—"

"Father?"

They turned to find Lizzie at the door, looking after them suspiciously. She was still wearing her torn, blood-smeared gown, and it had an absolutely garish effect.

"Lizzie," Mr. Bennet said, taking the end of the cut rope from Darcy's hand, "I would like to know why someone cut through the rope that was holding that chandelier in place."

Lizzie went pale and approached them slowly, looking at the rope in her father's hand as if it were a live snake.

"This place really is cursed," Bingley said, looking up at the ceiling where the chandelier had hung not an hour earlier.

"I don't believe in curses," Lizzie said.

"Then how do you explain this?" her father asked.

"You don't think Sally . . ." Bingley trailed off.

"I didn't see her," Darcy said. "Did any of you?"

They all shook their heads. Lizzie added, "She was below-stairs tonight, to avoid gossip. But I don't think she would do this to us—we saved her grandparents from jail."

"Then who?" Mr. Bennet asked again.

Darcy looked to Lizzie. It was her secret to tell. And judging by her horrified expression, he guessed she was regretting having kept it.

"Who else?" she said with a tired sigh.

Mr. Bennet needed no guesses. "Lady Catherine?" he asked,

incredulous. Both Darcy and Lizzie nodded, and Mr. Bennet's expression darkened. "Explain."

In halting sentences, Lizzie recounted the note she'd received nearly a week earlier. Mr. Bennet took the news in with a stoic expression, and when she'd finished, he turned to Darcy. "And you knew about this?"

"Yes, sir."

"And you didn't think to inform me?"

Darcy forced himself to meet Mr. Bennet's eyes. He read anger in there, but disappointment, too. The disappointment was what stung the most, because unlike when his own father was disappointed in him, Darcy cared very much about Mr. Bennet respecting him. He swallowed. "Lizzie asked me not to."

"Papa, it's not his fault—"

Mr. Bennet held up his hand, and she went quiet. "You both decided to keep this to yourself, knowing full well that Lady Catherine is dangerous and has made threats against us all. And in the face of multiple unsettling accidents and events, you decided to hold your tongues." He paused and shook his head. "What *possibly* could have possessed you?"

"I wanted to find out who the dead man was," Lizzie said, her voice small. "And I wanted to find the killer and restore Jane's reputation amongst her new neighbors. I thought if we told you, you'd insist on leaving and that would only anger her. I had every intention of telling you everything tomorrow . . ."

Darcy had never seen Lizzie so defeated before. He took her hand and squeezed it.

"Lady Catherine has infiltrated Netherfield Park?" Bingley asked. "But how?"

"I don't know, and I don't care," Mr. Bennet said. "We must leave immediately."

"I can't move Caroline," Bingley said. "You saw what state she's in."

"It's me she wants," Lizzie said miserably. "Everyone can stay here. I'll go."

"Nonsense. We will all go to your aunt and uncle Gardiner's. I wrote to them of our troubles, and they've already extended an invitation—"

"No." Lizzie gently withdrew her hand from Darcy's. "I won't go anywhere I might endanger more people I love. You and Mama and the girls should go to them, though. And Bingley, I'm truly sorry. I think you ought to send away all the servants except those absolutely necessary. Only keep those you trust."

Alarm spread through Darcy. "Lizzie, where do you plan on going?"

"I've given it some thought, and the Dashwoods have a spare room in their shop for me. I can keep a low profile while we—"

"No," Darcy and Mr. Bennet said at the same time.

"You're not venturing out alone, not with that madwoman at large!" Mr. Bennet said.

Don't leave me, Darcy thought selfishly. But was it selfish to want to face whatever was ahead with her by his side?

"Where would you have me go that's safe, Papa?" Lizzie asked. "I wouldn't trust a sea voyage—Lady Catherine has too many connections aboard vessels, and who knows where her spies might be?"

"Perhaps Scotland—"

"Scotland!" Lizzie cried.

"You don't have to go to Scotland," Darcy said. "You don't have to leave the country at all."

"Well, I certainly don't want to go into hiding, Darcy, but—"

"Come to Pemberley."

The words felt right the instant he spoke them. Everyone turned to look at him. "Pemberley is safe. I would trust everyone on the staff with my life, and Mrs. Reynolds knows everyone who works under her—there's not a chance that Lady Catherine could infiltrate Pemberley. We'd be far from London but still in somewhat easy contact with Graves, and we can strategize our next move in safety."

"Pemberley," Lizzie repeated. "But Darcy, your father—"

"Forget my father," he said. "I don't care what he thinks. I only care about your safety."

"I don't like the idea of you going off alone," Mr. Bennet told his daughter.

"Oh, Papa," she said. She crossed the few steps between him and took his hands in hers. "I'm not a little girl. Lady Catherine isn't going to forget me because I've managed to evade her. I know you're scared for me, but please. Let me try to catch her before it's too late."

Mr. Bennet was not a man of many words, but Darcy witnessed an array of warring emotions crossing his face—anger and sadness, stubborn resistance, and defeat. What must it be like to have a father who cared as much as Mr. Bennet cared for Lizzie? And not only cared for her but respected her. If Darcy were to ever become a father, he'd only be so lucky to be like Mr. Bennet.

"All right," Lizzie's father said, clapping a hand on her shoulder. "But you must promise me—"

"I'll be careful," she said, and hugged her father. "Thank you, Papa."

When her father finally released her, Darcy lowered his voice, casting a glance around the empty ballroom, strewn with the detritus of an evening gone awry. "We don't know who might be watching us. But if Lady Catherine or one of her spies is in the house, then we must attempt to deflect attention. Send Mrs. Bennet and the girls to the Gardiners', and send a carriage back to London. I'll leave for Pemberley, but make as if going elsewhere—Bath, perhaps. Pull the curtains of all the carriages and keep it secret which one Lizzie takes. It likely won't fool Lady Catherine forever, but it might buy us time."

"What about Georgiana?" Lizzie asked. "I don't want her to get hurt."

"Pemberley is safe, trust me. Even if word gets out that you're there, the staff can be trusted. We won't let anyone on the grounds. My father has more than just servants at Pemberley to watch over Georgiana, and they can keep you safe, too."

He looked into her eyes and thought what he wanted to say: *Don't leave me. Let me stand by your side. Let's fight her together.*

"I have to say, I like Darcy's plan far better than yours," Mr. Bennet said gruffly. "The Dashwood sisters are no wilting lilies, but what sort of protection can they offer you?"

Darcy expected Lizzie to protest. She was awfully loyal to her friends.

"However," her father continued, "it is your choice."

Lizzie held herself very still. Her eyes were fixed beyond them, on the fallen chandelier.

"All right," she said finally. "Let us go to Pemberley."

TWENTY-TWO

In Which Lizzie and Darcy Arrive at Pemberley

LIZZIE HAD BEEN VERY curious about Darcy's ancestral home, but she had not imagined that the first time she caught a glimpse of it would be after two long days of hard travel with a broken heart and a guilty conscience weighing her down.

They'd left in the early-morning hours after the ball, after some quick hushed discussions behind closed doors. Three carriages had been dispatched in three different directions. One went south to London, one east to the Gardiners' home, and one north to Pemberley. Charlotte's and Lizzie's trunks had been sent on the carriage bound for London, which had briefly stopped in the woods outside the estate so the two young ladies could disembark quickly with nothing but a valise each and Guy on his leash. They waited in the shadows, jumping at every small sound, until Darcy's carriage came rattling by and picked them up before whisking them north.

Lizzie had been grateful that when she had finally revealed the truth to her friend, Charlotte had opted to come with her to

Pemberley rather than return to London. She felt more at ease knowing that Charlotte was safe, but Charlotte, for her part, wasn't very pleased that Lizzie had elected to keep her note from Lady Catherine secret. She wasn't so petty as to give Lizzie the cold shoulder, but she was quiet the entire journey.

And Lizzie deserved this, she knew. She had chosen selfishly, putting a case above her friends and family. She was glad she'd been able to help the Burtons, and she could tell herself that she'd pursued the truth to help Jane, but it wasn't entirely true. She'd done so because she believed she'd known best.

And now she deserved the immense guilt she felt whenever she remembered Caroline shoving her to the floor seconds before the chandelier had fallen. *Caroline*, of all people! She ought to have let Lizzie take the chandelier on the head while she skipped away from the danger. To be sure, it would be Lizzie lying in a room in Netherfield, waiting to recover, but at least then the world would still make sense.

It was late in the afternoon on their second day of travel when Darcy leaned forward and peeked out of the curtains of the carriage. "We're close," he said, and there was no mistaking the eagerness in his voice.

"Thank heavens," Charlotte murmured, waving limply at her face with her fan.

They'd endured the entire journey with the curtains closed tight against prying eyes. Lizzie had wondered if the precaution was a bit much once they were a day away from Netherfield Park, but Darcy had remained strict, not wanting to risk anyone spotting Lizzie on her way north when she was supposed to be in London. As a result, the air in the carriage was hot and oppressive, and even poor Guy whined softly and panted on the floorboards.

But now the carriage slowed, and Lizzie leaned forward to gather Guy's leash as it came to a halt. "Not yet," Darcy said. "Stay here."

He jumped out of the carriage and Lizzie called, "What's the matter?" after him. But he didn't respond, and beyond the door she saw only woods. Lizzie and Charlotte exchanged puzzled looks. Guy sat up and gave one impatient woof.

Darcy was back after a quick conversation that Lizzie couldn't make out. "Is everything all right?"

"Everything is perfect," he said, grinning. It was the first time Lizzie had seen him smile since the night of the ball. "I had to speak with Travers, the gatekeeper."

"You have a gatekeeper?" Lizzie asked, incredulous. She pulled the curtain aside, caution be damned. There was indeed a small stone gatehouse, and an elaborate wrought-iron gate was slowly being opened. She heard hoofbeats and caught a glimpse of a lone rider taking off ahead of them.

"I told you that my father hired men to make sure Georgie was safe," Darcy said. "They'll ride ahead and let the house know we're here."

Lizzie was, for once, speechless. She had known that Darcy was wealthy. She had not understood that his family estate was surrounded by a great stone wall with a gate and a gatekeeper.

Multiple gatekeepers, it seemed, judging by the fact that there was an extra man and horse ready to ride ahead and warn the household of their impending arrival.

Once they passed through the gates and Lizzie heard them clank shut behind the carriage, Darcy threw open the curtains. All three of them blinked at the sudden light, and Guy hopped up on Lizzie's lap, pressing his nose against the glass.

The entrance to the estate was lightly wooded, and they drove through it for some time before the land gave way to green and gold countryside. Lizzie could feel the slight incline of the road beneath them, which added to her growing anticipation as the carriage crested the first hill.

Lizzie gasped.

From a gap in the trees lining the lane, Pemberley loomed in the distance.

In an instant, Lizzie understood how Darcy had considered Netherfield simply "well appointed." Pemberley, in comparison, was palatial. It had been constructed upon a gentle rise, and it was backed by wooded hills. As they drew closer, Lizzie could hear the insistent bubbling of the river that ran before the house. The sloping lawn between the river and the house was a vibrant green, with a well-kept walking path that led to the water. There were no excessive adornments on the front of the house, and the simplicity of its presentation made it all the more striking in Lizzie's eyes. What were the creations of humankind to the brilliance of their natural surroundings?

The carriage rolled over a stone bridge that spanned the river, and Pemberley was suddenly before them. Lizzie could scarcely breathe, she was so taken by the wonder of the estate. She tore her gaze away from the scene just long enough to look at Darcy. If all of this belonged to her, she'd been drinking up the sight of home. But Darcy wasn't looking out the window.

He was looking at her.

"What do you think?" he asked.

Lizzie opened her mouth to respond, but words failed her. She thought it was glorious, magnificent. She wanted to know how Darcy ever managed to leave it behind for London.

In that moment, she felt that to be mistress of Pemberley might be something!

But Darcy wasn't asking her to be mistress—he was asking her what she thought. And now even Charlotte was glancing at her with barely suppressed amusement at her lack of speech.

"It's truly beautiful," she managed.

"I'm glad you think so." Darcy's gaze was soft, and she felt something shift inside her. But before she could dwell on it, the carriage finally came to a halt in front of the house, and a footman opened the door.

Guy darted out, and the humans followed. Lizzie inhaled the sweet air, wanting to drink it all in. The view from the house was even more incredible, she found, as she turned and looked at the lawn spread out before them, and the water glistened in the sunshine. From this standpoint, one could see it wind its way through the valley like a shining ribbon.

"I don't think I've ever been so happy to be out of a carriage in my life," Charlotte remarked to her.

"Yes," Lizzie agreed. She was still dazed. Then she looked about. "Where's Guy? Guy!"

"He's all right," Darcy said, pointing to where the small dog was running happy laps in the nearby grass, dragging his leash behind him. "He's safe here."

The words, although directed at Guy, stirred something in Lizzie. *She* felt safe here.

A butler appeared from the front door. "Sir," he said, bowing slightly to Darcy.

"Charleston!" Darcy greeted, shaking his butler's hand. "It's been too long."

"We're very happy to see you," the butler said, offering a sidelong glance at the ladies. "Mrs. Reynolds will be along shortly."

"I'm sure I've thrown off her entire day. She needn't worry about everything being perfect. We are just happy to be here."

"Oh, she'll worry," Charleston said. "But she's glad you're here nonetheless. And I'm sure she won't be the only one."

"You're here!" came a screech from the front door, and Lizzie saw only a blur of a girl with dark brown hair hurling herself at Darcy. He caught her up in a giant hug and swung her around while she squealed in excitement. Finally, Darcy set her down, and Georgiana Darcy grinned up at him. She wore a plain day dress, and her hair fell loose in tangled, wild curls. She shoved

Darcy in jest. "Why didn't you write and tell me you were coming? If you wanted it to be a surprise, you managed that well."

"Is this what you're getting up to while I'm away?" Darcy tossed back. "Running around, half feral? I thought your lady's companion would keep you civilized."

Georgiana rolled her eyes dramatically. "Mrs. Watts is in bed with a headache, per usual. I've been dying for some proper companionship, and now you're here!" She reached out a hand to greet Lizzie warmly. "Welcome, Miss Bennet!"

"Please, at this point I feel as though you ought to call me Lizzie," she said, squeezing the other girl's hand. "We ought to have come much sooner."

Lizzie introduced Charlotte, and Georgiana welcomed her just as warmly before Darcy called Guy over. Georgiana was taken with the dog immediately, and earned his affection by rubbing his belly and calling him handsome before Darcy suggested, with a slightly nervous edge to his voice, that they go inside. Lizzie knew his edginess from their most recent ordeal would not fade away quickly.

Lizzie tried not to let her gaze stray as they passed through the intimidating halls adorned with tapestries and portraits. Georgiana chattered all the way as she led them past many formal rooms to a charming sitting room with comfortable furniture and a pianoforte in the corner. The windows were open, letting in a light breeze, and the view overlooked the river. They took a seat, and Guy immediately jumped up on the chair next to Georgiana.

"Guy, no," Lizzie said.

Georgiana laughed. "He is perfectly fine on the furniture—in fact, I adore him. We'll be best of friends, won't we, Guy?"

The dog settled in his seat and gave Lizzie a look that seemed to say, *So there.* Lizzie found herself quite incapable of protesting.

"Now, how long do you intend to stay?" Georgiana asked. "Please tell me a very long time."

Was it Lizzie's imagination, or was there an emphasis on *very long time* that seemed . . . suspicious?

"I don't know," Darcy said. "A few weeks, at least. Perhaps longer."

Lizzie tried to muster a smile. As beautiful as this place was, his words were a reminder of what they'd left behind, and the reason for their visit.

"What's the matter?" Georgiana asked.

Lizzie looked at Darcy. He winced, and said, "Well, I'm afraid things at Netherfield did not go well."

Georgiana promptly rang for a maid. "Then we shall have tea, and you can tell me all about it."

The last thing Lizzie wanted to do was drag Darcy's sister into this mess, but despite being younger than Lizzie, Georgiana Darcy was no child. After all, she'd proven herself more than capable last year in London. And once the tea arrived—with little cakes, and even cold roast pheasant cut up into small pieces for Guy—it was easy to tell her the whole tale. Georgiana listened, eyes wide, and interjected only a few times with clarifying questions. Her hand flew to her mouth when she learned of Caroline's injury, and by the time the telling was over, she was less lighthearted and more concerned.

"You absolutely did the right thing to bring her here," Georgiana told Darcy. "Pemberley is the safest place in all the world."

"Kew Palace might be a bit more secure, but she's right," Darcy told Lizzie. "You saw the stone wall coming in, and while the grounds are large, we are fairly isolated. I already instructed the gatekeeper not to let anyone in after us. I'll speak with Charleston about further safety measures."

"Thank you," Lizzie said to both siblings. "I hate to be a bother—"

"You're not," Georgiana insisted. "Really, this is the most interesting thing to happen since the last time we met."

Lizzie felt herself finally relax for a moment. The trip to Pemberley had been grim, and the shame and guilt she felt still clung to her. But here, perhaps, she could shed some fear and begin to strategize her next move. They'd find a way to draw out Lady Catherine without endangering any more people Lizzie cared for . . .

Suddenly, Georgiana looked uncertain. "There's just one thing I haven't mentioned yet, and I'm guessing since you haven't either, you don't know?"

"What is it?" Darcy asked, instantly concerned.

"It's probably nothing to worry about. I'm sure everything will be fine, and it shouldn't impact this plan at all . . . or rather, not too much . . ."

Lizzie and Charlotte exchanged perplexed glances, and Darcy sighed. "Just spell it out, Georgie."

"It's Father." She winced as she looked at her brother's confused expression. "I received a letter from him this morning. He's back in London, and he's furious that you're not there."

"Father is in England?" Darcy asked. "I knew he intended to return home soon, but I thought he'd be several more weeks at least."

"Apparently not." Georgiana rose and walked over to a small writing desk where she withdrew a letter with a heavy green seal, broken. She handed it to her brother and Darcy skimmed it. It was short—Lizzie knew the elder Mr. Darcy was not known for his loquaciousness.

Unease settled across her. Suddenly, coming to Pemberley was feeling less and less like a good idea.

"He took an earlier boat," Darcy muttered.

"What should we do?" Lizzie asked.

"Not a thing," Darcy said, crumpling the letter up. "I imagine he'll find his way here soon enough. Until then, all we can do is wait."

Georgiana's smile was stiff compared to what it had been just moments earlier, but she attempted to play off the awkwardness. "Charlotte, Lizzie, tomorrow I shall show you all of Pemberley. You'll love it here, I promise. We can have picnics along the river and pick berries in the gardens, and oh—do you ride?"

"Not well," Lizzie said honestly.

"All right, then we'll leave the horses. But wait until you see the library—"

Lizzie smiled and nodded to everything Georgiana said, but her heart was racing. Darcy's father had returned to England. He was coming here. She'd likely encounter him in just a few days' time.

If given the choice, she wasn't sure whom she dreaded facing more: Lady Catherine, or Darcy's father.

TWENTY-THREE

In Which Darcy and Georgiana Have a Heart-to-Heart

IT WAS GLORIOUS BEING home.

Darcy hadn't spent a night at Pemberley in nearly a year, and he'd forgotten, as he always did when he went away, just how much he loved it here. It wasn't just the fine house, or the familiar servants who'd known him since he was a boy, or how the bustle of London seemed very far when he was here—it was also being back with Georgiana once more. He felt proud and strangely sad to see how much she'd grown in their time apart. Despite her casual appearance when they'd first arrived, she poured the tea expertly and made brilliant and witty conversation with Lizzie and Charlotte. She efficiently saw that they were put up in comfortable rooms, informed the cook that there would be three additional people at dinner, and when she heard that they'd both arrived with little more than a change of clothes, she immediately saw to having spare clothing and garments placed in their rooms.

Darcy knew his sister hadn't been a child for a long time, but it was strange to realize she was a young lady now. Strange, but nice.

Given the strenuousness of their journey and their quick flight from Netherfield, Lizzie and Charlotte opted to turn in early after dinner, and Lizzie whisked Guy along with her. Darcy had a serious word with Charleston and Mrs. Reynolds in the library about the secrecy of Lizzie's presence and the need for caution, and he was walking toward the stairs, contemplating just how comfortable his bed here was, when he felt a poke in his ribs and turned to find Georgiana looking at him with something like mischief in her eyes.

"Brother. I think we need to talk."

He looked down the hall, where Charleston was instructing a footman. "Now?"

She rolled her eyes. "Unless you have more pressing business to tend to?"

He smiled. "All right. The grotto?"

Georgiana wrinkled her nose. "It's dark."

He looked out the window. It was a beautiful summer evening, and the sky was dusky, with pinpricks of stars beginning to dot the night sky. "Are you afraid?"

Indignation flashed across her face. "No, but you are."

"I'm afraid of dark, closed-in spaces," he corrected. "There's a difference—"

"Race you there!"

Georgiana took off down the hall, pulling up her skirts so

she could run. He rolled his eyes toward the ceiling. All right, she might be grown-up looking, but that didn't stop her from still behaving like a ten-year-old. "Didn't your lady's companion teach you it's impolite for a lady to run?" he called after her.

"I'm sure she would if she could catch me!"

Darcy took off after Georgiana, slipping out a back door to the gardens behind Pemberley. Georgiana eschewed the perfectly serviceable walking paths to run across the lawn, dodging bushes and benches and cutting through flower beds. He shook his head and followed her, feeling like he was twelve all over again. The ornamental gardens were large—one of Pemberley's many achievements—and they butted up against the woods. There, nestled among the trees, was a small grotto, half sunken into the earth. The outside was uninspiring stone covered in creeping ivy, but when he followed Georgiana through the door, which was sunken down three steps into the ground, it was as if they'd slipped into a different world.

Georgiana was already fiddling with a tinderbox, panting lightly as she struck the box and lit a candle. It let out a small ring of light that did little to illuminate the space. "You've gotten slow in your old age, brother."

"You won't live until old age if you keep up with those jokes," he said, picking up another candle and lighting it. "And besides, you had a head start."

"We started from the same spot," she argued. He shook his head. Lord help him if he had to contend with both Lizzie and Georgiana in the same house, arguing details with him.

They lit several more candles and carried them to various holders around the grotto. Intricately carved walls and ceilings boasted designs of seashells carved into the smooth rock. They were as familiar to him as his own childhood bedroom given the number of hours he'd spent in the grotto, which had been commissioned by his great-grandfather. This place had been his first refuge, and later, a place he shared with Georgiana when they both needed an escape.

"It's good to be home," he said in a quiet voice.

"Next time don't stay away so long," Georgiana said. The cadence of her words sounded lighthearted, but Darcy heard the hurt beneath it.

He winced. "I am sorry, Georgie. I wish I could say I had a good reason, but it all sounds like sorry excuses. I shouldn't have left you alone here for so many months."

She looked down. "What were you to do? Father gave us our marching orders."

Darcy was sick of marching. "Even still. How have you been? The truth, not what you tell others or what you think I want to hear. If things have been miserable—"

"Not miserable," she said. "I know I begged for you to visit, but it isn't as though I was left to waste away in a nunnery. Pemberley is an enchanting prison, and Mrs. Watts isn't entirely awful."

"What's she like?" Darcy asked.

"Sickly. And a bit pedantic, if I am being honest. But she's not terrible company. We would get the papers from London, and I'd share your exploits with her and she'd make a face"—Georgiana puckered her lips as if she'd just sucked on a lemon wedge—"and she'd say, 'A proper gentleman like your brother ought to settle down, not find himself running amok!' "

"She sounds like a delight," Darcy remarked dryly.

"Oh, you haven't even heard her expound upon her opinions of proper table etiquette," Georgiana said with an eye roll. "But she is right, you know. A proper gentleman like you ought to settle down. And now that you've brought Lizzie here . . ."

Darcy could see where this was going. "Georgie, I didn't bring her here to ask her to marry me."

"No, you brought her here to keep her safe. But why not ask her?"

"It's complicated."

Her face darkened. "Don't tell me you haven't asked her to marry you because of *him*?"

"No," Darcy said honestly, because even if his father were begging him to propose, he still wouldn't unless he knew Lizzie was ready.

But Georgiana didn't appear to be listening. "For someone who acts so indifferent to us, he's rather good at making our lives miserable. You know, for my birthday, he wished me a happy fourteenth year!"

Darcy winced. "He forgot."

"He's wished me a happy fourteenth year for two years in a row!"

Darcy opened his mouth to offer some words of comfort and found that he couldn't summon any. It was just as well, because Georgiana didn't appear to require them. "He left me here with no one but Mrs. Watts and nothing to do or look forward to. I should be in London, having a season at the very least, but instead I am locked up like one of his many priceless treasures he stashes away, only worse—because I am his daughter, not a plaything! And you are his son, and you should be able to marry the girl you love. Instead, we both obey his every command and live the lives he's imagined for us. Well, I don't want that, and neither should you—it's no way to live!"

It appeared that Georgiana was not as content as she let on in her letters. Profound guilt weighed upon Darcy, and not just over having abandoned her. He was just old enough to remember their father as he had been before their mother died. Sometimes the memories felt like dreams. He used to take Darcy to the river's edge, and they'd race wooden boats in the gentle current. He rode an impossibly tall horse, settling Darcy in front of him in the saddle, keeping him in place with his strong arm. He laughed. Darcy couldn't remember his father laughing after Georgiana's birth.

Everything changed the day Darcy's mother drew her last breath and Georgiana her first. From then on, there were nannies and nurses, and later a tutor for him and a governess for Georgiana. Their father never set foot in the nursery, and when he was home, he'd summon Darcy like he was a pupil and his father a headmaster. It had prepared him for school—but his father had ceased being a father.

Darcy wasn't sure whether he was lucky to have these memories or cursed because he knew what they'd lost. He'd never told Georgiana about them, afraid that doing so would hurt her even more.

But she was hurt now. He hadn't been able to protect her, not fully.

"You're right," he said. "I'm sorry."

"Don't you ever just yearn to break free and do what you want, for the sake of doing it? Consequences be damned?"

"Georgie!" he admonished.

"What? I read books. I can curse if I want."

"Hellion," he pronounced, but there was no bite in his words. "And yes, since you're asking—I do. All the time. And . . . I might have done a bit of breaking free, consequences be damned, as you so eloquently put it."

"Really?"

"Really. But the problem is, there *are* consequences. I love Lizzie very much. I want to marry her. But Father has threatened to disown me if I do."

Georgiana went still. "He wouldn't."

"Are you willing to test him?"

When Darcy had felt obligated to propose to Josette Beaufort, he'd thought they'd made a sensible match. He hadn't been prepared for the vehemence of his father's disapproval, although he hadn't threatened to disown Darcy then. But he hadn't needed to—instead he'd implied all the ways that Darcy would ruin his reputation, and Georgiana's, and Pemberley & Associates', if he went through with it. Would he have gone through with the marriage if his father had put his foot down? Probably not, he realized with shame. Josette had likely sensed it, too, which was why she had broken it off.

But with Lizzie, it was different. He was prepared to fight for her.

There was just one thing holding him back.

"So you won't have as much money," Georgiana said now, as if that were the only consideration. "He can't break the entail on Pemberley, so you'll have to wait until he dies to come back, which is unfortunate—"

"Georgie!"

"But you have the inheritance from Mother's estate, don't you? You wouldn't be destitute."

"No," Darcy agreed. Their mother had brought her own money into her marriage with their father, and it had passed to them both upon her death, although they'd never had cause to spend it before now. "But if Father were to disown me, it wouldn't be the money that concerns me. It's you. Father would do everything in his power to keep you from me."

She gave him a pitying look. "He couldn't keep us apart."

"Yes, Georgie, he could." Darcy kept his voice even. "He could forbid everyone around you from letting us meet or correspond, and then marry you off to some ogre of a man, and then your husband would keep me away."

"I'd run away rather than let that happen."

"I'm sure you would," he said, putting an arm around Georgiana's shoulders. She leaned into him. "And just think about what sort of holy hell he'd raise if you did."

"Holy hell," Georgiana said. "I like that."

He raised his eyes to the ceiling. "Don't repeat that in front of him."

"Perhaps I'll raise holy hell if he tries to prevent you from marrying Lizzie," she said tartly.

Darcy was certain she would—but less certain that his sister would prevail in such a battle. She was strong, but Darcy knew his father better. He was . . .

Ruthless.

"Don't worry about me," Darcy said. "Besides, Father isn't the only thing keeping me and Lizzie from marriage. We—"

"Really?" Georgiana spun around. "Darcy, do you mean—"

"We aren't secretly engaged, if that's what you're thinking! But rather . . . she'll let me know when she is ready."

"Ready for what? Why wouldn't she want to marry you?"

The indignation in her voice was gratifying. "She does, I think. But if she does, she'll have to give up many freedoms to be with me—her own money, her chance to own her property or business. Lizzie's independent. She won't sign that away lightly—and neither should you, for that matter."

"When have I had a chance to meet any eligible bachelors?" Georgiana asked peevishly.

"I'm just saying," Darcy said. "Don't rush things. Lizzie and I have no intention of parting ways. I told her I'd be willing to wait until she's ready."

"And when will that be?"

"I don't know! But you have to promise me not to meddle, Georgie. Leave it to me."

"I would, except I don't know that I trust Father not to interfere before it's too late."

Darcy didn't want to admit it, but he had a similar fear. What if his father intimidated Lizzie into not wanting to marry him at all? It wasn't just the disapproval over the marriage—the elder Mr. Darcy was well-respected in the legal field. If he didn't want Lizzie practicing, he could ruin Lizzie's career by calling in a few favors.

"Try not to worry," he told her. "For now, let's just focus on the problems at hand."

"Well, I think you ought to ask her to marry you," Georgiana said, leaning her head on his shoulder. "Do it before he arrives, and then marry her quickly, before he can put a stop to it. You could propose right here—it's the perfect spot, don't you agree?"

"Georgie, you're meddling," he said, but he couldn't help the teasing lilt in his voice.

"Fine," she said, heaving a sigh.

In the distance, they could hear the sound of a woman's voice calling out. Darcy turned toward the door. "What is that?"

"Georg-i-a-NA!" came the voice.

"Ugh, Mrs. Watts," Georgiana said, pulling away from her brother. "I thought she'd be laid up until tomorrow with that headache—they always last days. I better go see what she wants. Are you coming?"

"I think I'll stay out here a little longer." He wanted to linger in this place and try not to think about his troubles for a little while.

"All right," Georgiana said, and she stood up on tiptoe to kiss his cheek. "Don't stay out too long."

"Good night, Georgiana," he said, watching his sister turn to go.

"Good night, Brother," she said. She paused at the door and said, "Fitz?"

He turned back to her. No one but she called him that, and even that, rarely. "Yes?"

"I won't meddle, but I do think that you're making things more difficult than they need to be. You and Lizzie love each other, do you not?"

He nodded.

"Then be happy. Be together."

In the distance, he heard Mrs. Watts call out, "Georgiana! Where are you?"

"Thank you, Georgie," he said.

She left Darcy in the flickering candlelight. He wished he could see their circumstances as clearly as Georgiana. He wished it was as easy as love conquering any and all obstacles. But the truth was, marriage would create problems for them both, and he wouldn't pressure her into it simply because they loved each other. He wanted to know that Lizzie was ready to embrace that next step.

Behind him, Darcy heard the soft scuffing of light footsteps descending the steps into the grotto. He sighed and began to turn around. "Have you come back to harangue me some more, or are—"

He didn't get a chance to finish his sentence before a rush of movement overwhelmed him, followed by splitting pain, and then everything went black.

TWENTY-FOUR

In Which Lizzie and Georgiana Encounter a Pair of Trespassers

LIZZIE AWOKE THE NEXT morning with a rather embarrassing thought: She never wanted to leave Pemberley.

Of course, she wasn't being serious. Mostly. She really did miss London and its bustling energy, and she'd always wanted the chance to travel beyond the bounds of England. But if one had to be confined to one estate whilst figuring out how to avoid being trapped in the clutches of a murderous criminal, there really were worse places to be.

Her room was sumptuously decorated in a calming green, and the four-poster bed was like a cloud. The windows overlooked the river as it ran into the woods, and Lizzie imagined that view was as pretty at the height of summer as it was in the darkest depths of winter. And beyond her own bedchamber, she noted that every room she had been shown was beautifully furnished with elegant pieces that seemed sophisticated and timeless, chosen for their quality, not because they happened to be the height of fashion. Each room had a slightly different view of the grounds, none of which was anything less than astonishing. But grandeur aside, Lizzie felt an immediate ease at Pemberley. Guy, too, had seemed equally happy to traipse through halls the previous evening, finding new things to sniff and making friends with every servant.

In short, Pemberley was a dream. And Lizzie was intensely grateful that her mother was not here to see it, for if she were, Lizzie would surely never hear the end of it.

It was not lost on her, of course, the implication of Darcy bringing her here, beyond the need to see to her immediate safety. Darcy had made no attempts to disguise that he wanted to marry her—the only thing he hadn't done was propose. But Lizzie knew all he needed was some kind of signal from her, and he would. Then she could be mistress of this estate one day.

But probably not before Darcy was cast out of his father's life.

Lizzie loved her family, despite their many eccentricities and embarrassments, and she could not imagine the idea of being permanently cut off from them. And now that she had seen Pemberley, and spent more time with Georgiana, she wondered—how on earth could she ask Darcy to give it all up, just to marry her?

A knock on the door startled her from her thoughts. "Come in," she called, and the door opened and Georgiana peeked in. "Oh, good, you're awake."

Guy let out a happy bark and ran up to her, and Georgiana laughed and picked him up. "Did you sleep well?"

"It was the best night of sleep I've ever had," she answered honestly.

"Good. Now, it's rather late morning—no, don't look alarmed. You all needed your sleep. Charlotte came down for breakfast, and I set her up in the library. She's rather taken by my father's collection of travel diaries of various explorers of the New World, and I imagine she'll be absorbed until at least teatime. I was wondering if you'd like a tour of the grounds? We can sneak out through the kitchens and get you both something to eat, if you like."

"That sounds marvelous," Lizzie said. "But why do we have to sneak?"

Georgiana made a face. "Because if Mrs. Watts sees me, she won't let us go unchaperoned lest we run into my brother—she's rather prudish that way—and she'll insist we don't go outside until afternoon, and she won't let me take you to the woods, and she'll ask a whole series of boorish questions—"

Lizzie laughed. "All right, you don't have to convince me. She sounds rather unpleasant. Lead the way."

Georgiana kept up a steady stream of conversation as she led Lizzie through the back halls to the kitchens, which appeared to be a merry sort of chaos. A jolly-looking woman with hundreds of freckles on her face turned when they entered the kitchen and immediately tsked. "Miss Georgiana, what are you doing bringing a guest into the kitchens? You'll scandalize the poor lady!"

"This is Elizabeth Bennet, and she's a lady solicitor. You can scarcely scandalize her." To Lizzie, she said, "This is Mrs. Craig, and she is the best cook in all of Derbyshire."

"Oh, hush now, child!" Mrs. Craig turned pink.

"I am delighted to make your acquaintance," Lizzie said. "And I have to agree with Miss Darcy—the meal last night was excellent."

"Well, sit, sit," she said. "I'll rustle something up for you both and the pup."

Lizzie enjoyed watching the bustle of the kitchens and the warmness of Mrs. Craig's smile as she served them a simple breakfast, cooked to perfection. Guy got his own plate near the hearth, and everything felt . . . relaxing. Right. When they'd finished, Mrs. Craig shooed them out, and Georgiana took Lizzie out the back.

"Where's your brother this morning?" Lizzie asked as they rambled through the gardens.

"Oh, he's around somewhere, I imagine," Georgiana said. "He's likely gone to visit Holmes—that's our steward—or maybe into Lambton. He always has a hundred things to do when he comes home, and he hasn't been here much lately."

"I'm sorry," Lizzie said. "I feel as if I am partially to blame for that."

"What do you mean?" Georgiana asked, eyes wide.

"Just that . . . we've had so many cases as of late, and he's been an invaluable consultant. I worry he thought he couldn't leave London because of the work. But I know he's missed you terribly."

"Oh, no. I know he's been busy. And I'm glad you've been putting him to work with so many cases. Will you tell me about them? I only know what I read in the papers, and my brother is terribly reluctant to share the details in his letters."

"He probably worries I'll be a negative influence on you," Lizzie said, laughing. If Darcy were here, she could imagine his eye roll. "But all right. Which one do you want to hear about first?"

"The Pandemonium at the Pantheon! Did that man really try to stab a woman in front of an audience of a hundred people?"

Lizzie laughed. "Well, first I must go to the beginning of that case . . ."

Lizzie and Georgiana spent a pleasant morning walking through the grounds, swapping stories about Lizzie and Darcy's recent cases and tales from Darcy and Georgiana's childhood. Georgiana pointed out her favorite horses, and Lizzie told her about her ill-fated ride in Hyde Park upon Georgiana's borrowed mount, and then Georgiana led her on the walking path, which followed the river and led into the woods. Lizzie let Guy off his leash and the little dog romped through the tall grasses and chased squirrels and birds in the brush, always looping back to check in on Lizzie and Georgiana. It was the most pleasant morning Lizzie could remember, and the only thing that would have made it sweeter was if Darcy had joined them.

They had just rounded the bend in the wooded path when they came upon two men dressed in simple workwear standing at the path, speaking urgently between themselves. When they spotted Georgiana and Lizzie, Lizzie could read the alarm on their faces as plain as day. She called for Guy immediately, and the dog came bounding up to her.

"Miss Darcy," said one of the men. "You ought to go back on up to the house."

"What is it?" Georgiana asked.

"It might be nothing, but we've found two trespassers climbing the wall up ahead," he said. "The rest of the grooms have rounded them up and called Travers to come collect them. We'll keep them at the gatehouse until Mr. Darcy can question them."

Lizzie went cold, and the airy, happy feeling of the morning vanished. "Who?"

"Please, Miss Darcy," said the man, looking apprehensive. "Your brother wouldn't like it."

"Do you think it could be her?" Georgiana asked. "Lady Catherine?"

"Or her emissaries," Lizzie said, pushing forward. "Please, let us at least see who they are."

The man looked reluctant, but he wasn't given much of a choice—because Lizzie and Georgiana heard the sound of footsteps cutting through the underbrush, and two men appeared, walking what appeared to be two young ladies, their hands restrained behind their backs. Lizzie's heart nearly stopped just then. Could it be . . . could it be that simple? Would Lady Catherine really try to scale the walls at Pemberley? Had they caught her once and for all?

But then one of the ladies turned, and Lizzie got a good look at her face and her jaw dropped.

"Clara Jeffries?"

The men stopped, surprised at Lizzie and Georgiana's presence. Georgiana looked at Lizzie. "Do you know these ladies?"

The other young lady turned, and beneath her simple straw bonnet Lizzie saw another familiar face: Sally Burton. And she did not look pleased to see Lizzie.

"Yes," Lizzie said in shock.

"We found them climbing the wall back there," said the man holding on to Sally. "And they tried to run."

"Well, they wouldn't let us through the front gate, so we had to get creative," Sally said.

Lizzie set Guy down, no longer alarmed. "What on earth are you two doing here?"

Sally glared at Lizzie. "We've unfinished business."

"Miss, I think we really ought to take these ladies to the gatehouse now," said one man to Georgiana.

"Lizzie, do you think they are dangerous?" she asked.

"Dangerous? Us? That's rich!" Miss Jeffries looked affronted. Sally was still glaring.

"I don't think so," Lizzie said. "I'd prefer if you brought them back to the house so we can have a proper chat."

"But Mr. Darcy said—"

"We'll fetch my brother. But Miss Bennet knows these ladies, and she doesn't think they mean us any harm."

"Neither of them is the lady we are on the lookout for," Lizzie assured them.

In the end, Mr. Travers himself came to escort Miss Jeffries and Sally to the house, where they were brought into the library, disturbing Charlotte as she pored over an open book. She looked up in surprise when Lizzie and Georgiana entered, and surprise turned to shock when she saw Sally and Miss Jeffries follow after, their hands restrained. Lizzie quickly explained what had transpired, and then convinced Travers to remove the ladies' restraints. Charleston went to fetch Darcy, and Lizzie, Charlotte, and Georgiana sat down across from the detainees with Mr. Travers hovering nearby, refusing to leave them alone.

"Well, I have to say—you two are among the last people I expected to encounter today," Lizzie said.

"You were hoping for someone else?" Sally said with a sneer.

The vitriol in her expression took Lizzie off guard. "No. Not exactly. As you can see, the estate is . . . on edge."

"Oh, we saw," Clara said, giving Sally a not-so-subtle nudge. "The one at the gate wouldn't let us in and wouldn't even pass a message to you. I told Sally we ought to just go back to Lambton and write you a letter, but no. She had to climb the wall and get us caught."

"No unknown visitors pass through the gate," Travers said. "And Mr. Darcy told me last night that he wasn't expecting anyone."

"He wouldn't be," Sally snapped. "We came all on our own."

Lizzie had never seen Sally look so furious—except for when

Mr. Oliver had threatened her grandparents. "Why did you?" And then something worse occurred to her—what if they were bringing news from Netherfield? "Is it your grandparents? Caroline? Jane?"

"Don't pretend you don't know exactly why we're here!" Sally's eyes flashed dangerously. "You think you can just abscond in the night and get away with it?"

Lizzie gaped at her. Now she was truly confused. "Get away with what?"

Sally scoffed. "That's right—deny, deny, deny. I thought you were supposed to be a solicitor. What, you don't have a better argument planned?"

"I truly don't know what you're talking about," Lizzie said, looking at Charlotte with bewilderment. Her friend appeared to be equally confused.

"Fine." Sally leaned forward, her ice-blue eyes sharp. "I know what you stole."

"Stole?" Lizzie echoed. "I didn't steal anything!"

"You took the Netherfield treasure!"

It took Lizzie a beat to comprehend the words, and then she laughed. Charlotte looked concerned. Georgiana was perplexed. "You think I stole the silver?" Lizzie asked. "Last I saw it, it was secure in Bingley's lockbox."

"Not the silver," Sally spat. "I don't care about the damned silver!"

Travers cleared his throat. "I won't have swearing in front of the young lady of the house!"

"I've heard the word before," Georgiana protested.

"If you don't mean the silver, what do you mean?" Lizzie asked, growing impatient. "I left Netherfield with nothing more than a valise and the clothes on my back—I didn't steal a thing, and if I did, I promise you it was unintentional."

"I don't think she knows, Sally," Miss Jeffries whispered.

"She knows. She was over every inch of the estate, asking questions. And after how the ball turned out?" Sally's glare was stubborn. "She's playing coy."

Lizzie was growing more confused by the second.

"All right, we won't get anywhere with arguing," Charlotte said gently. "Now, clearly our visitors think Lizzie took something that was not hers when we left Netherfield, correct?"

Sally glared but nodded.

"And you call it the Netherfield treasure, but it's not the silver coins—are you implying that there was more to the treasure than the coins?" Charlotte asked.

More to the treasure. Lizzie had never considered this angle, but now it made sense—for a lady as cagey as Honoria Bingley was reputed to be, she would not hide the entirety of her treasure in one place. The risk of being robbed was too great, as she'd probably learned from George Oliver.

"There was more, wasn't there?" Lizzie asked, leaning forward.

"Speaking of convincing acts," Sally huffed.

"I think she's telling the truth, Sal," Miss Jeffries said again.

"Why do you think I'm the one who stole it, whatever it is?"

Sally continued to glare at her. "Because it's awfully convenient that it went missing at the same time that you left Netherfield."

"Correlation and causation are hardly the same thing," Lizzie said. "Although I agree that coincidence would be too much for me to ignore. But surely you must have proof beyond that?"

"No proof. But you were there when it all came crashing down. And then you were gone, and so was the last of Mrs. Bingley's fortune."

Lizzie stared at her, uncomprehending. *You were there when it all came crashing down.*

Crashing down.

"The chandelier?"

"Now she admits it!" Sally said.

"I don't know what you're talking about," Lizzie told her honestly. "The chandelier coming down *was* sabotage, but I had nothing to do with that—I was standing beneath it when it fell."

"But you took advantage of it and stole what wasn't yours!"

Lizzie stared at the other young lady, trying to piece together what she meant. The moment the chandelier had fallen was no longer quite so clear in her mind. It was as though one moment she had been standing, having a shockingly civil conversation with Caroline, and the next she was sprawled on the floor and Darcy was shouting her name and there was crystal everywhere and screams ripping through the air and . . .

Crystal everywhere. But it hadn't been broken. The crystals had stayed intact.

"The chandelier," Lizzie repeated, and now Charlotte and Georgiana looked at her with confusion. "It wasn't crystal."

"Now she comprehends," Sally said.

"I really don't think she knew before just now," Miss Jeffries insisted.

"I didn't," Lizzie said honestly. "But if you want me to help you, you have to explain."

She didn't think Sally would agree at first. But then she let out a resigned sigh. "*Fine.* You're right—the silver coins were hardly Mrs. Bingley's only treasure. In fact, she told me about them years ago, in case."

"In case of what?" Lizzie asked.

Sally shrugged. "In case I ever needed them. In case anyone I knew might need them. She didn't mind that Grandad had used a bit to try to pay off George, although she didn't like the outcome. I took a coin every now and then, and I'd use them to pay debts, or to ensure a family had fuel for the winter. They were doing no good sitting in that old house."

Lizzie looked between Sally and Miss Jeffries. Miss Jeffries must have read the question in her eyes. "Yes, she saved my father's business when he died. He had debts, and I couldn't possibly have begun to repay them. She didn't want to see me lose the only livelihood I had."

"That day in the churchyard," Lizzie said, remembering what had passed between them. "You were . . ."

"I was giving her the coins, yes," Sally said impatiently.

"But how did you use them?" Lizzie asked. "I think a few

people might have started paying attention if genuine silver Spanish cobs started appearing in a tiny village in Hertfordshire."

Clara shrugged. "The blacksmith's son melts them down for me. He thinks I'm stealing them, but he doesn't care as long as a nugget of silver is left for him."

Lizzie almost laughed. Of course. One could always count on greed to keep a secret. "And then what?"

"It's easy enough to find ways to exchange them for regular coin," Miss Jeffries said. "No one asks too many questions when you own a business. Then I give them back to Sally, and we use the money as we see fit."

"The gravestone," Charlotte said. "Was that you?"

Sally glared. "He was a thief and a lout, but I thought perhaps Mr. Oliver might leave us alone if he saw his father was buried properly."

Only that had turned out to be a miscalculation, for it had just enraged Mr. Oliver and fueled his suspicion about the Burtons using the treasure to pay for what they wanted. Which hadn't been inaccurate at all . . . he just hadn't had the proof.

"You've been working together this entire time, haven't you?" Charlotte asked suddenly. "I thought it odd that there was no mention of George Oliver's disappearance in any of the parish registers, especially after Mr. Thomas told me he was certain he remembered an entry."

"Sally asked me to remove all references to him in my reprintings," Miss Jeffries admitted. "It's why I offered to have them printed."

“Clara!” Sally said through clenched teeth.

“They already figured it out, Sal.” To Lizzie and Charlotte, Miss Jeffries said, “It was so that no one would ever suspect, you see. Sal knew that with your sister and brother-in-law moving in, it was only a matter of time before he was discovered.”

“I wanted to get rid of him before you all arrived,” Sally said grumpily. “But I didn’t have the time before the estate was swirling with estate agents and solicitors and your sister’s servants.”

“So you began to take protective measures by rewriting village history,” Lizzie said, almost approvingly. It was terribly clever. “And did Mr. Thomas know?”

“He never suspected,” Miss Jeffries said.

“And you’ve been using Mrs. Bingley’s stash of silver coins to fund various causes throughout the village, but all the while the real treasure was in the chandelier,” Lizzie said.

“Diamonds,” Sally said shortly. “She bought that chandelier with her silver, not long after she arrived at Netherfield. She told me she could tell how greedy her husband proved to be, and she wanted a way to keep her money close. In sight but concealed. The chandelier was meant to be revealed at a ball she hosted for Geoffrey’s birthday, but . . . well, the misfortunes struck.”

Lizzie let out a sharp little laugh. “Diamonds. Clever. Have you considered Mr. Oliver?”

“That was my first thought,” Sally interrupted. “But no. He was drunk at the pub the night of the ball. Multiple witnesses accounted for him. I went downstairs after helping the doctor stitch up Miss Bingley to find the chandelier picked over, and every guest in the house headed in different directions."

"And you suspected me?" Lizzie asked.

"You're not stupid. I heard your trunk went back to London, but you don't go anywhere without Mr. Darcy. I went to Clara and told her what I thought; we confirmed Mr. Oliver wasn't the thief, and then we took the first coach north."

Lizzie stood, the new information overwhelming. She needed to pace. "It never added up," she said. "Everything that happened at Netherfield. People said it was the curse, and at first I thought perhaps it was coincidence—or you," she said to Sally.

"What do you mean?" Sally asked.

"Getting trapped in the service door, the masonry falling, and now that chandelier . . . what if someone wasn't trying to hurt us but get at the treasure?"

"Who?" Sally asked. "Who could possibly know about the treasure?"

Lizzie didn't have any answers, but something else struck her just then. "You said you took a coach here?" she asked the other ladies.

"Yes," Miss Jeffries said. "Why—"

"Where's Darcy?" Lizzie asked. "I need to speak to him. If you've managed to find us in just a handful of days, then no doubt Lady Catherine isn't far behind."

"Who's Lady Catherine?" Sally asked. "Has she stolen the diamonds?"

"I'll ring for Charleston," Georgiana said. "He has to have found him by now."

It was but a few minutes before the butler returned, looking mildly frazzled. "I'm sorry, Miss Darcy. I've been unable to locate your brother."

"What? But where is he?"

"I don't know," he said carefully. "No one has seen him."

Unease pricked at Lizzie. "What do you mean, no one has seen him? Did he leave the estate?"

"He didn't pass through the gate this morning," Travers said.

Alarm began to settle in Lizzie's bones, and judging by Georgiana's expression, she was worried as well. "Would he have left by any other route?"

"There's a gate that remains locked," Georgiana said. "On the north side of the estate. But it's too narrow for a horse. If he went that way, it would be on foot . . . but he doesn't leave the estate on foot, ever. We're too far from anything else."

"When was the last time anyone saw him?" Lizzie asked the butler. "At breakfast?"

"Mr. Darcy didn't come down for breakfast."

Fear clawed its way through Lizzie's stomach. He wouldn't leave her, wouldn't leave Georgiana. Perhaps there was some reasonable explanation.

"Don't panic," Charlotte said, taking her arm. "We'll find him."

In short order, a small army of servants was dispatched to try to locate Darcy. It was reported that his bedchamber was empty and the bedclothes undisturbed. His horse was still in the stables, and none of the gardeners nor grooms had seen him leave. Panic was settling in, and Lizzie didn't know what to do.

Where was he?

In the midst of the worried bustle, Mrs. Reynolds approached her, something small and ivory colored in her hand. "Excuse me, Miss Bennet, but I found this on the hall table."

Charlotte and Georgiana gathered around her as she held out her hand. It was a small note on creamy linen paper. Lizzie's heart nearly stopped, and she took it from the housekeeper with numb, trembling fingers. She couldn't help but think of Lady Catherine and every taunting threat the lady had put to paper. Was this yet another one?

But then she saw the handwriting on the note, and she let out a gasp of relief. "It's Darcy's hand," she said, eagerly unfolding it.

My dearest Elizabeth, it read. *Meet me in the grotto as soon as you get this. I have something I must ask you. Yours, Fitzwilliam Darcy.*

"Oh!" Georgiana squeaked. "The grotto—this makes sense!"

"What's the grotto?" Lizzie asked, perplexed.

"It's on the edge of the woods—I pointed it out this morning, remember? It's one of Darcy's favorite places. You ought to go."

"All right," Lizzie said, looking at Charlotte, baffled.

"Alone!" Georgiana added.

Charlotte raised an eyebrow, and Lizzie felt her heart race. Alone? Why on earth did Darcy want her to meet him in a grotto, and why did Georgiana think she ought to go alone . . . oh. Lizzie bit her lip. Really, Darcy? Now was not the time!

"I'll go fetch him," Lizzie said. "Can you watch Guy for me?"

"Of course," Charlotte said, wearing a knowing smile. Lizzie wanted to roll her eyes but managed not to. "I'll tell them we can all call off the search as well."

"I'll show you where to go," Georgiana said, pulling on Lizzie's hand.

Lizzie allowed herself to be led out of the house and through the gardens. Georgiana was giddy, so clearly she understood what was about to happen. Lizzie found herself unable to push aside her anxiety about Clara and Sally's revelations and her fear of Lady Catherine. She felt vaguely sick, which was not at all an ideal state when one was about to be proposed to!

The grotto was an ivy-covered, subterranean stone structure with open, glassless windows. It looked secretive and alluring from the outside, but dim. Georgiana hesitated at the top of the steps leading down into the grotto. "You should go ahead," she said loudly. "I'll just . . . walk back to the house."

"All right," Lizzie said. "Thank you, Georgiana."

Her heart sped up as she made her way down the steps. Inside, the sunlight filtered in through greenery and the tall narrow windows set near the ceiling. Every surface was textured with the most enchanting designs of seashells, and under different circumstances Lizzie would have lingered and exclaimed over the craftsmanship.

"Darcy?" she called out, expecting him to materialize around a pillar.

But she heard nothing—no footsteps, no voice greeting her. "I would have expected a few candles at least," she muttered.

Then Lizzie heard a muffled grunt. She took three more steps forward, and as her eyes adjusted to the dimness, she saw something in the darkest far corner of the grotto. A figure, seated on the floor.

It was Darcy.

His hands and feet were bound, and he was awkwardly slumped against the rough-hewn wall. Dried blood flaked on his temple and cheek. When he spotted Lizzie, his eyes widened, and he made a sound against his gag that she could not decipher.

"Darcy!" Lizzie cried out in alarm as she ran toward him.

"Thank you for finally joining us, Miss Bennet," a voice from behind her said. "We've been waiting for you."

TWENTY-FIVE

In Which Lizzie Finally Comes Face-to-Face with Her Nemesis

LIZZIE COULD NOT FATHOM what she was seeing.

Her mouth was so dry that she could not have swallowed even if she'd wanted to, and her heart pounded in her chest so loudly that she could scarcely hear Darcy's muffled attempts at speech behind his gag. She stood protectively in front of Darcy.

Georgiana came running into the grotto, drawn by Lizzie's cry, and Darcy began trying to yell again, struggling against his bindings. "Lizzie, are you—"

She abruptly broke off when she saw her brother. Lizzie found her voice just then. "Georgiana, go."

"No, Georgiana, stay where you are," said the tall figure in the middle of the grotto.

"But Mrs. Watts—"

"That's not Mrs. Watts!" Lizzie said, her voice rising in fear.

The woman tutted, and Lizzie could see the gleam of the

pistol in her hand. "Miss Bennet, how rude. You're scaring the girl. As far as she is concerned, I am Mrs. Watts."

"You also go by the name Lady Catherine de Bourgh," Lizzie said. "I don't suppose you have any other names?"

"None that I am inclined to share with you."

"I don't understand," Georgiana said, and Lizzie realized now that the word that Darcy was trying to say behind his gag was *run*.

"This isn't your lady's companion," Lizzie said, never taking her eye off the pistol held casually in Lady Catherine's right hand. "This is Lady Catherine de Bourgh."

"Lizzie, Mrs. Watts has been with me for months," Georgiana said. Then she seemed to take note of the pistol. "Mrs. Watts, that's my brother! That's Lizzie Bennet—remember the lady I told you about—"

"She knows who I am," Lizzie said. "Georgiana, leave."

"No, Georgiana, stay," Lady Catherine purred.

"Don't hurt her! She's not a part of this."

"She very much is a part of this," Lady Catherine countered. "She's been telling me everything you've been up to these past eight months. Quite fond of her brother, this one is. According to her, he's hung the moon and stars. She'll take any excuse to boast about his accomplishments, and about the clever, the pretty, the resourceful Miss Bennet he's attached himself to. Why, I don't know why I bothered buying off Tomlinson when I had no better source on the activities of Mr. Darcy and Miss Bennet than Georgiana Darcy herself."

As she spoke, Lady Catherine pointed her pistol at Georgiana and motioned for her to join Lizzie and Darcy in the corner. Georgiana flinched when the pistol was pointed at her, and Darcy tried to shout something behind his gag, but it was muffled. "Come here, Georgie," Lizzie said, reaching out a hand. "It'll be all right."

Georgiana's shock made Lizzie's protective instincts flare up. "You've been here this entire time," she said to Lady Catherine, thinking back. Darcy and Georgiana's father had departed England eight months earlier. He'd hired Mrs. Watts before leaving London, but Darcy had never met the woman. Lizzie guessed it was no mere coincidence that Mrs. Watts had taken to her room at the moment of their arrival yesterday. "I'm happy to see your headache has cleared up."

"Oh, it hasn't, but I am certain it will by the end of the day." Lady Catherine hefted the pistol, and Lizzie tried her best not to flinch. "You've been quite the thorn in my side, Elizabeth. I suppose I cannot blame you for wiggling away from me in London last year and putting away Collins, but I was really quite angry when you put an end to the Mullins brothers' operation."

"That wasn't me exactly," Lizzie said. "That honor goes to Miss Leticia Cavendish."

"You also got Tomlinson arrested, which made me very cross." Lady Catherine stalked toward her, and Lizzie searched for her courage.

"I'm afraid I have that effect on people."

Lady Catherine was now close enough to trace the cool

metal of the pistol along Lizzie's jaw, and Lizzie forced herself to stare straight ahead, to not flinch. "You do. Which is why it's such a shame that you did not come with me voluntarily when you had the chance."

Lizzie wanted to move, wanted to fight back, but fear had rooted her firmly in place. Her abilities to defend herself were rudimentary, and no match against a pistol. Besides, if she did try to wrestle the weapon from Lady Catherine, it might discharge and hit either Darcy or Georgiana.

Faster than she expected, Lady Catherine's other hand tightened like a vise around Lizzie's upper arm and jerked her away from Darcy and Georgiana. Both the siblings cried out as Lizzie stumbled, but they didn't move. Lizzie felt the cold barrel of the pistol dig into her side. "You're coming with me. No tricks, no trying to escape. If you do, Darcy is dead. And if he's already dead, then Georgiana will be next."

Georgiana whimpered in fear, but Lizzie didn't look at either sibling. "If you kill them, you might as well kill me, because I won't work for you. Whatever you have in mind, I won't do it."

"Elizabeth, I am not to be trifled with. However insincere you may choose to be, you will not find me so." Lady Catherine gave her arm another jerk, and Lizzie bit her lip so as not to cry out from the pain.

"I decline," Lizzie said, attempting to wrench her arm from Lady Catherine's grasp. "What was it you said to me once? Often a lady's only choice is her refusal? Well, let me make it very clear to you—I refuse what you're offering."

"And I refuse to accept your refusal," Lady Catherine said, mouth set. "Trust me, you'll want the case I'm offering."

Lizzie actually laughed at that. "There's no case you could hand me that would make me go with you willingly!"

"Not even a case that could secure your own future?"

Lizzie had steeled herself to refuse anything Lady Catherine might offer, but she hesitated now, and Lady Catherine saw that tiny pause and pressed her advantage.

"You're curious," she said. "I thought you would be. It would only be a few years of work, I should think, and when the job is completed to my satisfaction, you'll be quite free to go back to your life and do as you please—even marry this simpleton, if that's what you choose."

"I'm not interested," Lizzie said. She wasn't going anywhere with Lady Catherine—but the woman had been right, Lizzie's curiosity was piqued.

"You could do more to help other women with this case than you ever could back at Longbourn, settling estates and contract disputes."

"Find someone else," she said.

Lady Catherine's laugh was mocking. "As if I haven't tried! Mr. Collins was the first person I attempted to recruit to my cause, but what a bumbling fool he turned out to be. The only good thing he ever did was lead me to you. Then I thought, perhaps it wasn't the man, it was the caliber of solicitor that was the issue. And Tomlinson was much cleverer than Collins, but he had no interest in my case—he said it couldn't be done, but moreover, it *shouldn't* be done. The audacity of that man! I wanted to shoot him myself, but no—instead he's in the custody of the Crown. You really are the most meddlesome girl!"

"And is that why you ordered him to kidnap me?" Lizzie asked. "To work this case?"

"Of course. And there's no need to play coy—if you're curious, just tell me."

Behind her, Lizzie could hear the muffled sounds of Darcy attempting to speak beyond his gag. She imagined him saying something like, *Don't entertain her delusions, Lizzie!* But it occurred to her that if she, Darcy, and Georgiana didn't return to the drawing room soon, the others might grow curious. And given the tensions on the estate, perhaps Mr. Travers would come to investigate their delay, and they'd have half a chance of escaping this madwoman.

She just had to buy herself more time.

"Fine," she said. "What's the case?"

"Property dispute," Lady Catherine said. "A very wealthy, well-connected man wrongfully seized my property. And while the possession might be technically legal, his methods are questionable."

Lizzie frowned. "Well, if his possession is legal, then I don't know what I could do about it. I'd need to know more about the methods and the property in question."

"A family home, and the income associated with it," Lady Catherine said. "As for the methods, he misrepresented his intentions."

Lizzie couldn't help it—her legal mind was already analyzing this scenario. "How large of a home, and how much land? Is there an entail? And what do you mean, he misrepresented his intentions? If there was fraud . . ."

Lady Catherine stared at Lizzie, and she smiled the moment that the details fell into place. Lady Catherine had referred to a case that could secure her own future. A case that no man would touch, that Tomlinson said shouldn't be touched.

"Are you referring to your husband?" Lizzie asked. "And is the property in question—"

"My family property, passed down to me," Lady Catherine said. "And that weasel stole it from me. I want it back."

Lizzie shook her head. "I'm sorry, I can't help—there are laws—"

"Unjust laws, wouldn't you agree?"

"Of course," Lizzie said. "But I'm just a solicitor. I can't change laws. You'd have to go through Parliament, and—"

Movement behind Lady Catherine caught Lizzie's eye, and hope leapt in her chest for a moment. It must have shown on her face, for Lady Catherine turned slightly. A figure appeared in the grotto doorway, backlit by the brilliant sunlight. Lizzie blinked, unable to make out who the newcomer was, until . . .

"Are you ready, madam?" The voice was female, although the figure was dressed in trousers and a men's jacket. "The horses are nearby."

The sunlight glinted off the newcomer's red hair. "Agnes," Lizzie breathed.

"Miss Bennet," she said crisply.

"But . . . how . . ."

"You aren't the only talented young lady I've collected," Lady Catherine said. "Agnes is quite the housebreaker. I saved her from the noose, and now she is committed to our cause."

"You were the one who took Guy, and the east wing—the accidents . . ." Lizzie realized she was making little sense, but it was all falling into place. Agnes had passed herself off as from the area, but she wasn't from Meryton. She had presented herself as friendly to Lizzie, gotten Guy to trust her, and had said that she didn't believe in the curse . . . "But you tried to kill me!"

Lady Catherine tutted. "Agnes, I told you I wanted her unharmed."

"I wasn't trying to kill her *specifically*," Agnes said. "I tried to do as you said—make it so unsafe that she'd have no choice but go to Pemberley."

"I could have been killed by that chandelier! You nearly killed Caroline Bingley!"

"Oh, I just wanted a closer look—after Sally insisted that no one polish it but her, I got curious."

"You're the one who stole the diamonds," Lizzie said.

Agnes gave a small bow and Lady Catherine said, "And they will fund our case for a good number of years. Now, enough talk. It's time to go. Agnes, you stay here and ensure the Darcys behave—no running off and warning anyone to be on the lookout. If you don't hear from me in five days' time, kill them and join us."

"No!" Lizzie cried. "You can't—"

Lady Catherine smacked Lizzie across the face with the pistol, the cold metal splitting the skin of her cheekbone. Lizzie felt burning pain and the trickle of blood on her cheek as she saw stars. Behind her, Georgiana let out a small yelp.

"You don't get to negotiate," Lady Catherine hissed. "I gave you many chances to join me without getting hurt, but you squandered them all. Now is the time for you to do as I say, or Agnes will kill everyone you love."

"I'm very good at poisons," Agnes said, blinking at her in an innocent fashion. "And at slipping into a house undetected at night. Honoria Bingley never even knew I was there."

Horror settled over Lizzie as she raised her hand to her face, wincing at the pain. "You killed Honoria Bingley?"

"Of course I had her killed," Lady Catherine said with a sigh. "I couldn't risk showing my face in London—I needed to find a way to drive you out of the city. I learned about Honoria and her fortune while I was working with Hurst."

George Hurst, Lady Catherine's first victim . . . that Lizzie knew of. Technically, Collins had killed Hurst, but it had been at Lady Catherine's behest.

"I had hoped that you'd find your way to Pemberley naturally in the last year, given how close you are with that one, but I suppose his father doesn't approve of you. He ought to thank me for this favor I'm doing him."

And with that, she yanked Lizzie's arm, dragging her toward the door. Lizzie's instinct was to go limp and drag her feet, but Lady Catherine simply let go of her, allowing Lizzie to tumble to the ground. She looked up at the sound of the pistol being cocked.

But it wasn't pointed at her.

"Get up," Lady Catherine ordered. "Or I'll shoot him."

Lizzie scrambled to her feet, risking one last look at Darcy and Georgiana, even though it broke her heart to do so. Georgiana's face was tearstained as she knelt next to her brother. And Darcy . . . oh, Darcy. His hair was frightfully disheveled, and he wore last night's clothes. He had been captive since last night and she hadn't even known! Worse than seeing him injured and helpless was the wild look in his eyes as their gazes met. His eyes pleaded with her, and it gutted Lizzie, but she couldn't look away. She had the desperate fear that she might never look upon Darcy ever again.

"I love you," she said.

Lady Catherine jerked her away. "Enough carrying on. Come along."

Lady Catherine dragged her out of the grotto, the barrel of the pistol digging into her side. Lizzie's mind spun—she needed to be smart now. If Agnes was staying behind, then she couldn't give her any reason to harm anyone she loved. But if she allowed Lady Catherine to whisk her away from Pemberley, then escape would become exponentially more difficult. She felt her breath coming in quick, short gasps. She was panicking, and the edges of her vision were going gray.

Breathe, she told herself. *Think*.

Lady Catherine's weaknesses—what were they? Right now,

as she marched Lizzie deeper into the woods behind the grotto, it didn't feel as though she had any. Lady Catherine had played a long game of cat and mouse, getting herself into position before Lizzie had even suspected danger. She'd been here the entire time, and all the while Lizzie had been back in London, afraid she was lurking behind every corner . . .

"How did you send the letters?" Lizzie asked. "If you were all the way up here?"

Lady Catherine let out an unladylike snort. "I wrote many letters. And then I simply had my associates choose which ones to deliver based on your reactions."

"Even the one at Netherfield?"

"That one was a gamble, but I thought you all might run to the countryside at some point. I told Agnes to be careful. She's rather overconfident, that one—but she does what she's told much better than you."

This, Lizzie realized, was Lady Catherine's weakness. She liked to talk. She liked to appear clever, and even more, she wanted everyone else to admire how clever she was. As long as Lizzie could encourage her to talk, then she might reveal something Lizzie could use in her escape. Something to use against her.

"This case you want me to work on," Lizzie said as Lady Catherine nudged her along. "Your husband? I thought he was dead."

"Good," she said. "That is what I want the world to think. It's far easier to style oneself as a widow than a separated woman. Society pities a widow. Doesn't expect much from her."

"Why don't you just have Agnes kill him? If she's so good at what she does."

"Because I'm not his heir," Lady Catherine said, bitterness heavy on her tongue. "If he dies, the entirety of his estate—including my estate—goes to someone else."

"Who?"

"The brat he had with the woman he married after he tossed me aside," Lady Catherine said as they emerged into a small clearing with one horse saddled and stomping its hooves impatiently. "Now, enough of—"

Thud!

Lady Catherine crashed into her with such force that Lizzie was knocked to the ground, the other woman falling on top of her. Instantly, the wind was knocked from Lizzie's lungs, and she writhed on the forest floor, struggling against the weight of the older woman on top of her, trying to breathe.

Finally, her gasp for breath drew in blessed air, and Lizzie coughed and panted until Lady Catherine's weight rolled off her, and she scrambled to her knees. Someone touched her shoulder and Lizzie whirled around, shoving at the hands that touched her.

"Easy!" came another voice, female.

Lizzie looked up and squinted.

Sally Burton stood before her, holding a hefty branch in one hand.

"Sally," Lizzie whispered. She heard the rustling of the underbrush and whirled around, only to find Clara and Charlotte hiding behind a bush. Guy came darting out, growling at the prone form of Lady Catherine. "Clara. Charlotte?"

"Is this Lady Catherine?" Charlotte asked, appalled.

"Yes," she said dully. Then the panic came back. "Darcy and Georgiana aren't safe! Agnes is in there with them. She'll kill them if she sees what we've done to Lady Catherine!"

"Agnes?" Sally asked. "Our Agnes, from Netherfield?"

"Yes! She was responsible for—well, everything! She stole the diamonds."

Sally's gaze darkened. "I never did like her."

"She was working with Lady Catherine this entire time?" Charlotte asked.

"Yes! I can't explain it all, but we need to get her away. But there's only one entrance, and if we all run in, she might hurt them."

Sally nodded. "So we lure her out. You wait here. But be prepared to move."

Before Lizzie could ask Sally what she intended to do, Sally slinked away, whistling a jaunty tune. Charlotte looked down at Lady Catherine. "Is she dead?"

"I hope not, because I would like to kill her myself," Lizzie said. She reached down and unclipped Guy's leash. "Help me."

With Charlotte's help, the two of them managed to awkwardly bind Lady Catherine's hands behind her back with the leash. Lizzie picked up the pistol. "Do you know how to use this?"

Charlotte nodded and held out her hand. "You go. I won't let her out of my sight."

Lizzie squeezed her best friend's shoulder once, then crept back through the woods toward the grotto. She wanted to run but was afraid doing so would draw too much attention. When she drew close, she sidled up to the back of the grotto and peered inside the glassless window. Georgiana and Darcy were still where they'd left them, but Agnes was looking toward the door, head cocked. Lizzie could hear Sally whistling, and Agnes was clearly suspicious. Agnes grabbed at Georgiana, who whimpered, and pulled her away from Darcy. Lizzie saw light glint off a blade that Agnes held under Georgiana's chin.

"Who's there?" Agnes shouted, making her voice sound high and scared—but Lizzie knew well enough by now that it was an act.

"It's Sally Burton, Agnes. I believe you stole something from me."

Lizzie saw Agnes go stiff and then propel Georgiana out the door and up the steps in front of her, knife still held to the younger girl's throat. "Sally Burton. You're a long way from home."

"I'd say the same about you, except that I'm beginning to suspect everything you told us was a lie," Lizzie heard Sally say.

"Not everything," Agnes said. "But most, I admit. I can't help it if Meryton is full of a bunch of blathering fools."

Agnes was fully outside the grotto now, and Lizzie couldn't see her or Sally or Clara, but she could hear them well enough. Darcy was left alone, still tied up. This was her chance. Carefully, she began to climb through the window.

“Aye, we have our share of fools, but they’re our fools. We don’t take kindly to people using us.” Sally still sounded unbothered, as if she were encountering a neighbor on a walk into the village.

“I would apologize, but it turns out I’m not very sorry,” Agnes said. “After all, it wasn’t as though any of the treasure was yours to begin with.”

Lizzie lowered herself into the grotto, dropping to the stone floor with a muffled “Oof!” Darcy turned to look at her, his eyes wide. She held up a finger to her lips.

“Well, it certainly wasn’t yours,” Sally said. “Three generations of my family have given our entire lives to Netherfield Park. That gives us more of a right to it than you.”

Darcy struggled against his bindings when he saw her. She reached for the gag first. When it fell from his mouth, Darcy gasped. “Georgie?”

“Outside, with Agnes,” Lizzie whispered, moving on to the knots at his wrists. “Sally is our distraction.”

“I left the silver,” Agnes said, her voice carrying into the grotto. “I had a feeling it wasn’t the extent of the treasure, and I figured I could rattle you all into revealing it. And wasn’t I right? The wealthy hang diamonds in their unused ballrooms while the rest of us struggle and starve for a living—and you were complicit!”

The ropes around Darcy’s hands finally began to loosen, and she helped him shed them and sit up. Darcy tried to work at the knot in the rope around his feet, but his hands were purple, and he was having trouble making his fingers work. "I'm sorry I lured you here," he whispered. "They made me write that note."

"Shh," she reassured him. She should have known—when in his life had he ever signed a note to her with his given name?

"Don't talk to me about being complicit," Sally snapped, and Lizzie heard the first hint of anger in her voice. "I used Mrs. Bingley's silver to make life better for the people of Meryton—with her blessing. That's a far cry from you, who stole what wasn't yours out of greed."

The knot finally loosened, and Lizzie pulled at the ropes, finding enough slack for Darcy to pull his feet free. He got to his feet but stumbled, and Lizzie clung to his arm, not wanting to draw Agnes's attention. "She has a knife!" she warned in a whisper.

But Darcy was wild-eyed, desperate to get to Georgiana. Lizzie picked up a length of discarded rope and pulled it taut in her hands. "Stay back," she warned. Lizzie crept across the grotto's stone floor as quietly as she could, and up the steps. Agnes's back was to her, and she held Georgiana tightly. Sally saw Lizzie coming, but her face betrayed nothing.

"You act as though you're so superior, but you're your mother's daughter. You concealed a crime for your own advantage. You protected a killer, and you have the audacity to lecture me? You're no better than me."

"At least she's not a killer herself!" Clara Jeffries shouted, popping out of the brush and hurling a rock in Agnes's direction.

Agnes jerked back, and Lizzie bit down on her tongue to hold in her gasp—Georgiana! But Clara's interjection was enough to startle Agnes, and Sally charged forward, grabbing at the arm that held the knife and wrestling it away from Georgiana's neck. Agnes was unbalanced enough that she let go of Georgiana, who dropped to the ground with a strangled cry. Agnes stumbled back, but she still held the knife, and she slashed it at Sally, the tip catching her forearm. The other girl hissed in pain, and Lizzie lurched into motion, throwing her length of rope over Agnes's head and pulling back with all her weight.

The shock of finding herself suddenly choked caused Agnes to swing around wildly with the hand holding the knife. White-hot pain seared Lizzie's hip and side, but still she held on. Georgiana managed to get to her feet, and Lizzie was afraid Agnes would stab her, but then Georgiana smacked the knife out of Agnes's hand. Now without a weapon, Agnes's hands flew to her neck, trying desperately to pull away at the rope. Lizzie held on long enough for Sally and Clara to rush forward and each grab one of Agnes's arms. It was no easy feat, wrestling her to the ground. She kicked and flailed desperately, but when she began to run out of air, she slumped. Lizzie loosened the rope—she wasn't keen on being the cause of someone's death, even a confessed killer. Between the three of them, they used the rope from Darcy's bindings to tie her hands and feet tightly.

Lizzie finally turned when the job was done to find Darcy, one arm slung around Georgiana's shoulders, hobbling toward them. "Lizzie!" Georgiana cried, and Lizzie ran to them. Darcy's other arm came around her and he held them both close.

“Thank heavens,” Lizzie murmured. “I was so scared she’d kill you both.”

“You’re bleeding,” Darcy gasped. And then: “Where’s Lady Catherine?”

Just then, the sound of Guy barking furiously reached them. Lizzie tore herself away from Darcy, wincing at the cut on her hip. Her dress was damp with blood, but she didn’t appear to be seriously injured. “Charlotte!” she cried, and began to run in her direction.

She was aware of Darcy and Georgiana following after her, but she didn’t wait for them. When she broke into the clearing where the horse had been, she found Guy standing over Charlotte’s prone form, barking.

Lady Catherine and the horse were gone.

TWENTY-SIX

In Which Lizzie and Darcy Pursue Lady Catherine, with Unlikely Help

LIZZIE SCREAMED AND RAN to Charlotte. Darcy was certain she was dead.

Lizzie managed to roll Charlotte over to her back and began shaking her friend. "Charlotte, no, no, no! Charlotte!"

His mouth was still dry from the gag, and his head pounded from the blow that wretched Agnes had landed on him the night before. But that was nothing to the emptiness he felt in that moment, watching as Lizzie shook a lifeless Charlotte.

"Lizzie?" came a hoarse whisper.

"Charlotte!" she cried, and Darcy dropped to his knees next to Lizzie. "Charlotte, are you all right?"

Guy pressed into Darcy's side and whined. He placed a hand on the small dog's head, and with his other hand he helped Charlotte sit up. She winced at the motion. "She got away, Lizzie. I'm so sorry."

"What happened?" he asked.

"We didn't tie her feet, and she ran for the horse," Charlotte said. "I hesitated—I didn't want to shoot the horse—and she swung up on his back. She kicked me as she went by, and everything went black."

"And the pistol?" Lizzie asked.

"I don't know," Charlotte moaned.

"I don't see it anywhere," Georgiana said, searching the nearby underbrush.

"Never mind that," Darcy said. His thoughts had felt as though they were all underwater, but they were becoming sharper now. "Where's Travers?"

"He left me and Sally and Clara in the parlor," Charlotte said, rubbing her temples. "There was some sort of commotion at the front of the house, and we took the opportunity to slip out the back, in case you needed help."

Darcy swallowed as he helped Lizzie get Charlotte to her feet. "She might have created a diversion out front. We need to—"

Charlotte swayed a bit but waved them off. "I'm all right."

"Georgie?" Darcy said, and she came over instantly, slipping Charlotte's arm over her shoulder.

"Go," she said.

Lizzie and Darcy ran back through the trees toward the grotto. Sally and Miss Jeffries were still in front of the grotto, Sally wielding the knife Agnes had threatened Georgiana with. "Is everything all right?" Miss Jeffries shouted.

"She escaped!" Lizzie shouted. "Stay put, we're going for help."

Darcy reached out and grabbed Lizzie's hand, pulling her

toward the house. "She has the horse, so she must be headed to the main gate. If we're lucky, one of the gatekeepers has a horse tied out front."

Darcy didn't waste any more breath on talking. They ran toward the house as quickly as the injuries they'd sustained and Lizzie's long skirts would allow. They entered through a back door and Darcy steered them through the gallery, shouting for help. His voice echoed off the walls, but he saw no sign of any servants—where were they? He reached the front hall and spun in a circle, trying to decide what to do next. Lizzie was wild-eyed beside him, and he knew what she must be thinking—they could not let Lady Catherine slip from their grasp again. They might not survive it.

"Out the front," Darcy decided. "I'll run to the gatehouse if I have to."

He ran out the front door, Lizzie on his heels. But when they spilled out onto the gravel drive, Darcy was confronted by a sobering sight:

Lady Catherine.

She stood before the house, a valise slung over her shoulder and her hair a disheveled mess. Her head had been tilted back, but when she saw Darcy and Lizzie spill out the front door, she turned and her expression darkened.

"Stop!" Darcy shouted.

Lady Catherine, unsurprisingly, did not. Faster than Darcy could have thought possible, she raised one arm, and they all saw what her valise had concealed: The pistol.

"Get down!" Lizzie shouted, and he heard a shot ring out as he fell to the ground, Lizzie tumbling down beside him.

I've been shot, he thought. For it seemed to be the only explanation for why his shoulder was on fire, and why he was suddenly flat on his back.

"Darcy!" Someone pushed him onto his back, and he saw Lizzie before him. Felt her hands running up and down his body searching for wounds. "You're not shot. You're all right!"

"No, I heard it," he mumbled. "A pistol shot—did you not hear it?"

"I heard it," she confirmed. He hissed in pain as her hands felt his shoulder. "I'm sorry! You landed on your shoulder when I pulled you down."

His shoulder screamed in protest as he struggled to sit up. Once upright, he saw that Lady Catherine herself was on the ground just as they were. Her valise had fallen, and spilling out of it were dozens of diamonds, glinting brilliantly in the sun.

Lizzie helped him to his feet, and together they limped toward her prone form, but cautiously. Lady Catherine was on her back. She panted heavily and groaned as she tried to sit up but couldn't quite manage it, for her left arm was clasping her right shoulder—from which a great deal of blood flowed.

A tall figure stalked over to her and kicked her fallen pistol away, out of Lady Catherine's reach. He made no motion to reach down and assist the injured lady but regarded her for a few moments. Then, he slipped his own pistol into its holster and turned his glower onto Lizzie and Darcy.

"Father," Darcy said, gasping in pain. He couldn't think of anything else to say.

"Fitzwilliam. Do you care to tell me why your sister's lady's companion just tried to shoot you?"

"For the record, I never liked her," Georgiana said from the end of the settee, sipping daintily at her tea. "I told you as much in all my letters, too, so there's a record."

Darcy smiled, then grimaced at the pain in his head. His entire body felt as though he'd been run over by a horse, but he was alive. And so was Lizzie, who sat in the closest chair to him, her hand cradling his, and Georgiana, who'd suffered little more than a scrape at the base of her throat from Agnes's blade.

Charlotte was also all right, although bruised and shaken. She sat in a chair with a blanket bundled around her, despite the summer heat. Mrs. Reynolds had tucked her in, telling Charlotte it was the perfect antidote to the shock she'd suffered, and then shoved tea into all their hands. Sally and Miss Jeffries—"Please, call me Clara at this point," she'd insisted—were completely unharmed. They were all gathered in the family parlor as Mrs. Reynolds fussed over them, even Guy, who was curled up on the settee next to Darcy.

"You never would have liked any lady's companion Father hired," Darcy told Georgiana.

"Well, at least any other lady's companion wouldn't have been a career criminal bent on exacting revenge against Lizzie."

"I would be worried if there were more than one," Lizzie said.

Darcy placed a hand over his face, then winced as the movement exacerbated the pain in his shoulder. "I can't believe she was here the entire time."

Mrs. Reynolds must have heard his hiss of pain, because she gently moved his hands aside and placed a cold cloth on his head, like she used to do when he was a boy. "You stay still now, sir."

"Don't worry," Lizzie said, taking his other hand. "I'll make sure he rests."

"Lizzie, I'm so sorry." He almost couldn't bring himself to look at her. Her cheek was puffy from Lady Catherine's blow, the cut still angry and the skin starting to bruise, although Mrs. Reynolds had helped her clean up the blood. "I thought bringing you here would keep you safe."

"It's not your fault."

"This is the perfect hiding place," Charlotte said. "When you think about, it's very audacious."

"The last place you'd look," Georgiana added.

"Downright devious if you ask me," Sally muttered.

"Thank you," Darcy said to the ladies surrounding him. "If not for you . . ."

"You're welcome," Georgiana said.

"It's the least I owe you and Miss Bennet," Sally said stiffly.

"Please, call me Lizzie."

"And we are sorry about accusing you of stealing," Clara added.

Sally nodded. "Although we will need the diamonds back."

"Diamonds?" Darcy asked.

"I'll explain later," Lizzie reassured him.

Just then, the door opened, revealing his father. Darcy was unsurprised to find his father's expression pinched and disapproving. In the months he'd spent abroad, his once-black hair had turned mostly gray, and the lines in his face were deeper. Darcy could scarcely believe he was here.

"I'd like to speak with my son," he said.

Mrs. Reynolds dipped a curtsy and hurried out of the room, and Sally, Clara, and Charlotte followed. Georgiana stood but she lingered. "Papa, I—"

"Not now, Georgiana."

"No," Darcy said, sitting up slowly. "Let her stay. She's the one who's been living with a criminal for nearly a year."

His father didn't have an answer to that, because Darcy's movement had displaced Guy, who hopped to the floor and trotted over the older Mr. Darcy to sniff his feet. The man scowled and stepped back. "What is this creature doing inside the house?"

"That's Guy," Darcy said. "He's my dog. Well, mine and Lizzie's. We both take care of him."

At the informal mention of Lizzie's name, his father looked her up and down. Lizzie stood and made a proper curtsy. "Miss Elizabeth Bennet, sir. I am sorry to be meeting you under these less-than-ideal circumstances."

"So you're the lady who fancies herself a solicitor, then?"

"No," Darcy said, clearing his throat. "She *is* a solicitor. With Longbourn and Sons."

His father ignored that. "Miss Bennet, I should like to have a private word with my children."

"No," Darcy said, taking Lizzie's hand in his once more and pulling her onto the settee next to him. "Whatever you say, you can say in front of Lizzie." His father glared, but Darcy didn't look away. "There are things you don't know because you've been gone so long, and I intend to give you a full accounting of my behavior and decisions. Once you hear the truth from me, then you can decide whether you approve. But Lizzie must remain here to be a part of the telling."

Beside him, Lizzie squeezed his hand. He clung to her.

"Fine." His father sat down in the chair across from him. "Begin."

It took nearly an hour for Darcy and Lizzie to reconstruct the entire tale, stretching all the way back to the day he and Lizzie met, working on Bingley's case, and encompassing the case of the Mullins Brothers and Mr. Tomlinson's deception. Some of this his father had known, thanks to the letters Darcy had sent abroad and the news his father had received from other solicitors at Pemberley & Associates, but there was a great deal of misinformation that Tomlinson had fed the senior Mr. Darcy over the past months. Darcy's voice gained strength the longer he spoke, and at first Lizzie was deferential to his explanation of matters, stepping in only to clarify. But by the time they were halfway through, she was speaking as often as he. And the entire time, his father just stared.

Darcy couldn't tell what his father thought—whether he

believed him or thought him mad or was angry with him or disappointed. When they concluded, Darcy's father regarded them for a long moment. Finally, he shifted his gaze to Lizzie, and to their tightly clasped hands. "It seems that I owe you a debt of gratitude today, Miss Bennet."

"No," Lizzie said. "I did what anyone would have done."

"No, you did not. Clearly not everyone would have put their own lives at risk for two people not related to them."

"Maybe not," Lizzie allowed, "but I think that most people would risk their lives for someone they love."

Love for Lizzie and all her bravery swelled within Darcy, and he squeezed her hand, scarcely willing to breathe in anticipation of his father's response.

"Love? You profess to love my son?"

"I do, very much." Lizzie's head was held high. "And I love Georgiana like a sister."

"And we love her!" Georgiana declared.

"Is that so?" Mr. Darcy asked.

"Yes," Darcy said, sitting up even straighter. "I love her."

"God help me," his father muttered. But they were saved from further declarations of any sort by a knock on the door. "Enter."

Charleston stepped in and bowed slightly to the elder Mr. Darcy. "Excuse me, sir, but there is a regiment at the front gates, requesting entry. They're led by a Colonel Graves, who said he has business with you."

"Business?" his father sputtered. "I don't know what he's—"

"Graves!" Darcy explained. "He's the man who has been

looking for Lady Catherine—Charleston, allow him entry. Tell him we have her."

Charleston looked to his father for confirmation, and his father nodded. "Very good, sir."

Darcy's father stood. "I suppose I shall go see what the man has to say. We're not done discussing this, Fitzwilliam."

He turned to march out the door, but Darcy got to his feet. "Actually, Father, there's one more thing."

He turned, annoyed. "What?"

"I love Miss Bennet, and as soon as she is prepared to say yes, I intend to ask her to marry me. And there is nothing you nor anyone else can do to persuade me otherwise."

He heard Lizzie gasp beside him, but he kept his gaze trained on his father. In the end, the man merely shook his head and said, "We'll continue to discuss this," before leaving, slamming the door behind him.

Darcy slumped back down in his seat. "Well, that went well."

"That went *so* well!" Georgiana cried, jumping up to hug them both.

"It did?" Lizzie asked. "I couldn't tell."

"I'm going to leave you for a moment," Georgiana said, releasing them. "But if you need me for any reason, I'll be just outside." Then she winked at him.

"Oh dear, I think your sister believes that you intend to propose this very minute."

Darcy reached out to grab Lizzie's hand once more. "And would you say yes?"

She pursed her lips, and Darcy could see that she was mulling it over. Her hair was a mess, and her cheek was now starting to turn from a dark red to a deep plum shade. There was dirt on her nose and her gown was grass-stained and torn, in addition to the bloody slit in her dress where Agnes's knife had grazed her.

She had never been so beautiful to him as she was in this moment.

"Not yet," she said softly. "But I think I'll be ready very soon."

"I can live with very soon," he said, leaning in to kiss her.

He felt her smile beneath his lips, and she wrapped her arms around him, pulling him tight. "Good," she whispered. "Because now that Lady Catherine is taken care of, we shall have all the time in the world."

TWENTY-SEVEN

In Which Lizzie Receives a Proper Proposal

THREE MONTHS LATER

IT WAS NOT A surprise, but Lizzie held her breath nonetheless while she waited for the final verdict.

"Guilty," declared the judge, and the entire courtroom burst into cheers.

Below her stood Lady Catherine de Bourgh in the accused's seat. Despite an entire courtroom celebrating her downfall, she held her head high. Her eyes roamed the courtroom, looking for something. Lizzie had a feeling she knew exactly what it was. Or rather, whom.

"Come on, let's go," she whispered to Charlotte, who stood next to her in the gallery.

"Don't you want to stay and hear the sentencing?" Charlotte asked.

Lizzie shook her head. She didn't want to give Lady Catherine the satisfaction of seeing her in the courtroom. Let her think Lizzie hadn't bothered to come. With a bit of luck, this would be the very last time they'd ever share a room, and she was eager for the moment to be behind her. "Darcy thinks there's a chance she'll get transportation to Australia. But if it's hanging, well . . . I don't want to stay to hear it."

"All right," Charlotte said, pushing through the many eager audience members pressing closer to get a glimpse of the famed criminal. Lizzie had gotten more than her fair share of Lady Catherine—not only in the past year and a half since they'd first met, but also in the last two days, as she'd finally stood trial.

They managed to reach the door and continued outside, into the autumn sun. The day was chilly but bright, and while the air held the promise of winter, London felt oddly cheerful. Lizzie liked to believe it was because justice had been done, but she knew it was just another day, and the weather had nothing to do with what had been decided in the courthouse.

"Are you relieved?" Charlotte asked, and Lizzie nodded.

"Relieved and sad. She hurt so many people. It's because of her that Mr. Hurst and Abigail and Wickham and Leticia Cavendish and Simon Mullins and Honoria Bingley are all dead."

"And it's because of you that she's no longer free," Charlotte reminded her.

"Paper?" a boy asked them, approaching with a large stack of cheap broadsides, chronicling the sordid details of the various trials. "Lady Catherine de Bourgh on trial, read all about it!"

"No, thank you," Lizzie said firmly, but tossed the boy a ha'penny anyway. She already knew what most of the papers said about Lady Catherine de Bourgh, about her, and about the trial. It had had enough shocking twists and surprise reveals to keep the public riveted, and Lizzie had turned down more than a few journalists and newspaper men who'd wanted her exclusive story. Everyone was rabid for details. But to Lizzie, perhaps the most shocking detail was the fact that Darcy's father had been the one to formally bring evidence against Lady Catherine in London, with supporting testimony from a myriad of others. The city's preeminent barrister, spearheading such a shocking case, had caused a stir. But when they had finished explaining their entire case history with Lady Catherine to Darcy's father and he'd spoken to Graves, the elder Mr. Darcy had insisted on filing a case against Lady Catherine himself. "If we leave this to the Crown, they'll try her for treason and nothing else," he explained to Lizzie and Darcy. In that moment, Lizzie could see where Darcy had gotten his serious, brooding expression. "And while that would certainly be serious enough, no one crosses a Darcy without consequence."

But Lizzie was not as naive as she had once been. There was only one punishment for treason, and Lady Catherine had signed her own death warrant years earlier.

"Are you all right?" Charlotte asked. "I know a guilty verdict was what we wanted, but . . ."

But it hardly fixed anything.

"I'm happy she's caught, and that she stood trial," Lizzie said. "I just wish we could go back to a time when I didn't think about her constantly."

"I know," Charlotte said, squeezing her arm. Just the month before, Agnes had been found guilty of murder and theft, and had been sentenced to hang.

Needless to say, Lizzie hadn't attended the execution.

"What you need is a new case," Charlotte told her. "Have you picked one out yet?"

Lizzie smiled, thinking of the stacks of letters and inquiries that had flooded the offices of Longbourn & Sons since they'd returned to London and news of Lady Catherine's arrest had broken. Charlotte had carefully screened and sorted them, pulling the most interesting cases out for Lizzie.

"Not yet," Lizzie said. "Papa is rather irritated that so many of them are criminal when he'd much rather deal with business law."

"Your father might grumble, but he is proud of you."

Lizzie smiled at that. Her father was still not thrilled with her interest in criminal law, nor was he happy to hear all that had happened at Pemberley, but he no longer tried to dictate which cases she took, which she appreciated. She valued his opinion, even if she sometimes disagreed with him.

"Perhaps something easy," Lizzie mused. "I promised to visit Jane and Bingley once the trial concluded. Have you decided whether you'll come with me?"

Her sister and brother-in-law had elected to extend their stay at Netherfield Park, in part because of Caroline's condition. She'd awoken after three days of sleep to a splitting headache, but Jane wrote that Caroline was not nearly as irritable as she'd expected. Lizzie had a feeling that wouldn't last, but she was relieved that Caroline was all right. She was indebted to her, and she'd have to tell the other young lady as much when she visited.

She tried not to think how Caroline might call in such a debt.

"I'll accompany you," Charlotte said. "As long as you don't insist on going into the east wing again."

"Jane says the repairs are underway!"

"That's hardly reassuring!"

Lizzie nudged her best friend. "I'm sure a certain vicar would be happy to see you."

Charlotte blushed. "I had a letter from him yesterday—he's coming to London on business next week and asked if he may call on me."

Lizzie gasped. "Charlotte!"

"Now, calm down. Nothing has happened yet."

"But it could, and that's the most wonderful thing." Lizzie wanted nothing more than to see her friend happy, and she couldn't remember the last time anything had made Charlotte smile as much as Mr. Thomas's letters. It was a good thing that she'd never been taken in by the awful Mr. Collins.

Just then, the doors to the courthouse opened and people began pouring out, spreading the news of the guilty verdict. Charlotte and Lizzie watched as the people went by, giddy with excitement. Lizzie couldn't bring herself to feel more than intense relief—despite everything that had transpired, she didn't delight in Lady Catherine's sentence.

Just then, a familiar figure emerged from the crowd, looking about. Lizzie smiled and raised a hand to wave. "Darcy!"

He turned and strode toward them, and Charlotte said, "I'll leave you to it. See you back at the office?"

"Yes," she said. "Tell Papa I won't be long!"

Charlotte took her leave as Darcy reached her and took her arm.

"Well," Darcy said. "It's finished."

"And?"

He grimaced. "It seems as though they're unwilling to transport or execute the wife of a peer, so it's prison. Indefinitely."

Lizzie shuddered, remembering the stench from within Newgate, which sat just a short distance away. "That is a punishment."

"Yes," he agreed. "And still probably not all she deserves."

There was a hollow tone to his voice, and Lizzie knew that the past three months had taken a toll on Darcy. He'd served as his father's junior counsel in bringing the case against Lady Catherine, and they'd uncovered more about Lady Catherine's misdeeds than they'd even suspected. Lizzie squeezed his arm. "You did very well today."

"Do you wish it had been you, before the judge?"

She shook her head, then stopped. "All right, maybe a little. But this was too risky a case to leave to chance and some judge's ill-conceived opinions on my capabilities when it comes to the law. Besides, I was too close to the case. I was happy to give my testimony and leave it that." She looked to the blue sky and then back at him. "You know, this is an important spot."

"Outside the courthouse?"

"No, this precise spot," Lizzie said, lips quirking into a teasing smile. "Don't you recall?"

He looked about them, and at the many people streaming past. "Did we have an argument here or something?"

She laughed. "No! But something very important did occur here. After another trial . . ."

He understood her then. "You mean, when we kissed for the first time?"

"Exactly."

"Well, shall I kiss you again? For tradition's sake?"

"You could." She stepped closer to him and took his hand, threading her fingers in his. "Or we could mark another memorable occasion here."

"What's that?"

"You could . . . ask me something."

His eyes widened and she tried not to laugh. "Really?"

"Only if it's really, really significant," she teased.

"Oh, I have just the thing," he said, turning so that they were facing each other. He gazed down at her and swallowed hard, then said, "Miss Elizabeth Bennet, would you do me the tremendous honor of . . . going into business with me?"

Her eyes widened and she laughed. "What?"

"I've been meaning to ask you, but I wasn't sure about the timing," he said. "I don't want to work for my father anymore—we've been getting along a little better, but the types of cases he wants me to pursue and the types of cases I want to take on are entirely different. You and I have been consulting on cases for over a year now. Why not combine forces officially?"

"You truly want to go into business together?"

"Why, was that not the question you were expecting?"

"You're teasing me," she accused.

"Always," he said, leaning in to whisper in her ear. "But not about that. Naturally, though, if we are to become conjoined in business, we might as well make everything entirely legal and . . . join hands in marriage?"

A thrill ran through Lizzie, not unlike the feeling she got when an enticing new case presented itself before her. But this wasn't some short-lived mystery to be solved. This was the future. Forever. With Darcy.

"Yes," she said, her lips finding his.

"Yes to what?" he asked in between kisses that warmed her to her toes.

"To all of it," she responded when she was able to draw a breath. "Yes, a thousand times yes, to everything with you."

ACKNOWLEDGMENTS

While it was not initially my intention to write an entire series about the adventures of Lizzie and Darcy, I'm truly grateful for the opportunity to have spent three books solving mysteries with them. The first person I have to thank is Claudia Gabel for taking a chance on me with *Pride and Premeditation* and loving these characters as much as I do—enough to suggest that I keep writing about them!

Thank you to Sarah Homer and Tara Weikum for taking on this series with enthusiasm and for bringing me under the Storytide fold. A special thanks to Sarah, who did not balk when I said I wanted to completely rework the plot after I'd already turned in a first draft! You reassured me over lunch that the new direction was great, giving me the confidence to forge ahead. Thank you for your steadfast support.

As always, thank you to my agent Taylor Martindale Kean and the Full Circle Literary team. Not only have you been a wonderful cheerleader throughout this entire process, but you're a savvy agent and a true friend, and that brainstorming call we had was crucial to cracking the plot for this book. I couldn't have done this without you.

After five books, I truly believe that I have some of the best people on my publishing team at HarperCollins, and I am so grateful to Taylan Salvati, Corina Lupp, Alison Klapthor, Jessica Berg, Maya Myers, Sam Fox, Shannon Cox, Roseanne Lauer, Meghan Pettit, Mary Magrisso, and everyone else who works so hard to get books in the hands of readers. You all are rock stars in my book. Thank you to Emma Congdon for creating yet another brilliant and beautiful cover and for lending your talents to this series.

Thank you also to booksellers, librarians, teachers, and bookish influencers who share the love of books every day with young people. You all are in the trenches doing the hard work, and it's because of you that the classics are still alive and relevant in our culture. Every time we've been able to connect over a shared love of Austen has been magical.

I'd be nothing without my writer friends encouraging me when writing feels impossible, celebrating the wins, and commiserating over the disappointments. Thank you to Molly Harper, Monica Roe, Melissa Baumgart, Annika Barranti Klein (who gave me the idea for the diamond chandelier!), Emily Martin, and Tegan Beese. And a special thanks to Laura Taylor Namey and Kathleen Glasgow for being the first to text when *In Want of a Suspect* hit the *USA Today* bestseller list!

My heartfelt thanks to my family for putting up with my erratic writing schedule (including skipping Easter to meet my deadline!) and supporting this dream. I want to especially thank my partner, Tab, for all of the big and small things you do for me—from sending me memes to painting my office while I was away at YALLFest so I could come home and finish revisions with a clean desk. I'm grateful for you every day.